ADVENT

THE EXLIAN SYNDROME SERIES

BOOKS BY SETH RING

THE EXLIAN SYNDROME SERIES

Advent

Dark Dawn (coming in 2025)

Apex (coming in 2025)

Evolution (coming in 2025)

Shattered Glory (coming in 2026)

Light's Ascension (coming in 2026)

THE IRON TYRANT SERIES

Chain of Feathers

Crow's Fortune

THE SOUL CALLER SERIES

Soul Caller 1

Soul Caller 2

THE DREAMER'S THRONE SERIES

Dreamer's Throne 1

Dreamer's Throne 2

Dreamer's Throne 3

Dreamer's Throne 4

THE NOVA TERRA SERIES

Mad Master Alchemist

THE TOWER SERIES

Forgemaster

Reforged

Arcanist

Ignition

Bloodline

Avatar

Challenger

THE BATTLE MAGE FARMER SERIES

Domestication

Germination

Cultivation

Fermentation

Transformation

Preservation

Separation

Conservation

Culmination

THE TITAN SERIES

Nova Terra: Titan

Nova Terra: Greymane

Nova Terra: Kingbreaker

Nova Terra: Guardian

Nova Terra: Liberator

Nova Terra: Earthshaper

Nova Terra: Stormbringer

Nova Terra: Stone King

Nova Terra: Catalyst

Nova Terra: Worldbearer

PRAISE FOR *ADVENT*

"Seth Ring kicks down the doors with *Advent*! This book has it all—wild action, bizarre aliens, relatable characters, and devious plot twists. Highly recommended!"

—JONATHAN MABERRY,

New York Times bestselling author of *NecroTek* and the Joe Ledger thrillers

"Seth Ring's writing is fast, fun, and entertaining. His stories are filled with engaging characters and great action."

—KEVIN J. ANDERSON,

New York Times bestselling coauthor of *Sisterhood of Dune*

"Seth Ring brings to life a new world that somehow still feels like home with heroes you can feel good about rooting for and a unique storyline that will keep you up well past your bedtime."

—JONATHAN YANEZ,

bestselling author of the Forsaken Mercenary series

"A masterful LitRPG adventure...Fans of high-stakes action and richly imagined worlds will find themselves hooked from page one!"

—NICHOLAS SANSBURY SMITH,

New York Times bestselling author of the Hell Divers series

ADVENT

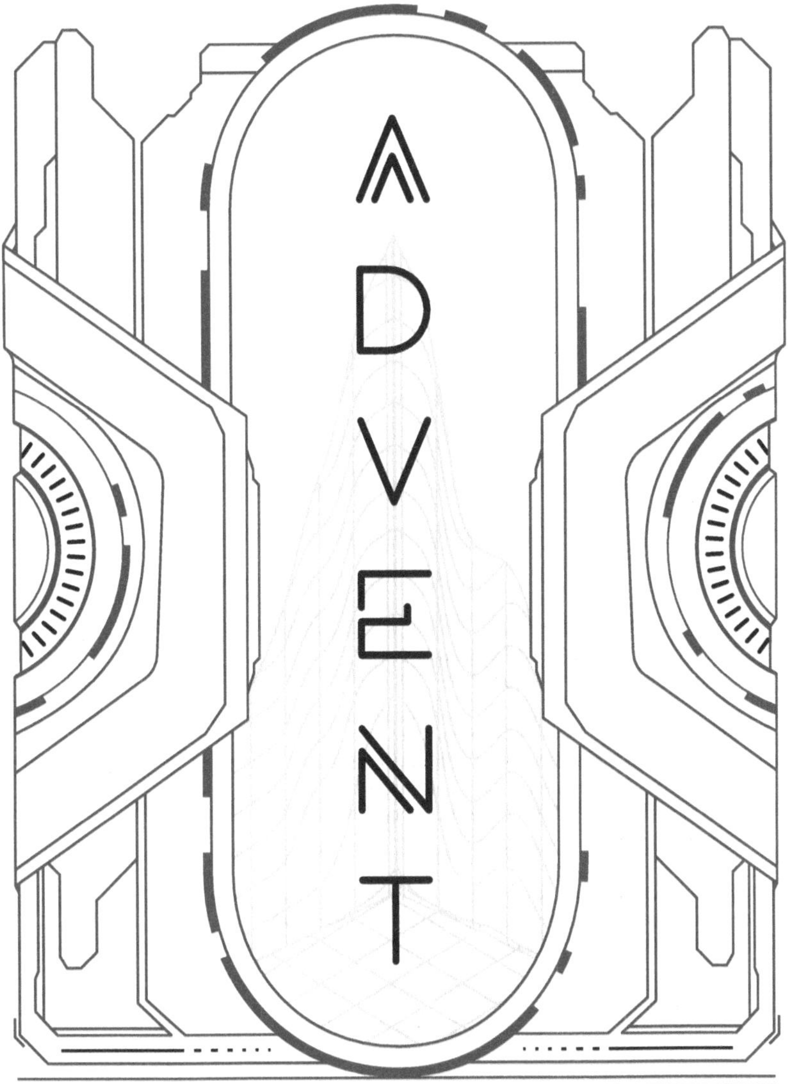

THE EXLIAN SYNDROME SERIES

Published in 2025 by Blackstone Publishing
Cover and book design by Larissa Ezel

Printed in the United States of America
Originally published in hardcover by Blackstone Publishing in 2025

First paperback edition: 2025
ISBN 979-8-8746-9477-7
Fiction / LitRPG (Literary Role-Playing Game)

Version 1

Blackstone Publishing
31 Mistletoe Rd.
Ashland, OR 97520

www.BlackstonePublishing.com

THE EXLIAN SYNDROME SERIES

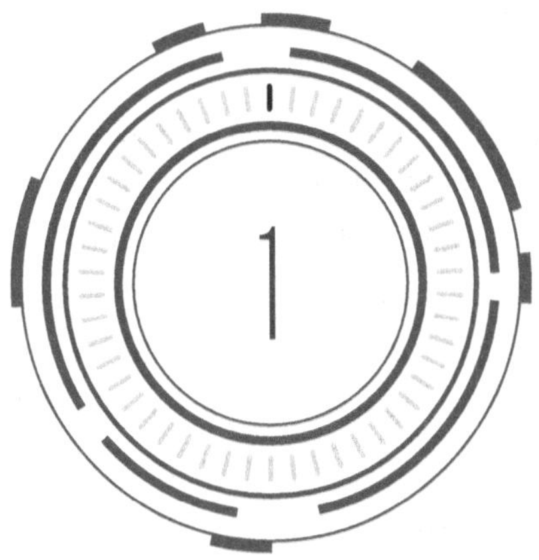

The terminal beeped softly, and Mark's shoulders dropped in sharp relief. He knew he had enough credits since he had finally gotten paid, but the possibility of rejection still haunted him. Hoping his relief wasn't showing on his face, he stepped through the open doors onto the train, looking around in a vain hope that he'd find a seat. Like normal, nothing available. With a sigh, he moved to the other end of the car, wedging himself between a seat and the exit door.

With barely a hum, the train took off, moving from a standstill to blistering speed in a fraction of a second without any noticeable shift in inertia. Catching sight of the faintly glowing mana circuit tracing its complex pattern along the ceiling, Mark idly wondered if they had built in the inertia-dampening effect or if the lack of movement was just a by-product of good insulation.

As always, the train cars were packed with commuters heading back from their jobs or from the training camps. A few young men and women, still dressed in bright-blue school uniforms, sat a bit farther down the car, chatting quietly with each other. Mark felt a pang in his chest, unsure if it was nostalgia, a desire to experience the camaraderie of school once more, or the dull pain of missing friends.

With a sigh, Mark turned away, looking out over the city that blurred past. New Emery was best described as strong, with little thought for the elegance of civilization, but to Mark's eyes, it carried a brutal and enduring beauty. Bright lights lit the center of the city, highlighting the massive skyscrapers that dominated the central district. That light, driven by the giant mana refineries hidden under the city, grew dimmer and dimmer the farther it got from the city center, and as his eyes moved out into the surrounding rings, the buildings got smaller as well. Everything in the city—every institution, every organization, every business—was oriented around one thing: the Exlian threat—the ever-present, ever-growing horde of mutating monsters who roamed the wilderness. Mark's life was no exception.

Catching sight of a bitter smile in the glass, Mark quickly tried to correct his expression. He knew from personal experience that it was better to keep up a chipper appearance, or at the very least something neutral that wouldn't automatically put others on guard.

Pushing aside the frustration threatening to boil up inside him, Mark tilted the back of his head against the cool glass window. He often caught this train after finishing up work, and the same tired faces that he always saw were present, heading to whatever home they had.

At the far end of the train, he spotted someone new—a young man with a firm expression and a crew cut that looked freshly done. He wore an olive-green uniform, undecorated, save for a simple patch on his shoulder. Mark was too far away to see what it read, but he knew its inscription by heart.

"For glory, for humanity," Mark whispered under his breath, a hint of excitement pushing aside his frustration.

The soldier must have noticed Mark's stare, because he suddenly looked up, his sharp eyes flashing with a strange power. Startled, Mark turned his head away and then, unable to resist, peeked at the young man from the corner of his eye, only to find that he was still staring straight at Mark, a small smile on his lips. The soldier nodded and then put his head down again, but the feeling of excitement persisted, even as the train car rang with the soft chime announcing Mark's stop. Stepping from the train onto the platform, Mark walked through the dark streets lit by flickering streetlights placed on the nearby buildings.

The environment, though it looked grim, was familiar to Mark. He had lived here almost his whole life, and his mind was occupied with the man on the train. That uniform and, more importantly, the badge that he wore marked the young man as a member of the city's Defense Force, the most prestigious of the three branches of the military, the one Mark desperately wanted to join himself.

When he arrived at his door, he punched in his key code and groaned when he heard the familiar, annoying whine of the lock on his door failing to disengage. The sound brought reality crashing back down on Mark, and with a frustrated sigh, he bumped his head against the door lightly. This area had once been nice, and everything had worked perfectly, but increasingly strict power rations left the mana circuits barely able to pull the mana they needed, resulting in their all-too-frequent failure. Waiting until the lock reset, Mark tried again.

When it failed for the fourth time, he just shook his head, annoyed, and walked around the building, hopping the fence to get into the small backyard. It was technically against the law to leave a door or window unlocked because of the ever-present Exlian threat, but Mark had spent one too many nights sleeping outside, unable to get into his home, to care.

He'd left a window on the second floor open a hair, hoping

it was a small enough gap that it wouldn't be noticed by any patrols or, worse, by an Exlian that had sneaked into the city. With practiced ease, he scrambled up the first-floor window, using a drainpipe to brace himself as he jumped to grab the sill of the second-story window, all the while balancing his backpack on one shoulder.

Wedging himself into place, he ran his fingers along the window. The tab he had left was still in place, which meant that the window hadn't been opened. It took a couple of tugs to get it open, but that was better than standing on his porch all evening, listening to the lock whine at him.

After the window was pushed up far enough, he shimmied himself up and rolled in, his hip slamming into the floor with a thud.

"Ouch."

Rubbing his hip, he stood up and closed the window, making sure to lock it tight. It was one thing to leave the window open when he wasn't around, another to leave it open when he was home and sleeping. The Exlian rarely got into the city, but he had heard enough horror stories about Exlian drones nesting in people's houses after dismembering them to run that risk, especially when he was on the fringes.

Tossing his bag onto his bed, he tried the light switch, but other than a dim flicker, there was nothing. Grumbling, he grabbed a small light from his desk and flicked it on. His heart sank as it flickered as well. Thankfully, a few taps later and it was shining brightly, casting a soft glow around him. The manastone that powered the lamp was advertised to last years, and Mark had only just bought it a few months before. Of course, one of the other risks of living on the outskirts of the city was that not everything worked as advertised.

Carrying his light, he headed downstairs, the familiar creak of the steps blending with the faint whir of the fridge. The house was simple, with a living room, dining room, and kitchenette on the first floor, along with a bathroom and a storage room. Upstairs, there were three rooms: Mark's room, his older brother Joe's room, and his parents' old room, now used as a storage room for all their stuff. The house was mostly bare, save for a few pieces of beat-up furniture long past their glory days.

The appliances in the kitchen had seen better days, but they still worked . . . mostly. Hesitating for a moment, Mark's hand touched the handle of the fridge. He braced himself and opened it up, feeling intense relief again when he was met by cool air rather than the stench of warming food. Too often recently, he had come home to find that the fridge had lost power as well.

After losing a couple of weeks' worth of groceries, which had put a massive dent in his already meager finances, he had taken to putting only the bare essentials in the fridge, but any spoilage meant going hungry. Scratching his head, he stared at his options. Since he had eaten the macaroni and cheese the night before, Mark pulled out a pack of instant noodles, whose colorful wrapper declared it as nutritious as it was delicious. Mark didn't believe either claim, but he still heated up a bit of water and let the noodles soak. As he was stirring the flavoring in, the lights flickered and came on, leaving him blinking in a suddenly bright room.

He wasn't sure why the power only ever turned on late at night, though he assumed it was because enough people had gone to sleep that the grid wasn't pulling as much power anymore. Taking his noodles, he walked over to the couch, avoiding the broken springs in the middle, and tucked himself into the corner where the last remaining cushion lurked.

Tapping his watch, he pulled up the InfoWeb screen on his wall, grimacing as he bit into something sour. As much as he wanted to spit it out, it was the only nutrition he'd get that evening, and so he swallowed it, getting up to get a glass of water from the sink. Behind him, he could hear a news anchor reporting on the state of the city.

"The threat level continues to climb, and we anticipate another major wave at some point in the next few months."

His eyes sharpening, Mark filled up his cup again and brought it back to the couch, paying careful attention to what the news anchor was saying.

"According to the experts, this next wave will be one of the largest seen in a decade and could last upward of six months. We have Dr. Edward Graham, an expert on the Exlian threat and specifically wave formation, here to share more with us. Dr. Graham?"

The camera panned over, settling on a familiar elderly scientist. Dr. Edward Graham was not merely an expert but *the* expert, currently running the Exlian Institute, the premier city laboratory that studied the Exlian threat to devise countermeasures against it. Turning to the camera with practiced ease, Dr. Graham spoke in a rich, calming baritone.

"We have benefited from more years of peace than we could have hoped for. Fifteen years ago, our city faced an extinction-level wave that threatened to destroy everything we held dear. But we stood strong and inflicted such grievous losses on the Exlian that it has taken them this long to regroup. Though this wave will likely be almost as strong, if not slightly stronger than the threat we faced fifteen years ago, we do not anticipate an extinction-level threat. Over the years we have learned a tremendous amount, strengthened our defenses, and devised new strategies and weapons to deal with the Exlian."

As Dr. Graham spoke, a window next to him showed footage of the terrible war humanity and the alien armies of the Exlian had waged fifteen years before and every year since. A faint pain and a deep, burning anger filled Mark as he watched the well-known images, and he barely heard what Dr. Graham was saying, until finally, the footage cut off, replaced with scenes of the city's current defenses, showing heavily armored soldiers, plasma blades in hand, guarding the walls of the city.

Letting out a breath he hadn't known he had been holding, Mark leaned back, a feeling of exhaustion coming over him. As Dr. Graham finished speaking, the camera panned back over to the newscaster, who appeared to stare straight at Mark.

"Given the emerging level of threat, recruitment will open once again, and the training camps for the three branches—the Defense Force, the Rangers, and the Engineering Corps—will open to the public. I would encourage every able-bodied young man and woman in this city, empowered or not, to step forward and do their duty: for glory, for humanity."

Mark mouthed the words along with the reporter, sitting up. With hurried fingers, he quickly changed the channel, beginning to search on the InfoWeb for more information. The city's forums were abuzz, rumors flying everywhere even though nothing official had been released yet. Still, Mark felt a glowing sense of excitement.

Two years ago, he had missed his chance to enroll in the Defense Force's training camp—his scores were more than good enough to secure a spot, but his finances were not. He'd been working furiously since then but was still far from what he needed. If the city was opening up the basic recruitment camps, however, there was a chance . . .

Spotting a post outlining the way the camps worked, Mark began to read, his excitement growing. The only thing that kept humanity from becoming just another dish on the Exlian threat's plate was the three arms of the military: the Defense Force, the Rangers, and the Engineering Corps. Each had its own training camp where young cadets could go to learn the tricks of each trade after graduating from the mandatory basic training.

The recent lack of waves had decreased the number of slots in the training camps, making it more expensive and competitive to attend, as doing so practically guaranteed a stable job with considerable upward social mobility. Those who lacked resources, like Mark, found themselves unable to get into any of the three camps. The basic recruitment camp, however, opened when a new wave had been identified and was used to bolster the numbers of soldiers during periods of crisis. The recruitment camp would let Mark get his foot in the door of the military, though it would be up to him to attract the attention of one of the three branches if he didn't want to stay a grunt. Unable to contain his excitement, Mark stood up and began pacing, visions of a new future dancing through his head.

As he was pacing, he caught sight of the only decor in the bare room. The photograph on the wall showed a powerfully built man with a green uniform that bore three shining silver stars on the breast pocket, each one representing a significant achievement. Next to him, tucked under his arm, was a woman with long brown hair and a smile that made Mark's heart ache. A thin, serious-looking boy with his mother's brown hair and bright eyes that glowed almost orange stood between them, and held in his father's arms was Mark, no more than a toddler, his tongue sticking out of the side of his mouth and one of his eyes squinting.

Though he had no memory of the picture being taken, Mark could distinctly remember being held in his father's strong arms. It had been fifteen years since he had seen his parents—fifteen years since his father had died on the wall, defending humanity from the largest wave the city had ever faced. The last time he had seen his father was when the alarm sounded, summoning all the off-duty Defense Force soldiers to the walls, and the last time he had seen his mother was a day later. She had received the news of his dad's wounds and rushed to the battlefield to see her dying husband, only to fall with him when their lines were overrun by a swarm of Exlian warrior bugs, led by a brand-new kind called terrors, more powerful than anything humanity could imagine.

Though the city had survived, Mark's family had not. After his parents' death, his brother had been consumed by hatred for the alien threat, disappearing into the military for years at a time, leaving Mark on his own. In truth, he didn't remember his parents overly well. He had only been five when they died, and though he still felt a dull ache when he thought of them, time had blunted the sorrow their death had brought. His older brother, Joe, however, was a different story, and Mark couldn't help but worry about him.

Heading back to the couch, Mark opened a new tab on the web and searched for the rankings. While the three branches of the military were responsible for keeping humanity safe, the true power that humanity wielded against the Exlian threat was held by the empowered. These were humans who had awoken the ability to channel mana directly through their bodies, transforming them into superhumans capable of feats beyond their imagination.

"Joseph Fields, ninety-seven . . . Huh, he's gone up a rank."

Pride filled his heart. To be within the top one hundred empowered in the city was a feat of tremendous proportions, one that would have made their father proud beyond belief. Joe's ability to manipulate flame had been awoken naturally, leaving little doubt of his genius. After staring at his brother's name for a moment longer, Mark sighed and began to scroll through the list.

There were two types of empowered: those who woke naturally and those who were forcefully awoken using the gems harvested from warrior-ranked Exlian. Unfortunately, the path to natural awakening was a mystery, though it was known that strong emotions were a potential trigger. Joe's awakening had coincided with his parents' deaths, and he had spent many long years training to use his ability before being assigned to the Ranger Corps and leaving the city on missions.

As proud as he was of his brother, Mark couldn't help but feel a thread of envy. Ever since Mark had turned fifteen, Joe had spent more time away than at home, and Mark had only been able to watch from a distance as Joe grew more and more powerful. More than anything, Mark wanted to join the military, to wear the armor of the Defense Force, just like his father. He'd even settle for the Rangers, like his brother, though their armor wasn't nearly as cool.

Mark scrolled through the list of empowered, seeing names he recognized and daydreaming, imagining what sorts of powers he might awaken. Elemental control, like his brother, would be great, though Mark would certainly prefer earth or air control to fire. Fire was great for damage but lacked the utility of earth and air's ability to fly. Superstrength or superspeed would be equally welcome, as both were priceless when defending against the Exlian. Even energy blasts or telekinesis would be fine with him.

Scrolling back to the top of the list, Mark looked over the top ten empowered, men and women with a level of strength that Mark couldn't even begin to imagine. The ability to control light, transforming it into a terrifying beam that could cut through anything, or stealing it to create pools of absolute darkness. Invulnerability to blade or claw. Telekinesis that granted its wielder the ability to crush even the hardest exoskeletons with a thought and transform simple chunks of metal into lethal storms.

By the time Mark had reached the tenth place, however, he found himself depressed instead of excited. The earliest known awakening was ten, and since both his father and brother were naturally empowered in their teenage years, Mark had once borne the delusion that he would have a natural awakening as well. Now, at twenty, he had been forced to accept that he simply wasn't as talented as his brother.

He hadn't lost hope, however, as even if he didn't awaken naturally, every member of the military was granted the opportunity for a forced awakening. It was only a chance, of course, as less than 50 percent of the population was able to awaken by consuming an Exlian skill gem, but Mark wasn't about to give up, no matter how old he was.

Checking the time, he saw that it was almost midnight and groaned, shutting the virtual window and heading to the bathroom to wash up. After a quick shower, he went to bed, only to dream that he was flying through the air, far above the city, wielding flaming fists as he battled an Exlian composed of floppy noodles that kept trying to stuff themselves into his mouth.

Waking up in a sweat as the morning light peeked through his window, he chalked it up to having eaten something on the edge of being spoiled and headed into the bathroom to freshen up. His days were mostly routine when his brother was deployed, consisting of working in the morning, training in the afternoon, and then picking up extra shifts in the evening when he could.

A thirty-five-minute commute on the train and then a walk through the crowded streets got him to a small restaurant tucked in a back alley that served off-duty military personnel. Heading through the back door, he scanned his watch at the computer and put his bag down on a bench by the back wall. The kitchen was small and cramped, and already three people rushed around it, frantically trying to complete their orders.

"What are you doing?" Mark's boss yelled when he caught sight of Mark. "The dishes aren't going to wash themselves."

Biting back a retort, Mark grabbed one of the rubber-covered aprons, knowing it would be entirely ineffective at keeping him dry, and hurried over to the sink already piled high with dishes. He was early today, but that didn't stop Jason from yelling at him, and for the next four hours, Mark worked as fast as he possibly could, loading and unloading dishes from the industrial washer that hummed in the corner. Once the lunch rush was over, Jason strode over, grunted at Mark, and turned the machine off.

"I'm not done," Mark said, pointing to a giant pile of dishes being stacked near the sink.

"Cost money to run that. More than I'm paying you," Jason snarled. "Wash the rest by hand."

As much as Mark wanted to lash out, it had taken him four months to land this job. He bit his tongue and began to fill the sink with soapy water. He was just beginning to dunk the first stack of plates when he saw a young woman approaching, carrying another giant stack.

"Oh, come on," Mark groaned.

He had never seen her before, and assumed she was one of

the ever-rotating waitresses who rarely stuck around long enough for him to learn their names. Jason wasn't an easy boss, and from the shouts Mark often heard drifting in from the dining room, he was much harder on the waitresses than on Mark, who had the fortune of being tucked out of the way in the back. Hearing his complaint, the young woman stopped, giving him a slightly frantic look as she held the plates tightly.

"Sorry, I'm just griping," Mark said, reaching out to take the plates from her.

She responded by flinching, nearly dropping the entire stack, causing Mark's face to pale. If any of the plates broke, they'd come out of his paycheck, and he'd be lucky if he made anything this week. Lunging forward, he wrapped one arm around the stack and the other around her, pulling her tightly to his chest as the plates started to dribble down toward the ground. Shocked by his sudden advance, the young woman froze and then began to struggle, causing the plates sandwiched between them to rattle.

"Don't move," Mark barked, much harsher than he intended. "Help me get them in the sink!"

It was a minor miracle that they managed to keep the plates sandwiched between them as they scooched over to the sink. As carefully as they could, they dropped them into the soapy water, and Mark winced every time he heard the thud as a plate struck the metal sides. Praying none of the plates had chipped, he said, "Sorry, I just—"

Mark looked up and realized she was gone. He fell silent and sighed, rubbing his forehead with a soapy hand. It was going to be a long day.

He didn't see the young woman for the rest of the day, but the next morning, when he jumped back into the familiar rush, he saw her flying in and out of the kitchen doors, balancing plates on her arms as if she had been doing it for years, and carrying stacks of dirty dishware in to drop next to the sink. She never looked at Mark and preferred to drop the plates as far away from him as possible before hurrying off, so after his first few attempts to apologize, Mark decided to forget it and buried himself in the suds and soapy water.

Every day after he finished the lunch rush, Mark would hang up his rubber apron, grab his bag, and head down the street to a local training center. Given the nature of life in New Emery, there were training centers everywhere, and they were always packed. This training center, one of half a dozen on this street, was the cheapest, resembling a large empty warehouse more than anything else. That didn't bother him, however, as for a modest fee of 100 credits, he could use it anytime he wanted. A fantastic deal considering that the next cheapest training center was a cool 500 credits a month.

Heading into the changing room, Mark didn't bother to change out of his wet clothing, knowing it would just get wet again later when he went back to work. After hanging up his bag, he unzipped it and pulled out his training gear. Weighted anklets were strapped around his legs, and a weighted vest went over his head. Getting out a pair of gloves, he held them in his hand as he walked out into the training area, nodding to another regular who always came during lunchtime. The middle-aged man greeted him with a wave before heading into the changing room to dress and go back to his desk job.

Adjusting the bulky and uncomfortable weighted vest, Mark sighed. There were much better options for training equipment, none of which he could afford, and it was with more than a little envy that he glanced at one of the coaches from the corner of his eye, seeing the man's streamlined training shirt that clung tightly to his muscular figure. Shirts like that were enchanted and could be carrying shards of manastones that allowed the wearer to adjust the weight at will. They also cost more than Mark made in a year.

Finding an empty corner, he began his warm-up, starting with some stretches and then working his way through his body-weight routine. Around halfway through his workout, one of the trainers wandered over and spent a few minutes half-heartedly showing Mark how to execute a side kick. Though martial arts were entirely useless against the Exlian unless one possessed superspeed or superstrength, they were still widely practiced, as they helped keep the body and the mind sharp.

After the trainer had wandered off to find someone else to instruct, Mark completely ignored everything that he had just been taught and began working through his forms. One of the advantages of having a brother in the Rangers was that Mark had been drilling his martial forms since he was ten years old.

Mark was soon lost in the flow of the movement, his mind forgetting his looming worries and the pressures of living on the periphery as he immersed himself in motion. This was one of the few moments during his day when life didn't seem so bad. Entirely too soon, his watch buzzed, shaking him from his trance and alerting him that it was time to head back to the restaurant to see if he could pick up shifts for the evening rush.

Hurrying to the changing room, Mark stripped off his shirt and toweled himself off. The one advantage to working in the back by the dish station was that nobody cared if he came in smelling of sweat, so after giving his shirt a moment to dry off, he put it back on and stored his training gear in his backpack. Pausing for a moment, he stared at his face in the mirror, his eyes tracing his lean cheeks and intense green eyes, hidden behind his dark-brown hair. He had gotten his hair from his mom and his eyes from his father. Though he wasn't as tall as his father, who had awakened a strength-based empowerment, Mark was well built, his shoulders broad, and his body muscular from his daily training. But he lacked the bulk of someone able to train with high-end gear, and his face was too thin to be handsome, though it had strong lines that hinted at good looks.

Brushing his hair out of his eyes, Mark sighed. He clearly needed to increase his food budget again. He had been trying to cut costs as much as possible to save every credit he could, but it was obvious that the cuts to his food budget were negatively impacting his workouts. Picking up his bag, he tossed it over his shoulder and headed out, noticing, as he did, a crowd by one of the trainers. Wondering if there was a new training routine, Mark wandered over, looking over the heads of those crowding around the paper the trainer was putting up. As the trainer stepped aside, Mark's eyes widened. It was a flyer announcing that the new basic recruitment camp was now accepting registration.

His fingers flying, Mark immediately opened up a virtual window on his watch and began to type in the InfoWeb address. The page stuttered as it tried to load, and Mark had no doubt that hundreds of thousands of other young men and women were doing exactly the same thing he was. Though it had been years since a basic recruitment camp had been opened, the slots always filled up quickly, and Mark could only pray that he was in time as he submitted the form.

Thankfully, it was a simple process, as the government already had all his information and would be able to look him up to determine whether he was a good candidate as long as he indicated he was interested. When he finished, he waited with bated breath for the confirmation to show up and grinned when he heard the ping. Closing the window, Mark said another silent prayer and, after giving the flyer a long look, headed back to the restaurant.

Along the way, his watch vibrated, and glancing down, Mark saw he had a call from an unlisted number. A grin lit up his face as he stopped and stepped to the side of the sidewalk, letting the people walking behind him pass. With a surprising amount of nervousness, he accepted the call and saw a familiar face appear.

"Joe! Where are you? Are you back in the city?"

"Hello, Mark. No, not back yet. We ran into a bit of a snag with our mission."

Mark's heart clenched as he noticed the exhaustion hidden in his brother's gaze. Though Joe's face appeared to be carved from marble, he couldn't hide just how tired he was or the nasty cut on his cheek.

"Are you okay?"

"Hmm? Yeah, fine. This is nothing. But like I said, we ran into a snag, so it might be a bit before I'm back."

A faint rumble from behind Joe caused the image above Mark's watch to shake as the signal cut in and out. Though he wanted to say something, Mark felt like his tongue was glued to the roof of his mouth, and for a moment the two brothers stared at each other in silence.

"Sorry I haven't been around more, Mark. This time, I'll take a real break, I promise."

The sounds behind Joe were getting louder, and Mark saw a flash of irritation in his brother's eyes.

"I can't stay on the call, but know that I love you. I'll see you soon."

Not wanting to call out his brother's lie, all Mark could do was offer a strained smile as the air around Joe erupted with flame and his brother turned away to deal with whatever that rumbling sound was.

"I love you too," Mark choked out, but it was too late. The call had already disconnected.

Standing on the sidewalk as people streamed past, hurrying about their business, Mark felt like his heart might burst. As a Ranger, Joe's whole life was about running into dangerous situations, and this wasn't the first call like this that Mark had received. Somehow that didn't make it better. It was only two blocks to the restaurant, but Mark was so distracted that he almost didn't make it.

The explosion came from the sewer system as a large Exlian burst up through the concrete, its sharp claws making short work of the street. Monstrous and terrifying as it was, the real danger came from the shards of concrete its entrance hurled across the street. The deadly projectiles tore into the crowd, one large piece scraping past Mark's nose with only inches to spare. Others walking nearby weren't so lucky, and cries of pain mingled with the terrified screams that filled the air.

This deep in the city, such attacks were rare, and the first thought that Mark had when his brain caught up to the chaos was that someone in the Defense Force was going to be punished. The second thought was about how stupid he was to be standing around thinking such useless thoughts when a monster was on the loose. Throwing himself to the ground and scrambling across the sidewalk to try to duck behind a car, Mark caught sight of the Exlian's legs.

They were covered in hard chitin plates and ended in a pair of wicked claws that gouged the street as it heaved its bulk by, leaving a trail of destruction. His heart pounded like a drum, filling his ears with a roar that drowned out the screams of the other civilians running for cover, and the fear coursing through him transformed his blood to ice. He was locked in place, not daring to move for fear he might attract the monster's attention, when he saw someone who had been hit by a piece of shrapnel just beyond the Exlian.

Middle aged, balding, and clutching his bleeding leg, the man lay on the ground, trying to pull himself away from the advancing monster. Adrenaline flooded Mark's system. Running out to try to save the man was suicide, as an unempowered stood no chance against even the weakest Exlian, but he wasn't thinking about survival anymore. The initial moment of terror had worn off, and all that was left was the desperate need to do something. Anything.

Feeling a loose piece of concrete, Mark grabbed it and lunged to his feet, vaulting over the hood of the car. As he landed on the other side, the Exlian came into full view. Eight feet tall, covered in spines, with a massive pair of mandibles and claws that could slice steel, the monster looked like something out of a nightmare. A nightmare about to eat the poor man who had been wounded.

With no chance of making it to the man before the Exlian attacked, Mark did the only thing he could. His arm came back, and he stepped forward, throwing the stone he was holding with all his might. It flew straight and true, slamming into the Exlian's carapace and causing the monster to jerk in surprise. Even as it began to turn, Mark was already diving to the side, his instincts screaming at him to flee as fast as possible. There was a screech and a blur, followed by the sound of tortured metal as the Exlian darted across the street and tried to cut Mark in half.

Without any apparent effort, its bladed arm sank deep into the car Mark had been standing in front of, tearing through the metal like it was paper. The rough concrete scraped at Mark's skin, but a few lacerations were the least of Mark's worries as he turned over, staring up at the Exlian that now stood over him. A million thoughts flashed through Mark's head, but they moved too fast for him to capture as the Exlian casually tore its bladed arm free and lifted it into the air.

There was a single instant of absolute stillness as man and monster stared at each other.

Then a blast of plasma tore through the Exlian's head, melting its carapace and frying the monster's insides, filling the air with a burning stench. At the same time, a figure appeared in the air above the street, half a dozen more balls of superheated mana flying around her like wisps dancing in the wind. Mark's mind hadn't yet caught up to what was happening when the Exlian collapsed in front of him, and the empowered woman floated down toward the street.

"Command, this is Aetherwisp. There appears to only be a single drone, though it was a big one on the cusp of transforming. At least a dozen casualties. No dead that I can see."

Mark gawked, still trying to piece together the abrupt reversal of fortune as the woman calling herself Aetherwisp looked over the street, her gaze settling on him. As their eyes met, Mark felt a wave of terrifying pressure that awoke a primal fear in his heart. This fear was much stronger than the terror induced by the Exlian drone and shook him to his core. He had never felt so small in his life.

The drone had been strong enough to end his life without him having any hope of surviving, and Aetherwisp had just ended its existence as if it were no more than an annoying bug.

"No, I'm not picking up anything else. We need an investigation team to figure out how a drone of this size got through the wall. All right, I'm heading out."

Closing her call, Aetherwisp flashed a smile at Mark, who was still staring at her in shock, and launched herself into the air, her wisps forming wings that carried her aloft. Then she was gone, leaving Mark and the wounded civilians in the street. The sirens started a moment later, and within a couple of minutes, emergency personnel were on the scene, patching everyone up and taking statements.

It was almost an hour before Mark was able to leave, and even then, he was only released after promising to get a follow-up exam within the week. His mind still numb from the shock, Mark walked back to the restaurant, where he was met at the back door by Jason, who looked him over carefully and then, with an uncharacteristic silence, jerked a thumb toward the massive pile of dishes that had been stacked next to the sink.

Mark's shift flew by, his thoughts completely occupied with the attack he had just lived through. He didn't regret throwing the rock, and he wasn't sure that there had been another option that would have kept the middle-aged man alive, but he couldn't shake the feeling of impotence that his encounter with the Exlian drone had generated. It was one thing to imagine how he would fare against an Exlian and entirely another, he found, to face one. Exlian were death incarnate, biological machines bred for war, and the only way to survive against them was with more power.

Placing one of the plates he had just scrubbed to the side, Mark grabbed another, his thoughts turning to Aetherwisp. He hadn't recognized her immediately, but given a moment to think about it, he realized he knew who she was. She was ranked eighty-seventh in the city and was assigned to the Defense Force, the military branch Mark desperately wanted to join, but seeing the gulf in power between them left Mark feeling like it might be hopeless.

The only chance he had to close that gap hinged on making it into the training camp. He knew that there was a high chance he would, since the basic recruitment camps were designed to take in as many people as possible, filling out the infantry ranks in preparation for the larger waves, and he had family in the military already. The city was constantly under attack, with small groups of Exlian attempting to break through the defensive lines to get at the citizens inside the city, so there was always a need for soldiers to guard the walls, and that was only more pressing during the waves.

Occasionally, some of the Exlian did sneak through, like the one that had nearly killed him that afternoon, forcing the Defense Force to comb the city until they were found, but such incidents were mercifully rare, and for the most part the Defense Force was able to keep the Exlian outside the city walls and humanity safe inside.

Only the Rangers and the Engineering Corps ventured out to set up hidden outposts designed to collect important resources that couldn't be sourced from the city itself. During the waves the Exlian would gather in vast numbers, covering the landscape, launching attacks against the city in rapid succession. Mark had never experienced it himself, but he had seen the videos of Exlian so thick in number they appeared to be a solid mass. These waves could last anywhere from a few weeks to months, and if the rumors flying around were anything to go by, the coming wave that was building beyond the city's walls would be the most dangerous yet.

Rumors were rumors, however, and even if they were true, Mark wasn't particularly afraid. The wave fifteen years ago had caught New Emery off guard, revealing gaps in the city's defenses that had now been plugged. New weapons had also been created during this time—weapons that proved devastating when deployed against the enemy. As long as there were enough defenders to properly man the wall, the chances of the city being breached were almost zero. Besides, even if the city wall was breached, the empowered who stood at the top of the rankings would step in to hold the line. His thoughts full of the future, Mark finished up close to midnight, earning himself a begrudging nod from his boss.

Wondering if the man ever slept, Mark began the trek home, only to realize that the train line he normally used wasn't running. Grumbling, he looked for the next closest stop and saw a train that would drop him off at a station that was a forty-five-minute walk from his house. It was that or take a taxi, which he couldn't afford. It was a common enough occurrence that he didn't think anything of it, and after boarding the train, he found a seat and set an alarm on his watch, trying to steal some rest. The train car was mercifully silent and mostly empty, save for a few late-night commuters, and he soon drifted into a fitful sleep, waking occasionally with a jerk as visions of massive, car-cleaving monsters crept into his dreams.

When his watch buzzed, Mark stood up with a yawn, walking to the door as the train came to a halt. He was the only one getting off and was soon alone on the platform. Standing there as the train pulled away, Mark opened his watch, pulling up a map of the city as he traced his route home. The last thing he wanted to do at this time of night was walk for forty-five minutes through the dark streets, but there simply wasn't another option if he didn't want to ruin his budget for the month. Until he got paid, money was too tight. With an annoyed sigh, he began trudging toward his house, focusing on putting one foot in front of the other.

The night was quiet, and this far out from the city center, the mana-fed streetlights were unreliable, often leaving the streets shrouded in inky darkness. The darkness contrasted sharply with the city center, which was so bright that it lit up the horizon, flooding the sky with just enough light pollution to block out the stars. Even if the light pollution hadn't drowned them out, the haze that hung above the city likely would have, leaving the night even darker. The farther Mark walked, the quieter the night became, until he suddenly realized that he couldn't hear any of the normal sounds he associated with the city at night.

Pausing at a street corner, he looked both ways, unnerved by the strange stillness. Seeing nothing, he shook his head and continued on his way, faster than before, trying not to recall the sight of the Exlian drone looming over him. Halfway down the block, he heard a sound that made his heartbeat speed up. From a nearby alley came the sound of rushing feet, and with bated breath, Mark paused.

The footsteps suddenly stopped, and Mark heard a light groan in the stillness. He was only a few blocks from his neighborhood now, and the desire to simply rush past and run home as fast as he could was strong enough to make him break into a run. Yet even as he started to move swiftly past the alleyway, he heard another groan. Someone was in distress. Wrestling with himself, Mark let out a light groan of his own and, against his better judgment, stopped. He peeked around the corner and caught sight of a figure, half collapsed against the wall.

"Are you okay?"

Jerking in surprise, the figure looked up, revealing a woman whose chin-length hair had obscured her features. She bore a nasty cut on her cheekbone that leaked blood in fat drops down her cheek, and purplish bruising around one eye that made one of her eyes disappear into shadow. She was clutching her side, which was bleeding badly, and when she saw Mark, her eyes widened in shock and a faint emotion he couldn't quite place. With a trembling hand, she lifted something that had been half concealed by her coat, holding it out toward Mark.

"Wildfire," she gasped. "Give this . . ."

Whatever she was trying to say was lost to the night as her eyes rolled back in her head and she collapsed like a puppet with its strings cut. Mark was a moment too late as he tried to grab her and winced as her head slammed against the ground. It was only then that he noticed how bad the woman's bleeding actually was as the growing pool of blood underneath her and her rapidly cooling skin told him that there was nothing he could do for her. Just to be sure, Mark crouched by her head and reached out to check the woman's pulse. Nothing.

His heart falling, Mark activated his watch to try to call the emergency line, only to find that no matter what he did, his watch simply wouldn't turn on. Staring at it in confusion, he pulled it off his wrist and tried to do a hard reboot, but the screen remained black. Frustrated, he nearly threw it against the ground. Of all the times for technology to fail him, he couldn't believe it was happening now. He didn't, of course, as watches were expensive.

A thought struck him, and he fumbled for the woman's watch, lifting her limp arm to try to send a message on it, but it was inexplicably dead as well. The frightening feeling of something being wrong washed over him, and Mark's breath caught. There was more to the situation than met the eye. Hoping he hadn't just stumbled into something dangerous, he rocked back on his heels and felt something by his foot.

The small box had tumbled from her hand as she fell. Simple and pure black, it carried an ornate set of carvings like some intriguing but useless ornament. Picking it up, Mark turned it over in his hands. The woman had said something about wildfire and giving, none of which made any sense. He could only assume that this box was to be given to somebody, and that it had something to do with flames.

Noticing a slight depression on one side of the box, Mark ran his thumb over it and felt a piercing pain as the box stabbed a black needle so deep into his thumb that it emerged through his nail on the other side. His breath caught in his chest as his entire body seized, and before his terrified eyes the black spike began to transform into dozens of waving tendrils. Mercifully, darkness overtook him as the pain coursing through his body proved to be too much for his mind to handle.

Had he been awake, he would have seen that as he collapsed backward onto the ground, the box continued to transform. Malleable tendrils extended from the sides of the box and burrowed into Mark's hand, pulsing as they were absorbed into him. It wasn't long before the box had vanished, merged into Mark's hand as if it had never been there.

Not more than five minutes later, the sound of footsteps

echoed in the alley, and three figures arrived on the scene, all wearing the black-and-green uniforms of the Rangers. A woman with close-cropped black hair and silver eyes led the group, and when she arrived by the body that lay in the middle of the alleyway, she held out her palm, activating her power. Threads of mana crackled as they emerged from her forearm, rapidly forming arcane symbols that created a pulse in the air, encompassing the surrounding area.

"Anything?" the leader of the Rangers asked.

"No," the woman replied. "There isn't a soul around, and no sign of the nest. Hold on, let me expand the search."

Closing her eyes, she activated her power again, this time causing a few sparkles to appear in the air around her. They were all faint, however, and after they had faded, she shook her head. "The only people nearby are in their homes. I'm not picking up any signs of life anywhere close."

Swearing under his breath, the older man, who had graying hair, a mustache, and a heavy jaw, looked at the third member of their group, a young man whose blond hair was tied up in a ponytail. "What do you think, Greg?"

"She is dead," the young man said, shaking his head. "Time of death approximately ten minutes ago. Died from blood loss. Your stab cut into her liver, and it's a miracle she made it this far, Captain."

"Miracle or curse? How she ran so fast losing that much blood, I don't understand. Did she meet someone here? Where was she going? And what happened to that blasted nest?"

Greg looked down at the woman's inert body and shrugged.

"No way to tell," he said, reaching down to tap the blood-stained concrete under her head. "There are no signs of anyone else. She staggered, caught herself on the wall, and then tried to take a step forward and collapsed. There are no signs of any nest. Are we sure that she actually grabbed it? Could it have been a false alarm?"

"No, she tried to run when we confronted her. And the alarm has been triggered downtown. All signs point to her as the culprit." Taking a deep breath to try to contain his anger, the captain looked over at the female Ranger. "What do you think, Laura?"

"I think that she was a diversion. She probably handed it off to somebody else and then ran to draw us away and buy them time to get to safety. It wouldn't be hard if the second person was an empowered with a stealth ability."

"If that's the case, we're in a lot of trouble. Who knows what these crazies will do with a nest in the city. Scan again."

"Yes, Captain."

When she held out her hand, another silver wave rippled out, vanishing into the walls of the alleyway. This time, there was a brighter sparkle in the air, directly in front of Laura, causing all three of the Rangers to draw their weapons. Holding a long silver dagger with a bright mana edge, Laura stared at a pile of debris at the other end of the alleyway, her eyes searching for whatever had triggered her power. After a tense moment, she suddenly laughed and relaxed.

"Just a cat," she said, pointing to a patch of darkness under a half-collapsed box. "Nothing to be worried about."

Peering at the box, the captain nodded and let out a long breath. "Nothing else?" he asked, though he knew the answer already.

"I didn't pick up anything else. There are no Exlian for at least a mile, and certainly no nests."

"Central is gonna have my hide for this," the captain said, sliding his blade into its sheath and rubbing his grizzled chin. "Come on, let's keep looking. Maybe we'll get lucky and pick up the tail of whoever she handed the nest off to."

When Mark awoke, it was morning. The events of the night before were fuzzy in his mind, and faint dread lingered in his heart. For a long moment, he didn't move, simply staring at the ceiling above his bed, his mind trying to come to terms with what had happened. An angry buzz intruded into his thoughts, and looking down, he stared at his watch, bleary eyed. Fumbling for the button to turn it on, he realized it was already on and blinking aggressively at him. When the numbers finally swam into focus, he realized that it was noon, and he had a dozen missed messages.

He jerked upright in shock, and his pounding heart sent a wave of excruciating pain through him that sent him tumbling straight to the floor. With his eyes screwed tight, a groan of pure anguish escaped his lips. Given ten years of aggressive workouts and martial arts, he was no stranger to sore muscles, but this was something else entirely. A terrible burning filled every single cell of his body, bringing with it a tremendous weakness and an overwhelming craving for food that overrode his desire to roll around on the floor in agony.

Unable to stand, it was all he could do to pull himself out of his room, half crawling and half sliding down the stairs, until he tumbled into the kitchen. His mind had no room for anything but the overwhelming need for food. Nearly tearing the fridge's door off in his haste to find something, Mark gobbled down everything in sight, and when he came back to himself ten minutes later, his fridge was empty. Though the terrible ache had not gone away, it had lessened enough that his mind was working once again. Remembering all the messages on his watch, he quickly opened them up, scrolling through them rapidly. They were from his boss, asking him, in increasingly irate terms, where he was. Paling and frantically tapping his watch, he called Jason.

"What?" Jason growled.

"I'm sorry," Mark said. "I'm really sick. I didn't mean to miss my shift."

There was a long moment of silence, and then, in a gruff voice, Jason said something that left Mark floored.

"That's fine. Just don't do it again. If you miss another shift, you're out. You're lucky someone was here to cover for you. She saved your butt, so make sure you buy her a meal or something to say thank you."

Before Mark could say anything, the phone disconnected, and he was left staring at it, unable to believe what he had just heard. Who on earth would have stepped in to cover for him? A moment later, that question was answered when his watch vibrated and a picture appeared, showing the new girl wearing a rubber apron at least two sizes too big, up to her elbows in soapy water.

Mark silently swore to himself that he would make it up to her, and he turned toward his pantry, looking for something more to eat. There was little there, but Mark didn't care, and after opening up a few old cans of vegetables, he scarfed them down.

With every bite he ate, the burning pain that filled his entire body receded slightly, but when he finished, he found himself still hungry. Checking his bank account, he grimaced. Whatever was happening to him would eat into his budget and affect his savings badly. He could feel that not eating would have catastrophic results, leaving him no choice. With a sigh, he looked at the empty fridge, then at the empty pantry. Hopefully, this terrible hunger would pass, or he was going to be in a lot of trouble.

Turning to the front door, Mark froze, his adrenaline spiking as he realized it was open. The still-engaged dead bolt had been ripped out of the wall, leaving the door open a crack. Mark had been so consumed with his hunger that he hadn't noticed it, and since he didn't remember getting home the night before, he could only assume that it had been hanging open this entire time.

There was a bit of movement on the floor, and ever so slowly, Mark's eyes fell, his heart beating loudly. Instead of the buggy features of an Exlian drone, he saw a tiny kitten sitting on the floor, staring up at him. Its fur was all black, except for its face, which had a large splash of white across its eyes and nose, almost like a mask.

The cat let out a large yawn and stretched. Feeling immense relief, Mark crouched down as the cat padded over to him. He held out his hand, curious how close it would get, and was astonished when the little cat climbed right up into his palm and sat down, its tail hanging over his fingers.

"Uh, hello?" Mark said, not quite sure what to do.

Blinking at him, the cat cocked its head to the side, then nodded to itself, as if quite pleased.

"Uh, sorry, little buddy. I, um, I don't have any food for you. I am about to go to the store, though, so if you hang around outside, maybe I could bring something back."

If the cat understood what he said, it gave no indication, and as carefully as he could, Mark carried it outside. It remained completely at ease as it sat on his hand, a tiny little thing, no more than six inches high. After trying in vain to shut his door behind him, Mark sighed, pulled it closed as best he could, and tried to put the cat down on the sidewalk. It didn't want to get down and raced up his arm, arriving on his shoulder, causing him to yelp. "Hey!"

As he tried to grab it, he felt claws starting to pierce his shoulder, and his yelp got louder.

"Ow! Hey, that hurts."

As soon as he stopped reaching for the cat, its claws retracted, and they fell into a stalemate. Mark was crouched, looking utterly ridiculous, on the sidewalk with his arms outspread and the cat perched serenely on his shoulder. Slowly straightening up, he started to reach for the cat again, only to feel its claws beginning to emerge and press down into his skin.

"Okay, you want to stay there. I get it."

The cat's tail lashed, and he decided that it would be better to go shopping with a cat on his shoulder than suffer under its claws trying to get it off. He imagined that it would jump down when it was ready, and strangely, having it on his shoulder made him feel less hungry.

The grocery store was only a couple of blocks away, and after checking his watch to make sure that he had enough time to both shop and get to his afternoon shift, Mark went shopping. His older brother had once told him that it was best not to go shopping when hungry, and an hour later Mark finally understood why.

Everything in the store had looked delicious to him. Everything. That feeling was disconcerting enough that he did his shopping quickly, afraid that if he stayed in the store he'd just start shoving things into his mouth.

He had the presence of mind to focus on high-protein, calorie-dense foods, as that was what his body was craving, and it was only when he got back to his apartment and began to put the bags on the table that he realized just how much he had purchased.

The little cat, who had remained on his shoulder for the entire trip, drawing quite a few looks from the others in the store, jumped down and padded its way over to the couch, where it seated itself in the most comfortable spot and then looked at Mark, clearly expecting some food.

"One moment, Your Majesty," Mark said sarcastically, earning himself a little nod from the black cat.

Rolling his eyes, Mark put the groceries away and got out a can of cat food. As he opened the can, the cat's ears perked up, and it sat up to look at him. Mark put the food on a small plate and carried it over to the kitten, who immediately began to eat. As he looked at the kitten happily biting into the food, he couldn't help but smile.

Taking out a pack of ground meat, Mark made some rice and poured a jar of sauce into it. He added the meat and some salt and pepper, stirring together a high-calorie meal that would normally last him a few days. Looking at the pot, Mark had a sinking suspicion that it would hardly last him this meal.

The cat resisted his attempts to move it from the comfortable spot on the couch, so Mark sat on the pathetic cushion next to it and began combing through the news to see if he could find any mention of what happened to him the night before, all the while shoving food into his mouth. In no time flat, he was finished, scraping the pot clean with his fork to get the last few grains of rice. To his dismay, he was still hungry, so he took out a large hunk of ham that he had purchased on a whim and proceeded to eat the entire thing. That was followed by half a dozen sandwiches and an entire bag of peaches.

When he finally began to feel satisfied, Mark forced himself to stop, afraid that he wouldn't have any food left if he didn't control himself. He had about an hour and a half before he needed to be at work, so he grabbed his bag, discarded by the stairs the night before, and went to the door. As he opened it, he felt a hint of pressure on his shoulder and realized that the little black cat had reclaimed its perch once again.

Mark should have been weirded out. He knew that any reasonable person would have been, but there was something comforting about the cat, so he walked out of the door, letting it be. The first thing he did after leaving his house was head back toward the alleyway where he had found the unconscious woman the night before. He was half convinced that what he had experienced was simply a nightmare, brought on by whatever strange condition had caused him to be so hungry, and that was reinforced when, arriving at the scene of the incident, he found nothing to indicate that it had ever happened.

There should have been a corpse, or at least an entire person's worth of blood soaked into the cement, but the ground was completely clean. Extraordinarily clean. His eyesight seemed sharper than ever, allowing him to pick up a clear distinction between the area where he had seen the woman fall and the ground a few feet away, which was covered in grime, as if someone had cleaned up the dirt in this area.

Unsettled, Mark traced the path the woman must have taken coming down the alleyway. A dozen feet away, he found what he was looking for—dark spots of dried blood that had dripped from the woman's side, falling among the debris that littered the alley. It hadn't been a dream, but what had actually happened, and how Mark had ended up back in his bed, he had no idea.

He hesitated to report the incident, as he could only imagine how crazy he would sound, claiming that a woman had been injured in the alleyway, then attacked him with a black box after dying. But apart from an overeager appetite, he had no proof that he hadn't imagined the entire thing. Unsure what to do, Mark made his way back into the city, arriving at the restaurant just as Jason walked out the back door, carrying a bag of trash.

"Sick, huh?" Jason sneered.

"I really was," Mark protested. "I am feeling better now, but I was really sick."

Rolling his eyes, Jason just jerked a thumb toward the door, telling Mark to go in. Not wanting to push the issue, Mark did and found the young woman who had stepped in to help him save his job standing by the sink, trying in vain to towel off her wet shirt.

"I think the towel's wetter than your shirt is, so it's not going to work very well," Mark said, dropping his bag on the bench.

Startled, as she hadn't heard him come in, the young woman looked up, freezing when she saw him, the barest hint of pink creeping onto her cheeks and the tips of her ears. Realizing he was staring, Mark quickly held out his hand. "I'm Mark."

At the same time that he introduced himself, the young woman dropped the towel and stepped back, leaving Mark's hand hanging in the air. Feeling slightly foolish, Mark stepped forward, just as the young woman, realizing that she had left Mark hanging, put out her hand and stepped forward as well, accidentally punching him in the stomach.

This time, the blush that flooded her face wasn't subtle, and in some surprise, Mark looked down at his stomach.

Overcome by curiosity, Mark grabbed the edge of his T-shirt and lifted, his eyes widening. Mark had always focused on functional muscle over building a chiseled but useless physique, so seeing a brand-new, well-defined eight-pack was a shock. For both—the waitress stepped back, eyes widening, and it was Mark's turn to blush. He quickly dropped the edge of his shirt, patting it to make sure his defined abs were completely covered.

"Sorry," he said, desperate to shift attention. "Let's try this again. My name is Mark."

"Sky," came the soft reply.

"It's nice to officially meet you, Sky, and thanks for covering for me. I wouldn't have a job right now if you hadn't."

Her expression slowly relaxing, Sky nodded.

"You covered for me," she said, "when I first got here. So I thought . . ."

She didn't finish her thought, as Jason yelled at them from across the room.

"You two can hold hands later. We've got a whole pile of customers, and half the staff lollygagging back here. Sky, get out front and start taking orders! And you, Mark, I want those dishes spit-polished!"

"Yes, sir," Mark called, giving Sky an apologetic grimace as he turned toward the sink.

Smiling, Sky turned and ran toward the dining room, leaving Mark to pick up the apron she had just put down. Tying it around his waist, he got to work on the giant pile of dishes. The rest of the evening passed swiftly, and Mark found himself moving faster and more efficiently than ever before. It helped, of course, that Sky popped back into the kitchen every few minutes and lingered for a moment after delivering dishes to Mark at the sink. She didn't say anything, but Mark felt happy about the attention she was paying him.

Halfway through the evening, he suddenly remembered the little black cat, but when he looked around, he didn't see it anywhere. With a shrug, Mark figured it had finally taken off, returning to wherever it had come from. Sky got off a few hours before Mark did, and after stopping by to ask if he would be in the next day, she slipped out the door before Jason could yell, leaving Mark looking after her.

"What are you staring at?" Jason growled from only a few feet behind Mark, causing him to jump and nearly drop the plate he was holding. "I don't pay you to gawk at the staff. Get back to work."

Strangely happy despite his growling boss, Mark spun around and saluted as best he could, causing a bit of foam to stick to his forehead. Jason had no patience for such fooling around, and with a glare he stomped off, no doubt to terrorize somebody else. Wanting to make up for the time he had missed that morning, Mark stayed well past midnight to help close the restaurant. Thankfully, the train that would take him home was running again, and it was a quick five-minute walk to his house from the station. The door was still broken when he arrived, but it didn't seem to have been disturbed, and as Mark was about to open the door, he suddenly found the small black cat on his shoulder once more.

"Okay, this is seriously weird," Mark said, speaking out loud to try to dispel some of the creepiness.

Giving him an arch look, the cat seemed to gesture with its head for him to go inside. As soon as they set foot in the house, the cat leaped down from his shoulder, landing on the couch, and took up its position on the best cushion, while it waited for something to eat. Mark's appetite had returned to normal, so he shared a quick snack with the kitten, then grabbed a bookshelf, the only other piece of furniture in the room, to pull in front of the door. It wouldn't keep it shut if someone was really determined, but it would at least give Mark some warning. With the door secured, he walked over to the stairs and was surprised to see the cat sitting at the top of them, staring at him.

"I can't just keep calling you 'cat,'" Mark said as he walked up the stairs and followed the cat into his bedroom, where it jumped onto his bed and curled up on his pillow. "And that's *my* pillow."

He was ignored, of course, as he'd assumed he would be, and so, with a sigh, he moved the pillow to the side and stole one from his brother's bed. Returning to his room, he sat on the bed and rubbed his nose as he considered the animal sharing a bed with him. He had acquired a new pet, though it might have been more accurate to say the cat had acquired him. Either way, he knew that he wasn't going to get to the bottom of all the weird things that had happened to him at two in the morning on a Friday night. He sighed and lay down, quickly falling asleep as he tried to come up with names for his new pet.

Unfortunately for Mark, the strangeness wasn't over yet, and he woke around four in the morning, two hours after he had gone to bed. Opening his eyes, he caught sight of the dark ceiling, his mind snapping into focus as he felt a familiar hunger surge within him, strong enough he knew it would be useless to try to go back to sleep. Grumbling, he stumbled out of bed and made his way down the dark staircase, not bothering to turn on the light.

The kitchen was shrouded in darkness, but it didn't pose any obstacle to Mark, and he headed straight for the fridge, squinting as the light hit his eyes when he opened the door. He grabbed a large block of cheese, intending to break some off to whet his appetite, but then, realizing how hungry he was, took the whole thing. A couple of minutes later, he had eaten the entire block of cheese, along with a full loaf of bread and the entire bag of apples that he had purchased at the store the day before.

"I'm going to go broke," he muttered.

Breaking into a box of energy bars that each contained enough calories to replace an entire meal, he ate every single one of them, determined not to stop until he finally felt full. Halfway through the last bar, he finally felt his stomach settle, and tossing the rest of the bar into his mouth, he chewed and swallowed as he stood up, reaching out to steady himself against the wall.

As soon as he stood up, he felt a flash, and his body grew warm. In a panic, he gripped the wall tightly as the world swam around him, heat waves seeming to obscure everything he saw. Then the sensation faded, and for a long moment, Mark stood in place, breathing heavily.

"I might need to go see a doctor."

Looking up, he caught sight of the cat sitting at the top of the stairs, staring at him. And for the first time, he realized that its eyes glowed with an eerie red light. Afraid he was seeing things, he blinked, but that didn't make it any better. In fact, it made it worse, as he noticed that the cat's right eye had another eye on top of it, slitted and alien. Jerking back in surprise, Mark looked closer and saw nothing but two completely normal cat eyes staring back at him.

"I really do need to go see a doctor," he said, shaking his head. "Or maybe I just need more sleep."

Letting go of the wall, he took a step forward and promptly fell over. Dragged to the side by a heavy weight, he landed on the ground with a yelp and rolled over onto his back. His left arm was strangely heavy, and it took considerable effort for him to lift it off the ground, to the point where he had to use his right hand to support it. Even stranger, the skin on his left arm felt much rougher than it should have been. After stumbling over to the stairs and nudging the light switch with his elbow, it was all he could do not to scream.

From the elbow down, his left arm had transformed into smooth gray concrete that matched the walls of his house. When he wasn't looking at it or feeling its weight dragging him down, his arm felt completely normal, and he had no trouble moving his fingers, but there was no doubt that his arm was concrete. The truth came in a rush, overwhelming him and causing him to sit down on the stairs. The changes to his body, his improved eyesight, the intense hunger, and the strange state of his arm . . .

"I'm empowered."

He had awoken a power naturally, and the realization left him too excited to sleep. For the rest of the night he paced around the house, and as soon as it was light, he rushed outside, barely noticing when the black cat hitched a ride on his shoulder. He had taken care to wrap cloth around his left arm, holding it in a sling to avoid accidentally slamming it into anybody and injuring them. He had already bruised himself quite badly when he hadn't been paying attention. Making his way toward the center of New Emery, he soon found himself outside a tall building. It was barely six in the morning, and a security guard, standing outside with a cup of coffee, watched him with a knowing gaze as he stared up at the tall building.

"Here to be tested?" the guard said.

"Yes, sir!" Mark replied, unable to temper his enthusiasm.

The guard jerked a thumb over his shoulder. "Head on in. Beth should be at desk three. She'll get you squared away."

"Thank you, sir!"

This was the New Emery testing facility, the place where every new empowered came to be tested for their ability, to discover not only their power but the potential their body contained. For a long time, Mark had dreamed of walking through the doors of the testing room, and it was finally going to happen. Heading over to the elderly woman sitting at desk three, Mark presented his identification.

"Mark Fields?" the woman said, looking at the information his watch had sent over to her screen and comparing the picture with Mark. "This must have been taken a while ago. You look like you've filled out quite a bit."

Mark knew it was the truth, but it was hard to appreciate just how much he had changed. Catching a glimpse of the picture, Mark realized that he had probably gained close to twenty pounds in the last twenty-four hours, all of it pure muscle. His face had filled out too, making him look much more like his late father.

"Fields . . . That name is familiar. Are you related to Joseph Fields?"

"Yes, ma'am."

"Oh, wonderful. Your family must be quite excited."

Mark kept quiet as the secretary finished registering him and waved him through the set of silver doors at the back of the building.

"Head on through there, and they'll help you with your test."

Taking a deep breath, Mark squared his shoulders and walked up to the double doors. There was a soft chime as his watch was registered, and then the doors slid open. The cat had disappeared at some point, but Mark was getting used to it coming and going without his noticing, and his mind was too full of anticipation to care. Inside, he was directed by a man in a white coat to go to testing room B, where he found two researchers who introduced themselves as Ellis and Gloria. Ellis reached out to shake Mark's hand and gestured for him to sit at the table.

"This assessment has two components," he said, getting right down to business. "Three, really, if you count the biological assessment, but that will only take a moment. The more important assessments are your power categorization and your power potential. Tell me, have you ever gone through this test before?"

"No, sir," Mark said, drinking in everything around him with an excited gaze.

Chuckling, Ellis tapped his watch, pulling up a virtual screen for Mark to see. "In that case, I have a few things to go over. I apologize if you know any of this information already, but I'm obligated to say it. First, we're going to be testing your power categorization. All that really means is we're going to be trying to identify what kind of power you possess. Just because you have become empowered doesn't mean that you necessarily know what your power is. And just because your power is manifested in a specific way doesn't mean that at its core that is your power. For example, someone who has the power of magnetism can make metal objects fly, which they might confuse for telekinesis. Two very different powers. So we're going to try to work our way through your power to really understand what it is. Does that make sense?"

"Yes, sir."

"Good. The second portion of the test is potential. In order to determine that, we have a series of tests that we'll put you through, depending on your power categorization, that will help us determine how much potential you have for learning and controlling powers in the future. That will be combined with your biological test to give you an overall ranking. Now, I know you know this part, since everybody knows this part, but as I said, I'm obligated to declare it and they're recording this conversation, so bear with me."

Tapping on his watch, Ellis brought up a new set of information on the screen.

"We categorize our powers, starting with the letter E, which is our lowest categorization, and rising from there to D, C, B, A, and finally, the ever-sought-after, rarely achieved S-level categorization. Why we use an S instead of an A-plus, don't ask me."

"It stands for 'supernatural,'" Gloria interjected, looking as if she did this all the time. "Because it is outside the scope of what we understand to be naturally possible."

"Well, there you go. S for 'supernatural.' Every power is categorized by one of these letters, which tells us approximately where it stands. On top of that, your maximum potential will also be categorized, though this is more for us than you. I know it's a little bit hard to understand sometimes, but those two categorizations together will tell us quite a bit about you. First, how strong is your power from the outset, and second, how high will you be able to raise it? Additionally, these will help us assign your starting grade. That is the letter every empowered carries throughout their life that will help identify how much of their power and potential they can presently access. Now, just because you have a low-ranked power doesn't mean that you will forever be stuck there. Skills can be acquired, granting higher degrees of power, though you'll be limited to a number of additional skills based on your potential rank. One for E, two for D, and so on and so forth. Now, with that out of the way, we can begin."

As he finished speaking, Ellis gestured to Gloria, who adjusted her glasses and looked at Mark. "Let's begin with power categorization. We'll start with the easy bit. Can you show us your power?"

Nodding, Mark began unwrapping the cloth that hid his arm, lifting his hand with some effort and placing it on the table in front of him.

"It looks to be transformation," Ellis said, poking at it with his finger. "Mixed material. Looks like concrete."

"Isn't that dangerous?" Mark asked.

"Concrete? Nothing particularly dangerous about concrete unless it hits you in the face," Ellis replied.

"No, I mean poking somebody's active power before you know what it does."

For half a second, Ellis looked genuinely confused, and then a wide smile spread on his face. "Oh, yes, normally it would be, but not for a null."

"Null? You mean somebody who cancels powers?"

"It's a little bit more complicated than that, but essentially, yes. I'm generally immune to powers below the A rank, so anything B and lower won't have an effect on me. Gloria is the same."

"Isn't that really rare?" Mark asked.

"Oh, exceedingly, which is why they pay us the big bucks to sit in here and test powers. You can't imagine the kinds of incidents we had before they started recruiting nulls to the job. Anyway, let's get back to it."

Mark sat in silence as they examined his arm and tested how

his fingers worked. Once satisfied, they asked him about how his power had been activated, questioning him in detail. When she had finished recording his answer, Gloria leaned forward with a smile. "And now the all-important question: Can you undo the transformation?"

"I'm not sure," Mark said, scratching his head. "I haven't actually tried."

"Why not?"

Mark could feel his cheeks heating up. "I guess I was just afraid that if I undo the transformation, it won't come back."

"Oh, that's not how powers work, sweetie," Gloria said, with a smile that told Mark she had heard the same statement before. "Why don't you go ahead and try to deactivate it?"

Mark had no idea how he had transformed his arm into concrete in the first place and only knew that it had happened when he had felt a sense of threat. Closing his eyes, he tried to will his arm to become flesh once more. Instead, the most remarkable thing happened. A faint spark emerged from his forearm, signaling the activation of his power, and the fingertips of his left hand glowed silver, reflecting the mirror sheen of the table his hand was resting on. The silver rapidly crept up his fingers, covered his palm and then the back of his hand, and began to work its way up his forearm until reaching his elbow. His hand suddenly felt much lighter, though no less strong, and in wonder, Mark lifted his metal-clad hand into the air, staring at it in surprise.

"And that is why we run these tests," Ellis said, leaning forward with excitement. "Gloria, are you getting this? At first, I thought it was a cladding, but no, this is a full shift. It looks like he's absorbing characteristics from the table and applying them to the entirety of his arm rather than just transforming the surface."

"And it's a nondisplacement absorption," Gloria replied, taking notes.

"Is that good?" Mark asked, still staring at his reflection in his silver palm.

"Oh, that's great. Otherwise, we'd have a giant hole in our table here," Ellis said, tapping the table. "Transformation and absorption are two different powers, and within the absorption category there are different sorts of absorption. What you're absorbing is the characteristics of something rather than the thing itself. I'm curious how many different materials you can absorb, so we'll orient some of our tests that way. More importantly, are you able to do anything beyond your left arm?"

"How would I know that?" Mark asked.

"Some people just do," Gloria replied, adjusting her glasses again. "Other people have to just do extensive testing. If you don't have a sort of feeling, a sixth sense that you can cover more of your body, then you probably can't."

"Wait, you mean all I'm gonna be able to do is turn my left arm into other materials?" Mark asked. His disappointment must have been revealed in his voice, because Ellis burst into laughter.

"For now, maybe," Gloria said, shooting a glare at Ellis. "But that's where it's important to test your potential. You might not believe me, but the power you're demonstrating is actually very significant, and if your potential is high, it means you'll be able to improve your ability with it until you match its rank. You might think of it like this: Currently, your power itself is like a small pool of water, but you are only rank E, which means that you can only wield a single cup at a time. Regardless of how strong your power is, you are limited in what you can use. The question is, are you going to be able to upgrade your cup and get strong enough to wield the full extent of your power? In a way, your potential is your limiter."

"Of course, it doesn't always go like that," Ellis said. "Sometimes it's the other way around. People have a really weak power, but their potential is off the charts. Thankfully, they can absorb more skill gems to make up the difference."

For over an hour, they asked Mark questions and put him through a series of increasingly complex tests using a variety of different materials. Twice they had to stop to let Mark eat something, as using his power caused his hunger to spike tremendously. When they were finally done, they announced that they'd be moving on to the next test to determine Mark's potential.

"What about my power?" he asked. "Aren't you going to tell me what it is?"

"Of course, just not right now. We have to put together a whole report and submit it for verification before we can give it to you," Ellis said, typing some notes into the virtual screen. "The good news is, they're working on it now, so it won't take weeks like it used to. You should have it by the time we're done with your potential test, or within an hour or so after. Time for the potential test. Let's get you strapped in."

Following Ellis, Mark walked to a small chamber, whose door he hadn't noticed before. Ellis punched in a code, and it hissed open, revealing a capsule with a comfortable-looking chair and dozens of devices that looked more like torture implements than scientific equipment.

"I know it looks scary," Ellis said, "but believe me, it won't hurt at all. In fact, there's a good chance you'll be unconscious for most of it."

"And if I'm not," Mark asked, "will it hurt then?"

"No, they're just gonna be testing a few different key metrics."

Letting Ellis strap him into the chair, Mark closed his eyes and tried not to think about what was about to happen. In truth, it wasn't nearly as bad as his imagination had made it out to be, and after a slightly uncomfortable forty-five minutes, the door slid open and he was freed. As he got up, he noticed Ellis had a fairly neutral expression, and with a sinking feeling, Mark walked out into the testing room, where Gloria was sitting at the table. Mark and Ellis joined her as she pulled up a screen.

"All right, Mark, we have your results. There's good news, and there's bad news. Which do you want first?"

"The good news," Mark said, taking a deep breath to fortify himself.

"The good news is your power is B ranked. Now, before you get disappointed, understand that less than one percent of the population of empowered have an A-ranked skill or higher. In fact, there are only five S-ranked empowered in the entire city, and you already know who they are."

Mark nodded. The five emperors, so titled because their powers could obliterate entire armies of Exlian, held the five top spots in the city. There were significantly more A-ranked empowered, including his brother, but just because Mark was disappointed didn't mean he was unreasonable enough to be upset. The chances of hitting even B rank were tiny, meaning the ability he had awakened was fantastic.

"Less than ten percent of the empowered are B ranked, so you're in a rare category, kid," Ellis said.

"He's right. Your absorption power would normally be ranked D at best. However, because you don't actually absorb the material but only absorb the characteristics of it, that raises it to C. What makes you B ranked is that you display signs of trait selection. Normally, when somebody with an absorption power absorbs a material, they absorb everything about it, which means they get all its strengths and weaknesses. For instance, the harder a material is, the less it can bend." Gloria held up her hand and began flexing her fingers. "You, on the other hand, are able to absorb tremendously hard material while also maintaining your flexibility. That's unusual enough to grant you a B ranking for your power. Unfortunately, to get an A ranking, you have to demonstrate the ability to generate your power from nothing."

"Like my brother," Mark said. "He can pull flame out of thin air."

"Indeed, that would categorize a flame-control power as A ranked, manifesting something from nothing. You have to be touching the substance you intend to transform your arm into."

Nodding slowly, Mark gripped the edge of the table as he leaned forward. "So what's the bad news?"

"The bad news is that your potential is, well, it's unstable," Gloria said with a frown.

"Unstable? What does that mean?"

"It means that our most consistent reading was in the D rank, with occasional spikes into C and dips into E."

When Gloria didn't continue, Mark frowned. "Okay, but what does that mean?"

Opening up a chart in the virtual screen to show Mark what they had been tracking, Ellis pointed at a spike. "It means that even if you manage to work your way into the D rank, you're probably going to have an almost impossible time making it to C. Now, potential isn't set in stone. It's just based on what we can currently understand about your power and your physical body."

"Exactly," Gloria said, adjusting her glasses. "From what we're seeing, however, this absorption power of yours is actually the culprit. It's currently stripping the potential out of your body every time you transform, which is why you keep getting so hungry when you use it. That's what we were testing by having you cycle your arm through various materials in the chair. Every time you use your ability, it eats away at your body a little bit, which in turn hampers your max potential. But it's not all bad news. It's highly possible that what's happening is something that we don't understand and can't categorize. That the power you possess is doing something to your body that we're just not aware of."

"B-ranked power and D-ranked potential?" Mark asked, his eyes downcast.

Sharing a glance with Gloria, Ellis nodded. "I'm sorry, kid."

"No, this is great," Mark said, excitement filling his eyes as he looked up.

"Great?" Ellis repeated.

"Yes. Great," Mark replied, plans already beginning to form in his head. "The cutoff for the Defense Force is D rank. And their recruitment page said that they value physical transformations. That means that I have a shot at joining."

"That's a great attitude to have, kid," Ellis said. "And if things change, you can always come back and get retested."

"Thank you," Mark said, standing up.

"Before you go," Gloria replied, "we have a couple of things to give you."

"Oh, sorry."

Mark quickly sat back down as Gloria picked up a case that had been sitting next to her feet and put it on the table. Spinning it around, she pushed it over to Mark, who opened it up and saw two items held in foam. The first was a small data stick that could be slotted into his watch. The second was a wire-thin bracelet formed from a squiggly line.

"The first is a gift from us. Not me and Ellis, of course, but our organization. Based on your results, we've generated a training plan for you, which we believe will help you unearth the highest amount of your potential. Included are physical exercises as well as a few mantras that you can try practicing to help you with your control. Also included on the data stick is a guide to Blackstar, the empowered forums, as well as your log-in credentials. Don't ask about the name. Even I don't know why they called it that. There's also a handy little guide on types of jobs that you might be able to take on if you're interested. Though from what you've said, it sounds like you have your heart set on defending the city."

"Yes, ma'am."

"I'll thank you in advance for your service," Gloria said with a smile, gesturing to the other item. "This is an activation bracelet. It's a tool that will allow you to harness your power more quickly. It goes on your right arm just below your wrist, and it'll sting for a moment when you put it on. Go ahead and slot the data stick, and then I'll show you how the bracelet works."

Taking the data stick from the box, Mark slotted it into his watch and after a moment heard a pleasant ding as a number of different operations were unlocked. Next was the activator, which he slipped onto his wrist, twitching as it shrank down and burrowed itself into his skin, biting at his flesh. The pain faded as fast as it had come, and Mark felt a strange sensation as a mana circuit was projected across his forearm.

"Hold your arm in front of you like you're looking at your wrist and say 'status,'" Gloria said, and Mark did what he was told.

"Status."

As soon as the word left his mouth, the mana circuit flared, and a simple screen was projected above Mark's wrist.

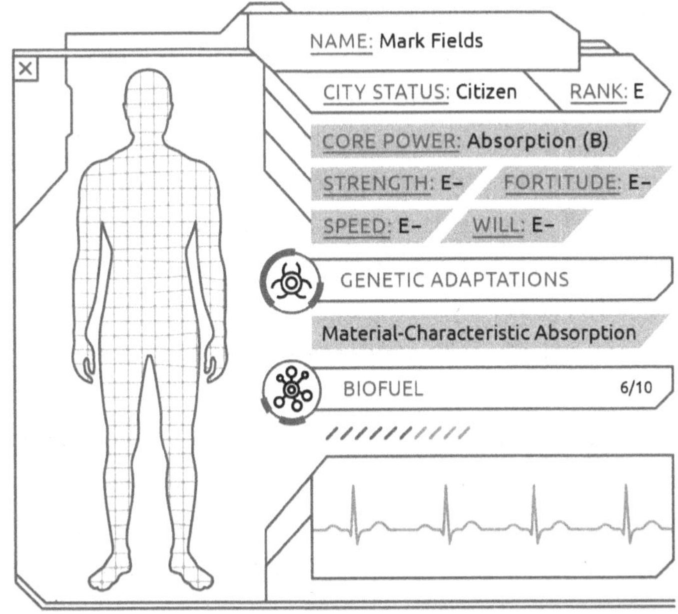

"This is your status screen," Gloria said. "It contains all sorts of vital information about you, and it can't be read by anyone except for you and authorized administrative staff. It can be used as a means of verifying your identity and will give you helpful information that has been customized to you. You'll see your name and the status you hold in the city. Your status screen should say 'citizen.' If you're able to join the Defense Force, it will change to reflect that. In the same vein, should you ever break any laws, you will be labeled a criminal. So don't break any laws."

"At least where people can see you," Ellis said, earning himself another glare from Gloria. He held up his hands with a smirk. "It was a joke, a joke."

"Pay no attention to him. You should also be able to see—and this is private information—your power as well as your categorizations for strength, speed, fortitude, and will. Most of the stats that you're going to see are self-explanatory, like strength and speed, but will is a collection of your mental fortitude and your intellect. The higher your will, the longer you're going to be able to sustain your powers, and the quicker you'll be able to activate them. Some empowered focus more on physical stats and use their powers to supplement. We categorize them as strikers. And then you have those who focus almost exclusively on training their will. We call them casters. The next section is your skills. As you gain additional skills, they'll appear on there as well, along with any other personalized information that the enchantment on your bracelet thinks it would be good for you to know."

Looking up from his status screen, Mark saw Gloria raise her hand.

"Don't tell me if you have anything in that section. It's important that you keep those things private, as they typically point to a weakness that you have and could potentially be exploited by others. You can explore them at your leisure. Finally, the activator will also assist you in absorbing new skills, should you have the chance. This is a basic model, and though the more advanced models are quite pricey, they also come with other features like built-in watches, or at least watch functionality, as well as a whole host of other things. Such activators have to be custom built for you, and if that is something you are interested in, you can find more information on the Blackstar forums."

Pausing, Gloria looked at Ellis. "Is there anything we're missing?"

"No, I don't think so," Ellis said. "Good luck, kid."

Mark's brain was practically bursting as he walked out of the testing room and made his way out onto the street. The sun gleamed on the tall glass buildings that surrounded him, casting a bright glow over everything that mirrored his internal excitement. Taking a deep breath, he couldn't help but feel as if he had stepped into a brand-new world, one filled with possibilities.

"Hey, get out of the way!"

Jerked from his daze by a growl, he turned around and saw a young man who had just come from the test rooms glaring at him, and Mark was immediately aware of how poorly he was dressed. He wore a simple T-shirt that had more than one hole in it, a pair of slacks that had seen better days, and frayed shoes held together with a bit of tape and the realities of his empty wallet. In contrast, the young man glaring at him was dressed from head to toe in designer clothing—one of his shoes was probably worth more than Mark's house. The watch he wore was an exclusive model, tastefully studded with gems, and behind him stood a tall, blank-faced bodyguard. Even stranger, Mark could feel the kitten on his shoulder, though he had no idea when the cat had reappeared. When he glanced at her, she was staring at the well-dressed young man with a curious expression, her head cocked to the side.

Quickly stepping out of the way, Mark didn't bother smiling or even responding. He had dealt with enough stuck-up rich kids in his school days to know that nothing good came from engaging with them. Better to hope that he was simply too insignificant to be noticed.

The young man walked past without so much as a glance, striding toward the car that had pulled up in front of the building. His bodyguard, however, didn't pass by so quickly, and his gaze lingered on Mark longer than was quite comfortable. Hearing the door to the car click shut, the guard turned and made his way to the front seat, where he joined the driver. A moment later, the car accelerated, joining the traffic in the street with barely a sound. Feeling the black cat's tail slap his cheek, Mark waved his hand.

"Knock it off," he said. "Where have you been, anyway?"

The cat stared at him silently for a second, then jumped down from his shoulder and crouched. As Mark watched with increasing astonishment, he saw the cat miming stalking prey, pouncing, and achieving a glorious victory as it caught and devoured its prey.

"You went hunting? What were you hunting?"

The little cat nodded, then lay down on its stomach, pulling its arms and legs in and wiggling them, accomplishing an astonishingly accurate impression of a bug.

"Oh, wow. Well, good job," Mark said.

Sitting up, the cat nodded and leaped onto Mark's shoulder, where it sat and licked its paw as it surveyed everything around them.

"You got a smart cat," said the guard, watching Mark over his still-steaming cup of coffee.

Feeling slightly silly, Mark nodded and took off, not wanting to embarrass himself further. Rather than head back to his house, he went straight to work, though there were still a few hours until he needed to be there. In his excitement, he had gotten to his testing early, so he had time to kill. Deciding he was hungry again, he stopped at a stall down the road from the restaurant to grab some cheap breakfast.

While he was eating, he perused the information that he had been given, first studying the basic facts that all empowered needed to know, then delving into the specialized training material that they had designed around his personal powers. He was so immersed in it that the stall owner finally rapped on his table. "I don't run a charity, kid. Either buy more food or get going so another customer can take your seat."

"Oh, sorry," Mark said, jumping up. "Sorry, I was just a bit lost in thought."

"I could see that. Don't sweat it—just be mindful next time. Hey, you work for Jason, right? Down the street?"

"Yes, sir."

"Ha, polite. Not like most kids these days. I got something for him. You mind taking it down for me?"

"No, sir, I'd be happy to."

Going behind his stall, the owner pulled out a bundle wrapped in cloth. "Make sure he gets this, and if you know what's good for you, don't peek inside."

"Yes, sir," Mark said, accepting the package.

As soon as he touched it, he knew exactly what it was, but he didn't say anything, instead turning and making his way down the street. Though most of the transactions in the city were done through the automatic credit system, there were still people, especially on the outskirts, who preferred to deal in paper credits. All the reasons that the shopkeeper might have wanted to give Jason cash raced through Mark's head, but ultimately, it wasn't his business, so he pushed his curiosity aside and handed the package over to Jason as soon as he saw him.

"Mr. Eberle asked me to give this to you."

Taking it, Jason tore it open, revealing a few thick stacks of paper credits, exactly as Mark had expected. Barely giving them a glance, Mark turned around and headed for the washing station, leaving Jason staring after him.

The next week passed in a blur for Mark. He maintained his normal routine, though he added two more training sessions, one early in the morning before heading to work, and the other after he got home. He had been discovering all sorts of interesting things about his new body, but the most important was the biofuel meter on his status.

It didn't take him long to understand what it represented, as every time he ate, it ticked up until it was full. It degraded slowly over time, regardless of whether he was doing anything strenuous, which suggested a baseline burn. While it was above the halfway mark, however, Mark didn't need sleep, and his mind felt unusually sharp. The lower it got, the hungrier he became, and if it ever hit three or lower, his body began to feel as if he were being stabbed by thousands of needles, the pain getting stronger as the biofuel degraded further.

He tested the meter rigorously, soon discovering that a day of regular activities would reduce his score by two if he didn't eat anything. On the other hand, when he did eat, keeping his biofuel close to full, he could operate for a full twenty-four hours before needing to grab a couple of hours of sleep.

The result was a rather unusual schedule, in which Mark slept for only four hours a night before getting up and beginning to train his body. According to the information he had been given, every empowered could reach at least an E level in all their stats, and that was what Mark focused on first, increasing his workout routine as he tried to build up to E-ranked strength, speed, fortitude, and will.

Despite keeping himself as busy as possible, he couldn't help but wonder if Joe was okay and wish that his older brother were around to answer his questions. Unfortunately, there had been no more information after his call, and he hadn't been able to reach Joe. He had no idea when Joe's deployment would be finished, so he did the best he could on his own, practicing controlling his power and, more importantly, increasing its activation speed.

Mark also began to look for scraps of material that he felt would be good for him to transform into. Initially, he had entertained fanciful ideas about getting his hand on a diamond or other equally precious material, but most of the materials that he had thought about transforming into were well out of his price range, even for a tiny amount. It didn't take him long to realize he was going to have to make do with what he could scrounge. That sent him hunting through a nearby hardware store, where he found a titanium screw made from an alloy that cost a couple of credits. Using a bit of string, he fashioned a simple necklace to keep it around his neck.

The screw was big enough to touch with all five of his fingers, which sped up the activation process considerably. He also found that holding on to something and using his activator allowed his arm to transform within a couple of seconds, instead of the minute it had taken in the tests. According to the training manual Gloria had given him, this was something that he could learn to do without the activator, though it would likely take him a long time. Titanium was very strong but also light, so Mark added a few other materials, including a chunk of reinforced concrete and a steel washer, which would both give his fist considerably more weight than the titanium.

The necklace was ugly, but he figured that it was better to be able to use his power than to not have any suitable material available. Throwing himself into his practice, he lost himself in the rhythm of it, and time passed swiftly. He was just toweling off after his afternoon exercise session a week later when his watch dinged, and glancing down at it, Mark saw a blinking message. His heart jumped in his chest, and he stared at it for a moment and then opened it before he lost his nerve. It was from the training camp, and the message was simple, ordering him to report for training in three days at the recruitment camp's intake center. Stifling the shout that rose to his lips, Mark rushed out of the training center and hurried to return to Jason's restaurant.

"What's got your panties in a twist?" Jason asked as soon as Mark walked up.

Carrying some dishes past, Sky paused, lingering at the door to the kitchen. Though Jason gave her an annoyed glance, he didn't say anything as Mark explained the situation.

"I've been accepted to the recruit training camp," Mark said, opening up the message to show Jason. "I was wondering if I could adjust my hours. The first stage of the training is only during the weekdays, which means I can work on the weekends. I'll work extra shifts to make up for it."

For the first time since he had known Jason, the owner's fierce expression softened slightly, and Mark could have sworn he saw a hint of nostalgia flashing past Jason's cold eyes.

"Fine, but I already told you, if you're late even once more, you're done."

"Thank you, sir," Mark said, turning toward the kitchen.

Sky had disappeared from the doorway, but when Mark got to the sink, she was standing there, a curious expression in her eyes.

"You're going to the training camp?" she asked, quickly adding, "I'm sorry, I didn't mean to eavesdrop."

"Oh, it's fine," Mark replied. "Yeah, I've been accepted to the basic recruitment camp. I'll be starting in a few days." Noticing a hint of disappointment on Sky's face, he hurried to assure her, "I'll still be working here. I'm not going to be gone for good."

"Oh, good," she said.

"I'll still see you on the weekends."

Sky didn't reply, but she nodded and hurried out to the dining room, just as Jason started to yell. Staring after her for a moment, Mark couldn't suppress the smile on his face, until one of the other servers dropped a giant stack of plates down next to the sink. Suppressing a groan, he finished tying the apron around his waist and grabbed the plates, dropping them in the soapy water.

All things considered, awakening B-ranked power and having a potential in the D rank was more than he could have expected. As much as he had secretly hoped for an A-ranked power or a high potential like his brother, Joe, the future really was looking good. Even with the piles of dishes threatening to bury him.

The training camp intake center was just as busy as Mark had imagined it would be. There were over two hundred thousand slots available in the camp, and according to some of the reports he had seen on the news, over five hundred thousand people had signed up within the first week. More were still pouring in, though many simply weren't eligible. Despite the high volume of people, the registration process was surprisingly smooth. After he'd waited in line for a couple of hours, it was finally Mark's turn. He stepped up to the desk, where a harassed-looking soldier was typing into his virtual screen.

"Mark Fields," the soldier said, not even bothering to look up.

"Yes, sir."

"You've been assigned to the eleventh camp. I'm sending the location to your device. You're expected to report for duty this afternoon for orientation."

Checking his watch, Mark saw both the directions and the time the orientation began. He still had a few hours before it would kick off, which would be plenty of time to grab some lunch and make it over to the camp.

"It says here that you're empowered?"

Hearing some confusion in the soldier's voice, Mark nodded. "Yes, sir."

For the first time, the soldier looked up, blinking a few times as he stared at Mark. "Did this just happen recently?"

"Yes, sir. Only about a week ago."

"Just in time," the soldier said. "Congratulations. That's a monumental thing. The eleventh camp is where they pull high performers for the three primary forces. If you do well, it's not impossible that you'll be sent to either the Defense Force, the Rangers, or the Engineering Corps, once your service as one of the basic infantry is done. Maybe even before, if you're lucky."

"Yes, sir," Mark said, saluting.

"Keep up that enthusiasm. You'll need it. All right, you're all checked in and ready to go. You'll get all the information you need at the orientation. I wish you luck, soldier."

"Thank you, sir," Mark said, and moved aside so the next person in line could step up to the desk.

He made his way out of the intake center and headed for the eleventh camp. Though it wasn't the closest of the camps, it was conveniently located near his neighborhood, and it would only take him fifteen minutes at a swift jog to travel between his house and the camp, saving him credits.

Since he was going to be working less, Mark was already trying to figure out how he was going to pay for all the food he had been consuming since awakening, making it a welcome surprise to find out that the camp was so close. Conscious of the money he could save by eating at home, Mark swung by his house and prepared a large pot of his normal beef, sauce, and rice mixture. When he offered some to the cat, who'd turned out to be female, she turned up her nose and even mimed gagging and dying, which amused Mark to no end.

"You're really good at this whole miming thing," he said, rising to get her a can of cat food. "Maybe that's what I'll call you. Mime."

She looked at him, her head cocked to the side, as if considering it, and then nodded as if she approved. After cracking the can open and placing it on the table, Mark grabbed a jar of protein-and-nutrition powder and sprinkled it liberally on his rice. It didn't do anything to improve the flavor, but Mark was too poor to care about that. After finishing the whole pot, he checked his status and saw that his biofuel meter was full. He still didn't quite understand what its use was, besides keeping him at peak energy, and he was also starting to suspect that there was something a little bit strange about his abilities.

According to what he had read on the Blackstar forums, the third section of his status should have listed the skills he possessed, based on his core power. Most empowered had a limited number of skills based on the rank of their power as soon as they awakened, and every time they would add or develop another skill, it would be added to that section. This meant that with a B-ranked power, Mark should have been staring at four distinct skills. After all, that was what gave powers their ranks. For an absorption power of the B rank, the four skills that should have been listed were trait selection, material transformation, characteristic absorption, and nondisplacement. Combined, these four skills would give him a B-ranked power. But instead there were no skills listed at all.

He wasn't quite sure what genetic adaptations—listed in the next section of his status—were, though he imagined that they had something to do with his body's ability to change. Somehow he had unlocked material-characteristic absorption with all the traits it possessed, and he had a sneaking suspicion that there might be ways to unlock other adaptations, granting him other abilities as well . . .

He was so busy thinking about all of this that he was almost late and ended up having to run rather than jog all the way to the eleventh training camp, burning off one of his biofuel units in the process. Grumbling to himself, he got out a few energy bars and began shoving them in his mouth. The guard at the camp's entrance held out a scanner, and Mark held up his watch. There was a pleasant beep, and the guard waved Mark through, pointing him toward the center of the camp, where a large open parade ground was slowly filling with the new recruits.

Mark joined the crowd, looking around to see if he knew anyone. There were a couple of people who seemed familiar to him and one he would have been more than happy not to see. The rich kid who had yelled at him after Mark's assessment. Though his outfit was different, it was just as expensive as before, and though he didn't have his bodyguard with him, it didn't seem to matter, as the area around him was empty. The others obviously felt as Mark did, not wanting to get close enough to get on his bad side. After a few minutes, a soldier walked up to the front and stared out over the crowd, which slowly fell silent as more of the recruits noticed him.

"Welcome to Training Camp Number Eleven," the soldier yelled, his voice carrying over the crowd. "I'm Lieutenant Cox, and I'll be in charge of all of you for the next few weeks. I've served for ten years in the city's Defense Force, and I'll be teaching you the basics of our strategies and tactics. By the time we are done here, you will have been welded into an impenetrable wall, fit to serve alongside the Defense Force and crush the heads of the Exlian scum. For glory!"

"For humanity!" the recruits yelled back, excitement building among them.

Examining the recruits with a critical eye, Cox nodded in approval. "At least I don't have to teach you the most basic thing.

Yes, we fight for our families, for our friends, for the citizens of New Emery, and for the city herself. Each of you will be assigned to a training team. You'll head there and meet your instructors, who will explain the schedule we will be following. While you are not technically yet part of the military of New Emery, I expect you to act as a soldier would. Remember, we will be watching and assessing your every move during this training camp. For those of you who perform well, there are countless opportunities to rise in the ranks. This is a rare and valuable chance, so do not disregard it. Am I clear?"

"Yes, sir," came the resounding shout.

Feeling his wrist vibrate, Mark looked down and saw he had been assigned to Team 1. The crowd quickly began to disperse, everyone heading for tents by the parade ground, where the teams were gathering. Spotting the rich kid heading toward the Team 1 tent as well, Mark grimaced, hoping that he wouldn't be recognized. There were close to a hundred recruits in total in the team, so Mark did his best to stay as far away as he possibly could, ending up in the back half of the group. It wasn't long before Lieutenant Cox joined them and called everybody to attention.

"Go ahead and take a seat," he said, "as this might get a little bit long. First, welcome to Team One of Camp Eleven. All of you are here because there is something distinct about you, making you the cream of the crop, at least when it comes to this camp. Don't let that go to your head, however, because if you don't perform up to the standard, you'll be demoted before you can blink. We have no time to play around in our training, because the Exlian suffer no fools. If you make a mistake out there on the battlefield, well, let's just say it's better to be demoted than dead. This stage of the training camp will run for six weeks.

"You'll have to provide your own housing, but you will be fed breakfast, lunch, and dinner here at the camp. Weekends are off.

You can do whatever you want, but understand that consequences are your own problem, and you'll be punished if you make them mine. I don't care if you're sick or hungover or whatever. Come Monday morning, you better be here bright and early, ready to work hard. We will be observing you throughout this time to determine whether you're worth investing more resources in. Some of you are empowered, and all of you, if you make it to graduation, will have the chance to either be empowered or earn a skill gem. As time goes on, we'll reveal how exactly you can earn that chance."

Mark listened intently as Lieutenant Cox continued his rapid-fire explanation of how the training camp would work. The first few weeks were to be dedicated to physical training to make sure that everyone met the minimum standard of fitness. After that would be combat training, team tactics, and even some class time where they would learn about the command structure of New Emery's military. They would be taught how to build basic defensive fortifications, drilled on the most common types of Exlian, and even have the chance to go out for patrols in some of the dead zone that surrounded the city. Mark paid careful attention, doing his best to note down everything that seemed important. Before he knew it, two hours had passed, and Lieutenant Cox clapped his hands and gestured for everybody to get up.

"All right, enough of this," he said. "We're going to begin our training right away, as I've always found that moving around helps you remember things the best. Each of you should have a number. Based on that number, fall in."

As he finished speaking, Lieutenant Cox pointed to a spot to his right, and the recruits quickly got to their feet. Checking his number, Mark hurried into the sixth spot. To his left, in spot number five, was a thin young woman with exceptionally piercing blue eyes, and next to her was a large teenager who must have stood at least six and a half feet tall and was easily twice as broad as Mark. Then there was a nervous-looking young man with sandy-blond hair that would occasionally shift as if a wind were blowing in it. In the second spot was a young woman whose forehead was permanently furrowed as if in anger. It was no surprise that standing in the first place was the rich young man who Mark had been trying to avoid. It took a few minutes for the recruits to sort themselves out, and then Lieutenant Cox pointed at recruit number one. "State your number and your first name, only your first name; otherwise we'll be here all day."

"One, Noah."

Nodding, Lieutenant Cox pointed at the girl in the second spot.

"Two, Phoenix."

Right on her heels, and with a considerable amount of nervousness, the blond young man blurted out, "Three, Glenn."

There was a long pause, and then number four spoke up. "Four, Danny."

"Five, Harper," said the woman next to Mark.

Feeling surprisingly nervous, Mark said, "Six, Mark."

The names quickly became a blur as they worked their way through until the hundredth recruit had recited their number and their first name.

"Well done," Lieutenant Cox said. "A few times in there where I wasn't sure if you'd be able to keep up, which is not a great sign, but you all did well enough. The number you have currently assigned is reflective of our assessment of your abilities. However, we would be delighted if you would prove to us that you are stronger than we think you are. As you progress through the training camp, you will be able to advance your position, and if our assessment of you goes up, so will your number. Every morning when we gather, and every evening before we dismiss, we'll gather here and repeat this exercise. Next time, I expect there not to be any pauses. All right?"

"Yes, sir," Mark shouted, his voice mixing with the rest of the recruits'.

"Good. Now we'll begin. Everybody down. Let's start with push-ups."

By the time evening came and they filed into the mess hall for their first meal as recruits, Mark was exceptionally glad that he had worked so hard in the years since high school. Lieutenant Cox seemed determined to push them to exhaustion, and many of the recruits could barely drag themselves to the tables. Typically, it took an entire day for Mark to lose two biofuel units, but their four-hour training session had wiped out four, and he could feel hunger starting to prick at his stomach. Sitting down at the tables, still in their numeric order, the recruits didn't have to wait long before soldiers began bringing trays out to them.

"It's all you can eat, kids," Lieutenant Cox said, "and believe me, you're going to need the energy. While it's not the tastiest food in the world, all this food has been specifically modified by our scientists to provide peak nutritional value. After you've finished what you have been given, hold up your hand if you want more."

Mark's hand immediately shot up, causing Lieutenant Cox to pause. Taking a step to the side so he could see Mark's tray, he saw nothing but empty plates and the people around Mark staring at him in bemusement.

"Get number six more food," Lieutenant Cox yelled, "and you better make it double."

It took five trays for Mark to refill his biofuel meter, and after it was full, he still shoved the rest of the food on the tray he was working on into his mouth, not wanting to waste anything. Seeing that he was finally done eating, the others at the table, many of whom were still working on their first or second trays, looked at him in amazement. The sharp-eyed young woman next to him, Harper, gestured to her tray. "You want to finish mine?"

"No, thank you," Mark said, holding up his hand. "I think I'm full."

"You think you're full?" Glenn asked from across the table. "Guys, he only thinks he's full. He's not actually sure."

"I've been meaning to ask you," Harper said as the others laughed. "Is that cat part of your empowerment?"

Freezing, Mark slowly turned his head and saw Mime sitting on his shoulder, calmly licking her paw. In truth, he'd had no idea she was there, as she seemed weightless. It was only after he saw her that he could feel the slight weight on his shoulder.

"Must be," Phoenix said, her eyebrows arched. "Otherwise, I doubt the instructors would let him bring a cat into the training camp."

"I've never seen an empowered who has a cat before," Danny said, his voice low and deep. "Though I do know someone who can turn into a tiger."

Feeling quite awkward, Mark tried to turn the conversation away from him and, more importantly, Mime.

"What about you?" he asked Harper.

"My ability is called farsight," she said. "Mostly, it means I just see really well. But if I concentrate, I can use it to spy on locations outside of my normal line of sight. I use a bow and have increased accuracy against any target that I can see."

"That's a cool power," Glenn said from across the table, his blond hair bouncing. "I have telekinesis. It only works within one hundred feet of me, and I can only really pick up small things. But I have pretty good control and can keep multiple things in the air at a time."

Growing interested in the conversation, Phoenix leaned forward. "I've seen somebody who has a power like that. Steel Storm."

"He's my dad," Glenn said.

"Wow, it's rather rare to have the same power in successive generations," Phoenix remarked.

"Well, we don't really have the same power," Glenn admitted. "His telekinesis isn't limited to one hundred feet, but he's only able to wield his knives. My power, though limited to a hundred feet, lets me manipulate anything that's a pound or less. What about you?"

"Energy control. Right now, it just means being able to shoot plasma blasts and pull up small shields."

"That's so cool," Danny said. "You guys all have cool powers. Mine seems lame."

"Superstrength?"

"Technically, it's growth."

"Wait, you get bigger?" Mark asked.

Grinning, Danny nodded. "Yes, right now I can only grow to about nine feet tall, but my strength increases accordingly."

As everybody else at their end of the table had shared their powers, the group's eyes turned to the only person who hadn't. Noah, the rich kid who was ranked first. He hadn't said a word the entire time and had just focused on eating. Mark noticed that he had cleared three trays of food and didn't seem at all perturbed that everyone was looking at him. Mark imagined he was used to being the center of attention.

"You're Noah, right?" Phoenix said. "What's your power?"

For a moment, Mark didn't think that Noah would respond, but everybody kept staring at him, so Noah pushed his empty tray aside. "I'm a paragon."

Mark let out a low whistle, impressed. A paragon was a particular category of empowered who had lesser versions of a considerable number of other abilities. It meant that Noah had multiple powers, though each probably wasn't quite as strong as another empowered who only had that specific power.

"A paragon?" Phoenix asked, her eyes lighting up. "What does it include?"

Looking like he wanted the conversation to be over, Noah frowned slightly. "Strength, speed, minor invulnerability, charisma, and basic energy manipulation."

"Oh man, that's crazy," Glenn said. "You're like a walking team, all by yourself."

Nodding, Noah got up and grabbed his trays to return to the soldiers. "I'll see you all tomorrow."

"Well, he's friendly," Harper said sarcastically, causing Mark, who remembered his last encounter with Noah vividly, to chuckle.

"Maybe he's just embarrassed," Danny said.

"Didn't look embarrassed to me," Phoenix replied, shaking her head. "But I do think it is time to go. It was nice to meet all of you, and I'm sure we'll get to know each other over the next few weeks."

One by one, everyone got up from the table, carried their trays to the kitchen, and then headed off. Mark, who felt full of energy, jogged home and spent the evening practicing his control over his power, switching his arm as quickly as he could between steel, concrete, and the titanium alloy. The training he had been given said it was more efficient to focus on reaching a basic mastery with his left arm before trying to extend the power to other body parts.

That hadn't stopped Mark from trying, of course, but every time he attempted to transform part of his body that wasn't his left arm from his elbow down, he felt an insurmountable resistance. There was a barrier in his way, preventing him from using the power, and a bit of research on the Blackstar forums revealed that this was fairly common. According to one post, this would likely change when he began to rank up, as each increase in rank would allow him to control his power more efficiently and affect more of his body. Feeling Mime brush up against him, he closed his virtual screen and picked her up.

"You know, this power is lamer than I thought it was going to be," Mark said. "I mean, eventually it'll be cool. You know, once I can transform my entire body into steel. If I'm ever able to, that is. But I honestly don't know what I'm going to be able to do with just one arm that's metal."

Mime didn't say anything and let out a great big yawn, causing Mark to look over at the clock.

"Huh, it's getting late," he said, "and I've got to be up in five hours for training. Time to get some sleep."

After taking a quick shower, he lay down on his bed and quickly fell into a deep sleep. As his breathing evened out, Mime, who had curled up next to him, slowly sat up, her eyes flashing red as she stared at his sleeping face. After a long moment, she lay back down with a tired yawn and curled up to go back to sleep. A moment later, Mark began to twitch, his body shaking and his face contorting, but she paid him no mind.

That night, Mark had the most vivid and terrifying dream of his life. It started simply enough. He woke in his bed and walked out of his house, only to find himself standing in an unfamiliar wilderness. Gone was the concrete-and-steel jungle he had known his whole life; gone were the mana lights and electronics that always surrounded him. In their place were thick plants, towering trees, and the gentle hum of nature. In the far distance, he could see mountains whose jagged peaks thrust into the sky like grasping fingers of a giant, wreathed in lightning-racked storm clouds.

The foliage around Mark was dense, blocking his sight no matter what direction he looked, hemming him in like a fence. The clearing where he stood was oblong and roughly fifty feet across at middle, stretching twice that to his front and back. Curious about the dream, Mark brushed a hand against his face, freezing when he realized that it felt no different from the waking world. He could taste the moist jungle air, hear the chatter of birds and insects in the distance, and feel the ground under his feet.

Feeling a bit of weight on his left arm, he looked down and realized that it was a glimmering silver he recognized as titanium alloy. Confused as to what was going on, he began to look around, when suddenly he heard a sound and spun, just in time to see a creature about the size of a large dog lunging toward him. The Exlian drone looked like a massive tick, with curved armor plates all along its back and a heavy set of pincers that it held out toward him. Though smaller than the last one he had encountered, it was still dangerous, and with a yelp, Mark jerked back. As he lifted his leg to block the Exlian drone, it brought its sharp pincers together, cutting into his leg and sending a burst of excruciating pain shooting through him.

The world warped as Mark fell to the ground, and suddenly

he was standing in the clearing once again, his breath coming in great gasps. This time, he didn't turn around, his gaze fixed on the bushes as the pain faded from his body. He heard the grass rustle, and a drone darted out of the underbrush toward him, pincers held wide. With a shout, Mark met it head-on, crouching and throwing a punch with his titanium-alloy arm.

His fist hit the drone, knocking it back far enough that Mark could reset his stance, but that was it. With an angry chitter, the drone launched itself at him again, its heavy pincers snapping like a pair of shears. This time, Mark slammed his forearm in between its pincers, hoping that it wouldn't have enough strength to shear straight through the alloy. His bet paid off, as the drone clamped down tight on his arm and began thrashing. Unfortunately, its wild movements sent a talon raking across his chest, causing the world to shift once more.

As Mark appeared for the third time, the stinging in his chest fading, he began to realize that there was something very wrong with this dream. Once again, the drone launched itself out of the underbrush toward him, moving with incredible speed, and this time, he elected to run, dashing toward the jungle to his side. The drone reached him just before he arrived in the jungle, leaping to land on his back. Driven face-first to the ground, Mark had no idea how the drone killed him, but it didn't matter. As soon as the dream reset, he took off, heading for the protection of the leaves. Maybe he could hide from it.

Diving into the underbrush, Mark felt the leaves brushing against him, filling his vision with green, and then he was back in the center of the clearing, staring at the blue sky overhead in a daze as the drone charged him. Unable to believe that he couldn't escape, he tried twice more before giving up. It appeared that whoever had designed this nightmare wanted him to get used to facing off against a drone.

Summoning his courage, Mark did his best but quickly discovered that no matter what he did, he was no match for the small monster. It was faster, stronger, and better equipped than he was, and the martial arts he had learned simply didn't work when facing Exlian. The drone had no sense of fear, a high tolerance for pain, and a considerable amount of resistance to blunt force. He learned all these characteristics the hard way, dying over and over again to the small death machine.

But it wasn't as if there was no benefit. The more he died, the less Mark cared. Constantly reviving meant that he could try anything that came to mind without worrying about the consequences, and that was what he did. With each death his fear of facing the drone lessened, and he began to pay closer attention to how it moved. Since he couldn't kill the monster, he focused instead on trying to stay away from it and soon became rather adept at dodging its fierce lunges.

Mark had stopped keeping track of the number of times that he had been beaten and was practicing anticipating when it would close its claws when he finally found a trick that worked. Rather than meet the drone head-on, he dodged to the side, dancing away from its snapping claws. As he did so, he swung his left arm, intending to knock the drone away. He misjudged the distance, however, and the tips of his metal fingers brushed against the drone's head. They were moving quickly, as he had swung with some force, and they tore into its tough exoskeleton, causing a thick green goo to dribble out. Wailing, the drone landed on the ground, and Mark stared at it in shock for a long moment before he leaped on it, pinning it down with his knee as he stabbed his fingers deep into the wound, hoping to finally kill it.

Instead, a flailing claw took his life.

Respawning in the center of the clearing, Mark's gaze grew intense, and rather than wait, he charged toward the spot where the drone would emerge. Though it took him a few more tries to replicate the attack, he quickly realized that he could use his metal arm like a blade of sorts, so long as he swung it fast enough. The fighting soon grew fierce, and when Mark finally managed to strike the drone down, he felt a thrill unlike anything he had ever experienced before. Lifting his arms, he howled in victory, the cry ringing far over the jungle. At his feet, the dead drone stopped twitching and faded away as there was another rustle in the underbrush and two drones emerged.

Mark didn't win a single one of the fights after that, though he came close on a couple of occasions. Fighting against two drones at the same time was simply too much for him, and finally, an hour before his alarm was supposed to go off, he jerked upright and awake, shaking terribly. Glancing down at his wrist, he pulled up his status and saw his biofuel was at two out of ten rather than at eight like it should have been. The dream was still vivid in his mind, and his body felt as if he had been fighting for hours.

"Okay, this is weird," he said as he staggered down the stairs to the kitchen.

Wrenching the door to the pantry open, he pulled out a box of energy bars and began shoving them into his mouth, barely managing to get the wrappers off before swallowing each down. That didn't seem to be quite enough, so he hurried to the fridge and pulled out a large tube of nutrient paste, a cheap food source generally considered unfit for human consumption. Steeling himself against the taste, he squeezed the entire tube into his mouth, gulping down large mouthfuls until it was empty. He felt his biofuel meter click back up, and the shaking subsided. Mark sighed, thankful he was able to process food into the nutrients and energy he needed so quickly.

As Mark sat in the kitchen, his biofuel meter slowly refilled until it hovered just below eight. Checking his watch, he saw that there was still an hour till his five o'clock call time, so rather than go back to bed, he began stretching in preparation for the exercise he expected that morning. When five o'clock came, he was standing at attention, along with everybody else in the first team. He had expected at least a couple of people to be late, and considering he saw more than a few recruits running toward their teams, he assumed that had been taken into consideration when the groups were formed. A moment later, Lieutenant Cox strolled into the tent and greeted them. "Good morning."

"Good morning, sir," came the shout.

"A bit weak, but we'll work on it. I hope you all got your beauty rest, because believe me, you're gonna need it. Now, I don't have a pep talk for you this morning, so let's get started with push-ups."

Hearing some faint groans from behind him, Mark dropped to the ground, waiting for the lieutenant to start the count. The morning workout was just as brutal as the evening workout had been, and by the time they were done running themselves ragged, it was nine o'clock and Mark's stomach was growling. Breakfast was a rather hurried affair, and Mark spent no time talking, instead shoving down as much food as he possibly could. He was still working through the sixth tray when a bell sounded and they were ordered to form up outside.

True to his word, Lieutenant Cox put them through their paces, doing all sorts of physical exercises, most of which Mark was familiar with. Lieutenant Cox was especially fond of push-ups, burpees, and odd sorts of squats, and every time anybody messed up or failed to follow one of his directions, he put the entire group through a grueling ten-minute regime of his three favorite exercises.

Though the exercises were hard, Mark was already in fantastic shape and, as an empowered, was slightly stronger than a normal human. He wasn't the strongest by far, as that title belonged to

Danny, who had no trouble with any of the exercises until the ever-observant Lieutenant Cox began to target the giant's weaknesses. Soon enough Danny was huffing and puffing along with everyone else.

Mark found this sort of training enjoyable, and he pushed himself as hard as he could, sparing no effort as he chewed through his biofuel meter, since he knew he would be able to refill it once mealtime came. At the end of the first day, he was well and truly exhausted, and rather than continue his training at home, he threw himself into bed immediately. Just before he fell asleep, a thought struck him, and he dragged himself out of bed and down to the kitchen, where he loaded up his arms with boxes of bars and a few tubes of the nutrient paste, which he carried upstairs to dump next to his bed.

"Just in case that dream happens again," he said to Mime, who was watching him with interest.

Thus prepared, Mark lay down and was soon asleep. A moment later he opened his eyes, finding himself in the wilderness once more. He groaned, frustrated that he was going to be forced into the same repetitive hell once more, but then a strange feeling welled up in him, filling him with a savage anticipation of the coming fights. It was such a foreign sensation that it threw Mark off, getting him killed twice before he calmed himself down.

Getting his surging emotions under control, Mark cracked his knuckles, readying himself for his next fight. The grass rustled, and a single drone shot toward him, claws clacking. He expected to be able to defeat it easily, but his first fight resulted in his death when he was sloppy with his dodge and it caught his leg.

Mark was more careful the fourth time, maintaining better distance, before once again eliminating the drone by tearing through its carapace and head. Two drones soon emerged, and so began another night of trying to defeat them.

It wasn't that Mark wasn't strong enough. After all, if they came at him one at a time, he could defeat them handily. The problem was, anytime he started fighting against one, the other would circle around, attacking him from a different angle. As the fights began to drag on, Mark's frustration grew, causing the fights to restart faster and faster as he took increasingly risky chances.

Finally, having died after practically throwing himself into one of the drones' mandibles while trying to dodge the other, he just charged forward as soon as he appeared, catching the drones just as they were emerging from the grass. Without thinking, he slashed down with his hand and happened to catch one of the drones in the head. With a keening wail, the drone died, its brain pierced by his fingers.

Mark was so surprised at how easily the blow had eliminated the drone that he failed to dodge the follow-up attack from its companion, and once again the dream reset. He had a moment between each spawn, and he sprang into action once again, rushing forward to try to repeat the move.

Of the dozen times that he tried it, he only succeeded four, and he soon realized that if he didn't hit a precise spot on the drone's head, the attack simply wouldn't work. The rest of the night, he committed himself to trying to find that spot, slowly raising his success rate until, seven out of ten times, he managed to kill the drone in one strike.

Right before the dream ended, he even managed to kill both of them, landing two successive blows targeting their heads that killed each of them instantly. Ecstatic, he barely had time to shout before three drones emerged and killed him in revenge for their companions. Instead of the dream restarting, he woke up, a familiar hunger in his stomach.

Rather than having to run down to the kitchen, he grabbed the nutrient paste he had placed next to him, unscrewed the lid, and ate the whole tube. Six energy bars followed it down his throat as he considered the repeating dream more fully. He wasn't quite sure how much time had passed in the dream, but his biofuel, which had been full when he went to bed, was now down to four. A rough estimation based on his physical activity told him the dream had lasted six hours, but when he checked the clock, it appeared that only two hours had passed, meaning that he had experienced time in the dream quite a bit differently than it had passed in reality. For a long time, he sat on his bed as he ate, trying to puzzle through what was going on, but no matter what sort of explanation he came up with, nothing fit.

He had an absorption power, the ability to transform part of his body, and a cat who came and went as she pleased. Mime had taken to riding around on his shoulder even while he was exercising, somehow managing to keep perfect balance no matter what position he put himself in. Yet nobody had commented on it, giving Mark the impression that he might well be going crazy. Additionally, he had accessed a strange dream training that had him fighting against ever-increasing numbers of Exlian drones.

By the time four thirty rolled around and he left for the training camp, he was no closer to understanding what was going on. What he did know was that he was starting to understand how to use his arm more effectively and had completely lost his fear of the drones. Instead of wasting his time on unknowns, Mark focused on what he could control, throwing himself into his training.

The first few days of the training camp were difficult, and it only got harder from there. By the time the first week ended, Mark was ready for a break. Physically, he was able to keep up fine, thanks to his unnatural appetite and ability to process nutrients at lightning speed, but mentally, he was exhausted. After getting used to the dream training, he enjoyed fighting against the Exlian drones, but after the fourth night it began to take its toll. The dream appeared every night and was relentless, never once allowing him a moment to rest.

As soon as he appeared in the wilderness, he was thrown against enemies, and there was no way to flee. If he didn't resist, he died within seconds, so for six grueling hours every night, he found himself being forced closer and closer to the edge.

Though he was still resting during that time, he found himself growing more mentally exhausted and would occasionally drift off into space for a few minutes before snapping back to awareness. Thankfully, at the end of the first week, just as they were finishing up dinner, the lieutenant came to their table to address them.

"You've all done well," he said. "Now that the first week is done, we're going to begin our daily assessments. On Monday morning, you'll find your new number. You've got the weekend off, so take it and rest. I can tell that some of you are building up a lot of fatigue, and I don't want you burning out."

Mark knew the lieutenant was talking to him specifically, but he was grateful that Cox didn't look in his direction. Heading home, he went to bed as normal, and though he still ended up in the dream, knowing that he'd have the next two days off made it much more bearable. The next morning, he arrived at the restaurant early and found Jason standing outside eating his breakfast.

"Our little soldier boy showed up."

"Yes, sir," Mark said, saluting.

Rolling his eyes, Jason just jerked his thumb over his shoulder. "There's still some food in the kitchen if you want it, but eat fast. Prep starts in fifteen minutes."

Heading inside, Mark found breakfast had been laid out on one of the tables, and a couple of the cooks and one of the servers who would be helping to open the restaurant were eating. They looked like they had just arrived and hadn't settled in yet, which meant that Jason must have made the food himself. Grabbing a plate, Mark piled it high and sat down at one of the tables to eat the best breakfast of his entire life.

He wasn't sure if it was the result of eating nothing but disgusting, high-calorie, nutrient-dense food at home or the terrible military food he had been getting at the training camp, but the eggs Jason had made were so good Mark nearly cried.

After breakfast had been cleaned up, everyone got to work, and Mark pitched in wherever he could. By the time they opened the doors, there was already a line halfway around the block, and Mark soon had more than enough dishes to keep him busy. Instead of using the industrial dishwasher, however, he washed them by hand, using the opportunity to practice his speed. According to the training he had been receiving, mundane actions done as fast as possible were one of the best ways to increase speed, and Mark could feel his body becoming more and more in tune as he completed each motion. Close to lunchtime, Sky arrived, her eyes lighting up when she saw Mark.

"Hey, how was training camp?" she asked, coming to stand next to the sink.

"It was amazing," Mark said, "but exhausting, and I hear it's only going to get worse from here."

"I wish I could go to the training camp," Sky said.

"You? Your twig arms would snap in half," Jason said, placing a tub full of dishes on the counter.

"What are you talking about? I'm strong," Sky retorted, lifting one of her arms and flexing.

"About as strong as a sick cat," Jason said over his shoulder as he bustled back into the dining room.

Sticking her tongue out at him, Sky went to hang her bag on the hook by the door. "He's right, though. I probably wouldn't last half a day in the training camp."

As much as he wanted to tell her that she'd be fine, Mark couldn't help but agree. Sky was slim if one was being kind, and skeletally thin if one wasn't. Mark knew the look well and could tell that Sky wasn't getting enough to eat and likely hadn't for a very long time.

Still, she looked better than she had the first time he saw her. Her complexion was starting to gain a bit more color, and her hair had picked up a bit of a shine. More importantly, she seemed much less flighty and scared at every loud sound and shouting voice. He was also surprised to see how well she was getting along with Jason. Their grumpy boss didn't yell at her much anymore, and even when he did, she often had a snappy comeback for him. Flashing a smile at Mark, Sky headed for the dining room, tying up her hair into a ponytail as she disappeared through the door.

"All right, enough standing around with a silly grin," one of the cooks said, bringing a stack of pots over to Mark. "You have too much work to do to be distracted."

Despite the busyness of the restaurant, Mark found it incredibly relaxing compared to the grueling physical workout that consumed every moment of his time in the training camp or the frustratingly fierce struggles he underwent in his dreams.

Over the next two days, Mark worked at the restaurant as much as possible, with only a short break between his shifts to catch a nap and die a few hundred times to the drones. On the second day, he carefully reconstructed the fights he had been in during his dream the night before as he washed the pots, looking for the differences between when he'd managed to pierce through the drones' heads and when he hadn't.

At first, it had seemed completely random, but with practice, Mark had been able to get his success rate up to around seven out of ten. There, it had stalled, and it remained stalled for days until finally creeping up to eight out of ten, where it got stuck once more. He felt like he was missing something, and he had just finished washing a big pot and was lifting it onto the drying rack when an insight struck him. Slowly putting the pot down, he stretched out his hand and made a chopping motion in the air. Then, frowning, he did it again, and again, and again.

"It's in the wrist," he heard a voice say, and looking over, he saw Jason standing there with his arms folded across his chest, a scowl on his face.

Staring blankly at his boss, Mark blinked a few times, causing Jason to grunt angrily and stretch out his hand, making the same chopping motion Mark was. At the last moment, however, his wrist twitched, completing the strike with a slight twist. Feeling as if a light bulb had gone off in his head, Mark repeated his chop again, this time including the slight shake of his wrist that caused his fingers to twist slightly at the last moment.

"I didn't know they were teaching Cutting Palm anymore," Jason said.

Mark just stared at him blankly. "I don't know what that is."

Eyes narrowing, Jason took a step forward and grabbed Mark's hand, examining it closely. He didn't say anything as he turned Mark's wrist this way and that, and when he had finished, he let go of Mark and stalked off, muttering something unintelligible under his breath. For the rest of the day, he completely ignored Mark, not even looking in his direction. Worried that he had somehow offended his boss, Mark stayed extra late, helping to clean up. Just before he left, Jason stomped back into the kitchen.

"Here," he snapped, throwing something through the air at Mark, who fumbled to catch it. It was a booklet, only fifty or so pages long, and on the front, written in simple lettering, were the words *Cutting Palm*.

Before Mark could ask Jason about it, his boss was gone, leaving Mark alone in the dark kitchen. Grabbing his bag, Mark headed out, catching the train back to his house. On the ride, he read the booklet cover to cover, twice. It was mostly diagrams of figures doing a martial art, with a few sentences explaining each diagram. The martial art was entirely focused on transforming the martial artist's hands into lethal blades.

According to the description in the front of the book, the Cutting Palm, at its highest level of mastery, could be used to slice through steel. At first, Mark scoffed at this idea. Until he remembered how his fingers had managed to break through even the tough exoskeleton of a drone in the dream. Of course, he couldn't do it with his right hand, only his left when it was transformed, as the fingers on his right hand weren't tough enough.

The booklet also provided numerous exercises to strengthen the fingers and the skin of the practitioner's palms, and when he got home, Mark couldn't help himself. Following the directions of the booklet, he got out a bucket and filled it with rice, practicing thrusting his hands down into it and making a fist as tightly as he could. It was exhausting work and used muscles that he hadn't even known existed.

That night, as he entered the dream, Mark found his success rate had dropped. At first, it bothered him, but then he noticed that the strikes that succeeded were almost twice as effective. Before, his attacks had occasionally been able to pierce through the chitin shells covering the drones' heads. However, it had been hit or miss whether the strike would hit their brains and kill them, or simply wound them. Now, however, each of his successful attacks was almost twice as powerful, practically splitting the bugs' heads in half.

When Mark reported for training that morning, he saw that his number had changed from six to three. Glenn had dropped to the fifth slot, and Harper had moved back one position to the sixth. It likely had something to do with his ability to push his body more aggressively than others, and Mark was quite happy when the other two didn't seem all that upset by the shift in their numbers. The change motivated everyone, however, and Mark found himself being pushed harder than ever during the training sessions. After everyone had stuffed themselves at lunch, they were gathered by the lieutenant and ordered to line up.

"We're going to be adding another dimension to our training, starting today. At the end of the day, the Exlian only respect one thing: deadly force. In light of that, we'll begin combat training, starting with basic hand-to-hand combat and then moving to standard-issue weapons like the mana sword and mana shield."

Pointing to a stack of gear that had been set nearby, Lieutenant Cox grinned. "Your results will impact your rank, so I expect you to do your best. Grab a sword and let's get started."

Joining the others in choosing a sword, Mark hefted his in

his hand as he examined it. The practice sword was identical to a normal mana sword in shape and weight, but the mana blade had been deactivated, ensuring it would remain blunt.

"One and two, come on up."

Noah and Phoenix both stepped out of the line and saluted the lieutenant, who gestured for them to square off.

"Rules are simple. You're trying to score a hit on your opponent's chest or take them to the ground. Powers are, of course, forbidden. You two can start whenever you are ready."

Phoenix didn't wait and immediately lunged toward Noah, the tip of her sword stabbing toward his heart. Unruffled, Noah took a step forward and to the side, his sword rising to deflect the attack. With a simple twist of his wrist, he cut down toward Phoenix's shoulder, then shifted the trajectory of his blade to a stab targeting her side when she moved her sword to block. Forced to backpedal, Phoenix tried to reset her stance, but Noah stepped closer once more and disarmed her with a quick chop. Rather than give up, Phoenix tried to punch Noah, but he was able to move at least twice as fast as she was and simply tilted his head to dodge as he lifted his sword to her neck.

"Done! Number one wins. You both did well, but it looks like you have a lot of combat experience, Noah."

"Yes, sir," Noah said as Phoenix returned to her place in the formation, a scowl on her face.

"All right, get back to your spot. Three and four, your turn."

Hearing his number called, Mark stepped out to stand in front of the group, Danny mirroring his movement. Glancing at the massive young man next to him, Mark had to fight to suppress his groan. Getting matched up against Danny was terrible luck, as the giant young man was many times stronger than Mark. Danny wasn't disappointed at all and grinned back at him. There wasn't anything Mark could do, however, so he took his place and waited for the fight to start. As soon as the lieutenant gave the command, Mark jumped back, avoiding a heavy swing from Danny, who had lunged forward, using his longer reach to his advantage.

Mark landed lightly and dashed forward, ducking low to try to get in close. Danny responded with a sharp kick, forcing Mark to block with the flat of his blade. The force of the kick lifted Mark into the air, and he nearly got caught by Danny's backswing, only managing to avoid it by twisting his body to the side. Off balance, he was forced to put one hand down on the ground to keep from landing on his side, and by the time he had gotten back up, Danny was attacking again.

Knowing he wouldn't be able to block Danny's heavy strikes directly, Mark focused on avoiding them, all while trying to get close enough to hit Danny with his sword. A couple of times, he was tempted to just drop his sword and use his fists, as he was much more adept with hand-to-hand combat, but he could only imagine what would happen if he accidentally tore a giant gash in Danny's body using Cutting Palm.

Mark managed to get close twice, but Danny's reach was simply too long and his swings too fast for Mark to break past. Eventually, Mark missed a dodge and was forced to block one of Danny's swings. The two weapons struck with a crack that sounded like thunder, and Mark went flying. Landing heavily, he rolled over and bounced up. He wasn't injured, but he had hit the ground, which ended the fight. Grimacing, he walked back to stand next to Danny, who gave him an apologetic smile.

"You hit like a truck," Mark said, returning Danny's smile to show there were no hard feelings. "Well done."

The rest of the afternoon was spent sparring, and Mark got to fight against the other members of the top six. He managed to win against Phoenix, thanks to his superior speed and strength, and beat both Harper and Glenn handily, as neither had ever trained in melee combat before. Noah, on the other hand, crushed everyone, including Mark and Danny, solidly cementing his spot at the top.

To Mark, the loss against Noah was much more demoralizing than his loss to Danny. He could use Danny's size as an excuse, but that didn't work against Noah. Though Noah was stronger and faster than Mark, it was his perfect technique that allowed him to win again and again. Consoling himself that there would be more chances to fight Noah and fired up to improve his martial arts, Mark threw himself into his routine, practicing his new martial art at home and undergoing grueling physical training during the day.

Mime accompanied him everywhere, her presence providing a surprising amount of emotional support. She understood his frustrations perfectly, as if they shared a connection, and Mark soon began to wonder if she truly was part of him. Occasionally, she would vanish, leaving him on his own, but invariably, he would look up and find that she had taken her place on his shoulder once more.

By the time the weekend came around again, Mark felt as if he had reached a basic level of mastery with the Cutting Palm martial art, which was good because the first thing that Jason did when Mark walked into the restaurant was pull him back out into the alleyway and have him demonstrate his forms. The scowl on Jason's face grew stronger every time Mark showed him one of the forms, and Mark worried that he was doing them wrong.

"Fine. Show me the next one," Jason growled, his arms crossed over his chest.

Taking a deep breath to calm his jumping nerves, Mark did as he was told, and he had soon displayed all the forms under Jason's critical glare. When he was done, Jason waved for him to move to the side and stood in the center of the alleyway. After taking a moment to center himself, Jason stretched out his hand and executed the first, second, and third strikes in succession, chaining the moves together as if they were one unbroken movement.

"Palm arts are about variations. Their strength lies in their adaptability and the speed with which they change."

Having delivered his wisdom, Jason turned and stalked into the restaurant, leaving Mark outside to try to replicate what he had just seen. A couple of minutes later, Sky stuck her head out of the door.

"You better get in here," she said. "Jason seems especially grouchy today."

As he washed the dishes, Mark continued to try to replicate the rapidly shifting strikes Jason had shown him. He didn't put any power into his hands but instead simply moved through the motions as smoothly as he could. Each transition felt quite clunky, but over time they started to become easier to connect as he began to understand how to make subtle adjustments to his wrists' positioning. He wasn't exactly sure what use he would get out of this insight, but it was clear from the way Jason moved through the forms that he had mastered the Cutting Palm, so Mark felt it was worth trying.

Occasionally, Mark had the sense he was being observed, and glancing over his shoulder, he saw Jason scowling at him as if deep in thought. Despite Jason's grumpy exterior, Mark was coming to genuinely appreciate his boss, and the sight of him effortlessly executing the Cutting Palm technique hinted at a mysterious past that Mark was quite curious about. There was no time to delve into that mystery, however, as the endless piles of dishes wouldn't wash themselves.

When Mark collapsed into bed that night, he easily dispatched the first and second rounds of dream drones. The three drones that followed, however, were another story, and though he was getting better at dodging their attacks, Mark wasn't able to keep up for long. When the three drones spawned, two rushing at him from the front and one from behind, Mark moved swiftly, jumping back as he turned and struck the drone who was alone. His hand sliced through the monster's head easily, its greenish ichor slipping off his titanium fingers as he spun around. The other two drones were almost on him, one lunging for his foot, the other his throat.

Lifting his leg, Mark instinctively shifted from a blade strike to an open palm, pushing the drone attacking him upward. The drone on the ground had already spun and was now attacking his other leg, but Mark had dealt with this before and agilely dodged to the side. The drone above him flailed with its sharp legs, and without thinking, Mark shifted his palm into a claw, grabbing one of the flailing legs and twisting, causing the drone to flip in the air. With a swipe of his hand, he brought it down, smashing it into its companion, leaving them both dazed.

It was strange, as if the attacks he had just made hadn't been separate attacks but instead had formed one continuous wave. Mark dropped to one knee, his hand flashing, his fingers straightening as he drove them down through the head of the first drone, straight into the second. Both drones went limp. The fact that he had managed to kill all three drones was so surprising that he didn't even notice when the new round of drones had manifested, and he quickly died.

Though he didn't manage to replicate the feat and died to the four drones that attacked him over a hundred times, Mark woke up with excitement burning away in his chest. Managing to kill the three drones had provided a glimpse of what was possible.

Emboldened by the idea of mastering this technique, Mark threw himself into his training with gusto, powered by the food provided by the training camp during the week. During the weekends, when he didn't have access to the training camp, he was forced to spend the little bit of money he made working at the restaurant on high-calorie nutrient paste to help him keep his energy up. Time flew by, but the tangible feeling of progress consumed Mark's mind, birthing a frightening level of focus that allowed him to sharpen his abilities even more. Every waking hour was spent training his body or improving his martial arts in one way or another, and during his sleep he ground out hours of grueling combat training.

Even his time at the restaurant became part of his practice as he worked on his speed and coordination, visualizing his Cutting Palm techniques as he washed dishes. It was toward the end of the third week of his intense training when Mark felt a burning sensation in his body and suddenly each of his movements seemed smoother, faster. Glancing down at his status, he saw a small note.

> Your speed has increased from E– to E.

Opening his status to confirm it, he couldn't help but grin, catching Lieutenant Cox's eye.

"Something funny, Mark?"

"No, sir," Mark yelled. "My speed just ranked up."

The lieutenant's face lost its grim expression, and he smiled just as widely as Mark.

"Congratulations," he said. "I'd expect most of you who are empowered to start seeing these kinds of rank-ups soon. As for those who aren't, keep working hard, and maybe you'll get the chance."

Like a fire had been lit under them, everyone began frantically pushing themselves even harder. There wasn't a single person there who didn't want to grow stronger, and the realization that they could achieve it simply by doing a few more exercises motivated them to no end. That suited Mark just fine, and he began taking advantage of his new speed to increase his pace on their runs and squeeze in extra sets of body-weight exercises during their workouts.

By the end of the fifth week, Mark had seen his strength and fortitude advance as well, increasing how easily he could complete the exercises the lieutenant assigned them. Mark wasn't the only one either, as almost every empowered in their team had ranked up at least one of their stats, if not more. During this time, Mark had also advanced to the second position, swapping places with Phoenix. As hard as she worked, she couldn't advance as fast as Mark did, since he could burn almost a dozen times more energy every day.

The only person he couldn't outwork was Noah, who held on to the top position with ruthless determination. Noah's paragon power, though not the same as Mark's biofuel, acted similarly, allowing Noah to learn everything more quickly than normal. His increased speed and strength gave him a significant advantage in the physical exercises, and his minor invulnerability allowed him to ignore many of the negative effects brought about by pushing himself so hard, which translated into the ability to push just as fast as, if not faster than, Mark.

After the final workout session, the lieutenant called everyone to form up, and Mark hurried to get into position. Despite his relentless efforts, Noah still stood to his left, in the first position, and Mark couldn't help but feel a flash of disappointment. He had been working as hard as he could, but the gap between him and Noah felt larger than ever. Up on the small stage, Lieutenant Cox looked over the group, a genuine smile spreading across his face.

"Congratulations to all of you. I didn't know if all of you would make it, but here you are, just about ready to graduate. However, this section of the training camp is, as you know, only the beginning. Within the week, those of you who have passed our test will receive a notification alerting you to your next assignment. If you've passed the preliminary round, it means we believe that you have everything it takes to be a good soldier. From here, you'll be pleased to know that the physical training will lighten, at least somewhat, but now, we have another six weeks of instruction. During this time, we'll be bringing in a few more instructors, who will be teaching you about the Exlian threat, the various monsters the swarm contains, and their weaknesses. You'll also learn to build defenses, raise buildings, gather supplies, and so on and so forth. Over the next six weeks, we will be watching you closely and adjusting your ranks on a daily basis. Anyone who ends the next section in the top twenty-five will receive a skill gem. Continue to work hard. Continue to persevere. For glory."

"For humanity!"

After being dismissed for dinner, Mark fell in beside Danny

and Harper and joined the line for the mess hall. Both Mark and Danny took multiple trays of food, and the soldiers in charge of portioning the food piled them extra high, used to how much they ate.

"Am I glad we're finally done with this section," Glenn groaned as Mark took a seat across from him.

"You know that we'll still have to exercise in the later sections, right?" Harper said, sliding into the seat next to Mark.

"Sure, but it shouldn't be quite so intense, which means that I'll finally get to take my position back," Phoenix commented, pointing her spoon at Mark's nose.

Smirking, Mark shoveled food into his mouth, too busy eating to voice a comeback.

"How crazy would it be if he was just as good at theory?" Danny asked, causing Harper to shudder.

"One superfreak is already too many," she said, lowering her voice slightly as she looked around for Noah. "If Mark turns out to be one too, I might just give up."

"Right? It's so discouraging having to constantly chase Noah," Glenn agreed. "I've been holding out hope that all of Mark's brainpower is being sucked away by his muscles and that he will turn out to be completely dumb when it comes to the theory work."

Seeing that everyone was looking at him, Mark paused with his fork halfway to his mouth and gave them a sorrowful look, shaking his head slowly as if he were confirming Glenn's words. As Glenn's eyes lit up, however, he finally responded to their teasing.

"I'm afraid to report that my grades were in the top three in my school."

Glenn's expression crumpled, and he picked up a bread roll from his plate to throw at Mark, who flashed a grin and lifted his hand to grab it. Just before he could, the roll jumped sideways, neatly dodging his hand and smacking him square in the cheek.

"Hey, no fair! Using powers is cheating."

This time, it was Glenn's turn to smirk as he controlled the bread roll to smack Mark again. "Gotta take my advantages where I can."

Mark, who was trying in vain to ward off the roll, saw something flash in front of his face and jerked back, his hands moving into a defensive position. Standing beside him, holding the offending bread roll, was Noah, his face as impassive as always.

"Using powers on your comrades is forbidden, especially in the training camp."

His tone was cold, and immediately the atmosphere around the table grew tense. Glenn looked stricken, and Harper and Phoenix both looked annoyed that Noah had stepped in. Only Danny was unperturbed, though that could have been because he had been busy eating the whole time. As the tension grew, he blinked and looked up from his plate, noticing Noah standing there. "Are you going to eat that?"

Noah shook his head and tossed the roll to Danny, who caught it and stuffed it into his mouth with a happy smile. Taking a breath, Mark did his best to relax his shoulders and leaned over as Noah took his seat.

"Hey, thanks," he said.

Noah slowly turned to look at him, his eyes narrowing as if he was trying to assess how sincere Mark was being. After a long moment, he nodded and then began to eat, ignoring everyone else at the table. Rolling her eyes, Harper gestured for the others to lean in as she spoke in a quiet voice.

"I heard something interesting about the next section of the training camp."

"Oh?" Phoenix leaned closer, her eyes lighting up with curiosity.

"One of my brother's friends is part of the training staff for another, and he was at our house yesterday. He let it slip that the next part of the camp is going to be divided into special groups. There will be one group that does mostly classroom time, but there will also be another group that gets specialized in-the-field training from active members of the three branches."

Both nervous and excited, Glenn leaned forward. "Whoa, are you serious? How are they splitting the groups up? What do we need to do to get in the advanced training group?"

"I'm not sure," Harper admitted with a shrug.

Listening carefully, Mark could feel excitement growing in his heart. The chance to train with active members of the three military branches would be much more valuable than any amount of classroom-based theory, and he could only hope that he would be chosen for the special training class. He was just thinking about what he could do to improve his chances when he heard a light ding from his watch. Looking down, he saw a message blinking at him and, with a shout, jumped up from the table, causing his chair to clatter to the ground.

"Everything okay, Mark?" Phoenix asked.

Mark, who had been staring at his watch, nodded mutely. He took a deep, shuddering breath and looked up, his voice filled with a low intensity.

"The Cerberus Battalion is back from deployment," he said.

Everyone at the table perked up at this, including Noah.

"How'd you get that information?" Harper asked, her eyes narrowing slightly as she stared at Mark. "Shouldn't the movement of a Ranger battalion be secret?"

"My brother's a member of Cerberus, and he just sent me a message that he's back in the city."

"You have a brother in Cerberus?" Glenn asked, his eyes wide. "Wow. See, I knew from the very beginning that you were a big shot."

"It's his brother, idiot, not him," Harper said.

"Still, that's really amazing."

Noah, who had finished all his food, pushed himself back from the table. He looked at Mark for a second, then nodded. "I'm glad he returned safely. Cerberus's missions are never easy."

Surprised by the sincerity hidden under Noah's cold tone, Mark nodded his thanks as Noah walked away.

"He's so stuck up," Harper grumbled.

"You would be too, if you came from a family like his," Phoenix said mysteriously.

"Sounds like somebody knows something," Glenn interjected, his eyes shining as he stared at Phoenix.

"Not something I'm foolish enough to go blabbing about," Phoenix retorted. "If you want to know, ask Noah yourself."

"Are you kidding? He'd probably snap my head off."

Too excited at the thought of seeing his brother again to sit still, Mark excused himself and ran off. He made it home in record time, only to find the house dark. Mark knew that since his brother had returned, he would see him soon, and for a moment, he considered asking Jason to have the next day off. He got as far as typing out the message before slowly deleting it. Even though he hadn't seen his brother in almost a year, he knew Joe wouldn't approve of him skipping work. As intensely disciplined as Mark was, he paled in comparison to his supersoldier brother. If he tried to use Joe's return as an excuse for not working, all he'd get was an earful.

His enthusiasm dampened, Mark looked around, trying to decide what to do before his brother came home. Mime, who had hopped down and taken her place on the couch as soon as they walked in the door, regarded him with curiosity as he paced back and forth, unable to contain his excitement. As he turned, he caught sight of the door, which was hanging slightly ajar. The lock was still broken. He kept meaning to fix it but simply hadn't had time. He could only imagine what his brother would say, however, if he returned home to a busted-open front door, so Mark ran to grab a few of the tools their father had left, then hunted around for a scrap of something that he could use to patch the broken doorjamb.

Thankfully, the lock itself was in good working order; it had just been ripped free from the frame, leaving it with nothing to catch on. It was a simple fix to Mark, who was used to patching things up around the house. For the next forty minutes, he occupied himself by cutting down a board to reinforce the holes and give the lock something to latch on to.

Every time he heard a sound outside, he would jump up, sticking his head out the door, hoping to see his brother, only to be disappointed when it was some random passerby. One of his neighbors, stopping at the house when he saw Mark working on the door, even asked him if he had any news of when his brother would return, but Mark just shook his head no and continued working.

It was technically the truth, he told himself, as he really didn't know when his brother was going to arrive. The movements of the Cerberus Battalion were always shrouded in mystery, and the city didn't look kindly on those who spilled any information about their whereabouts. So even though Mark knew they were back in the city, he wasn't about to tell his neighbor, who was often a little bit too nosy for his own good.

When he had finished repairing the door, Mark checked the lock to make sure it worked, then put away the tools. He sat on the couch, opening up his virtual screen, and began to watch the news. He only lasted a few minutes before nervous energy forced him off the couch to begin doing push-ups. As he listened to the news anchor drone on about the state of the city, he finished his push-ups and began squats, alternating between regular deep squats and pistol squats.

It was an hour and a half later when he heard a sound at the door, and the keypad beeped, causing him to spring up, brushing the beads of sweat from his brow as he stared at the slowly turning lock. The door opened, and his brother stepped in.

"Hello, Mark," Joe said, a smile flashing across his normally austere face.

His once-brown hair, now tinged with red due to the influence of his power, seemed duller than usual, and a general air of exhaustion surrounded him. Mark thought nothing of it as he jumped over the couch and wrapped his brother in a tight hug. For a moment, they stood in the doorway, and then Mark, feeling slightly embarrassed by the intensity of his reaction, let go and pulled Joe inside.

"Come in. Where's your bag? I can carry it up to your room."

"I don't have a bag," Joe said, shaking his head. "All my gear is still back at the barracks. I'll get it when I head back next week. I figured I had enough clothing here to last me through my time off."

"How long are you off?"

"A week," Joe said, following Mark into the kitchen and accepting the glass Mark filled with water.

"That's pretty generous. Last time you only had two days."

With a grimace hidden by the glass, Joe nodded and sat down, leaning against the table as he sipped on the water. "We have plenty of time to catch up. Word on the street is that you got into one of the training camps."

Nervous, Mark nodded. "It's only the basic recruit training camp, though."

"That's still something to be proud of," Joe said, placing the glass down on the table. "While they do open it to general admission, you still have to meet the minimum requirements. I've also heard that you were assigned to Camp Eleven."

Though each recruit's information was supposed to be private,

Mark wasn't surprised at all that his brother knew where he had been placed. It was hard to keep anything quiet in the military, especially when you got into the upper ranks.

Noticing Mark's disgruntled expression, Joe laughed. "An old instructor of mine sent me a message, wondering if you and I were related."

"Hopefully that's a good thing," Mark said, causing his brother to smirk.

"Honestly, who knows? It probably means he'll push you harder than normal. But Lieutenant Cox is a wonderful trainer, and you'll do well under him."

"I've really been enjoying his instruction so far," Mark said. "We've only gone through the physical-training section, but he really knows what he's talking about."

"Just wait until you get into Exlian biology. Cox has an eye for finding his enemy's weaknesses, so if you pay attention, you'll benefit quite a bit."

"What about you?" Mark asked, getting a drink of water for himself and sitting at the table across from his brother. "This deployment seemed really long."

"It wasn't supposed to be," Joe said, his expression darkening slightly. "We had some trouble out in the field."

Eyes wide, Mark listened carefully as Joe continued.

"We lost quite a few good Rangers to an Exlian ambush. We're not sure how they spotted us, but what should have been an easy scouting mission turned into months of siege. The only good thing is that we managed to identify a few more types."

Mark hoped Joe would go into detail about them, but his brother didn't indulge his curiosity.

"I'm lucky to have made it back alive," he said quietly.

From the heaviness of Joe's voice, Mark could tell he was still grieving those who had not been as lucky.

"I'm sorry," Mark whispered, but Joe just waved his hand.

"It comes with the territory." After taking a long drink of water, he placed his glass down, rotating it slightly on the table. "Anybody who joins Cerberus knows the risks. It's hard to lose comrades, but if you join the military, that's what you sign up for."

There was a faint bitterness in Joe's voice that Mark had never heard before, but before he could dig into it, his brother changed the subject.

"What is more important is that I also heard you have some exciting news," Joe said, staring intently at Mark, his orange eyes glowing slightly. "It appears that I'm not the only empowered in this family anymore."

Cracking a smile, Mark nodded. He'd known that he wouldn't be able to hide it from his brother, and someone, probably Lieutenant Cox, had already mentioned it to Joe. "Yes, I empowered right before the training camp started."

"What happened?"

Hesitating for a moment, Mark considered telling his brother about his strange experience, but given how fiercely committed Joe was to the military and the laws of the city, and how little Mark remembered about what happened, he ultimately held his tongue. "I don't know. I just woke up one morning, and something had changed."

Mark could feel the lameness in his answer acutely, and from the way his brother's eyes narrowed, he knew Joe had detected it as well.

"I got an absorption power," he said quickly, trying to shift the subject.

As he spoke, he held out his left arm, lightly touching his fingers against the metal dining room table. With a thought, he powered up his activator, and a few seconds later, his left arm had taken on a silvery sheen. Though Mark's will was still at E–, he could feel that the transformation was getting quicker and easier, meaning that his rank-up wasn't too far away. His brother reached across the table and tapped the back of Mark's hand, letting out a low whistle as his finger bounced off the metal skin.

"That's really cool. Is it just your arm?"

"For the moment, yes, but I have something called trait selection, which allows me to take only the advantages from a substance," Mark said, wiggling his fingers to demonstrate they could still move.

"So that means it's got to be what? A C-ranked skill?"

"B, actually," Mark said proudly. "Because I don't actually absorb the material itself, just its characteristics."

"Huh. That's a new one," Joe said, his eyebrows rising. "I've never seen anybody with an absorption power above C."

"The people doing the assessment seemed quite surprised as well," Mark admitted.

"It's understandable. While there is a nearly endless variety of powers, they typically fall into similar structures," Joe said. "And almost one hundred percent of the time, a variation to a power makes it weaker, not stronger. To see an absorption power that not only falls outside the norm but is stronger? That's quite interesting."

"It's not as cool as elemental control, but I'm pretty happy with it."

"You should be. I think the ability to transform into other substances is much more useful in combat than elemental control, except maybe at the absolute level."

Seeing Mark's skeptical look, Joe laughed and tapped on the table. "My guess is that you can maintain that transformation almost indefinitely, or at least you will be able to as you improve in your will. Using elemental control actively drains its wielder's energy, which means that if you can outlast someone in a fight, you'll be able to beat an elemental controller every single time, so long as you can catch them, of course. There are plenty of materials that are impervious to elements, which means once you have a full-body transformation, you'll be a walking tank. Take my flame, for instance. I can only get it so hot, and there are metals that I can't affect as a result. Plus, since you have trait selection, you should be able to take on the traits of nonsolid material."

Holding up his hand to stop his brother's theorizing, Mark shook his head.

"Maybe if I could get to the higher ranks," he said, "but my potential's not as good as yours."

"What do you mean?" Joe asked, his brow furrowing.

This was the part of the conversation Mark had been dreading, but rather than hide the truth, he took a deep breath and admitted it. "My potential's only rank D, and unstable at that. I might never make it out of E."

"Rank D?" Joe shook his head. "That shouldn't be possible. Both Mom and Dad had high potential. Mom's was A ranked, and Dad's was B ranked. You should be B at the very least."

Not knowing what to say, Mark shrugged. "When I took the test, they said that my potential was fluctuating, something having to do with my power, they thought. It was pretty solidly in the D range, and I'm happy with that. I really am. I only need to be in the D rank if I want to join the Defense Force."

"You don't want to join the Defense Force," Joe said, shaking his head.

Taken aback by the vehemence in his brother's voice, Mark raised his eyebrows. Joe caught himself, realizing he had misspoken, and after a moment of awkward silence, he flashed a smile. "I mean, the Rangers are so much better."

Though Joe tried to play it off as a joke, there had been nothing funny about what he'd said, but Mark didn't want to make it awkward, so he quickly changed the subject. "Hey, are you hungry? You must be hungry since you just got back."

"No, I'm fine," Joe said.

Mark had already jumped up and thrown open the fridge, freezing when he saw it was empty save for three boxes of the nutrient paste he had been buying. Since he had been eating all his meals either at the training camp or at the restaurant on the weekends, the only food Mark had been buying recently was the rather disgusting tubes of superprocessed food. Behind him, Joe looked on in bemusement as Mark rushed over to the pantry to see if anything was there. Opening the door, he found four neatly stacked boxes of energy bars and nothing else.

"Wow, I didn't realize you were so dedicated," Joe said, astonishment clear in his voice. "I knew we were poor, but that's another level."

Embarrassed, Mark shut the pantry door.

"Why don't I run out and get something," he said, "to celebrate you being home?"

"There's really no need," Joe said. "Actually, I'm pretty exhausted, and I think I might go and get some sleep. Maybe we can celebrate tomorrow. You don't have training camp, right?"

"I don't, but I do have to work."

"That's fine," Joe said. "I'll probably sleep most of the day anyway. I'll tell you what: I'll do a little bit of shopping while you're out, and when you get home, we'll cook up a nice meal."

Mark finally noticed how tired his brother looked. The bags under Joe's eyes were more pronounced than normal, and the way his cheeks and lips sagged spoke of tremendous exhaustion. His shoulders, normally straight and broad, were curled inward, as if he carried a tremendous weight upon his back. Pushing himself back from the table, Joe stood up, leaning heavily on it.

"I'm glad to see you, Mark," he said.

"I'm glad to see you too."

As Mark watched his brother slowly climb the stairs and disappear onto the second floor, he felt his heartbeat speeding up. He had been so excited to see Joe that he hadn't registered something was wrong. It was normal for Joe to be tired after getting back from deployment, but this was different. Something about Joe seemed fundamentally changed, but Mark couldn't quite put his finger on what.

After going into his room, Joe didn't come out, and Mark didn't bother him, though he did stand for a moment by his brother's door before he went to bed, hesitating as to whether he should knock and say good night. Eventually, deciding his brother was probably asleep, Mark turned and went into his own room, where he spent the night in the dream, battling against Exlian drones.

He had been fighting against four drones simultaneously for over a month, and while he still died every single time, which was tremendously frustrating, he was making just enough progress that he didn't want to quit. Not that he could quit. Mark had no idea why the dream had started or if it was possible to stop it. Even if he wanted to take a break, the drones would simply appear and kill him, sending spikes of pain radiating through him each time their sharp mandibles tore into his flesh.

Pain truly was a tremendous teacher, however, and Mark was getting close to the point where he felt that he could probably fight the four drones on equal footing. Killing them without dying himself was another matter, however, and though he hadn't managed to do it, Mark found himself getting better and better at staying alive.

In his military pants and shirt, Mark found himself woefully unprotected against the monsters' sharp bites and slashing claws. This lack of armor forced him to adjust his style, focusing more on avoiding enemy attacks while using his left arm to block. For a time, he'd found his right hand rather useless and stopped using it. However, when he didn't use both his hands and his feet to fight against the drones, he found himself dying rapidly.

Little by little, Mark had begun making instinctive adjustments to his fighting style, deploying the ever-changing strikes of Cutting Palm to deal with the drones' aggression, giving himself room to dodge. He wasn't sure if it was because of the emotion caused by his brother's return, but Mark found himself particularly energetic that night and came close to eliminating all four of the drones. His right hand simply wasn't quite strong enough to pierce through their armor, however, and though his palm strike managed to deflect the last drone's attack, one of its mandibles still caught the side of his chest, tearing a painful gash that caused his body to fade away.

Instead of reappearing as he expected to, Mark awoke, intense hunger seizing him. He felt a weight on his chest and, looking down, saw Mime sitting on top of him, staring at him with an intense gaze. Disoriented from being woken, Mark could have sworn he saw a red glow in her eyes. With a groan, he tried to turn over, and Mime jumped down from his chest and padded to the door.

Mark's stomach was screaming at him, as was normal after each of his dream combat sessions, but as he reached for a tube of nutrient paste, Mark got the oddest feeling. Mime had stopped next to the door and looked back at him, silent as always, and with a shiver, Mark had the distinct impression that there was a tremendous food source right outside his door. He had no idea how he knew, but he could tell that Mime wanted to go out and hunt.

Shuddering slightly as he thought of Mime dragging some poor unfortunate creature back to him for him to eat, Mark grabbed one of the tubes and ripped the top off, gulping it down. As he felt his body begin to absorb the nutrient paste, he sat up and shook his head.

"I don't eat creatures like that," Mark said. "I only eat cooked food."

Mime's head tilted to the side, genuine confusion flashing through her eyes, as she gave Mark an intense look.

"I'm serious," Mark said. "Don't go killing things and bringing them back here. I won't eat them."

Though she was just a cat, Mark felt as if her shoulders drooped, and slowly she turned back around, padded over to the bed, and jumped up, avoiding Mark as she returned to her pillow and curled up, clearly disappointed with Mark's decision.

Not feeling quite full, Mark sucked down another tube and went back to bed, where he managed to catch a couple of hours of actual sleep before dawn arrived. When he awoke, he saw the pillow next to him was empty. With a flash of panic, Mark wondered if Mime had ignored him and gone out hunting anyway.

Jumping up, he ran to the door and out into the hall, taking the steps three at a time as he ran down them. When he reached the bottom of the stairs, he caught sight of a standoff in the kitchen and froze. Joe was at the sink, a knife held in his hand and his body tense as he stared at Mime, who sat perfectly still on the dining room table.

"Everything okay?" Mark asked, stepping into the kitchen.

Joe never took his eyes off the cat. "What is that?"

"You mean my cat?"

Mark took a hesitant step forward.

"Stay where you are," Joe said, and memories of the years Mark spent training under his brother's harsh tutelage caused his body to freeze in place.

For a long moment, Joe and Mime maintained their locked gazes, until, with an almost comically large yawn, Mime turned and looked at Mark, giving him a slight nod. Leisurely standing up, Mime jumped down from the table and slowly walked over to Mark, rubbing up against him, before heading for the couch, where she took up her normal position on the one good cushion.

"Mark?"

Hearing the dangerous note in his brother's voice, Mark swallowed. "Yes?"

"Why is there an animal in our house? Don't you know that's against the law?"

If Mark had been frozen before, he was positively petrified now, his eyes going wide. He did know that. In fact, it was one of the most basic rules: Keep your doors locked, and don't let animals or strangers into your home.

"She's just a cat."

Joe slowly relaxed his tight grip on the knife he held. "I can see that."

Turning, he placed it down on the counter, and Mark noticed that his brother's hands were trembling slightly. Joe picked up the glass of water he had been filling and sat at the kitchen table. Mark joined him.

"Sorry for being so tense," Joe said. "Sometimes, after coming back from deployment, it takes me a few days to get used to not being under constant threat."

Sensing there was more to what his brother wanted to say, Mark didn't reply and just listened in silence.

"It's a pretty terrible thing to live under conditions where you could die at any time," Joe said, "and for the last six, maybe seven months, that's exactly what my life has been. I shouldn't have been so harsh yesterday about you joining the Defense Force. It's just, the military really isn't quite as glamorous as you might think."

Pausing to take a sip of his water, Joe looked across the table at Mark, his eyes full of mixed emotions.

"In the wilderness, anything that moves is a threat. You might think I'm joking, but I'm not. Plants, animals, and above all, Exlian.

They're everywhere and constantly on the hunt. But it's not just the Exlian. Mana has caused practically everything to evolve, to change, and it's all optimized for killing. Just because a creature is small doesn't mean it's not dangerous. Exlian drones aren't very big, but they can rip a person apart in a matter of seconds. Even an empowered, if they catch them without a mana suit. And the drones are the smallest and weakest of the Exlian. I've seen small flocks of birds tear a person apart until nothing remained except part of a hip bone."

With a slight shudder, Joe stared down at his water.

"I know most people don't pay attention to the rules about pets, especially out here on the outskirts of the city. And it's fine. I'm almost never around, so there's really no problem with you having a cat. I was just surprised, that's all."

Unsure what to say, Mark took a deep breath and stood up.

"Thanks," he said. "Mime is really nice, and I'm sure you two will get along great. I, uh, I have to go to work, but I'll be back this evening."

"Sure," Joe said with forced lightness. "I'll go grocery shopping while you're out. When you get home, we'll have a party. If you have any friends you want to invite, feel free. I might see if some of my buddies are still around. We can all celebrate together."

"Sure, that would be great," Mark said, a wide smile lighting up his face.

After rushing back upstairs to use the bathroom and getting dressed for his shift at the restaurant, Mark came down and grabbed a couple of the energy bars, saying goodbye to his brother before darting out the door. He was tremendously happy to have Joe back and in one piece and soon forgot the strangeness of the morning. When he arrived at the restaurant, he found it was busier than usual, and peeking out through the kitchen doors, he noticed a group of soldiers he had never seen before dressed in fatigues. Spotting a small patch on their shoulders depicting a dog, Mark's eyes widened.

"Same unit as your brother," Jason said, startling Mark.

Mark had been blocking the door, and Jason and a couple of the servers were waiting to go through. Mark mumbled an apology and stepped to the side. To his surprise, Jason didn't bite his head off, appearing preoccupied with something, which Mark didn't mind at all. Hurrying back to the dish area, Mark began to wash plates. His increased speed meant that he could wash the dishes by hand with no problem, saving his boss a considerable number of credits since he didn't have to run the expensive dishwasher. Plus, it helped Mark work on his coordination.

Closer to lunchtime, Sky came in, stopping by to say hi to Mark before she put up her hair and headed into the dining room to start taking orders from the lunch crowd. When he saw her, Mark was reminded about what his brother had said that morning, and decided to invite her to the party they would have that night. The next time she came through the kitchen to drop off a stack of dirty plates, he opened his mouth, but nervousness suddenly gripped him, and he found the words dying on his tongue. Seeing him staring at her with his mouth open as if he wanted to say something, Sky stopped and looked at him curiously.

"Uh, thanks," Mark said lamely, and with some confusion, Sky nodded and turned around to head back into the dining room.

Watching her go, Mark let out a small groan and leaned over, tapping his forehead against the metal edge of the sink.

"If it's too hard, just use the dishwasher," one of the cooks said, thinking that Mark was overwhelmed by the number of dishes.

Not bothering to correct his assumption, Mark stood up, wiped the suds from his forehead, and began to wash the dishes again. For the rest of the afternoon, he tried to work up the courage to say something, failing until she finally confronted him.

"Is everything okay, Mark?" Sky asked, pausing as she put her plates down on the counter next to the sink.

Feeling like an utter fool, Mark nodded.

"Yes," he said. "Actually, things are great. My brother's home, and he hasn't been home in quite a while, so we were thinking of having a party, and I was just wondering if you would want to come."

The words came out all in one jumbled rush, and it took Sky a moment to sort through them. Mark's heart plummeted as he saw Sky's conflicted expression, only to jump into his throat a moment later, when she suddenly smiled.

"Sure," she said. "That sounds like it would be great."

"Oh, good," Mark blurted out, "because I thought you wouldn't want to . . ."

Realizing what he was saying halfway through, he trailed off, staring wide eyed at Sky, whose cheeks carried the faintest hint of pink. Tongue tied, Mark grabbed half of the plates that she had just put down and dropped them in the sink, ignoring the loud clattering sound.

"Hey, be careful with those dishes! Any of them that break are coming out of your pay!" Jason yelled from across the room, somehow able to hear the clanking of the dishes over the hubbub of the kitchen.

Mark was thankful for his boss's sharp tone, which somehow always seemed to clear the awkward air. With a wry smile that Sky returned, he took the rest of the plates and plopped them into the sink. "I'm working a double today, so I don't get off until nine, but if that's not too late, we'd really love for you to join us."

"That's not too late," Sky said. "That's when I get off as well."

"Okay, great. Then you can just come with me to my house."

Looking quite happy, she rushed off, and for a few seconds Mark stood in place, looking in the direction she had gone. The thought of bringing Sky back to his house was strangely embarrassing, though Mark genuinely didn't understand why. An impulse struck him, and he quickly sent out a message to a chat group Phoenix had set up early in their training days.

MARK

Hey, since my brother is home, we're having a party. You're all invited.

Almost immediately, he began to get responses.

GLENN

Of course I can come. That sounds so fun. What's the address?

DANNY

Will there be food? Because I'll come if there's food.

HARPER

Sure. Send us the address, and I'll be there.

PHOENIX

Oh, that sounds so fun. Unfortunately, I've got a dinner already planned. But next time, let us know ahead of time, because I'd totally rather be hanging out with you guys.

Noah was in the group as well, though he had never once responded to any of their messages, so Mark didn't wait for him to reply and sent out his address. After dashing off a quick message to his brother to let him know how many people would be coming, Mark kept washing dishes, occasionally taking a break to chomp down on one of the energy bars to refill his biofuel meter.

At nine, he and Sky both grabbed their things and headed toward the train station, walking through the quiet streets lit by bright streetlights. Even though the restaurant was slightly out of the way, this area of town was quite bright, but the closer they got to the train station, the more nervous Sky became, until she stopped right before they entered.

"I'm sorry," she suddenly said. "I don't think I can come."

"What do you mean?" Mark asked. "Why not?"

Noticing her fidgeting with her hands, Mark glanced down and realized that Sky wasn't wearing a watch. Almost immediately, he figured out the problem. Without a watch, it would be impossible for her to get on the train, as she wouldn't be able to scan in.

"I normally walk everywhere," she said, blushing, as she saw Mark looking at her empty wrist.

With a level of smoothness that surprised him, Mark waved his hand and grabbed her arm, pulling her away from the train station's doors.

"That's fine. We can just take a car," he said.

Slightly stunned that he had slipped his arm around hers, Sky didn't manage to respond in time to stop him from ordering a taxi.

"I can pay you back," she said, but Mark shook his head.

"I'd have to get home anyway, and a taxi's really not that much more expensive, so don't worry about it."

That wasn't true, of course, and the taxi ride was guaranteed to eat into his meager savings, but right now he didn't care one bit. The car pulled up a moment later, and Mark opened the door for Sky, who nervously scooted in, sitting on the very edge of the seat and not daring to touch anything.

"You'll want to put your seat belt on," Mark said after getting in the car and shutting the door.

With a faint jerk, Sky watched as he buckled his own belt. Mark saw her slowly sliding backward until her back barely touched the backrest. She fumbled with her seat belt for a moment before figuring out how to pull it across her body, then carefully slotted it in. When it clicked, the driver, who was watching the two of them with a smirk, pulled out, and they were on their way. Mark tried to maintain pleasant conversation throughout the ride, but Sky was so nervous that she never said more than a word or two in response, and eventually the car lapsed into silence.

When the car pulled up outside Mark's house, Glenn and two of Joe's friends were already inside. Glenn was staring at the other two, twins with matching blond crew cuts and the builds of professional soldiers, with rapt attention as they chatted with Joe, recounting funny stories from their training days. Stepping inside the house, Mark realized that Sky hadn't entered behind him, and he turned around, finding her frozen on the doorstep.

"Come in," he said, but she didn't move, and he had to ask her again before she finally stepped inside.

Spotting them, Joe jumped up to greet them.

"Hey, Mark, who's your friend?" he asked, throwing his arm around Mark's shoulder.

"This is Sky," Mark said. "We work together at Jason's Pub."

"Nice to meet you, Sky." Joe held out his hand.

After hesitating for a moment, she took the offered hand and shook it. "Nice to meet you."

"Well, come on in and make yourself comfortable. There's food on the counter, drinks in the fridge, and you're welcome to sit anywhere."

Though she nodded and thanked Joe, Sky didn't leave Mark's side, hiding behind him as he approached Glenn and the twins, Kevin and Marvin, to introduce himself. Danny and Harper showed up not too long after, along with a few more of Joe's friends from his training days, and the party was soon well underway. Watching as everyone talked and laughed, Mark was pleased at how well the two groups were mixing. Sky was still shy, though at some point,

Mime found her and made a permanent home of Sky's arms. Holding the black cat helped Sky relax, and soon she was chatting with Harper on the couch, while Danny and Glenn bugged the soldiers for stories about their various deployments.

Close to eleven, Mark heard a knock at the door. Exchanging a glance with Joe, who shrugged, he got up to see who it was. He'd thought that everybody who was coming to the party had already arrived, so when he opened the door and saw Noah standing there with his hands behind his back, his bodyguard looming behind him, Mark just stared. For a long moment, the two of them just looked at each other, Mark not knowing what to say and Noah maintaining his characteristic silence.

"Who's this?" Joe asked, walking over.

As soon as the bodyguard spotted Joe, Mark could see his eyes narrowing and his shoulders tensing as he recognized the danger Joe represented. Noah's eyes lit up, and he quickly bowed his head slightly toward Joe. "My name is Noah Javesi. I'm a member of the same training camp as your brother, Mark."

"Oh, wonderful," Joe said, reaching out to pat Noah on the shoulder. "Come on in, and who's your friend?"

"This is Bandman. He'll stay outside."

"No need for that," Joe replied, gesturing for the bodyguard to enter.

Nodding in thanks, Bandman ducked through the door behind Noah and slowly surveyed the room. Though other people wouldn't have been able to notice it, as they were too far away, Mark, who was standing right next to the bodyguard, felt him tense again, both when he saw the twins, who were in the kitchen talking with Danny, and when he spotted Sky, who was sitting on the couch, Mime resting in her arms. He was also close enough to see the look that Noah gave his bodyguard, clearly warning him not to make a scene. Reaching into his pocket, Noah pulled out a small box, which he turned and handed to Mark.

"I was in a bit of a rush today," he said, "so I apologize. It isn't much."

"What's this for?" Mark asked, taking the small box and staring at it in confusion.

"Gift," Noah said casually. "Like I said, it's nothing big."

Mark had heard that among upper-class families, giving gifts when going over to somebody's house was a fairly normal thing, but he had never imagined anybody giving him one, so he didn't know what to do with it. Thankfully, Joe was more familiar with the customs of the upper class and took it from his brother.

"Thanks," he said. "I've got to run upstairs, so I'll drop this in your room, Mark. Why don't you take Noah over to get some food?"

Feeling surprisingly nervous, Mark nodded and jerked his head for Noah to follow him. In silence, they walked the five steps into the kitchen, and Mark introduced Noah to Joe's friends. Both Glenn and Danny were surprised to see that Noah had come, but as normal, Noah paid no attention to their astonishment and began happily picking through the food.

A moment later, Mark's watch buzzed, and he saw that Glenn had posted a picture of Noah picking up a sandwich in their group chat. A few seconds later, messages from Phoenix started to flood in, causing Mark's watch to buzz so much he had to mute it.

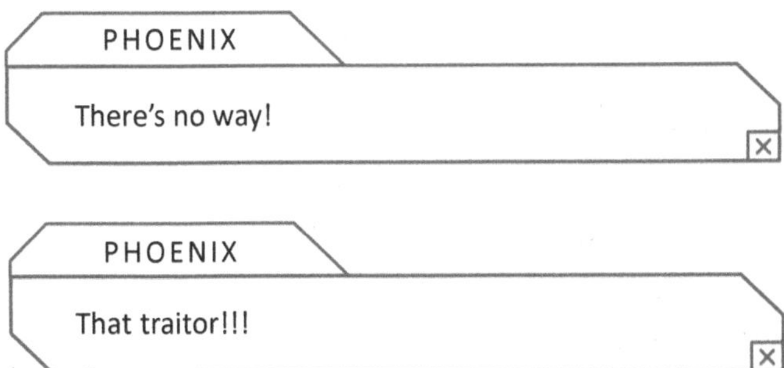

PHOENIX

He's supposed to be at the same event I'm at tonight.

PHOENIX

I wondered where he was. His dad said he wasn't feeling well.

PHOENIX

If he can come, then I can come. I'll be right there.

No more than twenty minutes had passed when there was another knock on the door, though this one was more akin to a pounding. When Mark opened the door, Phoenix swept right in, leaving Mark staring in shock. He had only ever seen her in the training fatigues, so when she stepped through the door in a sleek cocktail dress, a small fortune of jewels glittering around her neck, Mark found himself lost for words.

"Hello, Mark," Phoenix said with a bright smile, happy with the effect she was having on him.

Her eyes swept the room, a stormy look appearing when she spotted Noah, who was nonchalantly eating a chicken wing. Mark hadn't thought anything of it, but Noah was dressed in his casual street clothes, and though each and every item was no doubt worth more than everything Mark owned put together, there was no ostentation to any of it, allowing him to blend seamlessly in with the group.

"He even changed," Phoenix muttered under her breath,

before stalking up to Noah. "Does your father know you're here?"

Not bothering to put down the chicken leg he was chewing on, Noah shrugged. "Does yours?"

His reply left Phoenix speechless, and after growling at him, she decided the best course of action was to ignore him. By that time, Joe had walked over, and Mark introduced Phoenix, who said hello and then joined the group in the kitchen. The party was fairly low key, and Mark had a tremendous time. It had been years since he had spent time with friends, and having his brother home as well made things all the better.

Eventually it was time for people to start going, and one by one, they said their goodbyes and left. Finally, everyone had gone, except for Sky, who was still sitting on the couch with Mime asleep in her lap. Remembering that Sky didn't have a watch, and not knowing where she lived, Mark came over and sat on the armrest next to her. "Where do you live? I could take you home."

"Oh, there's no need," Sky said, brushing her hair behind her ear. "I just didn't want to wake your cat."

"Oh, don't worry about that," Mark replied, waving his hand. "Mime will go back to sleep, no problem."

Somewhat reluctantly, Sky scratched behind Mime's ears, causing her to open her eyes sleepily, then stretch.

"Come on, Mime, it's time to let your prisoner go home."

Giving Mark a long look, Mime leaped up onto his shoulder and perched there, watching Sky with glittering eyes.

"I wish I had a cat," Sky said, "but where I live, I can't really . . ."

Her voice trailed off.

"You gonna walk her home?" Joe asked from the kitchen, where he was cleaning up.

"Yes."

"No."

Their voices overlapping, Mark and Sky looked at each other.

"It's too far from here," Sky said quickly, shaking her head.

"Then at least let me call you a taxi," Mark said. "If it's that far, I can't have you walking all night."

Torn between her desire to not have to make the journey on foot and her worry about how much money it would cost, Sky didn't respond right away, and Mark quickly called up a car on his watch.

"You'll have to give the driver your address," he said, "since I don't know where you live, but they'll be here in a minute or two."

With a defeated sigh, Sky nodded. "All right, thank you. I had an absolutely wonderful time. Thank you so much for inviting me. And thanks for the taxi. And just . . . thanks."

As her voice trailed into silence, Sky stood up, tugging on her shirt.

"Of course," Mark said, walking with her as she went to the door.

"Come back anytime," Joe called from the kitchen, giving her a wave. "It was nice to meet you, Sky, and I really do hope I'll see you around."

By the time they got outside, the car was already pulling up, so Mark opened the door and Sky scooted in. Not wanting to pry, as Sky clearly didn't want to share her address, Mark said goodbye again and shut the door, heading back inside, where his brother was waiting for him with a wide grin.

"She seems nice."

Peeking out the window at the taillights vanishing into the night, Mark nodded. "She is."

"Phoenix seems nice too, and rich as well," Joe added.

"And absolutely not interested in me," Mark said, rolling his eyes.

"I don't know, she showed up to your party all dressed up."

Knowing his brother was teasing him, Mark just shook his head and walked into the kitchen to help Joe clean up. A little bit later, as he lay in bed, Mark couldn't help but review the evening in his head, Joe's words about Sky and Phoenix lingering in his mind. When he caught himself wondering what it would be like to date either of them, he laughed and rolled over, only to find Mime giving him a scornful look. Strangely embarrassed, Mark poked her nose with his finger, earning himself a bite in the process.

"Ouch! Oh, go to sleep. What do you know? You're just a silly cat."

The look that Mime gave him communicated very clearly that even if she was just a silly cat, she was infinitely superior to whatever lower life-form Mark was. Having expressed her disdain, Mime closed her eyes and snuggled down in her pillow, leaving Mark to his thoughts as he drifted off to sleep.

There was no time for fantasies in his dream, and Mark took a deep breath and stepped forward as the first drone burst from the undergrowth. With practiced ease, his right hand stretched out, and he used his palm to redirect the drone's mandibles away from him. As the bug shot past his side, his left hand flicked down, his metal fingers carving through its carapace and stabbing into its brain. The force of his strike split the drone's head in half, and as it faded away, he turned, getting into a stance as he readied himself to meet the charge of the next two drones.

They shot toward him a moment later, and he dodged to the side, maintaining an angle so he only ever had to deal with one at a time. With a furious hiss, the drone at the back scampered around its companion, but Mark kept rotating, never letting it get close. The first drone launched itself toward him, snapping down angrily on his forearm. He could feel the force of the attack, but the metal on his arm held strong, and with a twist of his wrist, Mark gripped the mandibles tightly, staying clear of the monster's wriggling legs as he grabbed one of the plates on its back and lifted it up into the air.

Just as the other drone leaped, unable to stop itself in time, Mark lifted the first drone into its path. The drone instinctively chomped down, its mandibles tearing through its companion's stomach. A moment later, Mark's arm was released as the first drone died, but rather than end the other drone immediately, Mark kicked it to the side and swiftly backed up to gain some distance.

For the next fifteen minutes, every time the drone would attack, Mark would simply block before knocking it aside as he tested his Cutting Palm technique. He was definitely improving, and as he practiced, he focused on defending with his left arm and attacking with his right, eventually managing to crack through the drone's shell and crush its head. With his metal left arm, he could kill the drones in one blow, but with his right, it took three attacks that all hit exactly the same spot. Though it was much less efficient, Mark was sure that if he continued to improve, he would eventually get to the point where even with his normal fist, he'd be able to break through the drone's armor.

The three drones attacked next, and Mark continued to fight against them, still using the same technique. Though he died twice, he eventually managed to kill all three of the drones, only using his right hand to attack. By this point, half the typical six-hour period had passed. For the remaining three hours, Mark just tried his best to survive. The drones were quick, their movements fluid, and their attacks sharp, but after fighting against them thousands of times, Mark felt as if he had an instinctive understanding of how they moved, and he was finding it easier and easier to avoid their chopping mandibles and slashing claws.

Monday came soon, and for the first time in a long time, Mark found himself with a free day. The trainees had the week off and would receive their new assignments that Friday. At first, Mark had been tempted to pick up some extra hours, but since his brother was home, he instead opted to hang out with Joe, who had mentioned having some errands to run. After eating breakfast, the two brothers headed toward the eastern side of the city, taking the train most of the way and then walking a few blocks to an area full of massive warehouses.

Joe met a few other soldiers, all dressed as civilians, including the twins Marvin and Kevin, and after he introduced Mark as his younger brother to the others, they headed inside one of the warehouses. As soon as the doors opened, the sound hit Mark in a solid wave, and when they walked in, the din grew even louder. There were massive cutting machines, blades whirring as they sliced up gigantic corpses. There were tables piled high with Exlian bodies as soldiers who wore the patch of the Engineering Corps cut into them with huge circular saws. Seeing Mark's astonished look, Kev patted him on the shoulder, hard enough to cause him to stumble.

"Is this your first time seeing a processing center?" Kev yelled over the sound of saws chewing through chitin.

Unable to even muster a verbal response, Mark nodded.

"Ha, I remember my first time seeing it."

Poking his brother's shoulder, Marv grinned and winked at Mark. "I remember it too! He puked his guts out for a week afterward, so don't worry, you're doing well."

The processing center was rather overwhelming, simply because there was so much going on and it was so loud, but nothing about it made Mark nauseous. They picked their way between the tables, stepping over channels filled with blood and viscera, discarded from the Exlian corpses. Mark had never seen so much blood in his life. He had the oddest experience of knowing that what he was looking at was genuinely disgusting yet feeling only faint hunger rather than disgust.

Joe led the way to the back corner of the processing center, where there was a small office, heavily soundproofed to keep the noise of the drills and saws from interfering with conversation. As the doors closed behind them, the air suddenly smelled much fresher, and they were met by a middle-aged man in a suit.

"Welcome. You must be Joseph Fields."

"I am," Joe said. "I'm here to negotiate the sale of the Exlian corpses we brought back."

Eyes narrowing, the man in the suit looked over their group. "Aren't those normally handled by the military?"

"Normally, yes," Joe replied, "but these are personal spoils."

Mark had the distinct impression that there was something going on he wasn't privy to from the way the man's expression grew somber. The soldiers who were with them seemed abnormally serious as well, but Joe was as relaxed as always.

"I see. My name is Gerry. Why don't you have a seat and tell me what you are looking to off-load?"

Sinking into the offered seat, Joe leaned back and looked around the office as he answered. "Twenty-five warriors between B and C ranks, five A-ranked warriors, and a terror."

The man's expression remained normal up until the end, but as soon as Joe mentioned a terror, he shot to his feet. "Are you serious?! You're not joking with me, are you?"

"No."

"Do you have a type for it?"

"Ravager."

All sorts of terms were being thrown around that Mark didn't understand, but he didn't ask any questions. Instead, he listened carefully to see if he could figure it out from context clues. Gerry, who had been ready to negotiate fiercely, was now agreeing to every single one of Joe's requests. In fact, Mark was convinced that Gerry would have happily handed over one of his kidneys if Joe had insisted on it.

A contract was quickly agreed on, and Joe signed it and then led everyone out through the processing center once more. The other soldiers said goodbye, leaving Mark and Joe alone. Looking up at the sky, Joe let out a deep sigh. "Come on, let's grab some lunch, and I'll explain whatever you didn't understand while we were in there."

After finding a small food stand nearby, Joe and Mark sat at a small table and made their order. While they waited for their food, Joe looked across the table at his younger brother.

"Go ahead and shoot," he said. "Ask me whatever questions you have, and I'll do my best to answer them."

"Were you selling the corpses of the Exlian that you killed?"

"Some of them," Joe responded, glancing over at the stall's owner, who was frying up some meat on a pan. "I killed a lot more Exlian than that, but of the corpses that we were able to bring back with us, that's my share."

"Did you kill a terror-ranked Exlian all by yourself?"

"Yes," Joe replied, his voice carrying a faintly bitter note.

"And why was the salesman so happy that you were willing to trade it?"

"Terror-ranked Exlian are hard to come by," Joe said, "especially the ravager type. The only way to put them down is with so much force that there's often nothing left of them. I managed to get a mostly intact corpse, which is worth a tremendous amount of credits. It's even harder to get them if you don't have a military connection, as they're rarely sold to the public. No matter how much I ask for it, he can probably get more at auction, if he even auctions it. There are a lot of families who have massive bounties for terror-ranked Exlian."

"Couldn't you have gone to one of the families yourself and just skipped the middleman?"

"No, soldiers are expressly forbidden from selling directly to the families," Joe said, his expression serious. "Now, that doesn't stop everybody, but if I was caught, it would be immediate execution or maybe even exile."

Shuddering slightly at the thought of being cast into the wilderness to fend for himself, Mark changed the subject. "I've never heard you mention having a share of the Exlian after coming back from a mission, and when we were there, everybody seemed abnormally somber. What changed?"

Joe didn't respond immediately, instead waiting as the stall owner placed their food in front of them. After the man had withdrawn, Joe picked up his fork and poked at the steak on his plate for a moment before beginning to speak.

"There's a tradition," he said. "When someone leaves the combat arm of the Rangers, they get a portion of their last mission's haul, based on the amount of Exlian they killed, at a ratio of ten to one."

"Hold on," Mark said, holding up his hand. "Are you telling me you killed ten terror-ranked Exlian?"

"Technically it was about fifteen, but they weren't able to bring back more than one terror-ranked corpse," Joe replied, cutting a slice off his steak and sticking it in his mouth.

Mark waited for him to finish chewing, all the while staring at his brother in astonishment. Looking up, Joe gestured with his fork. "They were all fairly low ranked, but still quite an accomplishment, isn't it?"

There was a dreadful calm on Joe's face, and he spoke of his deeds casually, as if observing them from a distance. Mark didn't have to be a genius to realize that something was wrong. Very wrong.

"Joe, what happened? Why are you leaving the Rangers?"

"I'm not, technically. I'm just not going to be fighting anymore. I mentioned we were under siege, right? Well, a few weeks ago, we had the opportunity to break the siege when we joined up with the Silver Strike Engineering Corps, about sixty miles outside the city. That's within the Defense Force Strike Zone, and we had already communicated with the city that we were returning. Unfortunately, there was a second ambush, this time with ten times the numbers of the ambush that kept us pinned down. We held on for two days of nonstop fighting, but then . . ." Joe fell silent, and Mark didn't rush him.

Picking up his cup, Joe brought it to his lips, and though the motion looked smooth, Mark could see the water inside of it shaking. After taking a long drink, Joe put it down and let out the breath he was holding, his words coming in a rush.

"Our reinforcements never showed up. The Defense Force was supposed to send out four battalions to provide a retreat corridor, preventing the Exlian from getting around behind us. They never came. My commanding officer realized that if something drastic didn't happen, none of us were making it back alive. My unit volunteered to break the siege, and that's exactly what we did. Unfortunately, we had to overcharge to do it, and I'm the only one who made it back to the city alive. Casualties were above seventy percent."

"You overcharged?" Mark asked, unable to believe what he was hearing.

"Yep." Joe was surprisingly calm about the situation. "I burned my power right out, and now . . ."

Stretching his hand forward, he turned his palm up, his fingers twitching as he tried to summon his flame. There was a faint wisp of power, and then Joe winced, his body shaking with pain.

"I'm being transferred," he said, his hand falling to the table powerlessly. "They'll give me a desk job in the Ranger office. It's better than leaving the military entirely, and it means I'll be around more."

"Giving you the corpses to sell . . ."

Mark's voice trailed off as Joe nodded. "It's their way of saying thank you. Doesn't quite make up for the nineteen friends I lost or the fact that I can't use my powers anymore, but at least it's something."

They ate the rest of the meal in silence, Mark feeling more and more miserable with every bite. Burnout, though rather rare, was a well-known phenomenon and occurred when someone pushed their power past its limit, overcharging it. This could allow an empowered to boost the rank of their power and their own body by a full grade but came at the cost of the power itself. Mark could only imagine just how strong his A-ranked brother had been. The only S-ranked powers in the city belonged to the top five empowered, and for a brief time Joseph Fields had been just as strong as any of them.

It was no wonder he had been able to kill multiple terrors by himself, and Mark had no doubt that Joe's sacrifice was the reason anyone had arrived safely home to the city. The right to sell a few of the Exlian corpses seemed like a pittance in comparison, and hearing that the Defense Force had never sent people out to rescue the Rangers explained the vehemence in Joe's voice when he'd told Mark to stay away from it.

As much as he wanted to explain the situation away, to come up with an excuse for why the Defense Force hadn't been able to send people, Mark wasn't so naive as to think that the military was without its problems. When Mark and Joe made their way back to their house, the air was stifling to Mark, and he genuinely didn't know what to say. His brother seemed abnormally calm about the whole situation, and Mark could only imagine how much of a mess he would be if he were in his brother's shoes. To go from being one of the strongest people in the city to not being able to use your power at all had to be soul crushing, and Mark genuinely didn't know how to comfort his older brother. Everything he thought of to say sounded trite, but he felt like he had to say something. When they stepped into their house, he grabbed Joe's arm. "I'm really sorry."

"I . . . It's okay," Joe replied, patting him on the shoulder. "It's not great, and I'm not going to stand here and pretend I'm actually okay with it. But life goes on. There are plenty of people who live without powers, and the knowledge I have is valuable. Besides, I've got an up-and-coming younger brother who can take care of me in my old age."

Despite feeling awful, Mark couldn't help but laugh.

"That's right," he said, patting himself on the chest. "Just you wait until I get to D rank. I'll earn plenty of money for both of us."

Giving his little brother a nod, Joe matched his smile.

"I'm counting on it," Joe said. "Unfortunately, one of the side effects of my burnout is I'm going to need medical treatment or my body's going to fall apart, and it's expensive. That's why they gave me the Exlian corpses to sell in the first place. But even with everything, it's only enough for a few years of treatment. But don't worry, we'll figure something out before that time comes."

Unsure what to say, Mark could only watch as Joe turned and headed upstairs toward his room. Mark waited until he heard the sound of Joe's door shutting and then slowly walked up to his own room, his mind full. Having Joe back should have been a wonderful and exciting thing. Now he wasn't so sure. It was hard to watch his brother, who he had always thought of as indestructible, look so defeated. Remembering how Joe's hand had shaken as he tried to activate his power, Mark couldn't help but shiver. He sat down on his bed, staring off into space for a moment.

Up until now, every ounce of his focus had been directed toward joining the military. But now, a new and more immediate goal had presented itself. Mark had already lost his father and mother, and there was no way that he was going to lose his brother as well. Getting up from his bed, he went to his desk and opened up his virtual screen. He began to search through the Blackstar forums, looking for any information he could find on burnout, and what he discovered wasn't encouraging. There were no documented cases of anybody recovering from burnout and being able to use their powers again, though some people were convinced that a cure existed. More importantly, Mark discovered that there was a drug that could prolong the life of someone affected by burnout. It was available through the military for 100,000 credits a bottle and through the Blackstar Exchange for 150,000 credits a bottle.

"I'm going to need a lot of money," Mark muttered to himself.

That thought led him down a long rabbit hole of the various ways that empowered could earn money. Mark had been so focused on joining the military that he knew very little about how the empowered interacted with the rest of society. To his surprise, he found that there were quite a few jobs that empowered could do that paid well.

Though he liked his job at Jason's Pub, it didn't pay much, and when he'd gotten it, he hadn't yet been empowered. Searching through the forums, he compiled a small list and leaned back in his chair to consider the options. The first was being a bodyguard. A good number of wealthy individuals, both unempowered and empowered, hired bodyguards. What they needed protection from inside the city, Mark wasn't entirely sure. Of course, he had heard rumors about vicious fights between the upper-class families, but he had always assumed they were just stories made for the shows and movies on the InfoWeb.

Another option was to become a freelance hunter, heading out into the dead zone that surrounded the city but still fell within the far wall. Dead zones were often inhabited by Exlian that had made it past the city's first line of defense into the ruined nest of buildings previous generations of humans had been forced to abandon. There were close to fifty miles of dead zone around the city in every direction, and freelance hunters supported the city's defenses by combing through them to kill Exlian before they could nest. That was dangerous work, however, and required a team, and Mark wasn't quite sure how his brother would react if he announced he wanted to become a freelance hunter.

The third job that had caught Mark's eye was one he hadn't known existed until accompanying his brother on his errand that very afternoon. He had seen it on a forum post and immediately written it down. Because of how difficult Exlian carcasses were to butcher, most of the individuals who processed their corpses were empowered. There was no minimum rank requirement, and Mark assumed that he would find mostly E-ranked empowered there, which suited him just fine.

That seemed the most stable and least dangerous of the three occupations, and so Mark crossed out the other two and circled the number listed in the post. As he got up from his desk, he noticed a small box sitting on its edge, and after a moment of staring at it, he remembered that this was the gift that Noah had brought the night of the party.

Curious, Mark unwrapped the paper, revealing a small case about four inches wide and five inches long. It had a clear plastic cover, and inside he saw three vials, each containing a glimmering blue liquid. There was nothing written on the box, and after turning it over, Mark logged on to Blackstar and began to search.

What he found left him speechless. What Noah had so casually handed him was called an elixir, a powerful medicine made from a very specific Exlian core. It came in three different grades. Yellow, the lowest, which was made from C-ranked Exlian cores. Blue, made from B-ranked cores. And red, which required A-ranked cores.

A single vial of the weakest C-ranked elixir purchased through the Blackstar forums cost no less than 10,000 credits, and a B-ranked elixir cost closer to 50,000. A-ranked elixirs were at least 500,000 credits and, from what Mark had read, were so rare that they couldn't be purchased. Noah came from a truly different world if he thought handing over a gift worth 150,000 credits wasn't much. As expensive as elixir was, it was worth every single credit, as a single vial would increase an empowered's strength by 10 percent. On the surface, 10 percent didn't seem like much, but even though the effect of each subsequent elixir lessened, with enough of them, it was possible for an empowered to boost their strength by almost 100 percent, making them twice as strong as they would otherwise be.

Pausing for a moment, Mark couldn't help but wonder if that was why Noah was so abnormally strong. If he had access to enough elixirs that he thought giving a few of them away was no big deal, then it would make sense that he was abnormally powerful compared to everybody else his own age. That didn't make Mark feel any better about being weaker than him, but it did give him a better idea of the wall he would have to overcome if he wanted to win against Noah.

Opening the case, Mark plucked out one of the blue vials. According to what he had read, the best way to consume it was to simply throw the entire thing in his mouth, where it would dissolve, flooding his body. Before he did, however, he paused, another thought occurring to him. After hesitating for a long moment, Mark jumped up and rushed out of his room to knock on the door of Joe's room across the hall.

"What's up?" Joe asked, opening the door.

Without a word, Mark held out his hand, the blue vial glittering in his palm.

"Is that what your friend brought you? Noah, right?" Joe asked. "I thought he looked rich."

"You should take it," Mark said. "Maybe it'll help you."

Giving Mark a gratified smile, Joe shook his head. "It won't; I've already looked into it. And besides, I've been stuffed so full of those things during my time in the military that they don't have any effect anymore. I've reached saturation. Come on, let's go back into your room, and I'll teach you how to absorb it."

Under Joe's guidance, Mark sat cross-legged on the ground, keeping his back straight against the edge of his bed. Taking a seat in Mark's chair, Joe looked over him with a critical eye.

"This is a classic meditation pose. You don't technically have to do this, and some people prefer other methods, but this is how I was taught. What you're going to do is drink the liquid and then meditate for about sixty seconds. You're going to keep yourself as still as possible as you allow it to move through your body. Then, from this position, you'll stand up and complete your martial forms. You'll keep up with your forms until you feel the burning in your body subside. How many of them did he give you?"

"Three."

"Wow, generous. All right, you'll want to take all three of them in succession, remembering to sit as still as possible every time you take one and then work through the burning feeling with your forms. You'll take the next one as soon as the last one has worn off."

Feeling quite nervous, Mark nodded and popped the first of the vials in his mouth, clamping his lips shut as the outer casing dissolved, filling his mouth with a small sun. The energy burned its way through him, starting as an intense warmth and quickly growing uncomfortable, until it reached his chest, where it felt as if a bonfire had been ignited. He carefully counted down the seconds in his mind, even as sweat began to pour off him. Every movement he made bled a bit of energy from the ball of flame inside him, and as he remained still, it continued to build, growing in intensity.

As the seconds ticked up, Mark understood why Joe had warned him about the discomfort. By the time he had reached thirty seconds of stillness, it felt as if he were being burned alive. When he reached forty-five seconds, that feeling had spread to every inch of his body, making him want to scream. It was incredibly painful, but Mark refused to waste this opportunity and held himself without moving, even as his body felt like it was being transformed into a charcoal brick.

Eventually the feeling of flames was simply too much to bear, and Mark jumped up, his hands thrusting out in front of him, as he began to execute the first martial art that came to mind: Cutting Palm. His feet remained in place as he threw out palm strikes in endless subtle variations, each movement easing the burning feeling in his muscles, and the effect of the elixir soon started to fade, bringing a measure of relief to Mark. Thick beads of goopy sweat ran down his body as the flames faded away, and a comfortable feeling shrouded Mark, making him want to lie down.

Before he could, he heard his brother's voice telling him to take another elixir. Without giving himself time to think, Mark sat down right where he was, keeping his back straight, and consumed the second vial when his brother handed it to him. Once again, the sun roared to life in Mark's mouth, but this time, instead of starting small as it gathered in his chest, it flooded through his entire body instantly, causing him to spasm. Joe had never mentioned anything like this, but Mark was in too much pain to ask him about it. He lost count of the seconds quickly as he did everything he could to keep from moving, and he had no idea how long he lasted before it was once again too much.

When he sprang up from his seated position, his hands and feet darted out, abandoning the Cutting Palm in favor of the katas Joe had taught him years ago. Yet even as he threw strikes and executed the kicks, Mark changed them, adapting each move based on what he had been learning about real combat in his dream fights against the drones. Watching from the side of the room, Joe's eyes slowly narrowed as he watched his brother launch strike after strike, each fist moving with such force that it caused a snapping sound in the air.

Mark felt his body beginning to calm down, once again leaving him feeling as if he were floating in a warm bath, completely relaxed. Out of instinct, he sat down again, and once more, an elixir was shoved into his mouth. This time, the sun exploded not in his mouth but rather throughout his whole body. It was exceptionally painful at the tips of his fingers and toes, and he could feel his skin being scorched. Still, he held on, using every ounce of his willpower to keep his body still.

There was a slight shake at his right wrist, letting him know that his status had an update, and Mark felt as if his mind settled. Vaguely, he could tell that he had broken through, but he didn't have enough mental bandwidth to care, as he just held on. The first time he had consumed the elixir, he had counted out sixty seconds before jumping up to begin his kata. The second time, having lost track of the count, he had sat in place for a minute and a half, and now, though his body gave off a faint, acrid smoke, he remained motionless for almost three minutes, completely oblivious to everything going on around him.

When his body finally began to twitch, Joe reached out and pushed his shoulder lightly. The forward momentum sent Mark springing into action, and once again, he began his imaginary fight, his body shifting through a combination of the Cutting Palm and his other martial arts forms as he battled imaginary drones. For almost ten minutes, the burning in his body lingered, dispersing little by little, until finally, every drop of potential had been wrung out of it.

When he faintly heard a voice say, "One more," Mark was too out of it to know that he had already consumed all three elixirs. As he sat down again, he felt something shoved between his lips, and Mark clenched his mouth shut as a supernova exploded in his throat.

"There's no way he's only D-ranked potential," Joe muttered.

In truth, he had fully expected his brother to fall unconscious after trying to absorb the first elixir. There was a certain level of danger in absorbing blue-ranked elixirs without first having absorbed the less potent yellow-ranked elixirs, but the effect of starting with the blue-ranked elixirs was known to be significantly stronger. Additionally, this method of absorbing multiple elixirs in one sitting was a military secret that only worked if the individual absorbing the elixir was able to maintain consciousness. If they were, however, it provided a qualitative improvement, making each elixir consumed twice as potent as the last.

The elixir he had just fed Mark had been Joe's last. The single red elixir he had been saving up for years to buy. With his power burned out, Joe had no longer had a use for it, and seeing just how his brother's body reacted to the elixirs, Joe felt as if he had been seized by madness. Pacing back and forth, Joe bit at his finger, occasionally glancing at Mark, who was sitting perfectly still in the center of the room, beads of black sweat dripping from his skin.

The first elixir had doubled the effect of the second. The second elixir had doubled that again for the third, making it four times more potent. The third elixir had been eight times more potent than normal, and it didn't stop there. The red elixir in Mark's mouth was now sixteen times more potent than it normally would have been.

Such intensity would have forced even the strongest soldiers to writhe, yet strangely, Mark remained perfectly alert but motionless. The acrid smoke seeping from his pores formed a thick cloud around him, forcing Joe to step back as Mark's muscles began to twitch, causing his skin to roll as if earthworms were crawling under it. It was a terrifying sight, and more than once, Joe reached for his watch for emergency response, but something about the calmness on Mark's face kept him from making the call. With a groan, Joe threw himself into the chair. "I must be going crazy."

Lifting his hand, Joe stared at his fingers for a moment and then clenched them tightly, his eyes blazing with anger. If the government ever found out that he had fed a red elixir to his brother, he'd be executed without mercy. They were simply too valuable to waste, as each one had the potential to upgrade someone in the B rank to an A-ranked empowered. But Joe didn't care anymore. It was the military's fault he had ended up like this, and he'd rather waste the elixir on his brother than give it anything more.

After almost ten minutes, Mark's muscles stopped spasming, and he returned to a state of calm. Worried that his brother might be burning up inside, Joe slowly approached, intending to nudge Mark once more. Before he could, a figure launched itself from the bed, landing lightly on Mark's head, without disturbing a single hair. Mime sat down and stared at Joe, slowly shaking her head back and forth.

Joe paused, his hand still outstretched, as he stared at the cat.

Ever so slowly, she lifted her paw and extended a single claw that glinted evilly in the light. Making sure Joe was looking straight at her, she carefully scraped the claw across her neck, causing Joe to fall back in shock.

Unable to believe what he was seeing, he asked, "Are you saying I'll kill him if I touch him?"

Disdainfully, Mime shook her head, then pointed at herself and then at Joe.

"You'll kill me if I touch him?" Joe asked incredulously. With a calm nod, Mime retracted her claw and then sat serenely on the top of Mark's head. Joe couldn't help but wonder again if he was going crazy. He had definitely seen the motion Mime had made, and though he didn't believe that Mime could actually harm him, he'd seen enough weird things to know not to chance it. Mark was the first person he had encountered whose power manifested as an animal, and the black cat had given him a strange feeling from the first moment he had seen her, a faint sense of danger that reminded him of many of his most lethal encounters in the wilderness.

Despite the feeling of danger, it was clear that if Mime wanted to harm Mark, she would have done so long ago. The fact that Mark was doing better than ever meant that this strangely intelligent cat was on his side. Still unsettled, Joe watched her carefully for a full fifteen minutes until Mark's eyes suddenly snapped open.

As awareness flooded back into his mind, Mark slowly held out his hands in front of him, looking down at them as if they were completely foreign. For a full minute, he stared blankly until, with a shiver, he came back to himself.

"Okay, so that was a weird experience," Mark said, turning his hands over a couple of times.

Joe crouched down near Mark but didn't reach out to touch him. "How are you feeling?"

"I'm feeling surprisingly good. How am I supposed to be feeling?"

"You should be feeling pretty relaxed, like you just exercised a whole lot and then got a massage."

"Yeah, no, that's not how I feel," Mark said. "I feel like I could run through a wall right now. My body is bursting with energy."

"Well, that's because you haven't worked it off. Do you still feel any burning?"

"Nope, no burning, just a whole lot of energy." Mark jumped to his feet, or at least tried to. He misjudged the jump and ended up nearly slamming into the ceiling, barely catching himself with his hand before falling back down to the ground, where he landed lightly, like a cat.

"We should go get you checked out just in case," Joe said. "Make sure there are no ill effects. How does your status look?"

Flipping it open, Mark was hit with rapid-fire notifications.

> Your will has increased from E– to E.

That must have been what he felt while taking the elixir.

> Your strength has increased from E to E+.
> Your strength has increased from E+ to D–.
> Your speed has increased from E to E+.
> Your speed has increased from E+ to D–.
> Your speed has increased from D– to D.
> Your speed has increased from D to D+.
> Your fortitude has increased from E to E+.
> Your fortitude has increased from E+ to D–.]

[Your fortitude has increased from D– to D.
Your will has increased from E to E+.
Your will has increased from E+ to D–.
Your will has increased from D– to D.
Your will has increased from D to D+.

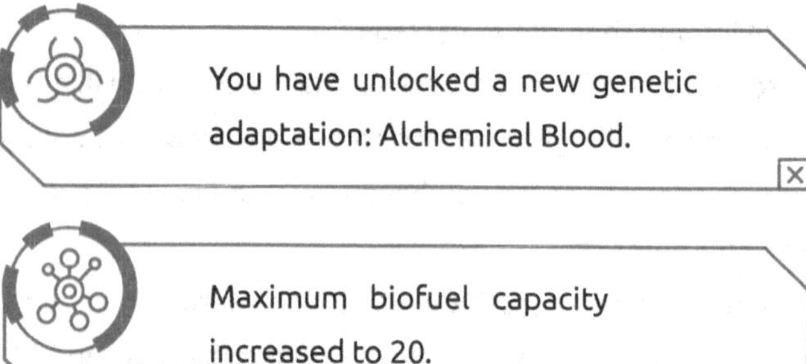

As the windows flashing in front of him cleared, Mark saw his new status.

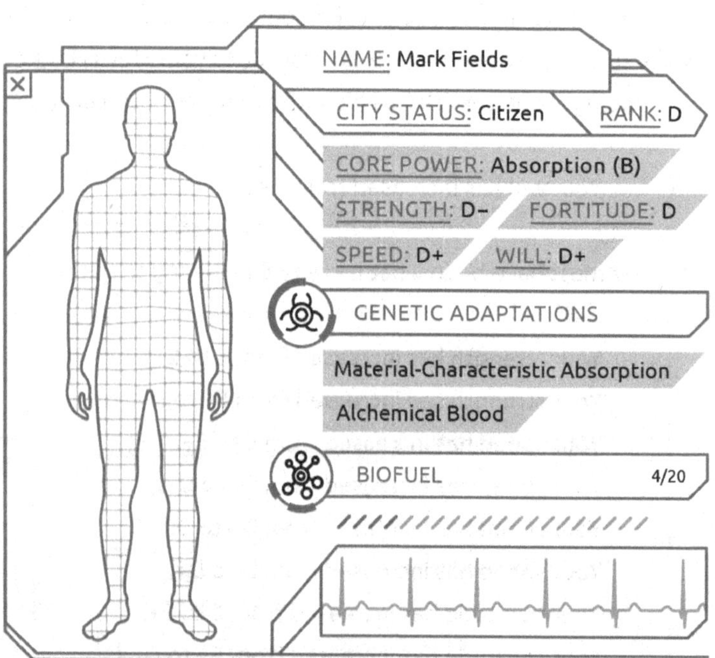

The first thought that occurred to him was how unbelievably unfair it had been to try to compete against Noah. Simply taking a few elixirs had completely transformed him, or so he thought, as he had no idea Joe had fed him a red elixir. The second thought was that he had earned a new power. Focusing on his new genetic adaptation, Mark felt his bracelet vibrate slightly, and then a new string of text popped up.

Alchemical Blood. Exposure to high doses of a mana-enhanced substance has caused you to absorb the advanced elixir's chemical composition, allowing you to transform your blood into a catalyzing agent that when added to a regular elixir will improve its quality by one rank.

Mark simply stared, reading the text over and over, as he tried to wrap his mind around it. Of course, he knew exactly what it meant, but it was the sheer absurdity of it that kept him staring, until Joe, who still hadn't touched him since Mime was perched on his head, cleared his throat. "Mark, are you okay?"

"Huh? What? Yeah, fine."

"Your status all right? No ill effects?"

"No," Mark said, slowly shaking his head. "In fact, all my stats have gone up. I'm in the D rank."

"You went up a whole rank?" Joe exclaimed. "Ha, I knew it. I knew there was no way that you had a D-ranked potential. If you only had a D-ranked potential, no matter how many elixirs you consumed, you wouldn't have leveled up. Elixirs can only take you so far toward your maximum potential; they can't take you the last bit of the way. Otherwise, everybody would just wait until they were right about to reach their potential and then cram as many elixirs as they could to make the last part the easiest. The stronger you are, the less of an elixir you can absorb, so the fact that you went up so fast means that your potential is a lot higher."

"But the assessment . . ."

"Forget the assessment. They have no idea what they're talking about. They told me that my flame power was B ranked. Of course, that was before I learned how to summon flame directly," Joe said, his eyes regaining some of their old luster.

Quite pleased, he reached out to pat his brother on the shoulder, stopping at the last second as he saw a flash of claw from on top of Mark's head. Pulling his hand back, he coughed into it. "Anyway, as I was saying, we should probably take you to see a doctor."

"I don't need a doctor," Mark said. "I'm totally fine. In fact, I've genuinely never felt better. Though I am a little bit hungry."

"In that case, let's get something to eat."

Feeling Mime shift from his head to his shoulder, Mark reached up to scratch under Mime's chin as they headed down to the kitchen. There still wasn't much food in the house, but after eating an entire pot of rice and every single vegetable they had, Mark still crammed down a dozen tubes of nutrient paste and six energy bars before his biofuel was finally full.

He could feel energy bursting from his body and felt as if he could run around the city. Probably a few times. His new D-ranked stats allowed him to move faster, be stronger, and withstand considerably more. But they also burned more energy, and Mark could only hope that as his stats continued to rise, the capacity of his biofuel meter would continue to increase as well.

He desperately wanted to ask his brother about his new genetic adaptation, but something in him told him to stay quiet, so instead he spent the rest of the afternoon talking to his brother about how to develop his powers. Joe was quite interested in the training module that he had been given after his assessment, and though Mark wasn't supposed to show it to anybody, he trusted his brother enough to lay it out for him.

"Overall, this is really good," Joe said, "though there are a couple of things that I would shift. You're not afraid of working hard, and you suffer well enough to take some of the shortcuts that the Rangers teach. I could get in a lot of trouble for teaching this stuff to you, so don't tell anybody, okay?"

Grinning, Mark held his hand over his heart. "I promise," he said. "I won't tell a soul, even if it kills me."

With a laugh, Joe rolled his eyes. "Oh, come on, it's not that serious. All right, let me work on this tonight, and tomorrow you'll have a brand-new training method. I'm going to warn you, though. It'll be brutal."

Buoyed by his newly increased biofuel meter, Mark slapped himself on the chest confidently. "No problem, I'll handle it, no sweat."

"We'll see about that," Joe said with a sinister smile.

Watching his brother disappear into his room to work on the new training system, Mark wondered if he would come to regret his boasting. Either way, it was too late, and all he could do was hope that he survived the coming week. Since he had a little bit of time and more energy than he knew what to do with, he decided to send Jason a message and see if he could pick up an extra shift at Jason's Pub.

JASON

Always room for another dishwasher. Get in here as soon as you can.

X

When he arrived at the pub and relieved the thankful cook who had been stuck washing dishes while Mark wasn't around, Jason walked over to dump a load of plates into the sink. "You off for the rest of the week?"

Mark was tempted to say yes, but he shook his head. "Not really. My brother's home, and he's putting together a training program for me to help me beef up a few of my skills before the second section of the training camp begins."

"At least you're not completely wasting your time," Jason said, frowning.

Hesitating for a few seconds, Mark firmed up his courage and spoke up just as Jason was turning to leave. "I actually want to talk to you about that."

Jason froze and then slowly turned around, his eyes narrowed. "What? You got a better job?"

"Honestly, I was thinking about it," Mark said. "You can get anybody to wash your dishes. But I was thinking about taking a job as a processor."

Jason was taken aback by Mark's words. Whatever he was about to say died in his throat, and his eyebrows rose. "Not a freelance hunter?"

Jason's surprise was understandable, as most new empowered favored hunting Exlian over spending their time buried in their guts.

"No, I'm not strong enough to be a hunter, and I don't know enough about Exlian to feel confident tracking them. While I'm at the training camp, they'll be teaching us what we need to know, and I figure by working as a processor, I can learn even more about them. You know, from studying their corpses, maybe figure out where their weak points are. Things like that. Plus, it pays a lot better than washing dishes, and frankly, I need the money."

Giving Mark a long, thoughtful look, Jason gestured for him to follow and led Mark out back, kicking aside a box in the alleyway.

"Let me see those forms," he said.

"You mean the Cutting Palm?"

"Of course I mean the Cutting Palm. What else would I be talking about? Your dishwashing form? Hurry up."

"Yes, sir!"

Sliding his left foot forward slightly and taking half a second to center himself, Mark began throwing out attacks, completely abandoning the kata that he had first learned. In his mind's eye, he saw drones emerging from the shadows and launching themselves toward him, and his flashing hands met them as they came. Empowered by his improved strength and speed, his fists tore through the air, filling the alley with a faint whistling sound that mixed with his controlled breathing. After two minutes of Mark fighting furiously against his imaginary foe, Jason held up his hand, something akin to praise in his eyes.

"Stop. All right, that's enough. You sure you want to work as a processor? If so, I can introduce you to a guy. He's a bit . . ." Jason paused and scratched his scruffy chin. "Well, he's a bit weird, but he's one of the best in the business, and I just so happen to know that he's behind right now. With a recommendation from yours truly, he might consider taking you on as an apprentice. Plus, he happens to work nearby."

Caught off guard, Mark let his hands drop. Jason never ceased to surprise him. Between the packs of money local businesses sent his way and the number of people Jason knew, it was clear there was a lot more to the pub owner than met the eye. "Are you serious? I would love that. That would be great."

Giving Mark an irritated glare, Jason waved a hand at him. "Enough. Don't turn all soppy on me. Come on."

Nearby, it turned out, was next door, in a massive building

that towered over the restaurant. Stepping inside, Mark was hit with a blast of cold air and realized that the entire building was refrigerated. Jason only walked in a few steps before stopping and banging on a large stack of barrels with the ladle he kept attached to his waist. "Abrams, you in here?"

"Hold on," came a shout, and a few minutes later, a thin, wiry figure approached them through the cold fog that filled the warehouse.

The man was old. So old his face was made of nothing but wrinkles and his frail limbs were little more than skin and bone. He had ruddy cheeks, a nose red from the cold, and a pair of piercing black eyes that stared at Mark from under two bushy eyebrows. "You here to collect another batch?"

"No," Jason said, lifting his hands. "We've got more than enough, thank you."

"Then what are you bugging me for? I was in the middle of working."

"I got a kid for you."

"What would I want a kid for?"

"You know how you were complaining that you have nobody to teach?" Jason asked, jerking his thumb toward Mark.

Abrams's eyes narrowed slightly, and his gaze shifted back to Mark, carefully examining him.

"The kid learned the basics of the Cutting Palm in only a few weeks."

"Ha, as if," Abrams said, spitting off to the side.

As soon as the spit touched the ground, it froze solid, causing

Mark to realize just how helpful having a high fortitude was. He could barely feel the cold, but if a regular person had been in the room, they wouldn't have lasted more than a minute or two before catching hypothermia. Abrams walked closer and stared at Mark intently. "Let me see your hands, kid."

Mark held out his hands, and Abrams grabbed them. While he was examining Mark's hands, Mark couldn't help but do the same. On first glance, there was nothing about Abrams that looked remarkable. He looked like the very picture of a crotchety old man who should have retired a decade ago. Until Mark saw his hands. His palms were wide and thick, his knuckles bony. His fingers were long and lean but contained the power to tear. They weren't pretty hands by any means, but Mark had the feeling they had been made to tear him apart.

Feeling Mark suddenly tense, Abrams looked up and stared at him for a moment and then, dropping Mark's hands, nodded. "Sure, if he wants to learn the trade, I can teach him. But I'll warn you, there's no quitting halfway through. You either learn it, or you donate your body to it."

As he spoke, he jerked his thumb at the wall, where half a dozen corpses were hanging on hooks, frozen solid. A couple of them looked like cows, but the rest appeared to be Exlian corpses, hanging motionless from the ceiling. Though Mark wanted to ask if he could back out, it was clear that both Jason and Abrams thought the deal was settled. The two older men bumped fists, and then Jason patted Mark on the shoulder. "You're lucky, kid. Luckier than you know. Whenever you need something to eat or to warm up, come on over. It'll be on the house."

Stunned by the sudden kindness of the restaurant owner, Mark could only watch in silence as Jason sauntered out of the freezing warehouse, a large smile on his normally sour face.

"Heh, he suckered you good," Abrams said. "Come on, I was in the middle of something. You can help me out."

Unsure what Abrams meant about Jason suckering him, Mark hurried after the old man, who moved surprisingly quick as they wove their way through stacks of frozen bodies. The entire warehouse, which was close to three football fields long, appeared to be jammed full of corpses.

"What did Jason tell you about this place?" Abrams asked as they reached a small room set in the very center of the warehouse, with walls made from thick plastic.

"He just said you were a processor."

"Processor?" Abrams asked, spinning around and pinning Mark in place with a glare. "He said I was a processor? No wonder he ran away so quickly. I am not a processor. I am an artist."

Mark's expression must have betrayed just how dismayed he felt, because Abrams suddenly burst into laughter and slapped Mark on the arm. "Ha, I'm just kidding, kid. But seriously, don't call me a processor. And I'm not joking about being an artist either. I'm an alchemical butcher. I assume you know what an alchemist is, right?"

"Yeah, someone who uses ingredients from Exlian or other natural sources to make potions."

"Exactly. An alchemist transforms mana-charged objects, usually harvested from nature, to create potions and elixirs. Exlian, as unnatural as they are, happen to form the primary source of our alchemical ingredients. However, in order to use them, an alchemist first has to extract them. And that's where I come in. I specialize in removing the very specific pieces of Exlian corpses necessary for an alchemist to do their work. Come on in."

Pushing aside the plastic curtain, Abrams revealed a gory scene. A table covered in blood, with an Exlian drone split open at the chest. Despite the gore, Mark didn't even blink, though he was, once again, filled with faint hunger. Out of instinct, he glanced down at his wrist but saw that his biofuel meter was full, leaving him faintly uneasy. Abram, noticing the calm expression on his face, nodded his head.

"Good. The first requirement for being an alchemical butcher is not getting queasy at the sight of blood. You'd be surprised at how many people, empowered even, get creeped out when they go digging around in an Exlian's innards. The second requirement"—Abrams held up his hands—"is having the right kind of hands. Hands that can perform the Cutting Palm. Unlike normal processors, we don't use tools, apart from our hands, to perform our job."

"We don't? I mean, you don't? Wouldn't a scalpel be better? Or even one of those big chain saws?" Mark asked, half expecting Abrams to blow up at him.

Instead, Abrams smiled and nodded. "It's a good question. And no, we don't. Alchemy requires precision above everything else. And by using a tool, it's possible to introduce something foreign into the ingredient. Metal has a tendency to leach mana from objects it touches and can also shift the elemental alignment of an ingredient without warning. By using Cutting Palm and coating our hands in mana, we can avoid changing the nature of the ingredients we deal with. For now, you can just watch me. This is my last one for the day. When I'm finished, we can talk about when you'll come and under what conditions I'd be willing to teach you."

Nodding, Mark stood quietly aside as Abrams stretched out his hands, a faint glow covering them, as he began to carefully pull the drone apart.

"As you can see here, this drone has a gland that can process high amounts of grit, expelling it from its body. That tells us it came from the far south, most likely a desert. That might leave you wondering, How did we get it up here? Well, drones move around a lot. And when I say 'a lot,' I mean a lot. They'll often migrate in massive herds, picking up more drones from wherever they go. Seventy years ago, one of those giant waves of drones happened to coincide with the waves that were attacking our city. That's what led to all those dead zones. We had to abandon our outer wall and pull back, losing the majority of the city as we did it. We still haven't recovered those dead zones, in large part thanks to the drones taking up residence underground. According to the rumors, there are massive subterranean labyrinths under the city outside of the walls."

Carefully separating out the gland he had pointed to, Abrams used his fingers to slice through the flesh and then placed the organ to the side on a tray. He removed four more parts from the drone before closing it up and shaking his hands. As the mana faded, any blood on Abrams's fingers dropped away, leaving his hands clean. Grabbing the tray, he told Mark to follow him.

"The alchemist who's coming to get these tomorrow wants them fresh, but if I leave them out, they'll freeze solid. We keep them in this little refrigerator, because it's not as cold as the warehouse. You're what? Rank D?"

"Yes, sir."

"Then you're strong enough. But before you commit to anything, you need to know what you're in for. That fool apprentice of mine probably didn't tell you anything."

"Jason?" Mark asked. "He's your apprentice?"

"Was my apprentice. The idiot gave up halfway and opened some crappy restaurant next door. You work there, right?"

"Yes, sir. I wash dishes."

"Dishwasher? Well, let me tell you, this'll be an upgrade. All right, kid, here's the deal. My name is Abrams, the last master of the Cutting Palm. And if you become my apprentice, I'll teach you the actual art. But the training is hard. Not only will you have to learn the Cutting Palm properly, but you'll have to take apart frozen monster corpses with your bare hands. It's brutally rough work, and it may take years to learn. On top of that, you're going to have to study alchemy, so you understand what it is you're cutting up and why, as well as anatomy, so you can learn about how bodies go together.

"The upside is that if you can hack it, you'll find yourself in one of the most lucrative businesses in New Emery. The only reason I'm talking to you is because you've shown a modicum of ability already. Not everybody can wield the Cutting Palm well enough to kill Exlian. Most people never even make it to the point where they can pierce flesh. But you've the aura of a killer around you, someone who's seen a lot of blood and death. I won't ask how or why, as I trust Jason wouldn't bring me a psycho. But I will say, if you do end up on the news for any of the wrong reasons, you'll be hanging from my rafters soon enough, waiting your turn on the chopping block."

Abrams's words were accompanied by a chilly glare that made Mark feel as if the temperature had dropped from cold to freezing. Mutely, he nodded, and the pressure eased as Abrams smiled. "Good. I expect you to be here every day."

"I'm sorry, sir—"

"What? You don't want to take this seriously?"

"No, sir. It's just that I'm a member of one of the training camps, so most days I'm not available. We just happen to be on break this week."

"Okay, fine. The camps are about to start stage two, right? That means you'll be doing the military's anatomy training. Even better. You'll come every night. I'll give you the keypad code so you can just come right in. Be here by nine o'clock tomorrow night. We'll work till two in the morning, and then you can get a couple hours of sleep before you go to your training."

Not seeing anything wrong with that routine, Mark nodded. "I can come earlier, sir. Dinner at the camp is done by six, so I could be here by seven."

"Okay, then come at seven," Abrams said, "but we're still working till two."

"Yes, sir."

Giving the eager young man a strange look, Abrams shook his head and muttered something under his breath. Mark assumed it was derogatory but didn't care. He was too excited about the chance to learn about alchemical butchering. He felt like he was walking on clouds, which lasted until he told Sky that he wasn't going to be working at the restaurant and her face fell.

"I'll still be hanging around. I'll just be working next door."

Only partially mollified, Sky glanced at the large warehouse. "What's next door?"

"Uh, it's a butcher? The owner deals in alchemical material."

A hint of envy flashed across Sky's eyes. "You're going to be an alchemist? I heard they make lots of money. I wish I could get a job like that."

Shifting nervously, Mark rubbed his palms on his shirt, unsure what to say. Sky must have noticed his discomfort, because she quickly changed the subject. "As long as you are still coming around, that's fine. I had a great time at your party, and I'd be sad if I didn't see you anymore."

"It was great to have you. My brother asked when you were going to come over again."

"Hey! Stop chitchatting with that freeloader and get out front! The orders won't take themselves."

Sticking her tongue out at Jason, who was glaring from in front of one of the industrial stoves, Sky waved to Mark and then hurried off to deal with the waiting customers. Laughing, Mark grabbed his stuff and said goodbye to Jason, who returned an annoyed grunt.

Mark had just gotten off the train and was walking back toward his house when he heard a faint sound in one of the alleyways, bringing an intense feeling of déjà vu. His senses sharpened as a feeling of excitement washed over him, catching him off guard. Riding on his shoulder, Mime crouched, her tail twitching as she stared toward the alleyway. Reaching up, Mark touched the screw he wore around his neck, and a few seconds later, his arm bore the silver sheen of titanium.

Mark stepped into the alleyway, his eyes scanning back and forth until he spotted a pair of legs sticking out from a pile of trash. His first instinct was to go over and check if the individual they belonged to was all right, but then his nose picked up the faintest scent of blood, as well as another scent he had never smelled before. Mime crouched lower, her butt slowly lifting into the air, and driven by some unknown instinct, Mark took a step forward. As soon as his foot hit the ground, the pile of trash exploded, and a small Exlian drone about the size of a large dog launched itself toward him, hissing fiercely as its mandibles spread wide, aiming for his neck.

Mark reacted instantly, his feet shifting to pull his head out of the way, even as he launched a slash that tore through the Exlian's exoskeleton, severing its head from its body. Half expecting the corpse to fade away, Mark spun his body on full alert as he waited for the next two Exlian to attack. It took him a full fifteen seconds to realize that there was no attack. No more drones were coming.

His heart should have been hammering in his chest, but Mark felt nothing, just an absolute calm, mixed with that faint hunger he had experienced twice now when he saw Exlian corpses. Ignoring the feeling, he stepped over to the pair of legs and began to move the trash aside, revealing a headless corpse. With a sigh, he crouched down next to the corpse and activated the dead man's watch, alerting public security that there was an incident. He was about to straighten up when Mime jumped off his shoulder and dashed into the darkness, her black fur blending perfectly with the shadows.

Annoyed, Mark shook his head and, after doing a quick scan to make sure he hadn't left any evidence behind, left the area. He felt unsettled by the whole encounter. This was the second Exlian he had encountered in the city, and he was starting to wonder what was happening. Worse, he felt like he should have been frightened by the encounter, but when adrenaline had flooded his system, he had gotten calmer rather than more excited.

To him, slaying an Exlian drone was no big deal, though that, in and of itself, was enough to alert him that something was off. Intellectually, he knew that he should be treating what had just happened with more weight, but his complete lack of feeling regarding the dead body he had just stumbled across made it hard. Public security would use the GPS tracker on the corpse's watch to pinpoint the body's location, and when they arrived, they would find nothing but the corpse and the dead Exlian. Hopefully, they would be able to figure out where the Exlian had come from.

Wrestling with his lack of feelings, Mark jogged home, and as he opened the door, he saw Mime sit up from the couch. Shutting the door, he stared at her, perplexed. "How'd you get home?"

"She came down from upstairs," Joe said, from the kitchen table. "Was she not supposed to be here?"

Still confused, Mark shook his head. "No, she's fine. She must have just taken a shortcut. I'll double-check to make sure the window isn't open upstairs." After walking over to join Joe at the table, Mark sat down. "Hey, do you know anything about an alchemical butcher?"

"You mean Grandmaster Abrams?" Joe asked without looking up from the paper he was working on. "Everybody knows about the grandmaster. Or at least they do if they deal in Exlian corpses."

"He's legit?"

"What do you mean by legit? He didn't offer to sell you something, did he?" Joe asked, finally looking up at his brother, his eyes narrowed.

"No, but he did offer me a job."

"A job?"

"Well, kind of. He offered to teach me, make me an apprentice."

Pushing the paper aside, Joe crossed his arms over his chest and leaned on the table, his faded orange eyes burning with curiosity. "Why don't you start at the beginning?"

It took almost an hour for Mark to explain all that had happened that evening, and when he was done, Joe let out a low whistle. "I wondered where you had learned an extra martial art, but Cutting Palm? That's a crazy one. You need to be really careful with it, as most people who practice it end up completely ruining their hands. Jason, your boss? I heard he stopped halfway, never reached mastery, which is why he can still use his fingers. Old man Abrams is the only one who managed to master it, which is why they call him Grandmaster. That's strange, though. Normally, people who practice Cutting Palm have abnormally enlarged knuckles because of the stress it puts on their fingers."

Stretching out his hands, Mark revealed his perfectly normal fingers and shrugged. "Maybe it's because I use it with my transformed hand," he said.

"Oh, interesting. That could be it. Maybe it's absorbing the stress that the martial art causes you."

Mark nodded, avoiding mentioning that he had done most of his practice in a dream that had no impact on his actual physical body. He had been doing martial arts long enough to have already figured out what was going on from Joe's comments.

Mark, unlike everyone else who practiced Cutting Palm, wasn't using the martial art in real life but instead was perfecting the technique in his dreams. Avoiding using Cutting Palm in the real world until he had mastered it would mean he wouldn't suffer any of the common ill effects. He made a mental note to only use Cutting Palm with his left hand until he could transform his right hand as well.

"There isn't anything wrong with apprenticing to him, per se, but just be really careful. You've got a promising future, and you shouldn't ruin it. On the other hand, that old man has more connections than nearly anybody in this city, as he is the only supplier of some really important materials. If what he's saying is true and you are actually able to master Cutting Palm, you'll inherit those same connections. Like I said, just be careful."

That night, when Mark slipped into the dream and faced the first of the drones, nothing felt particularly different, despite his recent upgrade. The bug jumped out at him, and he casually split its head in half with a swing of his left arm. The second and third groups of drones didn't pose a problem either. Mark only truly noticed a difference when he faced the four drones he had never been able to beat before. His speed had increased drastically. Now, when he dodged, he reacted faster and moved farther.

At first, this was a problem, as Mark's body was unused to this change. However, it only took him two deaths to adjust, and after a long and drawn-out fight, he managed to kill the four drones on his third attempt.

Just as he had anticipated, the next level was five drones. They came at him from all sides, striking him simultaneously, leaving him speechless. As his dream world faded back into focus after he reset, he immediately tried to move. But once again, no matter which way he turned, there was always a drone in his blind spot.

A dozen tries later, he found he was no closer to succeeding, though he had noticed something. While it felt like all the bugs were hitting him at the same time, one of them always struck first. It was the bug coming toward him from the back right. Its mandibles would sink deep into his kidneys as it tore through his flesh.

That meant Mark had a fraction of a second of reaction time between the first attack and the other four. Seizing on this, Mark tried escaping in different directions, buying himself time to eliminate the drone attacking from the back right. However, that just sent him closer to the other drones, allowing them to kill him faster. After accidentally impaling himself on their mandibles a few times, he finally grew frustrated and decided to try the opposite.

Instead of running, he threw himself back and to the right, turning in the air and slashing down with his right hand. Empowered by his new D-ranked strength, his right hand chopped through the drone's head. He didn't quite manage to reach the monster's brain, but it was as if a light had gone off in Mark's head.

For the rest of the night, he practiced throwing himself backward toward the drone and chopping down with his right hand as he turned. Strike after strike failed, and each time a piercing pain would send him back to the start. Rather than grow disheartened, though, Mark found his concentration just grew sharper with each iteration. The first time he killed the drone, he didn't even realize it and instinctively stopped, since he expected to be dead. A moment later, he was, as four sets of mandibles latched on to the back of his neck, his spine, and both his legs. Still, he had achieved it, and though he failed in his next attempt, that was enough for Mark.

It took four hours of grueling practice before he managed to kill the bug twice consecutively. But after that, it was as if his body remembered the exact motion, and it became an instinctive reflex. Of course, there were still the other four bugs to deal with; he died as soon as he turned around to try to deal with them. Instead of panicking, however, he began examining the scenario more closely. He tried to judge which bug would reach him first, depending on which way he moved. Then he used the location of the pain on his body to tell whether he was right. He woke without having made any more progress, but that didn't bother him one bit. He knew the next night he'd get another chance, and another the night after that, and the night after that.

Grabbing a tube of nutrient paste, he began eating it to take the edge of his hunger off as he went down to the kitchen, where he found Joe drinking a cup of coffee. The clock proclaimed it was four in the morning, and when Mark scratched his head and stared at Joe in bewilderment, his brother grinned. "I was curious what time you get up in the morning, but now that I know it's four, we can get to work. Get your water and put on your running shoes."

Taking a deep breath, Mark nodded and did as Joe said. This wasn't the first time he had trained with Joe, and there was a familiarity to it that got his blood pumping. The two took off as soon as their feet hit the sidewalk, with Joe setting a blistering pace that Mark had to sprint to keep up with. Both were tall, though Joe had a couple of inches on Mark, and while they had a relatively similar stride, Joe's steps ate up more distance, allowing him to pull ahead. Without even glancing back, Joe sped up, forcing Mark to increase his already maxed pace.

The game was simple: Keep a distance of less than two steps between them. Though Joe had burned out and could no longer access his power, that didn't mean that his A-ranked speed or B-ranked fortitude was gone. In terms of pure strength, he outclassed Mark by several orders of magnitude, and Mark quickly reached his limit. Yet Joe kept pushing, slowly decreasing their speed just enough that Mark could always squeeze out the energy needed to keep going. Feeling his biofuel meter ticking down, Mark gritted his teeth and pushed as hard as he could, not wanting to let his brother down.

Mark had no idea how many miles they had covered and was too winded to care when they arrived back at the house. He didn't bother flopping down and resting, however, as the run had only been the precursor. Instead, the brothers headed for the backyard, where a makeshift set of weights waited for them. The last time they had trained together, they had exclusively done bodyweight exercises. Now there were heavy plates and bars where there had once been dirt and gravel.

"Borrowed these from some friends," Joe said, hardly having broken a sweat. "Slap the plates on and let's get going. Since we just went for a run, we'll start with squats."

Suppressing his groan, Mark did as he was told. For the next three hours, he underwent the most torturous exercise regime he had ever experienced. He had always imagined Lieutenant Cox would be the worst trainer he would have to face in his life, but Joe made the lieutenant's training feel like a walk in the park. In three hours, Mark had eaten through ten more of his biofuel units, and his brother was staring at him like he was a monster. At least there was that.

"If you can still move, get up. We've got more to do."

With a groan, Mark rolled over and got to his feet. "As long as you give me food, I can go all day."

His brother's eyebrows rose, and Mark suddenly wished he had kept his big mouth shut.

"Challenge accepted," Joe replied, and sent off a quick message on his phone.

Then began the battle of wills between the two brothers as they each set out to outlast the other. Joe had a friend bring over boxes and boxes of energy bars, stacking them in the kitchen until there almost wasn't room to move. He told Mark he could eat as many as he wanted, and even brought them out to set down next to Mark as he worked out.

Mark gritted his teeth and began to repeat the exercise

routine Joe had created for him. He forced his screaming muscles to move even when they felt like they would tear. Eventually, however, no amount of coaxing would let Mark continue, even though his biofuel was full. His muscles had reached the point of absolute failure, leaving him unable to move. Mark could only lie on the ground, staring up at his smirking brother.

"Well, you almost made it to dinnertime," Joe said, picking up one of the boxes of bars. "You want me to peel these for you?"

Unable to even shake his head, Mark just glared, causing Joe to laugh.

"Not quite all day, but pretty close. I've no idea how this body of yours works, but it's certainly abnormal. And more importantly, if you cultivate it properly, it'll be the greatest asset you have. You know what the number one cause of people dying in the wilderness is? It's not a lack of power. It's the inability to recover quickly. Often, you only get a few minutes between fights. But your ability to process food and recover strength is simply insane."

As if to prove Joe's point, Mark let out a loud groan and pushed himself into a sitting position with trembling arms. He could already feel his full biofuel meter draining as the nutrients were broken down into his body. They rejuvenated his muscles and brought his strength back.

Glancing at his watch, Joe shook his head. "Two minutes. From absolute failure to being able to sit up in two minutes? You, brother, are a bit of a monster."

Though he hated to have lost, Mark couldn't help but feel a surge of pride. He knew better than anyone else that his brother was the real monster. Joe was in a league of his own, always had been. And though his power wasn't working, Mark couldn't even begin to imagine that stopping him. So to hear the admiration in his brother's voice was a victory, and Mark grinned so widely he felt his cheeks might split.

"Stop grinning and get to work on active recovery. Most people meditate when they want to recover. Do you remember how I showed you? This is your new mantra."

As he struggled to cross his legs and straighten his back, Mark focused on the simple set of words that Joe had written down and now held in front of him. Mantras were sets of phrases that helped focus one's attention. Some people claimed they had mystical properties, but Joe had explained that what really mattered was the practitioner's ability to visualize and believe in what they were saying.

Mark had never been able to feel any effect from any of the mantras he had chanted, and now, as he recited the words quietly in his head, focusing his attention, he found that it was no different. That didn't mean his recovery was slow, however, and instead, it began to speed up as his body gained more and more energy.

Halfway through his meditation, his biofuel meter began to bottom out, and rather than continue with what Mark felt was a pointless exercise, he quickly grabbed the box of bars Joe had been holding and unwrapped them, shoving each in his mouth as his brother stared.

"I'll take five more boxes if you have them," he said.

Shaking his head, Joe went into the kitchen and carried five boxes out, throwing them at Mark, who grabbed each one with ease. Soon there was nothing but a pile of wrappers and empty boxes, and Mark bounced to his feet.

"All right," he said, "ready to go."

There was a sharp beep as Joe stopped the timer on his watch, a small frown on his face.

"Ten minutes," he said, "which is too long, all things considered. Also, the amount of calories you consumed is too high. Admittedly, it's good for somebody in the D rank, but if you want to be able to survive out in the wilderness, you're going to have to cut the number of calories you're consuming by at least half, and you'll need to speed up your recovery as well. My recovery time is five minutes, and while I need more calories than you, that's only because I'm recovering more strength, going all the way from completely powerless to the A rank, whereas you're only going to D rank."

"Come on, that's not fair," Mark said. "You told me I had to be completely refilled, in peak shape."

His gaze skeptical, Joe held up his hand. "Hold on, are you trying to tell me that you could do all that exercise again? The whole training regime we just did for the last fourteen hours . . ."

"Well, yeah," Mark said, giving his brother a strange look. "Isn't that what you told me?"

"I'm definitely going to have to rebuild this exercise routine," Joe said, shaking his head. "You know what? Forget it. We'll leave it for tomorrow. Just be up at four and be ready to go."

The expression of frustration on Joe's face was a balm to Mark's soul, and with a wide grin, he snapped a salute. "Yes, sir!"

Since he only had an hour until he was supposed to show up for his first day of Abrams's training, Mark took a quick shower and got changed. He didn't know what to wear, so he brought his bag with some old clothes in it, while he wore one of his nicer outfits to try to show his new master some respect. Taking the train into the city, he stopped by Jason's Pub, walking in the back door, as normal. When Jason saw him, he crossed his arms over his chest and glared.

"Didn't take a fancy to you, huh?" Jason said, his tone cold.

Realizing there was a misunderstanding going on, Mark held up his hands.

"I'm not here for work," he said. "I just stopped by to say thanks. Tonight's gonna be my first night working with Mr. Abrams."

"He's not Mr. Abrams," Jason said, his expression softening. "Just Abrams, or you can call him Master, if you ever get that far. I hope you do, kid. I couldn't hack it, but maybe you can. Come on, I'll get you something to eat."

Walking over to the window where the food was being served, he grabbed one of the plates, seemingly at random, and slid it onto the counter in front of Mark. "Eat up, and then get over there."

"Hey, where'd my burger go?" one of the waiters asked. "It was right here a second ago."

"Shut up and make another one," Jason snapped, causing the cooks to hurry about and the waiter to sigh in exasperation.

Though he felt like he probably should have rejected it, Mark grinned and picked up the burger and took a big bite. "Thanks."

"Wow, you're really just eating that?" Sky said, sidling up to him.

"I saw him pick it up at random, so he couldn't have poisoned it," Mark replied between mouthfuls.

A few of the cooks laughed, and Jason glowered even more, but Mark was feeling pretty good and didn't let it bother him. After he and Sky chatted and he finished his food, Mark headed over to the warehouse, arriving just at seven. Punching the code into the keypad, he walked in and heard a loud voice bellowing from the center of the warehouse.

"Early is on time, and on time is late, kid. Don't let it happen again."

His breath catching in his chest, Mark quickly hurried over and saw a frozen corpse sitting on the table.

"Get the heaters turned on. We've got a big one to thaw."

"Do I have time to get changed?" Mark asked, but Abrams shook his head.

"If you wanted to change, you should have done that before you arrived. We've got work to do, kid. A full night ahead of us, if we're gonna get everything done by two a.m. Tonight you'll be getting your hands dirty, since nothing beats firsthand experience. I'll be guiding you on where you should be cutting, and I'll handle the actual extractions. Come on, hop to it."

Seeing Abrams gesture to a wall with a couple of switches, Mark hurried over and flipped them all.

"What are you doing? That's way too hot. For a corpse of this size, you only need two. Now turn it down before you fry us all."

Flipping the switches back down until only two were on, Mark heard Abrams yell again.

"Why would you leave it on two heaters right next to each other? You'll thaw out one side of the monster and leave the other completely frozen. Can't work like that. Even heat. Even."

Flipping off one of the switches, Mark tried the rest of them until he figured out which one controlled the light on the opposite side of the corpse.

"Now get over here, and let's get started. If we wait till it's completely thawed, we won't be able to refreeze it. We need it just pliable enough to work on."

Hurrying back over, Mark dropped his bag and rolled up his sleeves as far as they would go, not wanting them to get covered in blood. He looked around for an apron, but there was none in sight. Gesturing for him to get closer, Abrams pointed at the center of the frozen corpse. "We're gonna be taking this thing's liver out. The easiest way to access it? From the back. Its liver sits close to its spine, just under its ribs. We'll cut here."

With a finger, Abrams drew a line on the frozen corpse, then stared at Mark. "Well, what are you waiting for? Get that fancy hand of yours going, and let's see you do it."

Swallowing, Mark nodded and touched his screw necklace. A moment later, his hand flashed silver, and he positioned himself to try to cut into the frozen corpse.

"Move over. You're not standing in the right spot. How are you supposed to get any leverage from that angle? You're a tall guy, so you should be able to reach over it, right? If you were using your right hand, that would be correct, but you're using your left, so get over on this side."

As gruff as Abrams was, he was a good teacher, though no amount of good teaching could make it easier for Mark to chop his way through a half-frozen Exlian corpse, even with a metal hand.

It was brutally cold work, and soon, even Mark's D-ranked fortitude couldn't keep the chill from his fingers. Thankfully, his biofuel meter was full, though it began to tick down awfully quickly as the night wore on.

By the time Mark had gotten through the monster's tough exoskeleton and into the flesh below, a full four hours had passed, and he was exhausted. Abrams, on the other hand, was as fresh as ever and was perfectly ready to continue scolding him. When Mark's fingers finally broke through, he felt a hand clamp down on his wrist, preventing him from moving even an inch.

"Careful. You don't want to damage the ingredient we are after. Otherwise, we'd have to repeat this whole process, and believe me, neither of us wants to do that," Abrams said with a sneer. "Get your hand out of there, but go easy with it."

It took a surprising amount of force for Mark to be able to pull his fingers free, and when he saw the pathetically small hole he had made, any pride he had built up over the afternoon of training with his brother vanished, especially after Abrams looked at it and muttered, "A little bit small," under his breath.

With a casual grip, the old man tore the hole wider, doing it in a way that didn't damage anything but the monster's frozen skin.

"All right, once you've made the hole a little bit bigger, you can see the placement of the liver right here. There are four points where we'll need to disconnect it, and because this is a little bit delicate and I'd rather not have to do this again tomorrow night, I'm gonna handle it. You just watch. Pay careful attention to the way I exert strength through my wrist. Remember, fingers as blades, which means keeping them stiff. All the strength comes from my forearm and wrist, like so."

In truth, watching Abrams was a mesmerizing experience. The old man's fingers danced through the monster's flesh, leaving countless tiny cuts in their wake, and only a few minutes later, he held a complete monster liver in his hands.

"Grab the tray for me," Abrams commanded.

Mark's fingers were trembling from the cold that had invaded them, nearly causing him to fumble the tray, but he managed to hold it out for Abrams to put the liver down. Most of the creatures Mark had seen resembled giant insects. This Exlian, however, was quite different, appearing to have a layer of fur mixed in with the plates.

Noticing Mark's curious look, Abrams grinned. "You said you're about to enter the second stage of the training camp, right? Well, you'll learn all about the different sorts of creatures when you go, but this creature is called a war bear, and its liver is particularly useful for certain kinds of potions. Get those heat lamps off and help me haul it out."

By *help me haul it out*, Abrams meant *carry the entire thing by yourself.* As Mark struggled to lug the half-thawed corpse of the war bear back to its hook, Abrams walked along with him, explaining a few details about the liver. By the time Mark finally hauled the war bear back up into position, he was absolutely filthy, covered in blood and sweat, but Abrams didn't seem to care one bit, as he led Mark into a small office.

"Here," he said, getting a few books off the shelf by his desk.

The first one looked exactly like the Cutting Palm manual Mark had already gotten, just a little bit thicker.

"You'll find the next set of techniques in there. They also happen to be the final set of techniques. They'll either turn your hands into lethal weapons or ruin them beyond repair. If you have any questions, you can ask. This other book is a basic guide to alchemy. You'll need to know at least the basics if you want to be able to extract material that's usable. Study that in your spare time. If you head through that door, there's a shower. You stink something fierce, so you might want to take a shower before you head home."

"Thank you, sir," Mark said, bowing.

Abrams just grunted and waved him off, and Mark hurried into the bathroom. His clothing was practically ruined, but he still packed it up in a plastic bag to see if he could wash it out when he got home. After cleaning the war bear's blood from his body, Mark changed into his extra set of clothing, packed away his blood-covered garments, and headed out, catching the train back to his neighborhood.

It was close to two o'clock when he tumbled into bed, and he fell asleep almost instantly, finding himself in the dream wilderness, where he was assaulted by a drone immediately. Mark had spent the train ride home trying to memorize the new material in the Cutting Palm manual Abrams had given him, and now he began to put it into practice, all the while dodging the drone's attacks. Occasionally, he wasn't quite quick enough and got caught, forcing him to restart, but that served him just fine. He resisted the impulse to kill the drone and move up the chain, instead using the extra pressure to help him refine the technique.

Though he was in the dream, Mark found the most astonishing thing. When he used his left hand to execute the new palm techniques, they felt perfectly natural and were almost twice as effective as the first set of techniques he had learned. The first stage of the Cutting Palm transformed the entire hand into a blade, while the second stage focused on turning each individual finger into a blade. While Mark was using his metallic left hand, there were no issues. When he used his right hand, however, he could feel a faint pain tracing through his bones. Since he was in a dream, it would fade quickly, but Mark could only imagine how much damage practicing these techniques in the real world would do to him.

Deciding that he wouldn't move forward until he had mastered the technique with his right hand, Mark worked at it over and over, until, with a yank, he was pulled from the dream and thrust back into the real world. The dream only ever lasted two hours at most, and checking the clock, Mark saw that it was 3:55 a.m., meaning he only had five minutes until his training with Joe would begin. His stomach was rumbling, but he wasn't quite starving yet.

Thanks to the increase in the total amount of biofuel he could carry, he no longer ended the dream with an empty biofuel meter. Still, it wouldn't be a good idea to start the day on an empty stomach, so Mark reached for his nightstand, where a pile of nutrient paste sat. Precisely at four o'clock in the morning, he walked out of his room and found Joe standing in the hall.

"You know the drill," Joe said, and turning, he headed downstairs with Mark following closely after him.

After witnessing Mark's incredible recovery speed, Joe had rebuilt the training program once more. As they stretched lightly before their run, he explained the new plan.

"Your recovery is your greatest asset. I know I already told you some of this yesterday, but just listen. Having high endurance is incredibly important. However, the higher your endurance, the longer it is going to take to recharge. On top of that, no matter how high your endurance is, if you're only D rank, there simply isn't a way that you'll be able to compete with somebody who's above you in the ranks. The tyranny of ranks is a real thing, but that doesn't mean you can't outlast someone. This is a trick that we were taught early in the Rangers. If you want to run faster and farther than somebody or you want to escape from a pursuer of a higher rank, you don't need better fortitude. What you need is better speed and a faster recovery time.

"Imagine you're in a fight. You're fighting somebody who's a rank above you. Their endurance is naturally going to be two to three times yours, which means you'll get tired in half the time they will, maybe even a third, but imagine their recovery takes ten minutes, and imagine yours takes thirty seconds. How many times during the fight do you think you'll be able to recover? They will never get ten minutes of uninterrupted rest, but thirty seconds, you can squeeze it out with a bit of creativity. And as long as you can do that three or four times during the fight, you're the one who wins in the endurance battle.

"Maximizing your build around your recovery will also allow you to use your highest levels of speed, strength, and will. Most empowered can only reach their maximum level of ability once during a fight. After that, they're simply too tired to do it again, but if we can get your recovery down to an incredibly short amount of time, then you'll be able to burst with that peak power as often as you want."

"Is that actually possible?" Mark asked. "I've never heard of anybody with instant recovery."

"It's possible," Joe said, a strange look in his eyes, "though I don't know how successful we'll be. There are creatures who can do it, though. Including a really annoying creature called a psycho ape."

Leading Mark down the street in a sprint, Joe continued his explanation.

"Psycho apes are typically found in the jungles west of here, but occasionally they'll come out and we see them during waves, though thankfully not in large numbers. The psycho ape carries an innate skill called instant recovery that allows them to push their recovery to absurd levels. Unfortunately, their skill gems carry their uncanny agility ability, not their instant recovery, but I have some ideas about how to reproduce the effect. Normal people wouldn't be able to do it, but I have a sneaking suspicion you just might."

So began the hardest few days of Mark's entire life. All the training he had done up until this point, all the difficult hours spent sweating in the gym, had done nothing to prepare him for the excruciating level of intensity that was to come.

It started early every morning as Joe put Mark through a rigorous training regimen. As soon as he finished, he had no time to rest and had to rush over to Abrams's warehouse, where he assisted Abrams in disassembling corpses to harvest various important organs. Then, exhausted and cold, he would stumble back onto the train to head home for a couple of hours of sleep that wasn't actually sleep.

Had he not been empowered, Mark would have collapsed after the first day and a half, but thanks to his insane recovery and the margin granted by his biofuel meter, he somehow managed to grit his teeth and hold on. Joe continually refined the training program, using all sorts of tricks to keep Mark operating at peak efficiency until exhaustion overtook him. Once he collapsed, Joe would force him into active recovery.

At first, Mark was worried that the training wouldn't work and that he would simply break, but Joe, having spent a decade and a half working with some of the finest training the military could offer, understood Mark's limits perfectly and never carried him beyond them.

The only time Mark had to study the alchemy book that Abrams had given him was on the train ride, but he tried to recite it from memory while practicing the second stage of the Cutting Palm technique in his dream fights. When the weekend came, he was in such a daze that he got up normally and was walking out the door when Joe stopped him. Instead of their normal run, Joe sat him down at the kitchen table, passing a file with an attached data stick over to Mark. Joe leaned forward, resting his arms on the table as Mark began to read.

"This is everything I've collected from the last few days. You've been working hard, putting out a lot of energy and effort, which gave us the data to build you an optimal program. If you want to train your recovery, you don't have to keep up that same pace. Instead, I think we should be able to achieve this same effect with less time. However, it does mean that you're going to have to forgo cramming yourself full at every chance you get. Your body seems to have the ability to store calories and then use them on the back end. Normally, people do that through fat, but your body isn't getting fat.

"In fact, I'm not exactly sure what's going on with it, but however your power affects your biology, it's creating a situation where you have significant energy reserves. Your hunger acts as an advance warning, and once you fill it up, you can work through it over time. What we need to do is get you hungry and have you constantly expend and gain energy while maintaining that hungry state. By operating when you're hungry, as opposed to always full, your body will naturally start to optimize the way it spends calories. This is a slightly slower method than the one we're doing now, but you can't keep up this kind of training indefinitely, since eventually your willpower will collapse, and that can lead to psychological problems."

Thumbing through the pages, Mark nodded. "This makes sense. And I can see how taking this approach, where I don't fill up but instead just give my body little bits of nutrition at a time, will help train my recovery. I don't really like the idea, though. I'd much rather be exhausted than hungry."

"Sure, but it'll help train your willpower, too, which is one of the hardest things to train. That's not the only extra benefit either. At the end of the day, you're not always going to be able to rely on a constant food source. Sure, we have plenty of nutrient paste, but when you're out in the field, you might not have anything to eat for days. Currently, your body deals with the training by simply throwing a huge amount of energy at it. We need you not to do that.

"We need you to be hyperefficient. Because then, when you are full, the energy your body is going to use will be much smaller, allowing you to last much longer. Today we're going to rest. And tomorrow, I'll run you through a few hours of the exercises I have in mind. The goal will be to do them every day, at least once, twice if possible, though that might be hard while you're in the training camp."

"I was wondering what we were going to do about that," Mark

said, flipping the pages shut and inserting the data stick into his watch to upload the digital version of the report, along with a training checklist that identified each of the exercises that he would be doing.

"We're going to be watching your calorie intake very closely," Joe said, "so let's get that set up."

After setting up the monitoring on Mark's watch, Joe told him to relax for the day and went back to bed. Since Mark wasn't tired, he instead had to figure out what he was going to do that day. On Saturdays Sky didn't normally start work until the afternoon, so he opened his watch to send her a message, only to realize that he had no way of contacting her since she didn't have a watch of her own. Disappointed, he decided to go and do a bit more research on alchemy instead.

That meant spending the morning on Blackstar forums, searching through threads on the subject and trying to absorb as much information as he could. Alchemists, it turned out, were an incredibly important part of the empowered world, as they provided not only supplements to help with empowered training but also weapons, gear, and combat aids. Their ability to take material from the natural world that was imbued with mana and transform or magnify the mana's effects to produce wondrous results was highly sought after, and Mark soon began wondering if he should be training as an alchemist instead of an alchemical butcher.

That led down another rabbit hole, as he started to investigate what it took to become an alchemist. Finding a definitive guide offered for a couple of credits in one of the alchemist shops on the Blackstar forums, Mark spent the money and opened it up. For the next two hours, he sat at his desk, completely absorbed.

Alchemy was a highly specialized skill, and the most important feature of an alchemist was their ability to read the flow of mana through an object. Normally, this took the shape of an identification skill that allowed the wielder to uncover a mana-infused object's characteristics and abilities through examining it. Among the naturally awakened, these sorts of abilities were exceedingly rare, and anybody who had them was practically guaranteed to become a powerful alchemist.

Skill gems could be acquired for an exorbitant fee, mimicking the effect of the identification skill, yet the alchemists who possessed them would never be able to grow above rank C. Of course, there were alchemists who didn't have the identification skill, because they hadn't awakened it naturally and couldn't afford the skill gem that contained it. Their success rates, however, were abysmal, and it was a gamble every time they tried to create a potion, since they had no way of knowing the precise characteristics of the ingredients they used, which often led to their mixtures collapsing and becoming unusable.

Scratching his chin, Mark glanced down at his wrist. He had been holding out some hope that his alchemical blood adaptation would allow him to become an alchemist, as it was a tremendously lucrative career, but it had nothing to do with being able to identify materials. That didn't make it useless, however, and Mark already had a few ideas about how he might be able to use it to his advantage.

Closing the forum, Mark stood up and stretched, running over the plan in his head. First, he pulled up his map, looking for the closest alchemy shop, and then he checked his bank account to see how he was doing on credits. When he saw that he had barely over 15,000 credits, he grimaced. The money he made dishwashing had been barely enough to cover his expenses, and these 15,000 credits were the sum total of his savings, originally intended to pay for a spot in the Defense Force's training camp. Since he had already joined the recruit training camp, there was no need for him to continue saving up, but the thought of his savings disappearing still hurt. Of course, with the sale of the Exlian corpses,

Joe had plenty of money, but his brother would need it for the treatment he required.

Thinking it through, Mark decided it was worth the risk. Money was just money, after all. He could always earn more credits. After a quick train ride, Mark walked a few blocks to a small shopping center where one of the alchemy shops was located. He had walked through this area before, but money had always been so tight that he'd never bothered entering any of the stores.

When he arrived at the alchemist shop, he was a bit taken aback by how bright and well lit it was. He had expected something darker, more mysterious, as alchemists had a reputation of being rather eccentric. Instead, he was greeted at the door by a young woman in a uniform who gave him a slightly skeptical look but still smiled cheerfully as she asked him if he needed anything.

"I'd like to look at your elixirs."

"Of course, please come in."

She led him back to a counter where, arranged tastefully in a glass case, were three elixirs, backlit to make the liquid they contained glimmer brightly.

"Do you know what sort of elixir you'd like?" the young woman asked, already beginning to reach for the yellow vial.

Mark reached out and tapped the glass. "I'd like the C-ranked elixir, please."

"Of course, this is an elixir made from a peak C-ranked Exlian warrior, refined by our own personal master alchemist, guaranteed both effect and freshness."

Looking at the vial, Mark frowned. Since it was sealed, with no visible way to open or reseal it, he wasn't quite sure how he was supposed to carry out the next stage of his plan. Luckily, something caught his eye at that moment. In a nearby case was a specialized vial that contained three independent sections, along with a dropper that the larger vials could be slotted into.

"Do you have some way of dividing an elixir up?" Mark asked, gesturing to the glimmering yellow liquid the attendant held.

According to the forums, it was common for elixirs to be taken in small doses, though the effect wasn't quite as strong. Only the poorest of the empowered used such tactics, as every time an elixir was taken, it built resistance, making the ultimate effect lower, but it was common enough that a device had been created to assist with dividing the liquid up.

"This is a vial syringe. You can place the original capsule into the syringe and then attach the new, smaller vials down below. What's convenient about this is that it will prevent the elixir from encountering any air, thereby maintaining its potency. It costs four thousand credits and the C-ranked elixir ten thousand five hundred."

Unable to keep the grimace off his face, Mark stretched out his wrist with his watch. "I'll take them," he said.

With a sympathetic smile, the young woman packed up everything for Mark, throwing in a box of microvials, each one able to hold approximately a third of the elixir of a regular capsule. Mark scanned his watch, his heart clenching with pain as his precious credits flew away. Of course, if things worked out as he was hoping, he wouldn't be hurting for credits anymore, but in the meantime, he needed to be careful with his cash.

With his newly purchased elixir, Mark headed home, sighing as he paid fifteen more credits to take the train. Once home, he skipped lunch since his biofuel was still full and went up to his room, leaving Joe watching the news with Mime, who had claimed her normal spot on the nice cushion.

As he bounded up the stairs, Mark's excitement grew, and after closing the door to his room, he got out the case that contained the elixir and his new vial syringe. Reading over the instructions three times before opening up the syringe, he mustered his courage and decided to give it a try.

It was simple to slot the C-ranked elixir into place, and Mark prepared three of the small capsules that came with it. Now came the part Mark was unsure about. Getting out a knife, Mark pricked the end of his finger, carefully putting a single drop of blood into the bottom of one of the microvials. Pressing a bit of paper towel up against his finger, he waited for it to stop bleeding as he examined the blood drop at the bottom of the vial. It glimmered like a ruby, unusually bright, though Mark wasn't sure if that was just a figment of his imagination or if the color really was different from normal blood.

According to the description of his alchemical blood ability, all he had to do to upgrade the elixir from a yellow C-ranked elixir to a blue B-ranked elixir was add his blood, but Mark couldn't help but be skeptical. At the same time, if it actually worked, Mark would have a way to practically print money. So far, his other genetic adaptation had worked exactly as advertised, and though he was trying not to get too excited, Mark couldn't wait to try it out.

Quite nervous, he picked up the syringe and clipped the microvial onto the end of it. A slider on the side of the syringe could be set to determine how much liquid was extracted, and after clicking it into place, Mark took a deep breath and then squeezed the syringe's trigger. There was a soft hiss as the plunger shifted, and Mark saw the viscous yellow elixir squirting into the microvial, mixing with the blood. Almost immediately, it began to change color, yellow elixir and red blood forming a cloudy blue.

With a click, the injector stopped moving, and the microvial sealed to keep air out. With careful fingers, Mark pried the small vial loose and shook it, watching as the liquid tumbled back and forth. The blue was definitely there, but it was a bit lighter than it should have been, and Mark had the sense that this elixir was only about half as strong as the elixirs that Noah had gifted him. That meant this was a failed product, but at the same time, it was still stronger than a regular C-ranked elixir. Emboldened, Mark put the sealed microvial aside and put two drops of blood into the next vial.

Once again, he clipped it in place, made sure the dispensing dial was set correctly, and squeezed. This time, a deep-blue liquid glimmered with sapphire sparkles. Though it was slightly different in viscosity, the color was spot on, causing Mark's heart to leap.

Placing the vial carefully down next to the first one, Mark quickly made the third, then repackaged the first, adding a second drop of blood. Hunting about, he found the case that Noah's elixirs had come in and slotted the microelixirs inside. They looked much less impressive, only a third the size of the original elixirs, but Mark didn't care one bit. Closing the case, he slipped it in his pocket and left his room, pausing on the landing as he heard an unfamiliar female voice downstairs.

"What do you mean, Joe? You can't seriously be considering giving up."

Something about the tone of the speaker caused Mark to pause, listening intently as his brother responded quietly.

"Emily, it's not the same. What can I do?"

Whatever Emily said in response was too quiet to hear, but it must have infuriated Joe, because when he spoke again, his voice was suffused with anger.

"Don't you dare. I've been committed since before you joined. I've done more, given up more, than anyone else. But I refuse to take part in some half-baked scheme that's going to get a lot of people killed!"

"I didn't mean—"

"This conversation is over. You should leave."

Holding his breath, Mark remained still until he heard the front door shut and the creak of the couch. Reaching back, Mark grabbed his door and closed it loudly, hoping to give Joe a moment of warning. When he walked down the stairs, Joe was watching the news again, no sign of any anger or frustration on his face.

"Are you going out again?"

"Yes," Mark said, skidding to a halt in front of the door, his hand resting on the handle. "Do you need anything?"

"Yeah, I'm tired of eating energy bars, so pick us up something good. Maybe some steaks. We can grill them tonight. I'll send you the money."

"Sure," Mark said, his eyes gleaming. "I'll be back in a bit."

As Mark turned to leave, Mime scaled the back of the couch and leaped onto his shoulder, landing gracefully. A moment later, Mark was down on the sidewalk, running toward the train station. This time, his destination was farther away, at an alchemy supply store that offered an identification service. By the time he had gotten to the supply store, he was quite a bit calmer, though he still hadn't managed to piece together what his brother's conversation had been about. When he walked in with Mime sitting calmly on his shoulder, he was greeted by the shop's attendant, who was sitting behind a desk, half buried among shelves of all sorts of different ingredients. "Welcome to Botheby's. Anything you need, just ask."

Walking up to the desk, Mark nodded, his nervousness displayed on his face. "Do you do identification here?"

"Sure," the attendant said. "Well, not me. I'm not an alchemist, but we've got an alchemist on staff who does."

"How much does it cost?"

"It depends on how complex the item is, and it can range anywhere from five hundred credits to one hundred thousand."

Swallowing, Mark took out the case from his pocket.

"What about an elixir?" he asked.

Staring at the microvials, the attendant shook his head, a knowing smile on his lips. "Afraid you got scammed?"

"I am," Mark said, quickly nodding his head. "Look, see how these colors are different? I'm afraid someone pulled one over on me."

Taking the elixir shards from Mark, the attendant looked them over. "An elixir typically costs five hundred credits to identify, and you'll get a printout of all the sources so you can tell if it's pure or not."

Grimacing, Mark glanced at his watch. He was just shy of 500 credits, as the three train rides had put him at 485. On top of that, he still needed to pick up beef on the way home, and Joe's credits hadn't been transferred over.

"Are you planning on selling any of them?"

Mark heard a voice from the side and looked over, seeing a

young man about his age, wearing thick glasses and a robe stained with a variety of different splotches.

"This is Alchemist Henley," the attendant quickly said, introducing the shop's alchemist.

"Pleased to meet you, sir," Mark replied. "I was hoping to sell them, but I'm afraid one or more of them might be fake."

"Then it's good you came to check. Tell you what, if you're willing to sell them to our shop, we'll check them for free. If they're fake, no skin off your back. You won't owe us anything. But if they're real, give us a thousand-credit discount on each."

A full B-ranked elixir sold for approximately 50,000 credits, though he would probably only get 40 for it since he was selling it to an alchemist shop. Divided into thirds, that meant getting just over 13,000 per microvial. A thousand credits off each would bring that down to approximately 12,000 credits. And even if the lighter vial didn't sell for that much, Mark would be coming out well ahead, as he had spent just about 15,000 credits on the C-ranked elixir and vial syringe. Nodding quickly, Mark agreed. The alchemist took the case and gestured for Mark to follow him, walking into a back office full of various machines. "Have a seat."

Mark sat down as Alchemist Henley brought the vials over to a machine with a long, thin needle. Noticing his nervousness, Henley smiled. "In order to test the contents of the elixir, we will have to pierce the outer casing, but don't worry, it'll reseal perfectly."

Clipping the first of the vials into the machine, the alchemist started the machine up as Mark watched with interest. It didn't take long for the machine to run its assessment, and the light at the top of the machine blinked green and a small slip of paper printed out. Alchemist Henley handed the paper over to Mark without even bothering to look at it as he slipped the vial out of the machine and replaced it in the case.

As he continued to test the other two vials, Mark looked

over the paper, his forehead furrowing slightly. Listed were four separate Exlian, three with known types and the fourth with an unknown type. There had been a moment when Mark was concerned that the machine would have picked up his blood, and he was prepared to play it off as if he had been scammed, but nothing on the paper indicated that he was involved at all.

The next test came out the same, but when the last vial was placed in the machine, there was a warning beep and the yellow light on top of the machine flashed.

"It looks like there is a problem with this vial," the alchemist said, "though it's not actually a problem per se."

Showing the slip of paper it had produced to Mark, he tapped on the first line. "As you can see, this vial was made with a mixture of a B-ranked extract and C-ranked extracts. Either the alchemist mixing it didn't know what they were doing or, and this is more likely, you've been scammed."

Pasting a frown on his face to hide his elation, Mark nodded. "So how much is this one worth?"

"You're probably looking at about five thousand credits, unfortunately. Any mixed elixir is not worth very much since their effects are uncertain. The other two are peak B-ranked elixirs. Though you don't have quite enough here to form a full elixir, you could probably still get just under thirty thousand credits, say, twenty-eight."

"Will you give me thirty thousand credits for all of them?"

And with a wide grin, Alchemist Henley nodded. "Yes, we will," he said. "And if you have any more elixir shards you want to sell, bring them on over."

Trying to hide his elation, Mark stood up and shook the alchemist's offered hand. After he collected his credits, thanked the alchemist and the attendant once more, and walked out of the shop, he broke into a dance when he reached the sidewalk outside. His bet had been right, and Mark felt like he had just unlocked a gold mine.

On his way home, he stopped and picked up some steaks, along with a bunch of other groceries, reveling in his newfound wealth. The steaks were handed over to Joe, who was the better cook, and Mark headed upstairs to get on Blackstar Exchange, the sales platform attached to the empowered forums.

Filtering for C-ranked elixirs, he looked for a good deal, eventually finding a couple with an immediate purchase price of 9,500 credits each. Elixirs went quick, so Mark purchased them, entering his address for the delivery. It was common enough for D-ranked empowered to consume C-ranked elixirs that he didn't think it would pose any trouble.

As he waited for the delivery confirmation to go through, Mark began searching for elixir shards. It turned out there was a thriving market for them, as many empowered found it too expensive to purchase full elixirs, especially the B-ranked and A-ranked ones.

One of the best features of Blackstar was that it was anonymous, which meant Mark would have a natural sales channel for his upgraded elixir shards once he had made them. As excited as Mark was about this new business opportunity, he also wasn't foolish enough to think that it was without danger. He could imagine if anybody discovered what his blood was capable of, he'd probably end up locked in some basement, being bled dry until he died of old age. That was a fate he wanted to avoid at all costs.

The elixirs didn't arrive until the next day, and when they did, Mark didn't have time to work with them immediately, as he and Joe were still in the midst of his training. He had forgone refilling his biofuel meter after his dream training, instead bearing with the hunger gnawing at his stomach as his new training regimen required. It was intense for a while, but the longer Mark ignored it, the duller the feeling was, lending credence to Joe's guess that his body was simply reacting as it had been trained.

After an intense workout, his biofuel meter had bottomed out, and the real training began. It was simple and consisted of short, explosive workouts followed by eating enough to give him one unit of energy, then a few minutes of meditation as Mark tried to actively channel the nutrients he had just eaten into recovery.

In truth, he wasn't that confident that it would work, but about the fourth hour, he felt something faintly stirring inside of him when he began to meditate, and his recovery improved significantly.

Joe, noticing how quickly Mark recovered, slapped him on the shoulder. "Ha! That's what I'm talking about. We just need to keep doing that. Whatever you were thinking of in that moment, that's your new mantra. Over time, we'll try to refine it until you can recover in an instant."

Excited by their progress, they kept training for another few hours, until Joe finally called it off.

"All right, I think you can do it on your own now," he said. "Just remember the monitoring. Half of the strength of this regime is stacking consistency, so make sure you're keeping up with the stats I told you to track. You want to ensure that every single time you activate your ability, you're tracking how long it takes you to recover. It's a bit annoying to do without a trainer standing next to you, but I'll be able to help you during the mornings. Have you received your second assignment for the training camp?"

"Yes," Mark replied. "It came in last night. Camp Eleven again."

"That's good, because maybe we can talk to Lieutenant Cox about including some of this in your regular training. Now that I'm thinking about it, that's a really good idea. I'm going to go see if I can get ahold of him."

Watching Joe run into the house, Mark felt a bittersweet

happiness in his chest. In truth, the main reason he had agreed to act as Joe's guinea pig in trying to figure out this training method was that it had given his brother something to focus on besides his burned-out power. Training and growing in power had been Joe's obsession. But now that path had been destroyed, as his power would never be able to grow again.

From the way that he had launched himself into coming up with a training program for Mark, it was clear that he was using Mark as a bit of a stand-in. Though Mark wasn't sure that it was full-blown denial, he could tell that Joe preferred to pretend that everything was fine and normal. If his training helped, Mark didn't mind. His body had already recovered from his workout, and standing up, he stretched lightly and headed inside.

There was a simple brown box on his desk, and Mime was sitting next to it, staring intently at it. Wondering if she could feel the mana contained inside the elixirs, Mark opened the box and took out two cases, each with a single yellow elixir in it. Sniffing slightly, Mime lost interest and turned around, rubbing herself against Mark's arm before jumping to the bed.

"They may not look like much now," Mark said with a grin, "but just you wait."

After carefully opening the first package, Mark prepped three of the microvials and put two drops of blood in the first one. As he slotted the full vial of elixir into the syringe and adjusted the dial on the side, his excitement caused his hands to shake, so he put the syringe down for a moment and did his best to calm himself. Keeping his motions as deliberate as possible, he slotted the first microvial, double-checked the gauge, and squeezed, chuckling to himself as he saw the yellow liquid and red blood mixing into a glimmering blue.

It wasn't long before he had six shining blue elixirs on his desk, and with a deep breath, he picked one up, watching as the sun shone through it. The average market price for a shard on the Blackstar Exchange was 18,000 credits, which was a good bit higher than the 14,000-credit price he had gotten from Alchemist Henley. However, that was because the exchange sold directly to the end user.

The easiest, most lucrative way to sell the shards would be to set up a small shop on the exchange, but Mark had other ideas. He was okay giving up a little bit of profit as long as he could make a quick sale, and so instead he searched for individuals who had put up requests, asking for specific products and offering specific prices. He quickly found hundreds of requests for B-ranked elixir shards, most offering between 15,000 and 16,000 credits. Picking the six highest offers he could find, he accepted them and packaged up each elixir individually.

With a stack of boxes in hand, Mark waited until the courier was at his door and then ran down to hand them over to the slightly bored-looking middle-aged woman, who shoved them in her car without much care and took off. Each of the boxes had a special barcode on it, and once they were sent to the processing center, they would be linked to the transaction and sent off to the correct address, providing a layer of separation between the seller and the buyer that preserved the anonymity of the exchange.

Mark could see the credits on hold in his exchange account, but they wouldn't transfer until someone who worked for the exchange verified the items were real. Still, seeing just over 100,000 credits in the account made Mark practically giddy. He had to forcefully stop himself from immediately buying another vial of C-ranked elixir with his remaining credits. If something went wrong and the assessment came back that the elixir shards weren't what he promised, Mark could ill afford to spend his last remaining 10,000 credits.

His evening was spent as it always was, cutting apart half-frozen Exlian corpses and practicing his martial arts in his dream. As soon as he woke up the following morning, Mark jumped out of bed and headed for the backyard, where he began to run through the exercises he and Joe had come up with, once again focusing on training his recovery. Instead of reporting at five to the training camp, as he had during the first six weeks, Mark wasn't slated until nine, so he grabbed a light breakfast at home and, with his stomach growling, ran to camp.

Everyone was already there when he arrived, and Mark took up his spot between Noah and Phoenix as Lieutenant Cox walked onto the stage with two other soldiers. Of the original one hundred members of their group, there were a mere eighteen recruits. Where the others had been assigned, Mark had no idea, but there was no opportunity to ask, as Lieutenant Cox launched straight into his speech.

"Welcome back, recruits. Eighteen of you have passed the first section of our tests and will be entering the second. While the first section focused on physical training, this second section focuses on knowledge, specifically theory and its application. The military of New Emery is focused overwhelmingly on a single issue, the great threat: the Exlian, who swarm our world in numbers without end and constantly seek to destroy us. The Exlian are both a threat to humanity's survival and our greatest opportunity to rise above the creatures of this world and cement our place as the apex predators. That is what our military seeks to train: apex predators who can hunt the Exlian within our walls and without.

"Our hope is that the eighteen of you are on your way to becoming some of those elite. We'll have a bit of a different structure, necessitated by a change in the way this year's training is going to go. Unlike training structures in the past, you will spend approximately sixty percent of your time in the classroom and forty percent of your time in the field over the next six weeks. You'll be entering the dead zone as a team in order to begin getting used to fighting against the Exlian. Then you will have a one-week break, and in the third section of the training camp, you will spend sixty percent of your time in the field and the remaining forty percent training in the classroom, learning advanced tactics and information about the Exlian. Any questions?"

Glenn's hand shot up, and Lieutenant Cox gestured for him to speak.

"Sir, isn't it dangerous? I mean, to send us out in the field so early."

"Yes." Lieutenant Cox smiled. "It is dangerous, but each of your teams will have an instructor assigned to it. For the first six weeks, we will be with you every time you step out into the field in case there are issues. In the second six-week section, you'll be on your own. Now, this seems to be a good time for me to introduce the other two instructors who will be joining us. Lieutenant Rene is a member of the Rangers, and next to her is Lieutenant Wells from the Engineering Corps. All three of us will be training you during the classroom periods, and each time your team is sent out, one of us will accompany you. Now, if you have other questions, save them for once we're in the classroom. Let's get started with some light exercise."

The lieutenant's understanding of the term *light exercise* certainly wasn't anybody else's, though Mark found that after the training he had gone through the previous week, it wasn't quite so bad as before. Of course, he didn't have his biofuel meter full, which meant that he tired more easily, causing the others to give him curious glances. Lieutenant Cox appeared to have talked to his brother, however, and just as Mark was growing exhausted, the lieutenant walked around with a box of energy bars for everyone.

"What are these for, sir?" Harper asked as, beside her, Danny shoved an entire bar in his mouth.

"One of the most important parts of operating out in the

wilderness is recovery," the lieutenant said. "We're going to be including active recovery in our training. You're still expected to train on your own at home, but we won't be doing any of the sorts of physical exercise we did in the first six weeks. Instead, we're going to focus on smaller, more explosive workouts with active-recovery sessions between. Lieutenant Rene, would you mind demonstrating?"

With a nod, Lieutenant Rene stepped forward. She was a petite woman with dark hair pulled back in a tight ponytail and gray eyes. With a slight smile, she gestured for everybody to sit and then sat cross-legged on the platform in front of them. The rest of the morning passed quickly as Mark and the other trainees were immersed in the training. Their active-recovery meditation session transitioned straight into a theory class, in which Lieutenant Wells began introducing all the basic Exlian, starting with drones and their varieties, then moving on to warriors.

"As I said when I started the lecture, today we're going to mainly be doing an overview. We'll dive into more detail in later classes, spending an entire class on each of the various species of Exlian, but let's continue," Wells said.

He was a large man with incredibly thick arms and a barrel chest. Mark had been slightly surprised to discover that he was an officer in the Engineering Corps, as he was built more like a frontline fighter. As he spoke, he often ran his fingers through his brown beard, which fell to the center of his chest.

"After drones, we have warriors. This is by far the largest class of Exlian in terms of variation. Drones can reach as high as the D rank, but they can't get above that. If they do, they evolve into something greater, a warrior."

Seeing Harper's hand, Lieutenant Wells paused and pointed at her. "You have a question?"

"Yes, sir. Are all Exlian evolved from lower-ranked Exlian?"

"That is a wonderful question," Lieutenant Wells said, "and the answer is no. Some Exlian are evolved forms, but that happens on an individual basis, thankfully. Can you imagine what would happen if drones could naturally evolve? We would have been overrun years ago. The only time a drone can evolve is if it is hit with prolonged exposure to a tremendously potent source of mana. The same is true for warriors, though they typically find it easier to absorb mana than drones do, meaning they grow in strength at a more rapid pace. Thankfully, there aren't nearly as many of them, as each requires more mana for the nests to produce."

Seeing another hand, Lieutenant Wells waved for the recruit to put it down.

"We'll talk about what a nest is in a second. Let's get back to warriors. As I said, they have the greatest amount of variation. There are thousands of different kinds, and their purposes are just as varied. Some are optimized for hunting, some as frontline warriors, and some provide support to other Exlian. There are even warrior Exlian who are optimized for destroying fortifications. Some have wings and can fly, some burrow underground, and others are aquatic. No matter where you are in the wilderness, it's possible to encounter a warrior. And if you do, you better pray you've got the advantage, because all warriors share another characteristic. Just like drones, their death releases a specialized mana wave, a psychic scream that alerts other Exlian to their presence and pings the location where they died. Bear that in mind. If you ever kill a bug, your best bet is to get out of there as fast as possible, because if there are any other Exlian around, they're coming for you. Now, we call Exlian bugs, but that doesn't mean they are all completely insectile. Does anybody know what this is?"

Tapping his watch, Lieutenant Wells projected an image in the air in front of the recruits. It showed a massive monster, close to twelve feet high, with thick, furry legs, massive hulking arms, and a large, tooth-filled snout. Six insectoid legs extended from its back, and large patches of its body were covered in thick chitin plates. Mark recognized it instantly, having seen a slightly smaller version of the creature as a frozen corpse in Abrams's warehouse. Noah's and Phoenix's hands went up as well, along with those of a couple of the other recruits, whose names Mark didn't know. Looking over them, Wells pointed at Phoenix. "What do you think?"

"That's a war bear, sir."

"Good, can you tell what rank it is?"

Her hand slowly going down, Phoenix shook her head. Mark put his hand down as well, and soon, only Noah's hand remained in the air.

"Noah?"

"It's a B-ranked war bear, sir," Noah said calmly. "You can tell from the number of joints on the six insect legs on its back."

"Correct. War bears start at D rank, and you'll see a joint on their extra appendages for every rank above that. You can see there are two joints. It's B ranked. Do you know what you should do if you ever see a war bear with three joints?"

"Start running," Glenn shouted, causing all the recruits to laugh.

"No," Lieutenant Wells replied with a savage grin. "Nothing, because you'll already be dead. You just might not know it. All right, what about this one?"

The image in the air changed, revealing an eight-legged scorpion with a massive stinger on its tail and four sets of pincers. Apart from the hard armor that covered its body, the scorpion monster shared nothing in common with the war bear they had just seen, but Mark knew that both were Exlian, and moreover, they were Exlian that could be found in the local area. He had never seen a murder scorpion before, but they were a favorite of the entertainment channels, and so he had seen plenty of them on movies and shows.

"That is a murder scorpion, right?" Danny called out.

"That's right," Lieutenant Wells said. "This is a murder scorpion. They live mostly south of here, southwest to be exact. There's a swamp where they have their nest, and they venture out to search for prey. A couple years back, we had a particularly nasty attack on the southern wall that was made up primarily of murder scorpions. They're quick buggers, hard to hit because of the way their armor is shaped, and will tear you apart faster than you can blink. Worse, they swarm, so if you see one, you should assume there are a dozen more right under your feet. Now, let me introduce you to another warrior Exlian. This is what we call winged death. It's really just a murder scorpion with wings."

The monster hanging in the air in front of Mark and the others looked exactly like the previous monster, though without one of its pairs of claws. In the missing claws' place was a pair of large wings that looked like those of dragonflies, which could vibrate at high frequency to allow the scorpion a few minutes of flight. Laughing at the expressions on the recruits' faces, Lieutenant Wells turned to the next slide on the projector.

"All right, enough about warriors, though. We have other Exlian we have to worry about as well. The category above warrior is the terror level. Terror-level Exlian aren't actually different from warriors. They're simply A-ranked warriors. However, just as with the empowered, when an Exlian reaches the A rank, they go through a qualitative change, becoming considerably more powerful, so powerful that it often takes at least four empowered on their same level to take them down, or the might of one of the five, an S-ranked empowered. Everything you know about warrior Exlian can be assumed about terror-ranked Exlian, just multiplied by ten or more."

"There are two other types of Exlian that are important to understand. The first are the matrons. These are tremendously powerful Exlian, though their power doesn't lie in their ability to fight. That's what the warrior caste is for. The matrons instead act as control centers, and they are what transform the Exlian from mindless monsters into a lethal force capable of just as much discipline as our military. The matrons tend to favor brutish swarm tactics, as the main strength of their forces comes from the weight of numbers, but don't be fooled. The matrons are just as smart as we are, and craftier too. They know how to set ambushes. They understand scouting and denial of information. And worse, they seem to be getting smarter all the time, adapting to our tactics and devising new strategies of their own.

"Additionally, matrons have an innate ability to control mana, much like an energy controller, though their manipulation of it is fairly crude. They're able to summon shields and unleash a variety of mana blasts. If you ever come up against one, don't assume that it's going to be helpless. Now, our final type of Exlian is a bit of an oddity, as it isn't an Exlian per se. The nest."

Clicking his watch, Wells brought up an image of a strange black blob that pulsed and shimmered, stretching this way and that.

"The Exlian nest, which is where Exlian spawn, absorbs biological material and transforms it into Exlian. The primary job of a drone is to feed the nest, pulling biological material to it, where it will be engulfed and absorbed. Nests have no intelligence and can only ever produce a single type of Exlian. We have no idea how they form, though some people suspect they spawn from dead matrons, who use their tremendous psychic ability before they die to transform themselves, but again, that hasn't been confirmed and is only a theory. What we do know, however, is that nests need to be destroyed wherever they are found. They can grow indefinitely, and the larger they are, the faster they can produce Exlian. Let me show you."

Tapping his watch, Lieutenant Wells pulled up a video, which began to play. It appeared to be from the perspective of someone looking through a powerful set of binoculars, as Mark could see a faint shimmer of mana around the edges of the screen. Whoever it was peered into a swamp, and soon Mark noticed something odd. There was a dark shape in the water, and as the view zoomed outward, Mark realized that it covered the land as well. A massive blob, a few hundred feet across and as tall as a small hill. It vibrated endlessly, and every few minutes, a murder scorpion would come crawling out.

"How do you even kill something like that?" Danny asked, his voice a deep rumble.

"Good question," Lieutenant Wells said. "All you can really do is throw as much firepower at it as you possibly can, which is exactly what you'll see here in just a sec."

As the video continued, a figure suddenly zoomed into view, flying freely through the air. It was a man with close-cropped dark hair and a square jaw. He wore a tight mana suit, bright gold, with a white sun emblazoned on the chest, allowing everyone to identify him immediately. Coming to a stop over the massive nest, he stretched out his hand, and a single spot of light, so bright it hurt to look at even through the video, manifested in front of his finger. From it, a storm of beams rained down, cutting through the dark mass below, setting great portions of the nest on fire. It writhed in pain and began stretching out massive tentacles to try to envelop him, but with a wave of his hand, a curtain of light fell around him, chopping the tentacles into tiny pieces that swiftly turned to ash.

This was Ra, the undisputed number one on the empowered list. His power, as far as the public knew, was light control at the absolute level. Watching as he battled against the massive nest, Mark found himself holding his breath. He knew that the S-ranked heroes were in a league of their own, but seeing one fight was like watching a god descend to earth.

For almost ten minutes, the recruits watched in absolute silence as Ra obliterated the nest, using beams of light to incinerate massive swaths of it, all the while fighting off swarming flying scorpions and sparing the occasional beam for the murder scorpions rushing about below. Eventually, the video ended, and Wells gave the recruits a moment to process what they had seen.

"None of us are going to get to that level of power," Lieutenant Wells said, shaking his head. "But that doesn't mean we can't get strong enough to fight against the nests. Whenever we find one, depending on its location and what type of nest it is—and yes, there are different types of nests—we deploy one of the top five heroes to ensure its demise.

"Now, a common question we get is, 'If the Exlian are so powerful, how come we haven't been overrun already?' After all, aren't their numbers endless? They should be able to just drown us in bodies. And the answer to that is one of the greatest mysteries around. The Exlian appear to have factions of their own, and often the forces generated from different nests are seen fighting each other. Matrons war against other matrons, and warriors clash against other warriors. We've even had some success out in the wild pitting different Exlian factions against each other. Currently, there are five or so factions around our city, and they fight each other as often as they fight us, but we'll learn more about that later."

After lunch, there was more theory, this time taught by Lieutenant Cox and focused on how to identify Exlian weaknesses. Even though he had already learned much of the information the lieutenant shared from his work with Abrams, Mark still found it fascinating. The afternoon passed swiftly, and after the training camp ended, Mark swung by the restaurant to say hi to Sky and get some dinner before going to work with Abrams. She looked rather distracted and quite tired, so Mark pulled her to sit down with him for a moment. "Everything okay?"

She stared blankly at Mark for a moment and then looked down, biting her lip. "Yeah, everything is fine."

"You sure? Doesn't feel that way."

"I'm fine, Mark. Everything is fine."

Spearing a bite of meat with his fork, Mark smirked. "Funny thing about that word, 'fine.' The more you use it, the less believable it is. I may have believed you the first time, but the second time told me something was wrong, and the third told me that something was really wrong. What's going on?"

Grimacing, Sky leaned back and rubbed her arm, turning to stare out the window so she wouldn't have to look at Mark. He didn't push her, and they sat in silence while he kept eating. It wasn't until after he had finished that she spoke, her voice low.

"I'm just having a bit of trouble with one of my neighbors.

I . . . I don't live in a nice neighborhood, and one of my neighbors has been pretty annoying. But it's really not that big a deal. Look, you have to get to your job, and I have to get to work. Thanks for wanting to talk."

Flashing a smile, Sky pushed back her chair and got up, leaving Mark staring after her. He didn't for a minute believe that whatever Sky was going through was that simple, but he didn't know how to find out more without prying.

"You look like you got dumped," Jason said, sneering as he walked by.

Rolling his eyes, Mark tapped out a quick message on his watch and took his dishes to the back. He got to the warehouse with plenty of time to change and was ready to go five minutes before seven, but just as they were about to start, his watch vibrated.

With a snort, Abrams shook his head. "You can answer it. I see you looking at it, and if you can't concentrate, your work will be sloppy."

Embarrassed, Mark stepped back from the table where the frozen corpse of the large drone they were about to cut open lay and opened the message.

JOE

You know that sort of thing is illegal, right? But yes, I know someone who can keep an eye on her for a couple days. Most of the guys are getting restless, so this might be good for them. If I wasn't busy, I'd be tempted to do it myself. When does she get off her shift?

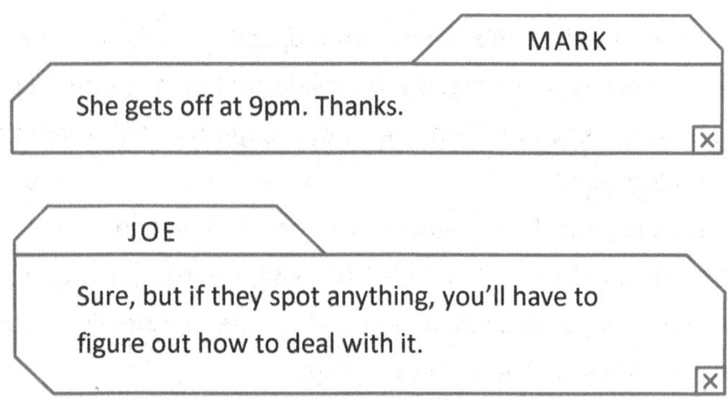

Closing the message, Mark rushed back to the table, smiling apologetically to his master, relieved that Joe was able to help. Turning off his watch, he took it off and put it to the side. "I'm ready."

"Good. Because we've got a long night and a lot of corpses to deal with."

By the time Mark got done, it was well after two a.m., and his hands ached terribly. Jason's Pub was already closed, and after peering in the window to make sure no one was there, Mark opted to get a warm drink from a nearby convenience store. When he turned on his watch to pay for the drink, he saw half a dozen messages, all from Joe.

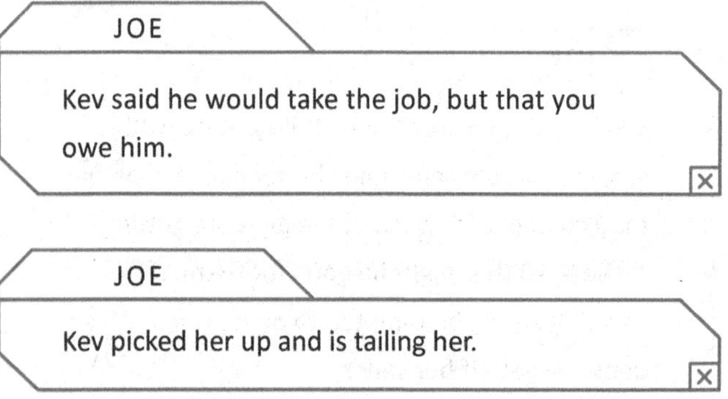

JOE

Ha! He got spotted. Seems she's really cagey.

JOE

We pulled Kev and got Perry to track her. He won't get spotted.

JOE

Some rough guys are hanging out near her route. They're on the lookout for someone.

JOE

Mark, when you get this, you should call me.

The last message was sent at just after one a.m. Holding his scalding coffee with both hands, Mark opened up his watch and hit Joe's image. There was a beep, and Joe's face appeared on his watch.

"Mark, I'm sending you an address. The guys from that message were on the lookout, and they were waiting for Sky. They dragged her into a club. Get here as soon as you can."

Hailing a cab with his watch, Mark gave the address that Joe had sent him and asked the driver to get there as fast as possible. Doing his best not to imagine the worst-case scenario, Mark kept himself occupied with warming up his stiff fingers, just in case there was a fight. The twenty minutes it took to get to the bar was torturous, and Mark jumped out even before the car had come to a stop.

"Over here."

Standing in the shadow of a nearby building was a small group, all dressed in nondescript dark clothing. Joe was there, along with Kevin, one of the twins who Mark had met, and a plain-looking young man whose face was strangely hard to remember.

"Mark, this is Perry. Perry, my little brother."

"Hey, kid."

Pointing across the street toward a neon sign, Joe spoke quietly. "Sky is in that club. She went in with a group of five guys who looked like a lot of the thugs that roam the outskirts. Her route home was a couple blocks from here, but they had spread out and then dragged her this way. One of them had his arm around her. Black hair, spiked, a couple piercings. You should go and get her out, because she didn't look happy to be going in there."

Slapping Mark on the shoulder hard enough to stagger him, Kevin grinned. "Your chance to play the hero. We'd help you, but if a couple Rangers started killing locals, there would be hell to pay."

"There will be no killing," Joe said firmly. "Mark, we'll be coming in as well, but we won't be acting unless everything goes bad. Kevin is right—if we so much as throw a punch, this could escalate really quickly. Kevin will go in first. Mark, you're next. Perry and I will follow. Keep your eyes open, and whatever you do, don't provoke."

"Sounds like you have done this sort of thing before," Mark said with a smile.

Chuckling, Kevin nodded, and Perry flashed a sly grin. Only Joe didn't crack a smile, but that was because he already had his game face on.

Watching Kevin head across the street, Perry glanced at Mark and then poked Joe. "He part of it?"

"No."

"Look at him. Not even a hint of nerves. He'd be great for—"

With a glare that could melt a hole in steel, Joe silenced Perry. "I said no."

"Fine, I get it. Pretend I didn't say anything."

Unsure what that had been about, Mark headed for the club when he got Joe's nod. The building was plain, with no windows and only a single sign hanging above the worn door. The sickly sweet smell of alcohol, tobacco, and regret hit Mark as he pulled the door open, along with a blast of air warm with sweat. He couldn't imagine anyone, let alone Sky, coming to a place like this of their own volition. The volume of the place let him know how mistaken he was, and as he stood in the club's entrance, trying to get used to the din and the dim lights, he felt someone brush past him.

"Back left corner. There is an emergency exit down the bathroom hallway. Leads into the back alley."

Mark heard Kevin's voice clear as day, but when he looked around, he couldn't see the large man anywhere, leaving him stumped. With a new appreciation for his brother's friends, Mark focused on what was important and headed for the back corner of the club, where a bunch of semicircular couches were arranged along the wall. He spotted Sky almost immediately, and she saw him as well, a panicked expression flashing across her face.

Just then, the man next to her tried to put his arm around her, and the panic turned into annoyance. As Mark walked over, she pushed the dark-haired man away and tried to get up, but he grabbed her waist. Two of the thugs who were sitting on the opposite ends of the couch stood up as Mark got close and stepped forward to block him.

"Slow down, champ. You—"

Whatever the thug was going to say was interrupted as Sky grabbed a bottle from the table and swung it as hard as she could at the black-haired man grabbing her. The crash of shattering glass cut through the din, silencing everyone nearby and causing the two thugs facing Mark to spin around. Wrenching herself free, Sky vaulted over the table in one smooth motion, slipping between the two thugs, who were staring at their drenched and bleeding boss in shock. Mark was just as caught off guard as everyone else, but when Sky grabbed his arm, he turned to run after her.

The dark-haired man, who had managed to lift his hand in time to keep the bottle from shattering on his head, let out a furious scream, pointing at Sky and Mark, who were pushing their way through the dense crowd. "Get them!"

Spotting the hallway that led to the restrooms, Mark switched directions and pulled Sky after him. Bursting through the back door into the alleyway, he hesitated, trying to decide which way to go. She didn't hesitate at all and grabbed his sleeve as she sprinted toward the street. Just before they made it around the corner, the thugs burst out of the doorway and looked around wildly. "They're going that way!"

Feeling his wrist vibrate as they ran down the street, Mark glanced down at it and saw messages streaming in.

KEVIN

Whoa, she's feisty. I like it.

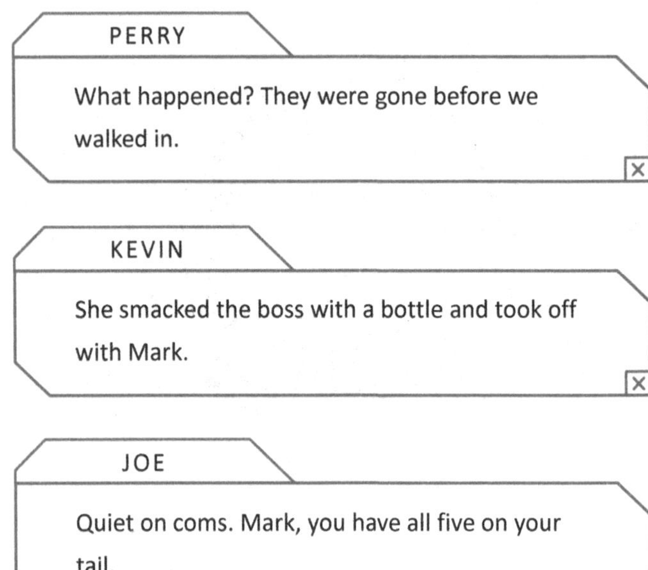

Sky was surprisingly fast, but it soon became clear to Mark that they weren't going to be able to lose their pursuers. The black-haired one who Sky had hit was catching up quickly, and his goons were trailing close behind. Glancing back, Mark took a deep breath and moved closer to Sky. "Sorry."

"What? Hey—!"

Scooping Sky up, Mark lengthened his stride and tore down the street, moving almost twice as fast as he had been a moment before. There was a startled shout behind him as the thugs started to fall behind. Seeing a corner up ahead, Mark took it so fast he nearly slammed into the wall, but he managed to turn just enough, running along the wall for a few feet before dropping back down to the street. Sky was holding on for dear life, her arms and legs wrapped around his waist and neck in a death grip as they left their pursuers behind.

When they were a couple of blocks ahead, Mark slowed to a jog and then to a stop, breathing heavily. Stretching out his hand to stabilize himself against a wall, he took a deep breath, then another, and felt his active recovery kick in. "You can get down now."

Sky was still wrapped around him, her eyes screwed shut, but at his words, she let go, tumbling to the ground and scrambling away. Mark thought he saw a blush on her face, but it was too dark to tell, and by the time she had straightened up and brushed herself off, she was back to normal.

"You're really strong."

Taken aback by Sky's sudden declaration, Mark slowly nodded. "It comes with being empowered."

"You're fast too. I wish I was that fast. Ha, then I could run away properly."

Spotting a bench in the distance, Mark pointed at it. "Want to sit down for a moment? Maybe tell me what is going on?"

"We better keep moving. Craig won't give up that easily."

Mark fell in beside Sky as they started walking, their path lit by the glow of the streetlights. "Was that Craig? The guy you hit with the bottle?"

"Yeah. He is . . . a guy I knew when I was little. We lost touch for a long time, and he just moved into the area."

Falling silent, Sky glanced at Mark, tucking a strand of her hair behind her ear. "Hey, Mark?"

"Yeah?"

"Thanks. For coming, I mean. Were the people following me earlier your friends?"

Rubbing the back of his neck, Mark nodded. "Yeah. They were supposed to stay out of sight. Hope they didn't freak you out."

"They did a little, though it isn't their fault. I've got a bit of a knack for knowing when I'm being watched." Sky's words were accompanied by a sly smile that set Mark's heart thumping. A blush followed as she peeked at him from the corner of her eyes. "It lets me know when someone is staring at me whenever I enter the room."

"Ha, well, that's embarrassing. I was hoping you wouldn't notice," Mark said.

As they came around the corner of the block, whatever Sky was about to say died on her lips. Spread across the street were Craig and his four goons. Sky grabbed Mark's arm, but before they could back up, another group emerged behind them, trapping them neatly. As the thugs closed in, Sky spoke in a whisper.

"I know you are strong, but be careful. Craig is dangerous."

"Is he empowered?"

Sky hesitated longer than Mark thought normal, but when he looked at her, she shook her head. "No, but he might as well be. Just be careful."

Stalking forward with an ugly expression on his face, Craig paid no attention to Sky, focusing instead on Mark. "You looking to die, kid?"

Facing down a dangerous-looking thug and nearly a dozen of his henchmen in a dark street in the middle of the night should have been a scary thing, but once again, Mark's fear was conspicuously absent. Instead, he felt a faint excitement that seemed to grow with every passing second, along with the disquieting hunger. Reaching up, he touched his necklace as he smirked at Craig. "Whoa, scary. You often assault people in the middle of the night? Because it seems like you've got it down to a science."

Frowning, Craig stopped a couple of feet from Mark, peering at him. "Give us the girl, and you can leave. No need for you to stick your nose in our business."

"Sky's business is my business," Mark replied flatly, his arm flashing silver as it transformed into titanium.

Seeing the transformation, a few of the thugs muttered something and began to back up, but Craig laughed and took a step forward. "I was wondering where your overconfidence was coming from. Turns out you got a fancy power. Well, you're not the only one who's got a fancy ability."

Craig's shoulders tensed up, and Mark lifted his hands and shifted in front of Sky, preparing for an attack. Just then, a door opened nearby, and a rowdy group of young men and women spilled out into the street. Distracted by the sudden noise, Craig hesitated and looked over, and the group slowly quieted down.

"Mark?" One of the young men stepped forward, coming into the light of one of the streetlights.

"Hey, Noah. Fancy running into you here."

His hands in his pockets, Noah sauntered over, looking every inch the spoiled rich kid. His bodyguard was nowhere in sight, but Mark had no doubt that he was lurking nearby.

"Noah, come on, we're going to be late," one of the young women called out, clearly not interested in getting involved in whatever was going on, but Noah waved her off.

"You go ahead. I'm going to talk with Mark a bit."

"Better listen to your friend before you get hurt," Craig growled.

Raising an eyebrow, Noah came to a stop next to Mark, one hand still in his pocket. The top buttons of his shirt were undone, and a gold chain flashed as it caught the light. Mark felt a twinge of envy as he stared at Noah, half disgusted by how cool he looked.

"Sounds like there is a problem here," Noah said, his eyes raking across the gathered thugs. "I'm really good at solving problems, so I'm going to stay."

Noah's friends had already moved down the street and soon stepped around the corner, vanishing into the night. Craig hesitated as he watched them go, and that cost him the initiative as Mark suddenly stepped forward. "If we're going to fight, let's do it. Otherwise, run off and don't bother Sky again."

Sneering, Craig hunched, and his hand went to his belt, emerging with a short dagger. Mark wasn't sure if Craig was posturing and didn't care either. His foot slid forward, and his fist lashed out as Craig started to raise his weapon. Mark's fist caught Craig on the cheek, snapping his head to the side and causing him to stumble. Mark immediately lunged for the next closest thug, kicking him in the stomach as he tried to close in.

The thugs behind them began to yell and charge, and Noah blurred, his body moving too quickly for most eyes to follow. There was a snap of breaking bones; one of the thugs fell to the ground, clutching his leg, and another was thrown backward, slamming into the street and sliding into the curb.

Mark still had three other thugs closing in on him, and Craig was starting to straighten up, so he pressed his advantage, blocking a blow from one of the thugs with his titanium arm and striking the thug in the throat. Instinct caused him to dodge to the side as a pipe whistled past his head, missing his skull by less than an inch. Annoyed, Mark grabbed it and shoved hard.

Ripped from his attacker's grasp, the pipe nailed the thug in the solar plexus, dropping him instantly. Spinning around, Mark blocked Craig's stab and snapped a quick kick to Craig's knee, hoping to drop him, but Craig twisted his leg and pressed in closer. The other thugs were all down, even the ones who had been about to attack Mark, and Noah was standing by Sky, adjusting his cuffs as she stared at him with wide eyes.

Unreasonably annoyed, Mark dropped the pipe, grabbed Craig's knife, and squeezed, his titanium fingers crushing the blade and a couple of Craig's fingers. With a sharp scream, Craig jerked back, cradling his broken fingers as he stared at Mark. An intense feeling of danger washed over Mark, and he jumped back, his hands coming up as Craig's hunched shoulders suddenly twisted, two more long arms growing from them. Craig's face transformed as well, his mouth extending outward to form a wide maw filled with sharp teeth that snapped toward Mark's neck.

The extra arms that sprouted from Craig's shoulders ended in sharp talons that slashed down at Mark, but he brought up his arm to block them, staggering as the blows struck. Craig's transformation had imbued him with increased strength as well as speed, and Mark found himself hard pressed to avoid the raking claws and snapping jaws as he stumbled backward. Thankfully, Noah dashed in from the side, slamming a punch into Craig's face that sent the monstrous thug tumbling sideways.

Bouncing to his feet, Craig let out a roar, and another pair of arms burst from his back, curling up from underneath his arms. Looking less and less human, the monster rushed forward, and Mark and Noah moved to meet him. They didn't need to waste time with words as they coordinated their attacks. Mark knew that when he attacked low, Noah would attack high, and when Noah pressed forward aggressively, he could retreat.

Landing a solid kick on Craig's shoulder, Mark dodged the counterattack as Noah's punch broke a couple of ribs. Grunting in pain, Craig tried to retreat, but Mark kept with him. Keeping his fingers on his left hand straight, he swiped, lacerating one of Craig's arms and causing a spray of blood. A faint shield sprang up around Noah, blocking the blood before it could get on his clothes as he kicked Craig's knee, driving the monster to the ground.

When Mark heard a faint rumble, his instincts kicked in and he grabbed Noah, yanking him backward as Craig's body began squirming and two more sets of arms burst from his back, grasping for their feet. Looking like something straight out of a nightmare, Craig jumped to his feet, no sign of sanity in his eyes, which had grown to nearly triple their original size and had multiple pupils.

"This is the last time I stop to help you," Noah grumbled as Craig spread his arms and roared.

"If we make it out of this, I'll owe you one."

"*When* we make it out," Noah corrected softly.

Any damage they had done to Craig's monstrous body had already been healed, and just when Mark was wondering how they were going to beat him, a car dropped out of the sky. It slammed into Craig, crushing him to the ground as Mark and Noah stared in shock. There was a muffled roar, and arms gripped the bottom of it, lifting it into the air, but before Craig could lift it up all the way, a stocky figure dropped on top of it, driving it back into the ground.

"Looks like you found a live one," Kevin said, grinning.

The sound of tortured metal had him springing to the side as Craig ripped the car in half, but no sooner had Kevin landed than he dashed forward, shoulder checking Craig so hard the two halves of the car were left hanging in the air as the monster cannonballed into the wall. Catching one of the car halves, Kevin grimaced as the other half clattered to the ground.

"Perry!"

Mark heard his brother's voice, then an answering voice from below their feet. "On it."

Rising up out of the street like a ghost, Perry extended his hand toward the stunned monster, mana coursing around it. There was a rumble, and the cracked bricks rose like a wave, wrapping Craig up until he was entirely covered. Tossing the remains of the car aside, Kevin sprinted over, picked up the bundle of bricks that trapped Craig, threw a wink at Mark, and then vanished into the night with a leap that carried him over the building. Feeling a tug on his shirt, Mark looked back and saw Sky staring after Kevin. "Was that . . . ?"

"Yeah, that was one of my brother's friends. This is another."

"Perry's the name. Pleased to meet both of you."

Joe came walking out of a nearby alleyway, his expression

somber and his eyes raking over the scene, as if he was looking for something. "Are you three okay?"

"Yes," Mark said, glancing at the other two, who each nodded. "But what was that?"

"The sin of New Emery," Perry spat, his expression dark. "Evidence of the corrupt—"

"Nothing you need to worry about," Joe said firmly. "Consider it a dangerous infection. Thankfully, it's not contagious, so you don't need to worry about it spreading."

"You sure about that, Joe?" Perry asked, obviously angry at being interrupted. "It seems like it's spreading to me."

"Perry, can we talk about this later?"

From the way Perry's jaw clenched, Mark thought that punches might start flying, so he stepped closer to Joe, watching Perry closely. Catching sight of his stare, Perry sighed, the tension leaving his shoulders as he held up his hands. "Fine. But we will talk about it later, believe me. You kids stay safe."

The ground under Perry's feet turned to soup, and he was gone, melded back into the ground. Turning to look at Joe, Mark raised his eyebrows. "Care to explain what is going on?"

Turning away, Joe shook his head. "No, not really. Sky might be able to give you a hint, though. Don't worry about Craig. He won't bother any of you again. I've got to go, and I might be gone for a day or two, but I'll be in touch."

Ignoring his brother's stare, Joe turned and jogged into the night, leaving Sky, Noah, and Mark standing in the street amid a bunch of groaning thugs. There was a long moment of silence between them, and then, with a laugh, Noah waved his hand. "Honestly? I don't really want to know. Seems like a lot of trouble, if you ask me. Sky, it was nice to see you again. See you tomorrow, Mark. Don't be late."

Shoving his hands into his pockets, Noah sauntered down the

street as his bodyguard emerged from a nearby shadow. As Noah walked past, he jerked a thumb over his shoulder. "Clean this up."

"Yes, sir."

Bandman walked over to one of the thugs on the ground and placed a foot on his chest. "You and the young lady are welcome to be on your way, Mr. Fields. I'll take care of everything here."

Sky was still holding on to Mark's sleeve, so he took her hand and led her away. It had been an eventful night, and when he saw a bench, he pulled her to it, and they sat down. He didn't know what to say, so he just stayed quiet, and Sky did too, until a black shadow jumped up in her lap and blinked up at her.

"Oh, hey, Mime."

Staring at his cat, who had appeared out of nowhere, Mark scratched his head as Sky started to scratch Mime's. Relaxing noticeably, Sky didn't look up at Mark as she started speaking.

"Thank you again. You, Noah, your brother, and his friends. None of you had to help, but you did. So thank you."

"Happy to."

"You know, sometimes things you've left behind come back to haunt you. Craig is . . . was . . . one of those things."

Hearing the hesitation in Sky's voice, Mark reached over to touch her leg gently. "Sky, you don't have to say anything if you don't want to. You're safe, and you can believe my brother when he says that Craig won't bother you anymore. Whatever is going on with him, Joe will take care of it. He is well connected through the military."

With a sad smile, Sky stroked Mime's stomach. "I know. I just wish . . ."

She never completed her wish, as Mark's watch vibrated loudly in the still night, and the moment was gone. Silencing his watch with a frown, Mark opened his mouth to ask her what she wished, but Sky shoved Mime into his arms and jumped up from the bench. "It's late and you have training tomorrow. I'm not too far from here, so you don't need to walk me home. I'll see you later, Mark. Thanks again."

Before Mark could protest, Sky had jogged around the corner and was gone, leaving him alone with Mime. Looking down at the cat, Mark saw Mime staring at him disdainfully. With a sigh, he stood up. "Yeah, I know, Mime. I know."

Mentally exhausted, Mark took a taxi back to his house and collapsed into bed, where he spent a fitful two hours dreaming of fighting ravenous Exlian drones. He slept in the following morning, finally managing to get some real rest, and then headed to the training camp. Noah clearly hadn't told anyone about their escapades the night before, and though he was still quite aloof, he picked a seat next to Mark at lunch and dinner and even added a few comments to the conversation.

As soon as dinner was over, Mark raced to the pub to see Sky. She still had thirty minutes until her break, and instead of waiting, Mark headed to a nearby shopping center. After looking around, he found the store he wanted and headed in to talk to the tired-looking young man at the counter.

"Hello, sir. Welcome to Everett's Custom Watches. How can I help you?"

"I'm looking for a new watch."

"Getting an upgrade, are we?"

"No. Not for me."

Mark glanced down at his watch. Even though it was an older

model, it had been a present from his brother, and he had no desire to get rid of it.

"I want a gift for somebody else. This will be their first watch."

"First watch. Got it. Do you need parental controls set up?"

"No, just a new, clean watch."

"Sure. What sort of model do you have in mind?"

Since he was flush with cash after selling the shards, Mark didn't worry too much about the price. He found a white one that he thought Sky would like but second-guessed himself and swapped it for an expensive but more rugged-looking watch that didn't stand out, and after having it activated, he paid the 6,000 credits and had the clerk wrap it up. He was sure that if he brought her to the store to try to pick out a watch, she would never accept it, so all he could do was hope he had picked correctly. He was leaning against the wall in the alleyway when Sky got off, staring up at the strip of dark sky that peeked between the alley walls.

"Sorry you had to wait so long," Sky said, still drying off her hands.

"It's no problem," Mark replied, straightening up. "I found plenty to do."

Sky looked slightly embarrassed as he approached, and Mark felt as if an ambiguous air were starting to gather around them. Starting to get embarrassed himself, he coughed and jerked a thumb over his shoulder. "Are you hungry for ice cream? I saw that there was a cart still open a couple of streets over."

"Sure, ice cream would be great," Sky replied, instinctively reaching for her wallet.

Though Mark wanted to offer to pay, he knew how independent Sky was, and considering he was hoping to force her to accept the watch he had purchased, he knew that offering to pay for her ice cream would only make her feel more uncomfortable. Pretending he didn't see as she surreptitiously peeked at the contents of her wallet, Mark led the way out of the alley and down the block. The box, squirreled away in his pocket, bumped against his side, sending waves of nervousness shooting through him. He hadn't thought about it much when he had picked out the watch, only thinking that it would be a great gift for her, but now that it was time to hand it over, he found himself freezing up. As always, Sky was strangely attuned to his fluctuating feelings, and after they had walked half a block, she looked over at him. "Is everything okay, Mark?"

Suddenly remembering that the last time they had been together, they had been facing down a monster, Mark felt like his concerns were silly. He rubbed his nose and nodded. "Yes, everything's fine. You know, it's crazy how I can face down someone trying to kill me with no fear, but then I get into a situation like this, and my heart is racing a hundred miles a minute."

Before his courage could fail him, he pulled the box out of his pocket and held it out to Sky. "I got you something, and I don't know why I'm so nervous about giving it to you, but I am. Anyway, I hope you like it. It's nothing big, but I think you'll find it useful."

Giving him a curious look, Sky took the box and cracked it open, freezing in place when she saw the brand-new watch inside. Mark had looked down after handing the box over, and it was only after he had gone ahead a few steps that he realized Sky wasn't next to him.

Turning around, he saw that she was still staring wide eyed into the box, her face rather pale.

"If you don't like it, we can go and exchange it for another model," he said.

"Mark, I—"

"Hold on," he interrupted. "Before you protest, let me explain. More than once, I've wanted to send you a message, to either hang out or just to chat, but I have no way of communicating with you. And last night, if you could have sent me a message,

I could have helped you avoid that situation better. Well, I got a bit of a bonus a couple days ago, and so I thought it would be a great opportunity to fix that problem. It'd be really nice to be able to contact you without coming to the restaurant and waiting around for your shift to end. There was another watch at the store. It was white, and I think you probably would have liked it better, because it was a lot prettier, but then I thought this one might be less eye catching, and I thought you'd prefer something more subdued, because, well . . ."

As he realized he was babbling, Mark's voice slowly faded, and Sky finally looked up, her eyes wet with tears. Flinching, Mark was caught completely off guard when she took three big steps forward and wrapped her arms around him, squeezing him tightly.

"Thank you," she said after a moment, her voice mixed with a sob.

Stepping back, she sniffed, wiped at her eyes, and gave an embarrassed laugh. "Thank you, Mark. This is a very considerate gift, and I love it."

"If you don't like the color, we can always go back."

"No," she said. "A simple watch like this definitely suits me better. Where I live, having anything flashy is a good way to get robbed."

"Yeah, that's what I thought," Mark said. "Not that the fancier watch wouldn't have suited you, I mean, but that this one might be a bit more practical."

"And I love practical," Sky replied. "Can you show me how to work this?"

"Sure. Let's go get our ice cream, and I'll help you set it up."

Sky demanded Mark let her pay for the ice cream, and he didn't argue, figuring it would help her accept the gift of the watch more easily. She couldn't stop playing with it, and when they had set up all the functions, she sent him half a dozen messages in a row. It was almost time for him to go to the warehouse when she suddenly stopped messing with her new watch and turned to look at Mark, who was watching her.

"Something wrong?" he asked, noticing her troubled expression.

"No, but I thought I should explain some things. About last night."

"Sky, you don't have to explain anything. We ran into a guy you used to know, who had a strange power. That's it."

"That's not it."

Grabbing Mark's arm, Sky leaned back, her eyes lifting to the darkening sky. The sun was just going down, and the last of its rays painted the clouds in pink and red hues.

"I told you I knew Craig, right? Well, that's because we went to the same school. It was a school for orphans whose parents had been killed in a wave. Orphans like me. Craig and I. We were good friends. He was a couple years older than me and really took care of me."

Sky didn't speak quickly, but it was clear she had thought long and hard about each of these words, so Mark didn't interrupt.

"None of us were empowered. We were just normal kids. But it wasn't a normal school. It was called Saint Vincent's and was run and sponsored by the city. And there was something going on behind the scenes. Something terrifying. They were constantly giving us medical examinations and shots, and kids would go missing all the time. Usually after having an 'episode.' After they vanished, they'd never show up again. Craig had one of these episodes, and I happened to see it. I was hiding in the room, and he got into a fight with another student. Suddenly, those arms grew out of Craig's back and . . ."

"Sky—"

"No, this is important. Craig killed him. Using those arms. I was hiding under a bed, and he turned and looked toward me, but before he could come and kill me, soldiers came and took him away. They injected him with something to make him transform back. Once it was clear, I ran as fast as I could and never went back. I've lived on my own ever since then, and I thought that was behind me until Craig suddenly showed up again."

Letting out a low whistle, Mark was at a loss for words. Sky's story was like something out of a horror movie, but Mark didn't think she was lying.

"The school closed down about ten years ago," Sky continued, her voice quiet, "but there are still more schools that haven't. I was going to tell you all this before you gave me the watch, because I think it's important you know what you are getting involved with."

When Mark arrived at the warehouse, his mind was full of thoughts. So full that he missed a cut and was severely berated for it. After he had finished the corpse he was working on and cleaned his hands, he turned to Abrams. "Master, do you know of a school called Saint Vincent's?"

Looking up from the ingredients Mark had extracted, Abrams's forehead furrowed. "Saint Vincent's? Yeah, of course I do. That was where they were testing on those kids, right? Nasty case, that. Trying to cross human and Exlian DNA to create supersoldiers. That school was shut down, and a couple others like it. How did you even hear about it? That is ancient history, and I don't imagine the textbooks teach it."

Without waiting for a reply, Abrams pointed at one of the ingredients Mark had pulled out. "You weren't careful enough with the intestines. It's ruptured here and here, which means it's ruined. Let's pull it again."

Mark's days began to take on a regular rhythm, each day starting when he woke from his dream to begin his recovery training. Then, at nine, he would report to the training camp, where he would listen to lectures on Exlian and theories around the empowered until dinner was served. That was followed by a quick second dinner at the restaurant before diving into work with Abrams. At two in the morning, he would stagger back into his room, exhausted, and rapidly sink into a deep sleep, during which he would relentlessly practice the second stage of the Cutting Palm art.

Mark found the schedule genuinely exhausting, especially since his training with Joe meant that he could never eat his fill. After the first week, he genuinely thought about giving up, but he could see the small incremental progress he was making across the board, including in the strength of his will as he learned to ignore the gnawing pain in his stomach. Joe had been right. He had come to associate the feeling of hunger with a need—the need to eat. He'd assumed that if his stomach was hungry, it meant that he had no calories to burn, but that wasn't true; instead, it was an indicator that he needed to refill his biofuel meter.

When he began to think of it that way, he started to notice the various sorts of nuance in the feelings of hunger and got better at judging when he had to eat something, versus when his stomach simply wanted to be full. He was also making slow but steady progress with Abrams, thanks to his incessant practice in the dream world. He felt he was close to achieving a basic mastery of Cutting Palm technique, and once he did, he'd be able to use it in the real world, regardless of whether his hands were titanium.

He hadn't made any progress in improving his absorption power, but he wasn't too worried about it, as he had enough other things going on that it wasn't a priority. Plus, it was becoming increasingly clear to him that his ability did not work like most others. The mantras that everyone else used to focus and polish their power had no effect on him, leaving him unsure how to proceed.

In his downtime, Mark's thoughts often drifted to the strange encounter he'd had with Craig and the few words his master had spoken about Saint Vincent's. In truth, he had no idea what to do with the information and was smart enough to know that digging through the InfoWeb to try to find out more would be dangerous. Craig's uncontrollable mutation was a clear sign that whatever program had been in place at Saint Vincent's had some success, and the fact that he had lived to return and find Sky was troubling. Not knowing what to do, Mark did his best to forget about it, focusing instead on what was right in front of him.

Though his days were full and he was often exhausted, there were a few genuine bright spots. Hanging out with Sky every day at dinnertime had become a habit, and on the occasional weekday when she wasn't working, Mark found himself feeling a bit lonely. Spending more time with the other recruits and getting to know them better was fun as well, but what Mark looked forward to the most was every weekend, when he had a few hours during the day to spend on his secret alchemy project.

He had quickly realized that even if he wanted to scale his

elixir-upgrading operation, he had to worry about supply and demand. With enough capital to invest, he could produce B-ranked elixirs endlessly, but doing so would only benefit him in the short term. Every 10,000-credit C-ranked elixir could be turned into 38,000 credits of pure profit, but there wasn't enough demand for the elixir shards to maintain their high price.

After some research, he found an alchemical device that would allow him to recombine the shards and spent the 50,000 credits necessary to acquire it. Thankfully, it wasn't very big, and Joe was rather preoccupied these days, so Mark was able to sneak it into his room and set it up in his closet. He also installed a couple of shelves and began buying boxes of vials in bulk.

After four weeks had passed, Mark had almost a million credits in his account, along with close to twenty full vials of glimmering blue elixir. In the meantime, the market for shards had been almost completely tapped out. Only a couple of new requests appeared, and since Mark wasn't the only one selling shards, the price had begun to drop drastically. That had affected the cost of elixirs as a whole, so Mark simply quit selling, watching nervously until it restabilized.

Since he had enough resources to deal in whole vials now, he decided to avoid making more for the moment and just sell the stock that he had. He was currently sitting on another million credits' worth of elixirs stuffed in a box in his closet and had plenty of credits in the bank, so there wasn't a need to rush things. Having so much money also gave him the chance to experiment a bit. He was curious if he'd be able to upgrade a B-ranked elixir to an A-ranked elixir, but after investing 50,000 credits in a blue elixir, he found his blood had no effect. It took a couple of experiments, but eventually he realized that his blood wasn't potent enough.

This suggested that as he continued to grow in strength, he would eventually get to the point where it would be possible, but at the moment, he was limited in what he could do. He also considered simply downing the twenty bottles that he had, working to increase his strength as much as possible, but a rather crazy idea had captured his imagination. Instead of maxing out his resistance with the B-ranked elixirs, if he simply waited until he was strong enough to upgrade them to A-ranked elixirs, he'd be able to get the maximum benefit, increasing his strength by as close to 100 percent as possible. Joe had mentioned the powerful effect of the red A-ranked elixir he had swallowed, and Mark couldn't wait to have the chance to take another.

When the fifth week of training started, Mark's team headed to the armory to collect the gear they would use in their field deployment. For the last couple of weeks, they had been learning about gear and the various roles the different branches of the military filled. The Defense Force was divided into three broad categories of tanks, strikers, and support, and members carried mana weapons and used shields. The Rangers followed a similar model, though they were divided into advance scouts, heavy scouts, and support scouts, all of whom used a variety of weapons. Unlike the other two, the Engineering Corps only had two categories: field engineers, which was the role Lieutenant Wells held, and research engineers, who typically stayed back in the city and conducted scientific research.

Lieutenant Cox gathered Noah, Mark, Phoenix, Danny, Glenn, and Harper together, informing them that they were Alpha Team. The other twelve recruits in the program were divided, based on their numbers, into Beta and Gamma Team, led by Lieutenant Rene and Lieutenant Wells, respectively.

"You'll be with me today," Lieutenant Cox said, "though we'll be rotating over the next couple of weeks. The goal is going to be to get you a taste of what it's like to operate as each of the squads. Of course, we'll be in the dead zone, rather than out in the wilderness itself, so you don't have to worry too much. We'll start with a simple patrol. Let's get everybody into their mana suits, and then we'll move out."

Mark followed the others with considerable excitement. In fact, everyone, apart from Noah, who was never excited, and Phoenix, who appeared to have worn a mana suit before, was ecstatic to finally get the chance to wear one. Each mana suit was composed of three main pieces. A skintight layer that hugged Mark's body closely, showing every single well-defined muscle. Over that, a slightly looser layer that kept the wearer's body temperature even. Then finally, the actual armor itself, a heavily enchanted frame covered in light plates of armor. The suits that the recruits were using were the lightest variation of the mana suits and included all the basic features, including an air-filtration system, a communications array, and a built-in wrist blade.

Noah, unsurprisingly, was in his suit within a minute or two, casually checking its range of motion, while the other three struggled to even put the armor on. Mark had no trouble with the first two layers, but figuring out how to slip into the armor was much more complicated.

Danny had a lot of trouble getting the skintight suit up over his massive shoulders until Noah casually pointed out that it was too small. They had to order another one in a bigger size, much to the quartermaster's amusement. Noticing that Mark and Glenn were both struggling to get into their armor, Noah walked over and showed them how to lean it forward and work their arms in first before standing up and closing it around their backs.

The more time Mark had spent with Noah, the clearer it became that Noah wasn't anything like Mark had imagined. As rich as he was, he had no real ego to speak of; he simply didn't care what other people did or thought. He was quick to step forward and help, though he never appeared happy to be doing it, and he was just as likely to completely ignore someone talking to him as he was to give them a short, clipped answer. He had been the hardest of the team to get to know, but Mark still felt they were slowly developing some rapport, especially after fighting together.

Once everybody was in their suits, they walked out to join Lieutenant Cox, who wore his combat-tested military-issue battle armor, which left their training suits looking like tin cans. Glancing down at his wrist, Lieutenant Cox punched a number into a virtual keypad the enchantments on his armor projected, and Mark felt a slight hum as his armor's mana circuits activated.

"Normally, when you're joining a group with a suit, you'll have to link in. Since you're in training armor, I'm doing it for you, but typically, it involves generating a proprietary code to make sure that only those with permission have access to the channels. Our voice communicators are now linked, so remember, anything you say, other people can hear."

"Hey, why are you looking at me?" Glenn protested, causing a wave of laughter to sweep across the channel.

"All right, I'll explain our voice protocols as we go. For the moment, let's just get used to how the suits move. It's not too much different from regular walking, but when we speed up, you'll find there's a bit of a trick to it."

Lieutenant Cox began to bound toward the gate of the training camp, and the team ran after him. Noah, who had obviously used mana suits before, kept up easily, and Phoenix was only a step behind. The others had considerably more trouble. It was a strange sensation, as the suit both compensated for Mark's balance and caused him to accelerate explosively. Walking didn't trigger the enchantments, but as soon as he started to run, he took off like a shot, and he stumbled for quite a few steps before he realized that trying to catch his balance was what was throwing him off, and he simply accepted the fact that he was going to crash. As soon as he stopped instinctively trying to compensate for his forward momentum, the suit stabilized itself, and Mark found his footing, quickly catching up to Phoenix. It didn't take long for the others to get it either, though occasionally Danny would stumble slightly, because he was so large his suit didn't quite manage to catch him. As they ran, Lieutenant Cox gave feedback.

"Mark, there's a balance between letting the suit do the work and being an active user. You're doing a good job letting it control the balance, but you need to control the power. Otherwise, you won't be able to reach top speeds. Same goes for you, Danny, just the other way. When you're adding strength, you're overwhelming the gyroscopic enchantment. Instead, focus on keeping your balance a bit more, and lower the amount of force you're putting into each stride. Glenn, doing flips is not part of our protocol. Harper, you're doing great."

He didn't bother saying anything to Noah or Phoenix, who had settled right in and were cruising along without any trouble. After twenty minutes of running, everybody had gotten the hang of it, and they arrived at the wall, a massive defensive structure that looped around the entire city. Stopping at one of the gates, Lieutenant Cox flashed his wrist toward the scanner, and a moment later, a small opening rumbled up. "Let's go."

The team paused once more when they were all outside, and the gate shut behind them. Giving them a moment to look around, Lieutenant Cox gestured to the silent buildings in front of them. "Welcome to the dead zone."

In truth, it didn't look that much different from the city inside the wall, at least when it came to how things were laid out. They were surrounded by buildings, some multiple stories tall, some shorter, and Mark could see skyscrapers in the distance, all in various states of disrepair. This had once been part of Emery, the massive city that served as humanity's capital. Far in the distance, surrounding the dead zone, was another wall, much smaller and breached in many places.

"We'll be doing a simple circuit," Cox said, "with the specific goal of trying to see if we can find a drone so you can see a live specimen, but we won't be staying out past dark. Come on, I'll show you the route."

With a flick of his wrist, Lieutenant Cox sent a map to each member of the team, and Mark projected the map so he could study it. It showed a six-block area and had a simple red line traced through the streets, with arrows to show which direction they would be going.

"This close to the wall is usually pretty clear, but I'd expect to run into some drones. Let's go."

Lieutenant Cox led the way forward into the eerily quiet city, the only sound the crunch of their armored feet as they walked across the cracked asphalt. There were plenty of plants climbing up and through the buildings, and Joe's warning came to mind, though Mark didn't see anything particularly dangerous looking. As they continued, Mark tried to keep his head on a swivel, looking back and forth across the wide-open street. As they proceeded single file, Lieutenant Cox was at the front of the group, acting as point, with Noah and Glenn right behind him. Then came Mark, Phoenix, and Harper, with Danny bringing up the rear.

Occasionally, scattered among the debris, he would see signs of the previous inhabitants. A half-crushed cup in a corner. A scratched sign, mostly buried in a pile of rubble. A torn-open briefcase, barely recognizable after years out in the rain and sun. Mark could only imagine how terrifying it must have been for those who had lived and worked in this part of the city when the swarms of Exlian broke through the outer wall and charged down the streets. Many signs of that fight still lingered, even all these years later. Smashed windows, entire sections of buildings that had been gouged out by massive claws. Tunnels burrowed into the ground, chunks of concrete thrown this way and that. There was an apocalyptic feeling to it, and from the tension Mark could sense from the others, he knew they were feeling it as well.

Lieutenant Cox was the only one at ease; he seemed just as much at home amid the rubble as he did behind the city's giant wall. That made sense, as Mark knew that they weren't in any danger. Not only did they have Lieutenant Cox with them, a powerful B-ranked empowered, but they were still within striking distance of New Emery's defenses, and a team could be sent to retrieve them at a moment's notice if the situation went bad. Still, he couldn't help but feel heightened tension, which was strange, as he hadn't even been this tense when he faced a drone inside the city. Somehow putting on the armor and leaving the confines of the city wall made him nervous.

"Hold up at the corner," Lieutenant Cox commanded.

The group came to a stop, their metal-shod feet screeching to a halt on the pavement and sending sparks flying.

"Each branch of the military has its own way of dividing teams. Leaving the Engineering Corps aside, both the Defense Force and Rangers have advance scouting units; tanks who act as the frontline bulwark; strikers, who deal most of the damage; and then the support roles, which typically focus on crowd control, shielding, and healing. Of course, the different branches have different names for the roles, but those are the four overall categories. We'll be patrolling every day for the next two weeks, and while we're doing that, I want you to think about what role you would be best in. Now, let's go over commands."

For the rest of the afternoon, the lieutenant led them through their patrol route, pointing out various dangers to watch out for and drilling them on the commands until they could react swiftly enough for his satisfaction. When they reached the point farthest from the city wall, Lieutenant Cox called a halt once more and began tapping on his right wrist as he slowly turned his head. It was faint, but Mark could feel little pulses of mana spreading out around them.

After a moment, Cox stopped and pointed off to their right. "About two buildings that way. I'm getting a ping. Why don't we go and say hi to our neighbors?"

Considerably more hesitant, everyone formed up and followed the lieutenant toward the building in the distance. It was a three-story office building, and near the top was a massive hole where it looked like something had either exploded or torn through the wall and ceiling. As they got close, Mark could feel his senses kicking into overdrive, and the strangest sensation enshrouded him, nearly causing him to stumble. A quick glance at those around him showed that nobody else in the group was having such an odd reaction.

Mark tried to shake himself free from it, but it persisted no matter what. It wasn't unpleasant, per se, but it was so odd that he couldn't help but shiver. It felt like a faint spiderweb overlaid atop his mind. Before he could explore it fully, however, Cox reached up and unsheathed his sword, a bright-red glow illuminating its edge as it activated. Made from a superdense alloy, the blade was normally dull, but as soon as the lieutenant's hand wrapped around the handle, the edge sprang to life, transforming from something that could only be used as a bludgeoning tool into a blade that could cut through solid steel like it was butter.

Seeing the lieutenant unsheathe his weapon, the others grabbed for theirs. Noah carried a sword and shield, though neither was as big as the lieutenant's, while Danny held a much larger shield and a mace. Glenn activated his knives, sending them spinning into the air, and Phoenix pulled mana to her hands, getting ready to cast mana bolts. Drawing an arrow, Harper nocked it on her bowstring, her eyes slowly scanning the environment in front of them for the enemy.

Mark, on the other hand, had been at a loss when it came to choosing weapons, as he was used to using his bare fists. Unfortunately, his left arm was currently wrapped up in metal gauntlets, which didn't give him that option. He had elected for a short sword, but he didn't bother drawing it. Instead, he figured he'd use the armor he wore as his weapon, though he could only use the second level of Cutting Palm with his left hand.

Just before the drone appeared, launching itself from a window on their left, Mark felt it, and his eyes darted over as he got ready to launch an attack. Lieutenant Cox was faster, and with a squelching sound, his sword pierced through the middle of the drone, pinning it to the stone wall. Before it could make a noise, he had grabbed the handle of his sword once more and, with a flick, bisected the monster. Its legs still twitched as it landed, and Mark thought he heard the faintest of screams.

"We only have a couple of minutes before other drones gather," Lieutenant Cox said, "so let's make this quick. This is an Exlian drone. They might not seem like much, but remember, they're all at least E ranked, which means they can chew through regular humans like nothing. This one is the weakest of the drones, but they should never be underestimated."

As the lieutenant continued to speak, Mark felt as if a dozen ants had suddenly started crawling on his scalp, and instinctively he lifted a hand to his head. Noticing his movement, the lieutenant looked over. "Something the matter, Mark?"

Not wanting to cause a scene, Mark shook his head. "No, sir."

"I think we've got company, sir," Harper called out, her eyes blinking as she scanned the area around them. "I'm picking up at least three different movements."

"A good rule of thumb," Cox replied, hefting his sword, "is to always assume there are four times as many Exlian as you can see with your own eyes. Point them out for us."

Her voice tense, Harper pointed out where each of the Exlian were coming from. They were closing in from three different sides, but Mark couldn't help but glance backward over his shoulder as he felt a faint tickle in the back of his mind.

Grinning, Lieutenant Cox nodded. "Mark here has the right idea. Exlian are sneaky buggers, and they'll ambush you from behind every chance they get. If they're surrounding us on three sides, you can guarantee they're surrounding us on four. Mark, Glenn, guard our backs."

"Yes, sir," Mark said, spinning and taking a couple of steps forward.

Glenn stood behind him, three glowing knives floating on either side of his shoulders.

"Look lively, team. We've got about fifteen incoming."

As Lieutenant Cox's voice faded, there was a rustle, and drones erupted from all sides, throwing themselves with reckless abandon at the team. Glenn let out a quiet shriek, and his knives flashed forward, most of them glancing harmlessly off the drones' carapaces. One of them, however, managed to stick deep into a small gap in a drone's neck, causing it to shriek and roll about.

Mark didn't hesitate and launched himself forward. He slammed his palm into the underside of one of the drones that was leaping at Glenn, at the same time stomping on the drone who had turned upside down, driving it into the ground and forcing the knife even deeper into its neck. A third drone jumped toward them, but Mark was already moving, spinning away from its claws as his left hand flicked out, tearing through the creature's skull with practiced ease. The dying drone on the ground was soon assaulted by the rest of Glenn's knives, even as the young man controlled the knife in its neck to saw back and forth, soon decapitating it.

As Lieutenant Cox watched, the team dealt with all fifteen of the drones. With some satisfaction, he looked over the group to see how everyone had reacted. Noah was breathing heavily from the sudden spike in adrenaline but had reacted calmly and with consummate skill, leveraging his increased speed and strength to tear two drones apart.

Phoenix and Glenn were a bit more tired, having used more energy than they needed to as they fought against drones for the first time. Harper had been the most nervous of all, and she'd missed her first two shots before falling into a steadier rhythm and helping Danny kill the drones he was defending against.

Though the large young man hadn't killed a drone of his own, he had done exactly what he was supposed to, which was keep the drones off his more fragile teammates, and his armor was slightly dented in a couple of places where he had used his body to block the drones' attacks.

When the lieutenant's gaze reached Mark, he paused. Mark was casually shaking Exlian blood off his gauntlet and showed no signs of worry or tension. Lieutenant Cox had been tracking the team's biometrics through their suits, just in case there was a crisis, but any tension that Mark had been under before the attack had vanished, and based on the numbers Lieutenant Cox was getting, he might as well have been out for a casual stroll to enjoy the flowers.

Mark didn't notice the lieutenant's attention, as he was focused on the faint web of energy that had been prickling at his mind. It had faded as the last of the drones fell, and though the energy wasn't gone, it was too faint for Mark to grab onto.

After making sure all the drones were dead, Lieutenant Cox called them back over, gathering the team up. "Now, I'm sure that some of you are thinking that that was easy, and in truth, it was. Part of the goal of this exercise is to teach you that you are stronger than you think you are. However, I want you to imagine something with me for a moment. What if there had been four times as many drones? Would it still have been so easy? And what if, halfway through your fight, an Exlian as strong as me showed up and decided you all needed to die?" He accompanied his question with a glare that sent a shiver down the spines of the entire group. "Just because you don't see the threat doesn't mean the threat doesn't exist. Still, you all did well. Come on, we're heading back to the city."

As far as first experiences outside the city wall went, Mark felt that it had been a good one. He was getting more used to the suit, and though it had been a little bit awkward to execute some of his martial movements in it, he found that as long as he stuck to the first stage of the Cutting Palm, he had no trouble. He was a little bit confused as to how he was supposed to use his power with a suit that covered every inch of his body, but he also wasn't about to start complaining. Having the extra armor all over was certainly worth it.

That night, when he walked into the warehouse, Abrams was

waiting for him, and rather than lead him to the table, Abrams gestured for him to follow.

"Come on, we've got some supplies to pick up," he said. "Carrying boxes of supplies is a bit too much for my old body, so I thought I'd wait for you to arrive."

That was a lie, of course, as Abrams was still able to handle the massive frozen corpses with ease. He was much stronger than Mark. But Mark didn't complain, as he knew this was part of his training as well.

They ended up doing very little carrying and instead went to a massive alchemy supply store. Walking through the racks, Mark listened intently as Abrams rattled off rapid-fire information about each material they passed. Rather than trust his memory, though he certainly did his best to remember it all, Mark recorded the entire conversation so he could play it back when he was on the train, then carried a small box of some rare ingredients the old man had ordered from the store. When they got back, it was only midnight, but rather than dive into cutting up corpses as he normally did, Abrams gestured for Mark to sit down. "I heard that you had your first experience out in the dead zone. How'd you feel about it?"

It was a complicated question, and Mark didn't rush to answer, taking a moment to think through his thoughts.

"I feel like it's sad," he said. "There's a sense of deep sorrow that shrouds the city, or at least what used to be a city. A sense of emptiness and distress, as if I can still feel the fear and panic of the people who lived there."

"It's a mana echo, and your mana sensitivity has to be pretty good to feel it. Anywhere that incredibly strong emotions exist, they'll often persist for a considerable amount of time afterward, so you can imagine just how awful it truly was if we're still able to sense it today. What about the Exlian? I heard you killed a couple of them."

Genuinely curious where Abrams was getting his information, Mark nodded. "Yes, I killed two. Just drones, though."

"Just drones, he says," Abrams sneered. "You ever seen what a drone will do to a man?"

The headless body that Mark had found in the alleyway flashed through his mind, and he nodded again. "I have, actually."

Taken aback, Abrams raised his eyebrows. "Well, maybe that's why you were so calm."

"Calm? What do you mean?"

"From what I hear, you barely even blinked when the drones jumped out, and then slaughtered them like so many bugs. Which they are, incidentally. But this wasn't your first time seeing Exlian, was it?"

Realizing that he had walked into a bit of a trap, Mark shook his head, trying to keep his expression as neutral as possible. He wasn't about to tell his master that he dreamed about killing Exlian every night, and instead tried to paper over his reaction with a bit of misdirection.

"No," he said. "I've seen a lot of Exlian, actually."

Eyes narrowing even further, Abrams leaned forward, his hands resting casually on his knees. "Oh, have you? Why don't you tell me about it?"

"Master, we're surrounded by Exlian," Mark said, leaning forward slightly to match Abrams's intensity. "They're all around us."

He gestured as he spoke, and Abrams cracked a smile, slapping his knee as he laughed. "All right, that was a good one. You're picking up on my kind of jokes, and I'm not sure if I should be happy or not. But that was a good one. You're trying to tell me that your time here, a mere few weeks, has completely hardened your heart against them?"

"No, not completely," Mark said, "but it's hard to be scared of something you understand. I've been studying Exlian here, tearing them apart with my bare hands." He lifted his hands to show his master. "I've been mastering the Cutting Palm, though I haven't quite reached mastery of the second stage, and I've been studying them at the training camp as well and learning from my brother. And besides, we were wearing armor that's too tough for the drones to get through. I probably could have let them chew on me for a few hours before they would have managed to crack through and bite into my flesh."

"That wouldn't have stopped them from crushing your bones," Abrams said, frowning. "But you're right. Thanks to the armor you were wearing, none of you were in any real danger. Against mana suits, drones really don't have a chance. If only we had had mana suits back in the day. All we had were bodies."

Looking rather sad, Abrams fell silent for a moment and then stood up. "Well, good. I'm glad there were no ill effects from your first foray out of the city. You're gonna have more of them, and over the next two weeks, I want you to do something. Be on the lookout for alchemical materials. Specifically, dead man's finger, which is a type of fungus that grows out in the dead zone. Looks like a bunch of skeletal fingers sticking up into the air. Do you know how to harvest it?"

"Using a mana blade, right, sir?"

"Yes. Make sure that you seal it up tight. We don't want any spores getting loose in the city. Also, you'll have to declare it once you get back to the gate. If you don't, you'll cause some real trouble, and we're not so poor that we need to resort to smuggling. Once you bring some back, I'll teach you how to make a potion. There's a really helpful concoction that you can build with dead man's fingers and the pheromone gland of any drone. All right, we've still got about an hour, so let's get to the table."

Mark had been hoping that he would be able to skip ripping apart a frozen corpse for at least one day, but Abrams wasn't about to let him off without getting his hands dirty. Before he knew it, Mark was covered in Exlian blood and guts once more.

The next day saw the team back out to patrol, though this time Lieutenant Cox didn't lead the way but left it up to the team how they organized themselves. To Mark's surprise, everyone except for Noah turned to him, clearly seeing him as the leader. Though technically Noah ranked above him, none of the rest of the team were quite as comfortable with the largely silent young man, and so they defaulted to Mark, who held the number two position. That didn't sit very well with Mark, however, and he tried to pass the torch to Noah. "Guys, I think Noah's gonna be a better leader."

"I don't agree," Harper said. "You've got great senses and can do a bit of everybody's job. Well, not so much the ranged attacks, but that's what Phoenix and I are here for. Oh, and Glenn too."

"But I'm more of a tank than a striker," Mark countered. "Our leader should be either support or a striker. It's too hard to see everything that's going on from the very front. Plus, Noah is the strongest among us and knows way more about Exlian theory than I do."

That was only partially true, as Mark had a much more intimate knowledge of Exlian biology, thanks to his time spent with Abrams. But Noah had a nearly encyclopedic knowledge of all the different kinds of Exlian, drilled into his head ever since he was a child.

"I don't know," Glenn said. "I think I'd kind of feel more comfortable with you as the leader."

"Enough of this," Phoenix interrupted. "We want Mark to be the leader. He wants Noah to be the leader. Why don't the two of you just work together?"

Sharing a glance with Noah, Mark saw a gleam in his eye and suddenly laughed.

"Or . . ." he said.

"You could be the leader," Noah finished, pointing back at Phoenix.

"Wait, what?"

"I think that's a fantastic idea," Mark said, patting Phoenix on the arm. "In fact, Noah and I both agree that you would make the best leader."

"Best vantage point," Noah said.

"And you're smart," Mark added.

"And passably good looking," Noah replied.

"Passably? What does that have to do with—you know what? Fine. If the two of you don't want to take responsibility, somebody has to step up. So I will," Phoenix said, glaring at Mark and Noah as they high-fived.

"Is it just me, or are those two weirdly in sync?" Harper whispered to Glenn.

Of course, they were communicating through their team channel, so everybody heard her loud and clear, but before Phoenix could blow up, Danny nodded.

"I think Phoenix would be the best leader. She'll have the best view of the battlefield and can send Noah to act as sweeper, since he's the strongest. Mark and I can tank, Noah can be our melee striker, and we have three ranged strikers. I think it's a good team setup."

With an annoyed sigh, Phoenix gestured for everybody to gather around.

"Fine. I think Danny has a good plan, so we'll go with that. Harper, I want you up with Noah. Mark, you're out front. Glenn, you and I will be behind them, and Danny will be bringing up the rear. Everybody stick to your positions, and watch for signs of the enemy. We have our route, so we'll begin our patrol, stopping at the spots I've marked."

Glancing at his map, Mark saw a few dots appearing along the route. Each was an easily defensible position, covered on two or more sides, where the team could rest without being concerned about being overrun. Mark's suggestion that Phoenix should take the leadership role turned out to be a good one, and she smoothly took command of the group and began issuing orders.

Realizing that he really didn't know much about her, except that her family was wealthy, Mark moved to the front of the group, leading the way down the abandoned streets. He had only gone a few blocks before that eerie, prickling feeling began to surround him once more, and he called for a stop.

"There's Exlian in the area," he said, scanning the street.

"Have you spotted them?" Phoenix asked. "How do you know?"

Instead of replying, Mark shook his head and slowly crouched, doing his best to sense where the prickles were. He was getting them from both sides of the street. Pointing ahead and toward the right, he whispered into the team channel. "Harper? Can you get eyes on that building? There should be a small open area in the back. Probably a parking lot."

"On it."

As she held her bow at the ready, Harper's eyes glazed over, and after a moment had passed, she nodded and held up five fingers, then made the hand sign for drones, indicating there were five drones on the right side.

"I think there are some on the other side too," Mark said, and a moment later, Harper confirmed that as well.

Their choices were simple: They could move straight down the street on the path they were on and face being ambushed from both sides, or they could take a circuitous route. Though there was danger in walking straight into the drones' ambush, it was much less dangerous now that they were aware of it than wandering out off the main streets that were commonly patrolled and into the narrow alleyways. There, an ambush could quickly turn into a siege, and it would be much harder for them to escape and much easier to be surrounded.

Thinking through the options in front of them, Phoenix gestured forward with two fingers. "Keep a sharp eye out. Let's move forward."

"Yes, ma'am," Mark said, getting to his feet and proceeding slowly.

In front of him were two buildings, one that looked like an old bank and another that had been a hotel. The drones they'd spotted were waiting in the bottom floors of both buildings, and as they passed between them, the doors suddenly shattered as the drones launched themselves forward.

A moment before they came, however, Mark called out the attack, giving everyone a fraction of a second to prepare. Glenn and Harper covered one side, while Phoenix launched a mana blast at the other. At the same time, Mark and Noah moved to cover Phoenix, while Danny thundered forward to plant his shield in front of Glenn and Harper. The street was so wide that by the time the drones got to them, there was little left of them, and Mark didn't even have to get involved as Noah stepped forward and slashed the mana-enhanced edge of his sword, cutting the last drone on their side in half.

On the other side, Danny crushed the last drone with his mace, sending a spray of bug juice across the concrete. The entire time, Lieutenant Cox didn't say a word, though his gaze did linger on Mark. With the ambush cleared, the team didn't stay in place but instead hurried on to avoid getting caught if more drones showed up to avenge their fallen comrades.

Twice more that day, they ran into drones, but in each case, Mark's advance warning and Phoenix's strategies carried them through with ease, and they made it back well before evening. The entire time they were out, Mark had been looking for the fungus Abrams wanted, but he hadn't spotted anything. It was a bit sad to have come back empty handed, but there wasn't anything he could do about it. After entering the training room, they stripped off their armor suits and met with Cox.

"You did well," he said, "especially for your first semisolo run. A couple mistakes that we'll address privately, but I have no notes except to say I think you made a wise choice with regards to your leader and the formation. Well done, Phoenix."

Caught off guard by the praise, Phoenix smiled brightly.

"All right, now, time for individual assessments. Come into my office, one after another."

One by one, members of the team entered, starting with Phoenix, then Noah. When it was Mark's turn, Lieutenant Cox was sitting at his desk, and he gestured to the chair across from him. "Take a seat, Mark. Before I give you your feedback, I'm curious: How do you think the rest of your team did?"

Mark had not been expecting to report on the rest of the team, but he replied as best he could. Lieutenant Cox didn't say anything, just noted down a few of Mark's answers. When Mark had finished, the lieutenant asked another question. "How do you think you did?"

"Overall, fairly well, sir. I was a bit slow to get into combat, though I don't know that that's actually a bad thing, as that meant I was able to be on the alert for new threats appearing. A couple of times I could have been more precise about where the enemy was, but I have a feeling that will come with practice," Mark mused.

"That is a surprisingly self-aware assessment, though I only say 'surprisingly' because it's rare to hear someone who's only been out of the city twice speak with such clarity. This is your second time out of the city, right?" Lieutenant Cox asked.

"Yes, sir," Mark said earnestly.

"Huh. All right, well, you did well. Better than I had any right to expect you would. If I didn't know any better, I would have assumed that you weren't a trainee at all and instead were a regular patrolman. Am I right in thinking that you want to be considered for the Defense Force?"

A surge of excitement filled Mark, and he nodded. "Yes, sir."

"Well, keep up the good work, and I'd be happy to make a recommendation. We need good patrolmen with sharp senses. They're the main line of defense that keeps our city safe. You've got a cool head, and whatever sense skill you're using is top notch. We don't typically pry, but I assume you got it from your brother. Just be careful with skills. You can only rely on them so far. Your actual personal strength is where your focus should be."

Dropping his head to avoid showing his panicked expression, Mark tried to calm his rapidly beating heart. "Yes, sir."

"All right, that's it. We'll be heading out tomorrow for another patrol, so make sure you get good sleep."

As the door closed behind Mark, he took a deep breath.

The conversation had been gratifying, and hearing Lieutenant Cox speak of a Defense Force recommendation sent a thrill through Mark's body. But at the same time, the conversation had woken a thread of caution in him. He hadn't even thought about how strange it was that he could sense the Exlian without needing to see them. Moreover, he had no idea why he could sense them either; he'd assumed that the faint prickling he felt was a completely normal thing. As he thought back on it, none of the others had shown any reaction when coming within range of the Exlian, while he was able to pick them up from a distance.

Mark's D rank meant he could have two skills: his base power and an additional skill beyond that. Cox was under the impression that he had picked up a second skill already, gaining something that would allow him to sense the presence of the Exlian. While pretending he had a second skill was a good cover for his bizarre new ability, Mark knew that excuse wouldn't stand up to scrutiny. Skill gems were insanely expensive, and even the cheapest was almost a million credits. There was no way that someone in Mark's position could afford one, unless his brother had helped him.

Of course, Mark had more than enough money to buy his own, but explaining how he got that money would lead to even more trouble. Mark was growing fast, and he had been quite excited about it. But talking with the lieutenant had poured a bucket of cold water on him, leaving him sputtering mentally as he tried to figure out what he was going to do. At the very least, he needed to be very careful in how he showed his abilities going forward so he didn't end up attracting the wrong type of attention. With how strange his powers were, the last thing Mark wanted was to turn into a test subject in some secret government project.

Thankfully, nothing out of the ordinary happened for the next few days, and soon the training camp came to a close. Mark and the rest of the team had spent the entire last two weeks on patrol, tracing different routes through the dead zone outside the western gate as Lieutenant Cox trailed after them. For the last mission, Lieutenant Cox sent them out alone, giving them a crisis code they could enter into their communicators if things went sour. Though he didn't have any proof, Mark had a nagging feeling that Lieutenant Cox had followed them anyway, watching over them from afar in case something did happen.

Under Phoenix's leadership, however, everything went

smoothly, and they passed through their last patrol of the training without issue. When they got back to camp and got unsuited, they gathered together to chat before splitting up for their week off, and Noah surprised everyone with a casual invitation to a party that evening to celebrate. After spending twelve weeks together and fighting together for two of them, everyone had more or less accepted Noah, and they quickly agreed. Noah gave them an address, but when Glenn looked it up on his map, he was confused.

"This isn't your house," he said. "This is a club."

"It's a club my family owns," Noah replied calmly. "And I'm afraid my house isn't really suitable for gatherings. We have a private room at the club we can use. I'll see everybody there at eight."

It was only after everyone had already left that Mark realized that if he went to the party, he would miss his session with Abrams. After considering it, however, he decided to ask for the night off. Rather than send a message, he hurried to Abrams's warehouse, punched in the key code, and stepped inside. He could tell from the glow of the heat lamps in the center of the warehouse that Abrams was in the middle of butchering a humanoid Exlian. Not wanting to interrupt, he waited off to the side.

It was a full hour before Abrams finished, and when he did, he gestured, and Mark ran over and grabbed the tray for him, holding it out as his master pulled what appeared to be a complete circulatory system out of the dead Exlian and laid it carefully on the tray.

"What do you want?" Abrams asked, staring at his apprentice through narrowed eyes.

"One of my teammates is having a party to celebrate finishing up our second stage of training. And I was hoping I could go attend. It's at eight o'clock tonight."

"Sure, but if you go, you're going to have to come all day on your week off."

"That's fine," Mark said, nodding excitedly. "That's totally fine."

"Huh, fine. Go to your party. You're lucky you didn't mention his last name. Otherwise, there's no way I would have said yes."

With those cryptic words, Abrams shooed Mark off and carried the tray toward his office. Watching Abrams's hunched back until the door closed behind him, Mark tried to puzzle out what his master had meant. Noah's last name was Javesi, a name that Mark had never heard before. Wondering if there was something between Abrams and the Javesi family, Mark took a taxi home, changed into his best outfit, and let his brother know where he was going. Mime, who had been sitting on the couch like normal, jumped up onto Mark's shoulder. Reaching up, Mark grabbed her and took her down.

"I'm going to a party. You can't come," he said, but she slipped out of his hands and sat on his shoulder, glaring at him until he finally gave up. "Okay, fine, you can come. But you're not going to have any fun," he warned.

Wrinkling her nose as if to say, *We'll see about that*, Mime pointed imperiously at the door. With a sigh, Mark opened it and walked out. Another quick taxi ride and twenty-five minutes later, he was standing outside the club where they had agreed to meet. Glenn and Danny were already there, dressed in clothes that were about as nice as Mark's, which was to say, not very. Phoenix and Harper showed up not long after, and it was clear that the girls had been shopping. While Phoenix looked completely comfortable in her slim-fitting dress and high heels, Harper looked a bit like she wanted to crawl right out of her clothes and down the nearest drain. Her arms crossed protectively across her chest, and her three-inch heels gave her an unsteady walk.

"The two of you ladies look lovely," Glenn said with a wide grin. "Hey, we should get a picture."

"Should we wait for Noah?" Danny asked.

"No need," Mark said, jerking a thumb toward the club's

entrance, where Noah was waiting for them. "Let's get the picture inside."

The club didn't appear to have a name and looked entirely too upscale for Mark to feel comfortable. They stepped inside and were greeted by a woman in a tasteful but revealing dress, who greeted Noah with a slight bow.

"We've reserved the Crimson Dragon room."

"Of course, Mr. Javesi," the woman purred.

With an elegant gesture, she turned and walked away, all grace and swaying hips. Mark was too busy looking around to particularly care, but it was clear from the way Noah's teeth clenched that he wasn't particularly happy.

By the time they got to the Crimson Dragon suite, the woman had gotten the memo, because she was all business as she ushered them in and informed them that the food would be there shortly. The Crimson Dragon suite was large, though not so big that the six of them felt lost in it. There were couches and a wide balcony that overlooked a garden, where a live band was playing for the enjoyment of the guests. Walking over to the balcony, Mark leaned on the railing, his eyes slowly scanning over the grounds. Noah walked up beside him and stood silently. His thoughts, as always, were a mystery.

"It's really pretty," Mark said.

"My mother designed it before she passed away," Noah replied. "I quite enjoy coming here. It reminds me of her."

"I'm sorry to hear that. May I ask what happened?"

"Fifteen years ago," Noah said, "during the wave. She was the commander of the Cerberus Battalion and led it to plug one of the gaps. She didn't have to fight on the front lines, but she chose to."

Taking a drink, Mark shook his head. "I'm sorry to hear that, man. Sounds like she was a brave woman."

"The bravest. I just hope that I can follow in her footsteps, in some small way."

The air had grown heavy, and in an effort to lighten the mood, Mark grinned and reached into his pocket. "Hey, that reminds me. I brought something for you. I didn't have time to wrap it, but I hope you'll forgive me."

Taking the case that Mark offered, Noah raised his eyebrows. Slotted inside of it were three blue elixirs.

"Yours came in really helpful," Mark said. "And when I say really helpful, I mean really helpful. I'm a D-ranked empowered now because of them. So I thought I'd return the favor. Oh, and flip it over."

Turning the case over, Noah saw a piece of paper with a contact number scrawled on it, pasted onto the back of the case.

"I picked up a new job at Abrams's warehouse. If there's ever any special ingredients you're looking for, give me a call. I'm sure I can hook you up."

There was no doubt in Mark's mind that if Noah wanted an alchemical ingredient, he would be able to get it. From the casual way he treated credits, it was likely that there was nothing Mark had access to that was out of Noah's reach, so what Mark was offering was a chance for Noah to form a connection with his master, Abrams. From the quick smile that flashed across Noah's face, it was clear that he liked the gift.

"Thank you," he said. "I'll treasure this."

As the night wore on, the team talked and laughed, discussing their missions and their lives. Under Harper's goading, Phoenix finally began to share a little bit about herself, revealing that she belonged to the Borner family, a large merchant family who specialized in building the mana suits they had been using for training. One of her great-uncles on her father's side had been part of the team that had created the first of the mana suits, and the Borner family had been mass-producing them ever since. Just as it was going on ten o'clock, there was a heavy pounding on the door, and then a young woman swaggered in, an ugly smile on her face.

"Well, if it isn't my dear brother and his friends," she said, smirking at Noah. "I tell you, though, this is really a first. I didn't actually think you had friends, Noah."

Noah's expression was so cold Mark thought he saw ice forming on his eyebrows as he stared at the young woman. "Hello, Amy."

"Hello? Is that all you have to say? You finally crawled out of your hole, and the only thing you have to say is hello?"

Noah, who was still sitting, ignored his sister, his eyes

wandering over the five people who had come in after her. None of them looked close to as confident as Amy did, but Mark could only suppose that was because Amy was part of the family who owned this club, and they were not. As he waited to see what would happen, Mark assessed the group carefully. Each of them wore designer clothing, though none of it quite as expensive as the silky dress Amy had on. They were all well built and gave off faint traces of mana, indicating that they were empowered. Mark found that odd, as it was rare to see so many empowered together outside the military. Amy's next words cleared that up.

"You know, it's really unkind of you, brother. Here I am, slaving away in the Defense Force training camp, and rather than come and share some of my burden, you've run away to a little basic recruitment camp. It's going to be really hard to win Father's favor like that."

"You can have it," Noah said, his voice just as cold as his stare.

Glancing over, Mark saw that Noah appeared completely relaxed otherwise, lounging in his chair, his arm hanging over the back and legs extended. With a laugh, Amy shook her head. "You better not let him hear you say that, or you'll be in for a whole pile of pain. This must be your team. I've heard all sorts of things about them."

Her eyes only rested on Mark for a moment, but he felt something deeply malevolent in her gaze. Just then, Mime, who had been out exploring the garden, leaped up onto the balcony wall and then down to the floor and trotted over to Mark without a care in the world. Reaching down, Mark picked Mime up, causing Amy to turn and stare at him.

"Is that your cat," she asked, seeing Mark scratching behind Mime's ears.

"It is."

"A boy with a cat. What are you, a two-bit villain? Brother, your friends are hilarious. It's unfortunate that they're not as strong as they are funny. Otherwise, you might actually have a chance."

Phoenix had heard enough, and in a moment, she was on her feet, Harper and Glenn shadowing her. Danny was slower, but as he stood up to his full height and towered over Amy's companions, a few of them took a step back. Noah remained seated, but Mark got up as well, lifting Mime to his shoulder, where she sat calmly, her tail swishing back and forth across his back as she stared at Amy.

"Ooh, it looks like you have some backbone, at least. Unlike my dear brother here. What do you think, Noah? You going to let your team fight your battles for you? It wouldn't be the first time, would it?"

Noah didn't reply, and for a long moment, silence stretched in the room until Mark couldn't help it and chuckled.

"What's so funny?" Amy asked, her gaze sharpening as it snapped to Mark. "Why don't you share the joke?"

"I'm sorry, I just think it's humorous that you're here blabbing so much your lips are going to fall off to try and provoke your brother when he clearly doesn't care."

Mark wasn't sure what sort of signal Amy had given, but one of the brawny young men next to her suddenly lunged forward, his fist flying toward Mark's chin with explosive force.

The fist was moving much faster than Mark should have been able to react to, but he had done this so many times in his dreams that he moved without thinking. His right foot kicked out and his left knee bent, causing his entire body to lean backward. Just before the fist reached Mark's chin, the young man's thigh ran into Mark's foot, causing him to halt in place. That brief moment allowed Mark just enough time to get his chin out of the path of the strike.

At the same time, his hand instinctively curled, two fingers extending like a blade as he jabbed upward at the offending elbow.

He hadn't even thought about attacking, but it was so ingrained in his body that he couldn't control it. Right before his fingers pierced straight through the young man's arm, he felt his wrist grabbed. Blinking, Mark came back to himself. Noah stood next to him, his hands straining as he held Mark's wrist. The tip of Mark's middle finger had barely touched the young man's elbow, and in the frozen stillness, a single drop of blood rolled down his finger and dripped to the floor. Jerking back in fear, the young man who had attacked kept his hands up warily, as Mark slowly straightened. Somehow Mime was still sitting on Mark's shoulder, creating a surreal picture.

"There's no need for this," Noah said, releasing Mark's wrist.

Amy's expression was awful, and she stepped forward with a sneer.

"You're always looking down on me," she said, "but that ends today. Your pathetic team is no better than you are, and I aim to prove it."

"And how do you intend to do that?" Noah asked, no expression on his face.

"With a fight, of course. It looks like you've got some skilled people, which is how you like it so you can hide behind those stronger than you are. You've always been too cowardly to come out and face your problems yourself. Well, brother, I'm your problem. Are you gonna come and face me, or are you gonna leave it to these pathetic commoners to regain your honor? Unless all of you are too scared to fight? Maybe my brother surrounded himself with people just like him."

"Do you think anybody will care if we kill her?" Phoenix asked Harper, just loud enough that everyone could hear.

That sent Amy into peals of laughter. "Kill me? You think you could kill me? You're just as delusional as he is. Come on, I'll give you a chance. You and I can fight right here if you'd like."

"Absolutely not," Noah said.

"If you don't want me and her to fight, then you'll have to do it yourself," Amy replied. "I'll go and arrange the ring."

Glancing across Mark and the others disdainfully, Amy turned on her heel and stalked out of the room, her five teammates following her. From the way Noah's jaw was working, Mark could tell he was quite upset. He reached out and patted Noah on the shoulder. "Some things, no matter how hard we try to avoid them, will just come. I'm assuming you can shield us from any repercussions if we beat the snot out of them?"

"Yes," Noah said, a thread of anger appearing in his voice for the first time, "but that won't be easy."

Danny, normally mild mannered, grinned and cracked his knuckles.

"It's been a while since I got to cut loose," he said. "Let's go show them what it means to grow up tough."

"Speak for yourself," Glenn replied. "I am strictly middle class, and there was nothing difficult about my childhood. Besides, those guys looked like they could rip me in half."

"You'll be fine," Phoenix replied, punching him lightly in the chest. "You might not even have to fight. There are six of us, so winning four matches will do it."

"Hey, Noah," Mark asked, causing his friend to stop at the door. "All this food. You don't mind if I eat it, do you?"

"Are you hungry? At a time like this?" Harper asked incredulously, but Noah just shrugged.

"Do what you want."

"All right, thanks," Mark said, rubbing his hands together as he eyed the fancy platters of meat and grilled vegetables. "I'll follow in a sec."

Mark had been doing his best to hold himself back for the last few weeks, forcing his body into what felt like near starvation to work on his recovery ability, but now that a fight was on the horizon, he threw all of that out the window and started shoving food in his mouth as fast as he possibly could. In less than ten minutes, he had cleared half the table, and the rest followed soon after. By the time he caught up with the others, they were already changed and ready to fight. Noticing his faintly bulging stomach, Phoenix raised an eyebrow.

"I know you like to eat," she said, "but do you think that's wise right before a fight?"

"Give me like ten minutes, and I'll be good," Mark replied, burping lightly.

To his surprise, Phoenix didn't snap back but looked toward Amy and her friends. Their opponents had already changed, and a couple of them even held practice weapons.

"What kind of fight is this?" Phoenix asked.

"Just a friendly spar," Amy replied with a nasty grin. "No need to use powers, right? Just our natural strength and speed."

Mark frowned, his eyes raking across the well-built men and women on the other team. It was obvious from their physiques that all of them had strength and speed powers, and likely other powers as well. He had his martial arts, so he was confident enough in a fight without using his powers, and Noah and Danny would both be fine, as they had enhanced physiques, but Harper, Glenn, and Phoenix all lacked physical advantages, and if the teams were to go up against one another in one-on-one matches, there was no way they'd be able to beat their opponents. He was about to protest when Phoenix nodded.

"Sure," she said, "let's do that."

Harper and Glenn both disliked the idea, but Phoenix waved for them to be quiet and called the team together.

"Danny, you're up first," she said. "Noah will go second, and I'll go third. Mark, you're fourth."

"What about me and Harper?" Glenn asked, looking quite nervous.

"We won't get there," Phoenix said. "If we do, we'll just give up."

"No way, are you serious? I can't believe you're leaving me out of the fight," Harper said, anger blazing in her eyes.

"If it makes you feel better," Phoenix said, "I'm planning on going up there and getting my face beat in, but I have a trick that'll allow me to win. Amy looks like she's too clever for her own good and will probably bait out our stronger fighters with weaker fighters on her end. As long as Mark wins, we'll be fine. Of course, if any of us lose, then our strategy is not going to work, and you guys can decide whether you want to go up there after you see how the fights turn out. How does that sound?"

Mollified, Harper nodded. "Sure," she said.

"I have a more important job for you," Phoenix said, lowering her voice to a whisper. "Harper, I need you to pay careful attention to the opponents. I have a feeling they're not above cheating to win. Glenn, you have a hundred-foot range to your telekinesis, right? There's an emergency stop button behind that desk that'll put the whole ring into stasis. If things get dangerous, and I don't mean like 'somebody's getting beat up' dangerous but 'somebody's about to die' dangerous, I need you to punch the button."

"I can do that," Glenn said, casually glancing at the unmanned desk.

"Thanks, we'll be counting on you." Turning around, Phoenix took a couple of steps forward and pointed to the empty desk. "Hey, where's the attendant? Shouldn't there be somebody here?"

"It's just a friendly spar," Amy called back. "Why would we need an attendant?"

"Fine. Danny, get on up there."

"Happy to," Danny replied, stretching his neck as he sauntered up to the stage.

The only young woman in Amy's group was chosen to go up onstage first, and when she looked at Danny, there was clear fear in her eyes. Mark had a bad feeling about the match, as Danny already looked troubled.

"Do you think he'll go easy on her?" Glenn whispered.

"It'd be a mistake if he does," Mark replied.

"I don't know," Glenn said. "I feel like it'd be hard to hit a girl."

That earned him a disdainful glance from Phoenix, but Mark couldn't help but feel the same. Up on the stage, Danny lifted his hand.

"Hello, my name is Danny."

"My name is Jamie," she replied, blinking up at him. "I don't really want to fight."

As she spoke, she took a step forward, getting close to Danny.

"Good," he said, and backhanded her out of the ring.

The blow was so quick nobody saw it coming. One moment, he was completely relaxed, and the next, there was a short, sharp scream, and Jamie landed in a pile outside the ring, bleeding from her cheek. Still smiling, just as pleasantly as before, Danny nodded and pointed at her. "That means she's out, right?"

His question was met with pin-drop silence, as everyone stared in horror at the giant.

"I think that counts as our win," Phoenix replied finally, breaking the silence.

Chuckling, Danny nodded and turned to walk off the stage. Just before he got down, he paused and looked back at the other team.

"Sorry about your face," he said, speaking to Jamie, "but I've got six sisters, and I've been sparring against them since I was old enough to tie my shoes. That kind of trick only works once."

"That was awesome," Glenn said, slapping Danny repeatedly on the arm as he walked down from the ring. "I seriously thought you were just gonna talk to her, and then *bam*, right out of the ring."

"It only worked because she thought I would hesitate," Danny said. "My guess is that she's got superstrength herself. If she had set up, it would have been an annoyingly long fight."

"Still, you did it. Well done," Mark said, giving Danny a fist bump.

About to walk up onstage, Noah was stopped by Phoenix.

"I think it'd be better if I go up first," she said, "because now that I've had some time to look at them, I genuinely don't think my trick is going to work."

"Why not?" Mark asked.

"Because they're all stronger and faster than I thought they'd be. I figured we'd be facing a team of regular people. While Danny was up there, I've been looking them up. They're the first squad in the Defense Force training camp. Every single one of them has an A-ranked ability and talent."

"Then you shouldn't be going up at all," Mark said, frowning. "There's no reason for you to get up onstage and fight."

"I don't know," Phoenix said with a small smile. "There's something fun about pushing your limits. Thanks, Mark. I appreciate your concern, but I'll be fine."

Taking a deep breath, Mark stepped back. "All right," he said. "I won't stop you."

By the time Phoenix walked up onstage, her opponent was already there. He was handsome, with dark hair and eyes and a sun-kissed complexion. He looked like just another pretty boy, but the way he moved told Mark that he had plenty of experience in live combat, which didn't bode well for Phoenix.

When he saw Phoenix standing across from him, her opponent let out a dramatic sigh. "Of course they had to send a girl. Here I was hoping for at least one of the two remaining men in your group."

Not rising to his provocation, Phoenix took up her stance, causing her opponent to laugh. "Oh, come on. Do you really think something like that's going to work on me?"

He punctuated his sentence by moving so quickly across the stage it looked like he had teleported, appearing right in front of Phoenix and grabbing her chin between two fingers.

"Tell you what, pretty lady," he started to say as Phoenix whipped up her leg, intending to knee him in the crotch.

He'd been expecting it, however, and he simply twisted his hips, blocking her attack as he pressed closer, using his elbows to lock out her arms so she couldn't strike at him. With a fierce look in her eye, she tried to headbutt him, but he simply tightened his grip on her chin, keeping her from moving her head forward. He was still moving, and as she stumbled back, he kept pace with her, clearly adept at this type of fighting.

Suddenly, Phoenix, who was backpedaling as fast as she could, tripped, and with a laugh, he tried to slip his arm around her waist. He was still moving forward, and one of his feet just so happened to land on the edge of her toes, rolling slightly, as her other foot tangled with his. Unable to stop himself because of his momentum, he suddenly stumbled off balance, but his arm was already around Phoenix's waist, and as the two of them tumbled down into a pile, there was a fierce howl, and he leaped back, his eyes murderous. As they had fallen to the ground, Phoenix's elbow had come down full force on his crotch, and now, legs clenched tightly together and bent over in pain, he glared at her as she nimbly jumped off the stage.

"I surrender," she said as Glenn and Harper both laughed. "It's your win."

"You!"

Practically growling, the young man stepped forward, only to see Danny standing in his way.

"Take another step, and I'll slap you so hard you'll have to wear your head backward," Danny said, his voice a deep rumble.

Having seen his companion already batted off the stage with casual ease, the young man wasn't going to risk it, no matter how angry he was, and with clenched teeth, he slowly backed up, going back to his side as Danny gave Phoenix a thumbs-up. The score was now one to one, which meant that it would be difficult for their team to win, as their opponents were much stronger than Glenn and Harper, but none of them particularly cared anymore.

Noah was grinning as he walked up onto the stage.

"Why bother with all this," he said to his sister. "Come up, and we'll settle this. You and me, as the tiebreaker."

Rolling her eyes, Amy shook her head. "Brother, brother, when will you ever learn? Desmond, you're up."

One of the young men who had been standing beside her quietly nodded, his face impassive, and slowly walked up onto the stage. Mark's eyes narrowed as he watched Noah's opponent. Until he moved, he had given off no sign of being any different from the others, but now Mark could sense something dangerous. Trusting his instincts, he jumped up on the stage.

"Let me face him," he said, causing Noah to raise his eyebrows.

"What are you doing?" he asked.

"I'm taking over your fight," Mark replied, his eyes never leaving his opponent.

On the opposite side of the stage, Amy scowled. "Get down, kid."

"Why would I do that?" Mark asked. "We hadn't finished choosing who was going to go up first, me or Noah. We were just planning on discussing it here onstage, and now we've settled it. Me and the stone-faced killer here are going to fight while Noah watches from down below."

From the hard set of his jaw, Mark could tell that Noah felt embarrassed that someone had come up onstage to replace him, but Phoenix jumped in, too, before he could say anything.

"Noah, come down," she said, her tone insistent.

Biting his lip, Noah gave a curt nod, turned, and walked off the stage, his fists so tightly clenched his knuckles were white. Seeing that his opponent was looking at his shoulder, Mark saw Mime was still sitting there and, with a laugh, poked her in the stomach.

"Go wait on the side," he said. "I might need you to carry me home after this is done."

Giving Mark an arch look, Mime nodded and jumped down, quietly padding to the edge of the stage. Down below, Amy was positively furious.

"Desmond," she snarled, causing Mark's opponent to turn and look over his shoulder. "I'll bear the consequences."

Hearing her sinister words, Desmond nodded, his face still impassive, and got into his combat stance. Neither he nor Mark spoke as they stared at each other. And then, at the same time, both shifted forward a single step. The difference was Mark stopped while Desmond sped up, his body blurring as he raced across the arena. As soon as he saw his opponent move, Mark knew he was in trouble. Desmond clearly wasn't E ranked like most of the trainees. He wasn't even D ranked like Mark. Instead, judging by how quickly he was moving, he was at least C ranked.

That ruled out a physical contest, which meant that Mark's only option was relying on dodging. Shifting to the side as Desmond launched his attack, Mark struck out with his hand, aiming to parry the blow. Though he successfully managed to brush it aside, the residual force sent him stumbling back, his palms shaking. Desmond didn't pause, following up his first strike with a second and then a third. Each one clipped past Mark, who was dodging desperately, with enough force to crush him if he was hit.

Lunging away from a blow, Mark scrambled to the side, throwing his center of gravity ahead of himself and using it to twist his hips at an odd angle, barely dodging a lightning-fast kick that probably would have crippled him had it hit. It was clear that Desmond was playing for keeps, and Mark was genuinely at a loss as to what to do. His only advantage was his unnatural stamina, but already he could feel his biofuel beginning to drain as he pushed his body to the absolute limit to try to avoid Desmond's full-power strikes.

Barely managing to avoid a punch by flopping backward, Mark skidded across the ground and then rolled over as fast as he could as a boot landed where his chest had been a moment before. There was a crunch as the floor under Desmond's foot cracked, and despite Phoenix's shout, Amy just grinned and waved for the fight to continue.

"Are you crazy?" Phoenix yelled. "Are you trying to kill him?"

"Huh, is that a gnat talking?" Amy asked, looking around in confusion.

"Amy, stop this," Noah said, but his sister just laughed.

"Oh, now you want to talk to me? Now you want to ask me for something? He butted in where he didn't belong, so he has to pay the price."

Mark, realizing there was no way he could win the fight and that his opponent genuinely had it out for him, tried to scramble to the side of the stage, but before he could, a hand grabbed his leg and yanked him back. Spinning, he snapped a kick that slammed Desmond in the face. He caught sight of a pitying look in Desmond's eyes right before pain exploded through his leg. Gritting his teeth, Mark ignored it, his fingers raking across Desmond's leg. He could feel the pain in his wrist as he activated the second stage of the Cutting Palm, but even as his hand tore through Desmond's protective garment, it was deflected by a glimmering sheen that covered Desmond's legs.

Realizing that his opponent had been using his powers from the beginning, Mark was dumbfounded. Before he could say anything, however, a kick caught him in the chest, and he heard his bones crack. Spitting out a mouthful of blood, he writhed in pain, but his leg was still being held tight. The look of pity was gone from Desmond's eyes, and as he lifted his fist, aiming to bring it down on Mark's head, Mark genuinely felt as if he were going to die.

In that moment, three things happened: He caught sight of a faint flash of black by the side of the stage, the door burst open, and then everything froze as Glenn punched the emergency stasis button. Thick mana flooded across the arena, crashing down on Mark and Desmond with such force Mark's vision darkened. Desmond tried to move, managing to shift only an inch before the mana locked him in place. In excruciating pain, Mark stayed awake only long enough to give Desmond a savage grin. His teeth were stained with blood that he had coughed up after being kicked in the chest.

As Mark fell unconscious, Amy spun to stare at Noah and the others, who weren't even close to the emergency stasis button. She was about to speak when the man who had thrown open the door beat her to it.

"What, dear children, is happening here?"

Amy's face paled, going white as a ghost as she slowly turned to stare at her father. Noah's reaction was much more muted, but the cold look was back on his face.

"As you can see, my sister is having one of her hired thugs

kill a friend of mine," Noah said calmly, as if it were just another run-of-the-mill experience.

Andre Javesi, councillor of New Emery and one of the richest and most powerful men in the city, sighed lightly and rubbed his forehead.

"Will the two of you ever stop causing trouble?" he asked. "What am I going to do with you? Do you realize how hard this is going to be to clean up?"

His eyes completely ignored the group of people behind Amy and instead turned toward Noah, narrowing slightly when he caught sight of Phoenix.

"And you even brought someone from the other families into this."

Though he spoke calmly, his clenched jaw told both of his children just how much trouble they were in.

"It's not my fault," Amy muttered, her expression growing petulant. "I hired Desmond to teach my brother a little lesson. He was going to fight with him fairly, but that commoner Noah brought jumped in, getting involved in our family business."

Glancing at the stage, where Desmond was still struggling against the stasis and Mark had passed out, Andre raised his eyebrows slightly before turning away, completely unconcerned with Mark's fate.

"We need to get him into a healing tank," Noah said quietly, causing his father to sigh.

"We have much bigger problems to deal with," Andre retorted, his calm mask almost cracking.

Completely unfazed, Noah shook his head. "I don't think so. I think you need to save him. Otherwise, we're going to have much bigger problems."

This time, Andre's expression did crack, fury twisting his face as he stared at Noah, then at Mark's body. Before he could speak, there was a sound from behind him, and he spun around.

"I thought I said nobody was to bother us," he snarled, and in response, the head of one of his bodyguards tumbled into the room, his neck neatly severed.

A wrinkly-faced old man walked in after it, paying no mind to the streak of blood splattered across the polished marble floor. As soon as Abrams stepped into the room, the temperature plunged, and icy fingers of fear gripped everyone. Looking around casually, Abrams nodded to Andre, then turned to Noah. "Thanks for the call, kid. Now I won't have to kill all of you. Tell me, was she the one who set this up?"

"No, wait!" Andre blurted out.

Before he could reach for Abrams, the old man was already across the room, his hand locked around Amy's neck. The guards began to lift their weapons, but Andre roared for them to stop, his face pale and his hands shaking. Amy was frozen in place, her eyes wide with terror, as she hung from Abrams's bony grip.

"So you do value her," Abrams said, grinning at Andre. "And here I thought you were intentionally trying to get her killed by having her mess with my apprentice."

The word dropped into the frozen room like an Arctic wind.

"I know you care about your family honor and all that garbage," Abrams said to Andre. "But there are some things that are more important, and my apprentice is at the top of that list. I've made it my practice to stay out of city business and let you and your cronies run things. But I swear on my dead wife's grave that if Mark and his friends don't show up for training on Monday, as good as new and maybe even better, I will tear your little empire apart, brick by brick."

"I understand," Andre said. "Please, let my daughter go."

Turning his cold gaze onto Amy, who could do nothing but shake in terror, unable to even fall unconscious because of the biting cold that surrounded her, Abrams stared at her for a moment.

"I must be getting soft in my old age," he said with a soft sigh. "This is your single and only chance. Don't make me regret it."

By the time his words had faded from the air, Abrams was nowhere to be seen, but the chill lingered for quite a while.

"Get that stasis off, and get him to a healing tank," Andre said, his eyes blazing with fury.

Taking a deep breath, he slowly exhaled, closing his eyes as he straightened his shoulders and adjusted his coat. When he opened them again, he had returned to the calm man who had first entered the room. Giving his kids dispassionate glances, he smiled slightly. "I'll speak to the two of you later. Let's get this mess cleaned up. Noah, why don't you escort your friends out? Amy, go change."

Seeing her father looking down at her feet, Amy glanced down, her face turning scarlet as she realized she had wet herself without even realizing it.

"You don't need to be embarrassed," Andre said, lifting his chin slightly. "I probably would have done the same thing."

By the time Noah had arranged rides for the others and rushed back, Mark had already been transferred to a state-of-the-art hospital located in the attached estate. He paused at the door and turned, eyeing one of his father's bodyguards.

"Where's Desmond?" he asked.

"He slipped out in the chaos," the bodyguard said impassively.

Gritting his teeth, Noah could only hold his anger in. It had taken him too long to recognize Desmond, one of his father's cleaners. The Javesi family had many people like him who were engaged in all sorts of nefarious tasks. It appeared that his father didn't want to lose a valuable chess piece. Mark was suspended in a healing tank in the center of the room, and as Noah caught sight of his own reflection in the glass, he grew bitter. He was the firstborn of the Javesi family, yet he felt entirely helpless. If Mark hadn't shared that he was working at Abrams's warehouse, Noah wouldn't have called Abrams, and his friend might be dead right now. Feeling his calm mask slipping, Noah leaned his forehead against the cool glass of the healing tank, trying to calm his surging emotions.

"Ah, Noah! I was hoping to find you."

Straightening up, Noah turned, his gaze hard as he watched a short, potbellied man in a white coat approaching. If the doctor noticed the ice in Noah's gaze, he gave no indication of it and instead stared fervently past Noah at the tube that held Mark. "Have you seen the numbers coming out of this tank? They're incredible. I've never seen such high adaptability. This kid's body is a gold mine. I have a feeling we could advance our research by decades if he was in the program. You have to convince your father—"

"Dr. Kramer," Noah interrupted, practically shouting, "he is off limits."

"Off limits? What do you mean? He can't be off limits. We need his body—"

"I will not repeat myself," Noah growled, taking a step forward and staring down at the balding doctor. "Mark Fields is on the no-touch list."

Giving Noah a sour look, Dr. Kramer nodded. "Fine, I understand. But believe me, it's a mistake to let him go."

As Noah stepped into the infirmary, Desmond was stepping out of a car, almost four miles away.

"Head down the alleyway; take a left and then a right. The entrance to the safe house will be on your right," said the driver before peeling off.

Desmond swore under his breath. He hated the Javesi family, each and every last one of them. That was why he had jumped at the chance to permanently disfigure Noah. Mark's intrusion had been both unplanned and unwelcome, but it wasn't like he had something against the kid. Shaking his head, he walked into the alley, his senses on full alert. It had come as a complete surprise to him that the kid had an old monster for a master, and he was desperately hoping that he had managed to slip under the radar. As long as he made it to the safe house before it occurred to that frightening old man to look for him, he'd be fine. He'd lie low for a while, and then, when things blew over, he'd get back to work.

About to turn the corner, he paused, realizing that the night was abnormally still. Normally, in the back alleys of the city, there were little sounds. Mice scurrying up and down the pipes, the wind rustling the trash, even the hum of insects. He heard nothing at all. Fearing what he might find as he turned the corner, Desmond thought about running, but if it was Abrams waiting for him, then no amount of fleeing would work. Better to play the pity card and hope that the old man hadn't wasted it all on that insane Javesi girl.

Fortifying his courage, Desmond stepped around the corner, a relieved smile breaking across his face as he saw a cat sitting at the other end of the alleyway, watching him with curious eyes. Its fur was pitch black, except for a patch of white on its face that looked like a skull mask. Desmond felt that it was familiar, but it took a moment to place where he had seen it before.

"Hey, aren't you that kid's cat?" Desmond asked, the feeling of strangeness crashing back down on him.

Nodding her head, Mime smiled, her mouth stretching wide in a decidedly uncatlike smile with entirely too many teeth.

When Abrams arrived a few moments later, grumbling about how much slower he had become as he walked up the alleyway, he found nothing but a hand that had transformed into gleaming steel. Crouching down, he picked it up and looked around. It had been bitten off cleanly, and there was no sign of the rest of the body. With a sigh, Abrams stared at the steel hand for a moment as frost began to cover it, and it grew colder and colder until it shattered, falling to the ground as unrecognizable scrap.

"Looks like someone beat me to it."

Mark's awareness returned in a slow, hazy fashion, like waking up from a long dream. His eyes felt sticky, and he had trouble opening them. He could hear vague sounds around him, including an odd bubbling that made him feel like he was underwater. It was rhythmic, and every few seconds a rush of bubbles drifted past his head, threatening to lull him right back to sleep.

He could feel his body acutely, and the pain was gone. The last thing he remembered was the feeling of the stasis field locking him down, sending prickles of electricity racing through his body. Beyond that, there was nothing. He honestly hadn't expected to wake up, as the damage to his body had been tremendous.

Prying his eyelids apart, he found himself floating in a tank of viscous liquid. It was clear, allowing him to see through it, and to his surprise, it didn't sting his eyes at all. In a curious way, the liquid around him felt as if it didn't exist, and it didn't take him long to realize that he was in a healing tank. His tank was set up next to half a dozen others, all currently empty, in a large room with a variety of state-of-the-art medical equipment shoved up against the walls. He didn't recognize any of the doctors who were nearby, but he must have set off an alarm, as one of them noticed he had woken up.

"Welcome back to the land of the living." Mark could see the relief in the man's eyes. "Can you tell me how many fingers I'm holding up?"

Seeing all five fingers of the man's hand extended, Mark shook his head and pointed at the breathing apparatus currently covering his mouth.

"Don't worry, you can talk normally. I'll be able to hear you."

"Five?" Mark croaked, his voice feeling dry.

"Perfect, how about now?"

"Two?"

"Good. And what is your name?"

"Mark . . . Mark Fields."

"Perfect. Our scans didn't detect any damage, but you never know. We expected you to be in the tank for another, let's see, eight hours, but your recovery is impressive, and you've been absorbing a much higher flow of mana than normal. I'd say you should be good to go in another thirty minutes or so."

"What happened?" Mark asked.

"I don't know, but it looked rough," the doctor said. "They brought you in, and we got you in the tank just in time. If we had waited even half an hour longer, you probably wouldn't have made it."

With a sigh, Mark leaned back slightly, his eyes drifting toward the ceiling as he tried to imagine what could have taken place after he went unconscious. Somebody had clearly stepped in, as there had been no one in the room who would have been able to pull Desmond off him. The gap between D rank and C rank was simply too great.

As dreadful as the experience had been, Mark couldn't seem to find it in himself to be angry. Instead, he was just frustrated. He should have recognized the gap in their power earlier and gotten off the stage immediately. Thinking back over the fight, Mark realized that he could have used one of Desmond's early attacks to give him the boost he needed to escape the ring. Instead, he had stuck around, overconfident in his ability to survive.

It didn't help, of course, that Desmond had been using his power from the beginning. Mark remembered the flash of metal as his hand bounced off Desmond's calf. His opponent had a similar power to that of Mark himself, though it covered the majority of his body, which explained why his attacks were so sharp and heavy. At the C rank, controlling where a power was applied wasn't unheard of, and Mark couldn't help but feel a flash of envy. His power only worked on his arm, while Desmond had been able to cover his whole body while excluding his face and hands. Annoyed, Mark reached out, meaning to touch the glass, but before he could, he noticed a faint blinking notification on his right forearm. Curious, he brought up his status and saw that he had a new alert.

Your genetic adaptation, Alchemical Blood, has improved.

Bemused, he pulled up *Alchemical Blood* and saw that it now had a *2* next to it. As he mentally selected it, it unfolded, revealing a surprising gain.

Exposure to high doses of healing potion have caused you to absorb the healing potion's chemical composition, allowing you to transform your blood into a catalyzing agent that, when added to a regular healing potion, will improve its quality by one rank.

This was the same as his elixir ability and caused Mark's eyes to widen slightly. Healing potions, while not as expensive as elixirs or nearly so rare, were still tremendously valuable, as demand for them was constant and voracious. They were particularly important to freelance hunters, and as many empowered made their living by venturing outside the city to hunt down Exlian, Mark could just imagine how many credits would come rolling in if he began mass-producing improved healing potions. The rest of his stay in the tank was consumed with thoughts of how to set up that business, and when the tank finally drained and they pulled him out, he had already come up with a plan.

An elegant-looking middle-aged woman was waiting for him at the door, dressed in a suit with a skirt and holding a clipboard. "Mr. Fields, I hope that your stay in the Javesi Medical Center was rejuvenating."

"It certainly was," Mark replied, flexing his body. "I feel in practically perfect form."

"You should," she said as she glanced down at the clipboard, "as you consumed three times the normal amount of healing potion, but given that your incident happened on our property, we feel that it's a small price to pay. I have your watch and clothing here, as well as a small token of our remorse."

Taking the bag that she offered, Mark saw that laid on top of his neatly folded clothing was a card with the Javesi family logo printed on top of it.

"What's this?" he asked, picking it up.

"That is a VIP card that will get you into any of our clubs around the city. Additionally, I've taken the liberty of transferring two million credits to your account."

Realizing that they were doing their best to buy his silence, Mark looked at the woman for a moment and then smiled widely.

"Thank you," he said. "That's so kind of you."

His calm acceptance allowed the woman to relax, and the hint of tension in her shoulders faded. "I have a car waiting to take you back to your house, if you'll come this way."

Carrying his things, Mark followed after her, and forty-five minutes later he was standing on the sidewalk in front of his house. Mime was sitting on the porch, clearly waiting for him, and as he walked up, Joe opened the door. His brother's expression was calm, but Mark could see the anger burning in his older brother.

"I'm totally fine," Mark said, spreading his arms and turning around so his brother could see.

"Hard not to be, after you spent a day and a half in a healing tank," Joe said, the corners of his lips twitching. "Come on in."

Walking in after his brother, Mark picked Mime up and began petting her. She felt slightly heavier than normal, but Mark just assumed that it was a lingering weakness after having spent so much time in the tank.

"I'm just about to cook lunch," Joe said. "What do you want to eat?"

"Something quick," Mark replied. "I'm already late for training with Master Abrams, and I want to get over there soon. I'm really just here to drop my stuff off."

"Are you sure that's a wise idea?" Joe asked, his eyes narrowing. "Shouldn't you be resting after such a terrible fight? Just because you spent some time in a healing tank doesn't mean there aren't lingering problems."

The question stopped Mark in his tracks, causing his brow to furrow as he considered it deeply. Joe was correct. He had just gone through an intensely traumatic experience of having his bones shattered and being helpless in the face of a much more powerful fighter, but there was no lingering shadow of fear, no ill effect that Mark could sense. Instead, when he thought about what he had gone through, the only thing he felt was deep frustration that he hadn't been able to rip Desmond's leg off with a single strike. Odd, but not important. Now, more than anything, he wanted to throw himself back into training, to keep growing, to get stronger, so that the next time he faced an opponent like Desmond, he'd be able to take them apart without risking life and limb.

"You know, I genuinely think I'm fine," Mark said with a shrug.

"You know yourself better than I do," Joe replied. "I'll make you a quick sandwich, and you can get going, but Mark—"

Pausing at the stairway, Mark looked over his shoulder, meeting Joe's intense gaze.

"You need to be careful with the Javesi family. They don't take well to their name being smeared, and you just made them eat crow. I know you think that Noah is your friend. He might even think that you are friends, but there is no such thing in the aristocratic families. They'll skin you as soon as look at you, and joke around while doing it."

Taken aback by Joe's vehement tone, Mark didn't know what to say.

"The people at the top get a lot of benefits for being there," Joe continued, his expression firm. "Benefits they are willing to go to any lengths to protect. It has transformed this city into a poisonous swamp, more dangerous than any Exlian nest. And the Javesi family sits at the center of that swamp. Anyone who gets on their bad side has a habit of vanishing, and they've had their hands in more than a few of those dirty projects we were talking about before."

Though he didn't think his brother would lie to him, Mark couldn't help but wonder if Joe was exaggerating things. His brother seemed convinced that the city was filled with nefarious forces, but to Mark, the evidence just wasn't there. Even Sky's story about the strange place she had grown up and the tests they had undergone was from years ago, and according to her, that program had been closed.

Joe must have been able to see his skepticism on his face, because his expression hardened, and he turned away. "Some things need to be experienced to be learned. I just hope the lesson doesn't cost you as much as it cost me."

Watching his brother disappear up the stairs, Mark shook his head. Joe was seeing danger where it didn't exist, likely a side effect of having burned out. Figuring it would be better to give him some time, Mark dropped off his stuff, shoved a sandwich in his mouth, and caught a taxi to Abrams's warehouse, where his master was waiting for Mark in the small office, a scowl pasted across his face.

"About time you showed up," Abrams grumbled.

Mark stopped in front of Abrams, clasped his hands together in front of him, his left hand wrapping around his right fist, and bowed deeply. He had seen the gesture in the Cutting Palm manual and knew it was a measure of respect.

"Thank you," he said, meaning it from the bottom of his heart.

"For what?"

Mark didn't know what had happened after he fell unconscious, but it didn't take a genius to know someone had stepped in. The only person he knew with enough influence to force the Javesi family to help him was his master. In truth, he didn't really understand the extent of Abrams's influence, but he did know that Abrams was well known all over the city. Of course, he might be completely wrong, but if he was, he could always play it off as just being grateful for his master's teaching. Seeing the slight twinkle in Abrams's eyes and the faint curl on his lips, Mark knew he had guessed correctly, and instead of replying, he just bowed deeper.

"I should have told you not to get involved with them," Abrams said, "but, and I can't believe I'm saying this, that Javesi kid you're friends with, he's not so bad. So long as he doesn't follow in his father's footsteps, he will make a good friend. If he does follow his father, then there will come a day when either you'll have to bury him or he's going to bury you."

Standing up, Abrams looked Mark up and down. "How are you feeling?"

"I'm feeling great. I've made a full recovery, and if anything, I feel like my strength has improved."

"Good, and do you feel like they treated you fairly? They didn't just shove you in a tank and then kick you to the curb, did they?"

"No, sir. I feel quite well compensated for what I experienced."

"Good. That means we can put this incident behind us and get back to what's important: taking apart Exlian corpses."

Staring at his master's wide grin, Mark could only smile weakly, knowing he was in for a long afternoon of digging through freezing bodies.

Whether because he was still concerned about lingering effects on Mark's health or for some other reason, Abrams kicked Mark out at around eight o'clock, and after taking a shower and getting changed, Mark wandered over to the restaurant to see if Sky was working.

It was midnight by the time Mark got home, and after flopping down in his bed, he saw that he had almost a dozen missed messages, most of them in the team chat group, asking him if he was okay. He opened up the chat and typed out a message.

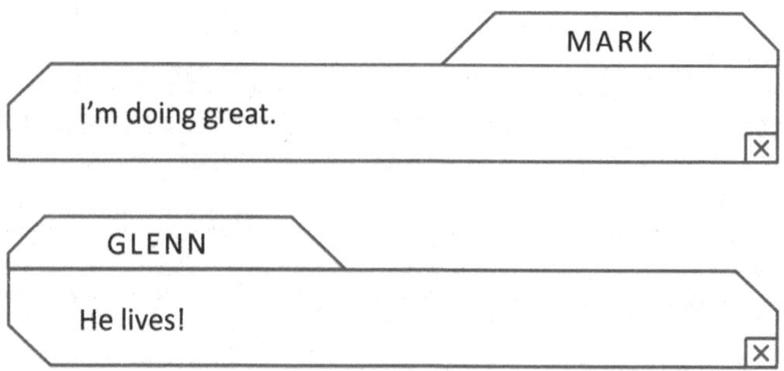

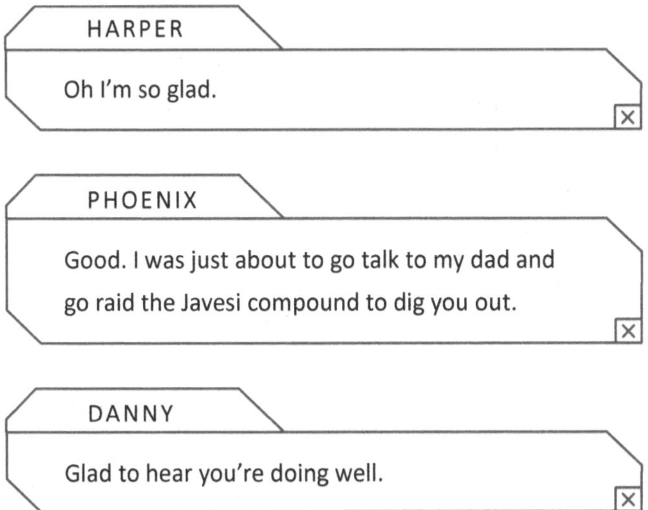

Noah was the only one who didn't respond. Mark didn't let it bother him, as Noah's situation was incredibly complicated. He imagined that his friend probably felt terrible for what had happened. He thought about sending Noah a message but ultimately decided to let it be. Instead, he sent a message to Sky, asking if she'd gotten home safely.

It took her a while to respond, but when he saw that she had, Mark let out a long sigh and closed his eyes, quickly drifting off into sleep. The next few days passed with relative normality, and Mark threw himself into his work with Abrams, immersing himself in his master's trade as he continued to practice the second stage of the Cutting Palm at night.

He had more free time in the evenings, and he and Sky began regularly hanging out after she got off her shift. She still was strangely hesitant to speak about where she lived, but Mark didn't mind. They began to roam the city, chatting and exploring as they got to know each other better. Mime often accompanied them, and Sky grew particularly attached to the small black cat.

Sky also adored high spaces, and most of their evenings ended with them finding a tall building to climb. They would perch on the roof and stare out over the city, admiring the glittering lights. As the week drew to a close, Mark and Sky were sitting on top of a tall building, thirteen stories off the ground. Mime was sitting comfortably in Sky's lap when she turned to Mark.

"Hey, Mark," she said.

"Yeah, what's up?" he replied.

"Why doesn't Mime make any noise? Is that why you named her Mime?"

It took a moment for Mark to understand what Sky was talking about. He was about to protest when it suddenly struck him. He had never actually heard Mime make any noise, at least with her mouth. Even her paws were unnaturally silent.

"I'm not sure. Maybe that subconsciously did play into my naming her Mime."

"Do you think she's mute, or is she just quiet?" Sky asked. Mime sat up and looked at them, each in turn.

"No idea," Mark admitted. "It could be that there's something wrong with her vocal cords, as now that you mentioned it, I've never heard her purr either."

"A cat who doesn't purr, huh? Well, even if she doesn't make noise, she sure is cute," Sky said with a smile. "Mime, can you say 'meow'? Say 'meow.'"

Mime's head slowly tilted to the side, and then, in an almost perfect replica of Sky's voice, she replied, "Meow."

Mark and Sky both stared at Mime in shock.

"Okay, that is *not* what a meow is supposed to sound like," Mark said, slightly creeped out.

Before either of them could continue to press the matter, the city shook, and a fireball rose in the distance, lighting up the night. A moment later, the shock wave hit, knocking Sky and Mark from their place on the edge of the building.

Grabbing the edge of the wall behind him, Mark slipped an arm around Sky, holding her tight as the shaking sent her tumbling forward. Sky's weight pulled him from the edge of the building, and for the briefest of moments they were falling before his hand tightened on the edge, catching them. Sky shrieked, clutching Mime tightly, as they hung thirteen stories above the ground.

"Hold on! I've got you."

Trying not to scrape Sky against the side of the building, he pulled up, lifting Sky high enough to push her up and over the edge. Once she was safe, he grabbed the ledge with two hands and climbed up, tumbling over the small ledge. Sky's eyes were wide, her breath coming fast. Mark, on the contrary, was completely calm, and once again he was struck by the strange discrepancy between what he felt and what he thought he should have been feeling.

Sky stared toward the center of the city as sirens started to sound in the distance. "What was that?"

Standing up, Mark brushed off his hand and pointed. It was hard to see the dark cloud of smoke rising into the air, but the occasional flicker of flame and the bright lights made it faintly visible against the night sky.

"There was an explosion, a really big one," Mark replied.

He tapped on his watch, pulling up the news feeds, and watched as reports rolled in. The explosion was at one of the major train terminals, mercifully mostly empty at this time of night, but at least a dozen people had already been confirmed caught in the blast. There was no doubt in Mark's mind that they had been killed instantly, as the explosion had been powerful enough to shake the entire city. That station was one of the central hubs, and Mark quickly saw reports of the entire mass transit system grinding to a halt.

"Well, that's not good."

Sky, who had been reading about the situation as well, shook her head. "No, it's not. Do you think it was an intentional explosion?"

"Most people are saying it's a gas leak, but we probably won't know for sure until later tonight."

Glancing at the smoke rising in the distance, Sky let out a bitter sigh. "You know, there are some times that I wish I could just disappear from this place. Or fly away into the sky." With a light laugh, she shook her head. "I just feel so powerless."

Shutting down his virtual screen, Mark walked over to stand next to her.

"I get that," he said. "Last weekend, I ran into a situation where I was genuinely powerless, and it was awful. I got into a fight with somebody I shouldn't have been fighting, and they crushed me without even trying. That feeling of powerlessness is really terrible, but you know, there is a way to overcome it."

Her face illuminated by the bright lights of the city, Sky turned and looked at Mark, waiting for him to continue. Reaching up to touch his necklace, Mark's left arm transformed into gleaming titanium, and he slowly clenched his fingers into a hard fist.

"And that is to get more powerful ourselves. To increase our own power and the power of our networks. Not so we can rule over others but so we can be genuinely free from the system."

"Is that actually possible?" Sky asked skeptically as her eyes drifted back to the billowing black cloud in the distance.

"It is," Mark said. "I know two people who are free. My master, who is so strong and so important that nobody can touch him, and my brother, who's free in here"—Mark tapped his chest—"and up here." He tapped his head. "And no matter what happens to him, those two things can't be taken away, but it's a lot easier said than done, and if I'm honest, I have no idea how to get there."

"That's fine for you to say, Mark. You're empowered." Sky's voice was quiet. So quiet, Mark had to strain to hear it. "But for regular people like me, the future isn't so rosy."

Though he felt an overwhelming desire to grab Sky and

promise that he would help her gain the power and freedom that she wanted, Mark kept quiet. He was confident in his own ability to rise, but he knew better than to promise something he might not be able to fulfill, and though he liked Sky and genuinely wanted to see her happy, she wasn't wrong. For a human, New Emery was rough. He knew from firsthand experience. After all, it hadn't been that long since he was in the same place, barely scraping along at the bottom of society's barrel.

It was with a subdued heart that he walked into his house. Joe was at the kitchen table, but his eyes were glued to the screen in the living room, where the news anchor was sharing details about the explosion.

". . . authorities arriving on the scene were able to rescue six people, who are in critical condition, but at least a dozen more are suspected to have been killed in the blast. Details are still sparse, but as the fires are brought under control, the authorities expect to learn more."

Tapping his watch to turn off the screen, Joe looked at Mark. "Why the long face?"

Joining Joe at the table, Mark shrugged. "Things just seem a bit bleak at the moment. I had a conversation with Sky that ended on a down note, and now this whole explosion in the city. Just a bit unsettling."

"I'd brace yourself," Joe said, his tone severe. "This feels like a harbinger of things to come."

Taken aback, Mark gave his brother a confused look, but Joe didn't elaborate. Standing up, he patted Mark on the shoulder as he headed upstairs.

Mark was still thinking about what Joe had said on Monday morning when he headed back to the training camp. Arriving in the changing room just before six a.m., he saw that Danny was already there. His big friend looked him over with a critical eye, worried that there had been lingering ill effects, but Mark, who had already stripped off his shirt, spread his arms out and turned around. "See, doing better than ever."

"You're not joking," Danny said. "How on earth did you get that muscle definition?"

Looking down at his body, which appeared to have been sculpted from stone, Mark flashed a lopsided grin and shrugged. "Good genetics?"

"Ha, it must be. Because I'm at least a dozen times stronger than you, and I look like a lump of clay."

Danny's physique certainly wasn't as bad as he made it out to be, but the level of rapid definition in Mark's musculature was truly incredible. He had just finished putting on his bodysuit when the door opened and Noah came in. Without hesitating, Noah walked right up to Mark and held out his hand. "I'm sorry for what you had to go through. It won't happen again."

"Don't worry about it," Mark said with an easy smile. "I was well taken care of afterward."

"Not well enough, in my opinion," Noah replied. "I want to personally thank you for what you did for me. I was too late in recognizing Desmond, and I should have known that Amy was planning something. If you hadn't stepped up, I would have ended up in just as bad shape as you did."

"Really?" Mark asked, his forehead furrowed. "Your sister would do that to you?"

"It wouldn't be the first time," Noah said with a grimace. "She knows little restraint, though she's been much more tolerable since Master Abrams put the fear in her."

"You didn't get in too much trouble with your dad, did you?" Danny asked Noah from across the room.

Flashing a brief smile, Noah shook his head. "Just the normal sadistic training sessions and starvation."

The calm way he spoke made Mark's heart hurt. Taking a deep breath, he patted Noah on the shoulder. "It sounds like you suffered more than I did. Come on, let's get suited up."

Together with Glenn, who arrived a few minutes later, the four of them got into their mana suits and went to the training ground to meet up with the girls. They found Lieutenant Wells waiting there for them and quickly fell into formation.

"For the next three weeks, I'm going to be with you," he said. "We'll be patrolling every day except Fridays, when you'll have classroom instruction. I'm going to be primarily teaching you about fieldwork—how to build fortifications, how to assess positions, how to identify resources or the signs of resources, things like that. I believe in on-the-job training, and so I picked up a few missions for us that we'll be trying to complete as we're out. Of course, at the same time, we'll be doing our anti-Exlian training.

So never forget: Keep your head on a swivel. Any questions?"

Seeing there were none, he clapped his hands together. "All right, follow me."

As they ran toward the city gate, Mark observed the suit that Lieutenant Wells was wearing. It was rougher around the edges than Lieutenant Cox's suit and didn't move quite as quickly, but its limbs carried a greater feeling of strength, and Mark could only imagine it was just as dangerous in combat. Wells carried two axes on his back and a massive metal pole in his hand. After scanning them out at the gate, he gestured for Phoenix to step forward. "I've read your profile and Lieutenant Cox's assessment. It sounds like you've already settled into a good team formation, so I'm not gonna throw any wrenches in your plan. Here's your mission."

There was a beep, and Mark held up his wrist as details of the mission Lieutenant Wells was assigning flashed across his helmet's visor. It was a search-and-secure mission. Wells had identified a building a few dozen blocks from the city, and the team was to search through it and secure it. It appeared straightforward enough, but the Exlian made sure nothing was ever straightforward. Phoenix clearly felt the same way, because she took a long time to speak up, reading over the mission multiple times. "Sir?"

"Yes, Phoenix."

"Is there a particular reason we are trying to secure this building?"

"That is exactly the question you should be asking," Lieutenant Wells said. "The Engineering Corps is not like the Defense Force or even the Rangers. We don't just blindly follow orders, but instead, we think about what we're doing. Our greatest advantage over the Exlian is not our mana tools, though that certainly is an advantage. It's not the strength of our arms, because frankly, we're outclassed there by at least a couple of degrees. Instead"—Lieutenant Wells tapped on his helmet, producing a ringing sound—"it's our minds.

You may have heard that there are some Exlian who are just as smart as humans. They may be just as smart, but they don't display creativity the way we do. Understanding why you're executing a mission is one of the most important facets of being able to execute it well. To answer your question, we're establishing a forward base there. Your team is securing the location and clearing any Exlian you find, as well as establishing the perimeter. In about six hours, another team will be coming through, transporting gear, and they'll need a place to stop and rest."

Raising his hand, Mark waited for Lieutenant Wells to gesture to him before speaking up. "Does that mean we'll be spending the night outside the city, sir?"

"No, once the perimeter is established and we've rendezvoused with the second team, a third team from the Defense Force camp will be coming to relieve you. That is, assuming all goes according to plan."

"Got it, sir. Thank you," Phoenix said, turning to the team. "All right, anybody have any concerns with the way we have been operating? If so, speak up now."

Nobody responded, and so she assigned everybody their tasks. Mark found himself out front again, which suited him just fine. He quite enjoyed having the open city before him and occasionally found himself moving too fast for the others to keep up through the broken buildings and twisting streets. The team was supposed to keep up a sedate pace, making sure they had plenty of energy when they finally reached their destination, which meant Mark had to suppress his desire to run ahead. One of the challenges of having such a tremendous amount of energy was the constant drive to expend it, but he forced himself into the pace Phoenix set, recognizing the wisdom in preserving his energy for when they faced the enemy.

Of course, there was no guarantee that they would find an enemy at their destination, and it wasn't until they were roughly a block away from their target building that Mark sensed something. As he stepped into the strange mental webbing he had come to recognize as the Exlian overlay, there was a faint prickling from up ahead. During his downtime, he had been looking into what he was feeling, and what he had discovered had left him more confused than ever. Research on the Exlian suggested that they communicated through a psychic web projected by each Exlian. The stronger the Exlian, the larger the web they produced, and when Exlian gathered, these webs would combine, extending out even farther.

Mark was able to sense that web, though no amount of searching revealed anyone else who had ever reported such a thing. As oblivious as he sometimes was, Mark was starting to understand just how different his powers were. If he was right and he was tapping into the Exlian's psychic network, then he was experiencing something no other human had ever experienced before.

After he took a few steps forward, the feeling of prickling in the front of his mind got stronger, and Mark held up his hand, signaling for the team to stop. "Exlian ahead. Probably inside the building we're looking to occupy."

"Harper, can you check it out?" Phoenix asked, and the team waited as Harper cast her vision forward.

"I'm seeing a few dozen drones," she said quietly.

"What about in the other buildings?" Phoenix asked.

"Let me check," Harper replied as she began to extensively scan the surrounding buildings.

The last thing the team wanted to do was enter their target building and then find themselves swarmed from all sides, so they waited in silence as Harper checked the surrounding buildings thoroughly.

"Nothing," she said, "but just because I can't see them doesn't mean they're not there."

"Exactly, and you said about three dozen? That's more than we've ever faced before. Thankfully, we should be able to fight through them piecemeal," Phoenix mused, pulling up the layout of the building they were about to assault.

Feeling a shift as the Exlian overlay abruptly expanded, Mark spun around, pointing to the southwest. "We need to get into hiding. There's a massive group of drones heading this way. They're gonna pass through this location in a couple of minutes."

Without questioning him, Phoenix nodded.

"Let's go, folks," she said, and took off running, leading the group into a nearby building half a block down from their target.

As quickly as possible, they climbed the stairs until they were on the roof, where they hunkered down to wait. Only two minutes after they took their positions, Harper, who had been watching the streets below, let out a gasp. "There are hundreds of them!"

Soon the team began to hear chittering and the clack of drone legs on the asphalt as the monsters crawled by. For ten tense minutes, they waited, not daring to move lest they attract the attention of the mass of drones passing by. Even Lieutenant Wells appeared nervous. When they were finally gone and a few minutes had passed, Phoenix sat up and looked around at the group. "What do you think?"

Noah spoke up first, his tone calm and certain. "There's a high chance that there's a warrior in the area. We only get concentrations of drones that large near warriors. What are our options?"

"We can continue with the mission, or we can call it off," Phoenix said, glancing at the lieutenant, who nodded.

"What's the likelihood we can beat a warrior?" Glenn asked.

"We should be able to overpower a D-ranked warrior without too much trouble. A C rank will be a lot harder, and B . . ." Phoenix shook her head. "Let's hope we don't meet a B-ranked warrior."

"I concur," Lieutenant Wells said gruffly.

"There shouldn't be any B-ranked warriors this close to the city. There shouldn't even be any C-ranked warriors this close to the city," Harper added. "I say we risk it."

"I vote to keep going as well," Danny said.

When Phoenix looked at him, Mark shrugged. In truth, if the decision were up to him, he never would have considered backing down. It was better to leave the choice up to others. Thinking for a moment, Phoenix nodded. "All right, let's keep going. We'll wait for another two minutes, and if the way is still clear, we'll head toward our target."

They occupied themselves for the two remaining minutes by adjusting their suits and making sure their weapons were working. Mark didn't bother drawing the short sword, as his metal gauntlets would be much more effective against the drones. He still couldn't use the second stage of the Cutting Palm technique, but the first stage was more than enough to deal with drones, thanks to the hard alloy gauntlets he wore.

When the two minutes had passed and the Exlian overlay had shrunk again, he stood and led the way down the staircases, pausing before he exited the building to scan the street. As quietly as possible, he began to make his way along the side of the street toward the target building, paying careful attention to the prickling sensation in the psychic web. Unfortunately, there was no way to kill drones silently without alerting the rest of them, so there was almost no reason to employ a stealth approach.

Instead, the team stacked up by the door as Mark gave the signal for seven drones, which was the number he counted inside the main lobby. On Phoenix's command, they kicked open the door and rushed in. Mark headed straight for the closest drone, accelerating rapidly, and hit the drone with the force of a high-speed train, crushing it into paste with a well-placed kick.

The next drone, only a few feet behind the first, let out a shriek and launched itself toward him, but a quick strike split it down the middle. The others were already fighting, arrows and daggers flashing through the air, accompanied by Danny's roar and Noah's flashing blade. Phoenix didn't engage, instead watching the team's back and getting ready to shield if anybody fell into a troublesome situation.

As each drone died, Mark could feel the psychic network trembling as they let out a shriek, and the faint prickle that marked their location winked out. The drones upstairs had been alerted and were already beginning to rush down, tumbling over one another as they raced toward the bottom floor.

"Danny! Block the door!" Phoenix yelled, and shouting his acknowledgment, Danny ran forward, planting his shield in the doorway that led to the stairs.

The drones hit him a moment later, crashing against the massive shield and splitting to either side, where they were met by Noah, whose sword was supported by Harper's arrows, and on the other side by Mark's fists and Glenn's dancing daggers. Despite dying in droves, the drones threw themselves forward with no hesitation, until eventually their numbers dropped to manageable levels. When only six were coming from the upper floors, Mark felt something shift in the psychic network, and a second bright light began to blaze . . .

If the drones had been tiny pricks in the psychic network, then the new presence that suddenly appeared was like a small sun, causing the psychic network to suddenly strengthen.

"We've got trouble!" Mark yelled, realizing what he was sensing.

"What—?"

Cutting Phoenix off, Mark pointed to the ceiling. "Warrior coming through!" he yelled as the ceiling exploded, showering them with shards of cement, and a large Exlian monster dropped through the hole.

It had six legs, much like the drones, and a pair of heavy claws, an extra pair of arms extended from its back, each ending in a scything talon. The mantis warrior was one of the more common warrior-ranked Exlian, though that didn't make it any less dangerous. It had dropped behind Danny and was rearing back to strike at Harper, who was standing nearby, when Phoenix yelled, "Danny, hit it!"

Spinning with surprising agility, considering his bulk, Danny lowered his shoulder and charged forward, his shield ramming into the side of the warrior, sending it tumbling across the lobby floor, its legs scrabbling to find purchase on the slippery, polished concrete. Mark and Noah, without needing to be told, stepped into the gap Danny's exit created, both striking a drone that had made it to the bottom of the stairs.

"I've got this!" Mark yelled, and with a nod, Noah spun around and launched himself into the fight between Danny and the massive mantis.

"Hit it with everything you've got!" Phoenix yelled, beginning to summon blasts of mana from her fists that seared the air as they melted chunks of the mantis's armor.

Glancing over his shoulder, Mark saw the fight was going well, which meant the warrior probably wasn't above the D rank. Judging from how relaxed Lieutenant Wells was, Mark felt pretty good about the situation. This lasted all of two minutes, when suddenly he felt the psychic network flare again and realized there was another warrior heading toward them quickly.

"We've got another warrior incoming!" he yelled, and a moment later, one of the walls of the building exploded as a second mantis, this one bigger and considerably faster, burst into the room.

Worse, its carapace gleamed red, causing Mark's breath to catch. This was a clear sign of a mutation, and his mind spun through what he had learned with Abrams about assessing elementally active Exlian.

"It's probably got a flame attack!" Mark yelled, and just in time, Phoenix pulled the mana in front of her together, forming a barrier as a blast of flame rolled across her and Harper.

Danny, tangled up with the first mantis, wasn't able to respond in time as the second warrior mantis threw itself forward, darting past him and raking him with one of its sharp blades. Mark had just killed the final drone on the stairs and now turned and charged toward the fight, even as Danny let out a pained roar and fell to one knee. There was a blur as Noah intercepted a claw aiming at Danny's head, managing to deflect it with a twist of his blade. Abandoning his shield and gripping his sword in two hands, Noah let out a shout and unleashed a vicious chop that sliced straight through the weaker mantis's claw arm.

It hissed in pain and scuttled backward, all the while pelted by arrows. As Danny struggled to get to his feet, blood dripping down his back, Mark found himself facing the stronger of the two mantises. It didn't seem to be in the C rank, which he was immensely grateful for, but was still a mutated D-ranked mantis, which made it about twice as dangerous as normal.

With Phoenix behind him and Glenn off to one side, Mark's focus narrowed. He could feel a fierce boiling in his chest, a strange mix of excitement and hunger that left him confused. Just before the mantis moved, Mark sensed it. Whether from a twitch of its muscles or a premonition through the psychic network, he wasn't sure, but it meant that he was a fraction of a second faster. He stepped forward, bringing him inside the mantis's range, neatly avoiding its stabbing blade. It responded by trying to snip him in half, but he twisted out of the way, his palms warding the two claws away from his body to snap empty air.

With arms and legs flying, he fought against the drone in close quarters. He used the faint precognition he possessed, along with the thousands of hours of practice fighting against Exlian in close combat, to keep himself from getting snapped in half while Glenn and Phoenix peppered the monster with their attacks. Risking a glance toward the other fight, he saw that Danny had recovered his feet and was currently using his shield to great effect, slamming it repeatedly into the one-clawed mantis's face. This kept it off balance as Noah went to town on its carapace, his mana-infused blade tearing great chunks out of the monster.

Harper's arrows, more effective against smaller Exlian, didn't have quite enough power to do significant damage. However, whenever an opportunity presented itself, she would send an arrow deep into its body, targeting the wounds Noah was making. The Exlian Mark was fighting suddenly let out a hiss and abandoned its attacks against him, lunging for Phoenix, who quickly erected a shield. Mark, who was half underneath the giant creature, took the opportunity to whip out his short sword, thrusting up and burying it in the monster's neck.

With a screech of pain, it fell back, trying to grab at the handle of the sword with its claws. Sensing an opportunity to go in for the kill, Mark did just that. His left arm had long since transformed into the same alloy that formed the plates on his armor. Now he darted forward, dodging past a slashing blade and vaulting up and onto the mantis's back. He thrust his left hand down, tearing straight through the hard armor that covered the Exlian's head and driving his fingers into the monster's brain.

With a heavy shudder, the Exlian dropped to the ground, and a moment later, Noah's sword lopped the other mantis's head off. Mark jumped down from the top of the mantis, staying well clear of its claws, just in case touching them triggered a death reflex. One of the hidden dangers of Exlian warriors was that they often spasmed after death, and if you were not careful, you could get caught in the flailing.

The rest of the team was slowly gathering up, trying to calm down after the fierce fight, but Mark was already scanning the psychic web, trying to sense if any other Exlian were nearby. As the two warriors fell, there had been a muted shriek, as if coming from the other side of a wall. The network faded as well, though Mark could still faintly sense it on the periphery of his mind.

"I think we're safe," he said after a moment, causing Glenn to let out a large sigh.

"Ugh, that was terrible."

"You're telling me," Danny said, unclipping his helmet, as Harper checked the large slash that had torn straight through Danny's armor and laid open his back.

From the pouch she carried at her side, Harper pulled out a bottle with pale-red liquid in it, and Mark watched with interest. As she dripped it into the wound, Danny hissed, clenching his teeth as the painful process of healing started, but within a couple of minutes, the healing potion had caused his skin to knit back together, leaving a faint scar.

Phoenix, working with Noah and Glenn, had begun to move the corpses, and once Danny was healed, he helped Mark flip the mutated mantis on its back so Mark could retrieve his short sword. After cleaning it off, Mark looked at the corpse of the mutated Exlian with interest. After a moment of thought, he walked over to Lieutenant Wells. "Sir, are we allowed to butcher the Exlian corpses during our missions?"

"Can I ask why you're asking?" Lieutenant Wells asked, his brow furrowing slightly.

"I'm curious about this mutation, sir," Mark said. "Normally, fire mutations like this only happen when there's a source of extreme heat nearby. However, if the monster ate something that has a high amount of fire mana in it, that could have caused a mutation as well. I'd like to see if there are any traces."

Smiling, Wells nodded. "Sure, go ahead if you think you can."

"Thank you, sir."

Taking off his gauntlets, Mark asked Danny to help him position the mantis, then began cutting through its chest. Butchering an Exlian corpse on the battlefield was very different from doing so in the warehouse, and as Mark's fingers stabbed through the outer carapace into the softer flesh below, he felt a jolt run through him, nearly causing him to gasp.

Taking a deep breath as his hunger surged, he forcefully controlled it and began working through the mantis's chest, looking for its stomach, which he extracted with a practiced hand. The rest of the team watched in silence as he tore the stomach open gently, revealing what appeared to be a mash that he examined with a critical eye.

"Find anything?" Lieutenant Wells asked, leaning over Mark's shoulder.

"Yes, sir. It looks like we have fire moss nearby," Mark said, using his pinkie to point at a trace of red fiber mixed in with everything else.

"Sharp eyes, kid," Lieutenant Wells said, tapping Mark on the shoulder. "That's actually why we're here. There's a cave underneath this building, and it's got fire moss in it. The base we're setting up is so that the Engineering Corps can harvest it."

"In that case, we better get our perimeter set," Phoenix said, and the team quickly split up.

Mark, Noah, and Phoenix combed through the floors above, while Harper, Glenn, and Danny guarded the lower lobby. There weren't any other Exlian in the building, and soon the team had gathered once more.

"At this point, it's just a matter of waiting," Phoenix said. "We have three hours before the Engineering Corps team arrives, and our replacements shouldn't be much further behind. Stay alert, and make sure you eat something."

Unbuckling his helmet, Mark sat down on a chunk of rubble and pulled a tube of nutrient paste out of his bag.

"Ugh. How can you eat that stuff?" Harper asked as she peeled a bar.

"I'd rather be full than hungry," Mark replied, shrugging.

He had spent the majority of his biofuel in the fight against the mantises and was quite happy for the opportunity to fill up a bit. At the same time, he kept having the strangest sensation, as if there were a deliciously tasty meal sitting nearby, but every time he looked around, all he could see were the mutilated corpses of the Exlian.

With Danny's help, he pulled the mantises outside the building, dumped them in a shallow grave along with the other drones, and covered them with rubble. It wouldn't keep the scavengers from picking at them, but it would keep the lobby from festering as they began to rot.

He had just turned away when he felt a faint shift that caused him to stop and slowly turn around, his eyes scanning the environment. Failing to notice the small pair of glittering red eyes peering at him from under a gap in the pile of rocks he and Danny had just thrown together, he shrugged and went back into the building. A faint sound of crunching drifted into the air, quiet enough that it went unnoticed.

The rest of the mission went smoothly, with the two teams arriving one after another. Mark and the others even got a chance to go down into the cave below the building, accessed through the basement, and check out the thick carpet of fire moss that filled it. Fire moss was a subbreed of elemental moss, a strange type of moss that had evolved to be able to filter specific kinds of mana out of the air. It had a considerable number of uses, both for alchemy and for consumable products in general, and so long as this base could be maintained, the cave would provide a steady, albeit small, supply of fire moss to the alchemists of New Emery.

It was with high spirits that the team returned to the city. Their first mission and, more importantly, their first encounter with warrior-ranked Exlian had gone smoothly. After peeling themselves out of their mana suits and washing the dirt, grime, and blood from their bodies, they gathered to debrief. Lieutenant Wells stroked his beard as he scanned the group.

"I'm genuinely at a bit of a loss," he said. "You operate together as well as any team I've seen. Your skills are balanced. None of you fight for leadership, but you all think independently. Lieutenant Cox had high praise for you, but I must admit I was a little bit skeptical. But you successfully fought against not one but two warrior Exlian and completed your mission perfectly. I'm going to have to tell him he sold you short. Even though they were only in the D rank, it's important to understand just how much of an achievement killing Exlian warriors is. Exlian ranks are different from human ranks, and it takes, on average, four empowered to beat one Exlian of the same rank. Not only did you defeat a D-ranked Exlian warrior, at the same time you fought off and killed a mutated warrior.

"Phoenix, your calm assessment in the midst of battle and your assignment of soldiers were impeccable. Shifting Danny from blocking the door to using his strength to suppress the first mantis was exactly the right move. Mark, that sixth sense you have that tells you when an enemy is approaching and in what quantity is something you need to focus on cultivating, as it will make surviving in the wilderness much easier. The rest of you, your attacks were strong and consistent, without any sloppiness at all. Noah, especially, you have quite the skill with your blade. Glenn and Harper, the same is true for your accuracy.

"Overall, you did phenomenally. Of course, there's always more to learn, but genuinely, if this had been your final test, you would have all passed with flying colors. However, just because you've done it once doesn't mean your job is done. The next few weeks are going to be about doing exactly what you did today over and over again. I'll have a new mission for you tomorrow, and it'll be a long one, so I recommend you go and get some rest."

Time fell into the familiar rhythm, passing in a blur and leaving Mark wondering where the days went. He was as busy as always. During the day, he would be deployed with a team, combing through the dead zone, killing Exlian, and learning from Lieutenant Wells about everything from building fortifications and entrenching positions to performing demolitions and collecting resources. His nights were spent with Abrams, who had begun to increase Mark's alchemical training, making him memorize volume after volume of ingredients and their uses.

Halfway through their six-week training period, Lieutenant Wells bid them farewell, and Lieutenant Rene joined them to teach them Ranger-specific skills, such as scouting, information collection, and tracking. Over the course of the six weeks, the team faced down warrior-ranked Exlian three more times, but in each case, it was only a single monster in the D rank, and with careful tactics, they managed to bring the Exlian down without trouble each time.

The only major change in Mark's life was that his incessant dream war against Exlian drones had ended, and to his dismay he now faced Exlian warriors once he fell asleep. Killing an Exlian warrior on his own was practically impossible. He had been able to kill the mutated mantis with relative ease, but only because it had been distracted by Phoenix and Glenn. Facing it solo, it was all he could do to survive, and he felt as if he had been thrust back into the early days of his dream battles.

After six hours of being repeatedly crushed by the single mantis that spawned, Mark would wake up, lie in bed for a second as he tried to reorient himself, and then, with a sigh, begin his personal training for the day. He was seeing tremendous progress on that front, and after two months of solid practice, his recovery speed had already improved. Before, Mark had needed to use five units of biofuel to recover fully, which took about half an hour for his body to process. Now, after two months, he had cut that number down to three and could recover fully in just ten minutes. He was a little bit worried that he would reach the end of his improvement, but since the training program was still working, he kept at it.

When their six-week training period ended, the team was called into a room to meet with Lieutenant Cox, Lieutenant Rene, and Lieutenant Wells. All three lieutenants had already expressed their appreciation for Mark and his team, and six small boxes sat on the table in front of them.

"You know," Lieutenant Cox said with a smile, "you've put us in a slightly awkward situation, as it's very rare for a team to get perfect scores across the board, but watching you shore up your weaknesses and polish your strengths over the last eighteen weeks has been a wonderful experience. As promised, graduating in the top twenty will get you a skill gem. However, the top twenty slots are for all the training camps in the city, not just Camp Eleven."

Immediately, the tension in the room rose.

"Now, the three primary camps for the Defense Force,

Rangers, and Engineering Corps are not included, but the competition was still fierce. After an independent assessment and on our recommendation, I'm pleased to announce that all of you have made it, though some only by the skin of their teeth," Lieutenant Rene said with a grin, looking pointedly at Glenn. "Glenn squeezed in at twenty, thanks to the fact that he had three glowing recommendations."

With a huge sigh of relief, Glenn bowed. "Thank you."

"No need to thank us. You deserve it," Lieutenant Wells said. "As is tradition, the six stones will be randomly distributed, starting with our first-place slot, Noah."

Mark wasn't surprised that Noah had gotten first place, as he was practically perfect in everything he did. He had no idea whether Noah's family ties had anything to do with his position, but even if Noah had been some unknown kid from the slums, Mark believed he would have gotten first place. Noah was incredibly smart and had a suite of powers that allowed him to fight up at least one level, making him one of the strongest recruits in the training camps.

"And in third place, Phoenix."

Bowing slightly, Phoenix stepped forward and picked up the box directly in front of her.

"Next, we have Mark, who came in seventh."

Heart hammering, Mark stepped forward, his eyes scanning over the boxes. Of the four left, the one on the far right called to him, and even though he had to cross the room, he walked over and picked it up before returning to his place. Danny had gotten the twelfth position, Harper the thirteenth, and Glenn, of course, was last with spot twenty. Once everybody had their boxes, Lieutenant Cox cleared his throat.

"Now," he said, looking at each of them in turn, "you're going to be given an assessment to fill out. That assessment will have some questions about your experience, but more importantly, it'll ask you about your plans for the future. There are really three potential paths. The first is that you join the basic infantry. As you know, New Emery is preparing to face a wave, and we expect it to be a big one, which is why we've opened up so many camps, and this is just the first phase of the training camps. More will be starting up in a couple of weeks.

"Joining the basic infantry will put you on the front line in the fight against the Exlian. I know everybody knocks the infantry, but in reality, the infantry forms the core of our military, manning the walls against the threat and keeping our city safe. The second option is that you elect to join one of the three special branches: the Defense Force, the Rangers, or the Engineering Corps. Now, you don't get to actually choose, but you can indicate on the form which branch you're most interested in. I assure you, especially since you're among the top twenty in the city, your wishes will be taken into consideration.

"The third option is one that I don't recommend but is always available. You can elect to be a Reserve member. The Reserves are groups of empowered individuals who don't serve actively in the military but agree to participate in the battles. Most hunters are Reserve members. While it can be a lucrative path in the short term, it tends to produce incredibly short-lived careers, as the Reserves tend to be stuck into the worst situations and the most dangerous gaps, but it is always a path if you wish to pursue it. Let me congratulate you all once again on your graduation from the training camp. I sincerely hope I'll get to see you around."

Saluting, the team filed out and for a moment simply stood in the hall looking at each other with excitement.

"I think it's time for another party," Phoenix said. "But this time *not* at Noah's place."

That earned a chuckle, and even Noah smiled.

"How about I host," Phoenix said. "I haven't gotten a chance to show off like Mark or Noah."

"It sounds fun," Mark said. "But I'll have to ask my master. He's a bit of a stickler for training. Do you have a free day coming up?"

"Sunday I should be free most of the day. If that works for everybody else, we can do it then," Phoenix said, looking around at the group. Seeing everyone's nods, she punched something into her watch. "All right, I'll send out the location, and I'll see you all Sunday."

After saying goodbye to everybody, Mark jogged home, holding the box containing the skill gem tightly. Even though it was random what sort of ability would be produced, Mark was incredibly excited. Despite being D rank, Mark didn't have any skills, and he was hoping that he would be able to unlock something cool to supplement his more passive genetic adaptations.

When he arrived home, he saw Joe sitting on the couch and was greeted by Mime at the door. Stopping to pat his cat on the head, Mark glanced at Joe. Recently, Joe had been looking stressed, as if there was something weighing on him. Now, he was hunched forward, staring intensely at the newscast.

"I got into the top twenty."

Glancing up, Joe blinked at Mark as his mind caught up with what Mark had just said.

"They gave me a skill gem."

"Hey, congratulations!" Jumping up, Joe slapped Mark on the shoulder and then pulled him into a hug. After a tight squeeze, Joe held Mark at arm's length. "I'm really proud of you, Mark. You've been working so hard. I'm not surprised you made it."

A flush of pride caused Mark to grin. "Thanks. I got number seven."

"And you got a gem for it?"

Nodding, Mark held out the white box, trying to put it into Joe's hand. "Here. I have a really good feeling about it."

"It won't help me."

"But can't you . . ."

Flashing a smile that didn't manage to mask the sadness in his eyes, Joe shook his head. "No. I didn't just burn out my flame ability, Mark. I burned out all my skills too. I don't have any free slots anymore, and with them burned out, there is no way to get rid of them. I really do appreciate the thought, but I can't use it."

Slowly pulling the box back, Mark felt strangely embarrassed. He had been sure that this was the solution to Joe's troubles, but reality was harsher than he'd realized.

Later that night, he sat cross-legged on the floor of his room, carefully opening the box and gazing down at the glimmering green gem inside. The gem carried a sense of freedom about it that appealed to Mark, and with careful fingers, he lifted it out of the box, holding it in his palm.

Even though he had never used a skill gem before, he had been taught in one of his theory classes how to absorb it, and Joe had given him some notes as well. Mark cupped his hands in front of his stomach, holding the glowing green gem loosely in his palm as he began to concentrate on it.

Guided by the mana in his body, the gem should have transformed into a dense mist, flowing up and into his nose and mouth as it began to build a skill in him. Instead, it sat completely inert in his palm. Figuring that he wasn't concentrating hard enough, Mark doubled down, but as the seconds ticked into minutes, he realized something wasn't right.

According to what he had learned, he should be able to feel the energy of the stone, but apart from looking like a rock filled with various shades of dancing greens, it looked perfectly ordinary to Mark. With a frown, he lifted the gem and sniffed it. It smelled perfectly ordinary as well. Shaking it did nothing but cause beams of green light to scatter around the room, and with a sigh of frustration, he put it back in his palm and tried again.

After nearly five minutes of absolute concentration, he felt something shift near him and quickly closed his palm as Mime pounced on it. Her sharp teeth pricked his hand, but he didn't open his fingers and instead pushed her away. "Ow, stop that. It's not for you to eat. This is not for cats."

Managing to look both despondent and offended that Mark would even dream of thinking she wanted to eat the skill gem, Mime sat by the door and looked away from Mark, occasionally peeking at him from the corner of her eye.

Sticking the gem back in the box, Mark made sure the lid was tightly on and then kept it with him as he walked over to his desk to begin searching for more information on the empowered forums. Every single thing he read led him to believe that it should be a simple process to absorb a skill gem. In the videos, it took less than a minute for the gem to transform into fog that seeped in through the ears, nose, and mouth of the person activating it, granting them a new skill. Walking across the hall, Mark tapped on Joe's door.

"One second."

The door opened a moment later, and Joe poked his head out. Behind him, his room was a mess, and it looked like he had been pinning something to the wall. His curiosity piqued, Mark looked closer and saw that the wall was a huge map of the city, with a number of locations circled and one crossed out. Before he could see which place had been crossed out, Joe pulled the door shut. "What skill did you get?"

"Uh, about that . . . Does it normally take a while to absorb a skill gem?"

Giving Mark a strange look, Joe shook his head. "No. Maybe a minute or two. Why?"

"No reason. But are there people who can't absorb skill gems?"

The strange expression on Joe's face grew, and Mark caught a hint of suspicion in his gaze. "Everyone can absorb skill gems. Even the unempowered. Is something wrong, Mark?"

Swallowing, Mark shook his head and took a step back, grabbing the handle of his door and opening it. "Nothing is wrong. I got a pretty interesting ability. I think it's related to alchemy. I'm going to go ask Master Abrams about it."

With that bald-faced lie, Mark stepped into his room and shut the door behind him. Feeling a headache developing, Mark was gazing glumly at the closed box when he felt his watch vibrate and realized it was time to leave for Abrams's warehouse. Sensing his bad mood, Mime jumped up on the table and rubbed her head against his arm. Then, looking over her shoulder disdainfully at the box, she kicked it off the desk with her back leg. Yelping, Mark grabbed it out of the air before it hit the ground. Skill gems weren't particularly fragile, but they were way too expensive to risk breaking.

"Come on now," he said, feeling a bit better. "Let's get ready for work."

He figured he'd ask his master about it, so he stuck the box in his bag and then, after changing into his work clothes, left the house with Mime and caught a taxi. When he arrived at the warehouse, he was surprised to see Sky waiting by the door.

"Hey, Sky, what's up?"

"Hey, Mark, I was wondering if you could do me a favor."

Noticing how nervous Sky was, Mark quickly nodded. "Sure, what do you need?"

"I . . . I'm applying for one of the training camps, for the next round," she said, her words tumbling out in a rush. "I've been hearing more about them, and before, when I didn't have a watch, I couldn't sign up, but now I do have a watch. I even got a bank account and everything, but I don't have family, and they were asking for a reference, like a recommendation, and I was hoping that, you know, I could put you."

"Of course," Mark said. "Yeah, that's totally fine. You should put Jason as well. I'm sure he'd give you a glowing recommendation, but are you sure you want to join?"

"Yes." Sky nodded. "I've been thinking about it for a while, and after seeing you go through it and how much it's helped you, I want to give it a shot myself."

"I think that's a great idea, though it'll be a lot harder if you're not empowered," Mark said.

Nervously playing with the hem of her shirt, Sky shrugged. "I don't really have much choice about that. Neither of my parents were empowered. I just . . . I don't think it runs in the family. Besides, I'm already nineteen. There really isn't much hope for me to awaken naturally."

About to nod, Mark suddenly remembered the skill gem in his bag, but before he could say anything about it, his watch beeped, signaling the top of the hour.

"Shoot, I'm late. Sorry! Hey, what are you doing tomorrow? Do you want to meet me in the morning?" Mark asked, rushing past Sky and punching in the code to the door.

"Sure," Sky said.

"Great, see you then," Mark said, and the door slammed behind him, leaving Sky staring at it in bewilderment.

Figuring he could always play it off as a general hangout, Mark thought long and hard that night, but he decided that even if he couldn't use the skill gem, Sky probably could. If she was able to use it and it actually worked, it would mean that she wouldn't be naturally empowered. Most empowered weren't, and since Mark didn't need the money, he thought it would be a good use of the skill gem. Part of him was still holding out hope that he would be able to absorb it, but deep in his heart, he knew he couldn't.

The next morning, after his training, he sent Sky a message, and they met at a small park near his house. She was sitting on a bench when he arrived. Sitting down, he held out the box with a skill gem. As soon as she saw it, she drew back a bit, worried that he was about to give her another present.

"Hold on," he said. "Don't get all excited. This is for you, but only if you want it, and it probably won't make your life any easier. In fact, it might make your life a whole lot harder, but I want to give you the option, which is why I wanted to talk to you this morning."

"Mark, Mark," Sky said, interrupting his babbling. "What are you talking about?"

Taking a deep breath, Mark put the box down between them, on the bench, and tapped it with his finger.

"There's a skill gem in here," he said quietly, then quickly grabbed Sky before she shrieked and leaped to her feet. "Quiet. These things are worth a lot of money, and I don't want to get mugged. Like I said, there's a skill gem in here. I don't know what skill it is, but if you want it, I'm willing to let you have it. Don't ask me why, but there's some really complicated circumstances as to why I can't use it, and the same is true about Joe. If you take it, there's a decent chance that it won't even work and you won't become empowered, but I think ultimately it's worth the risk. If you do become empowered and gain a skill, life won't necessarily be easier, but you will be able to trade your current problems for better ones.

"You won't have to work as a waitress anymore, that's for sure. Plus, if you're about to get into the training camp, doing so as an empowered will really improve your chances of getting a good career afterward. Again, it all depends on your skill, and before you look at me like that, I'm not offering this for free. The average market price for a skill gem is two million credits, which seems like a lot now but really isn't that much. Most empowered will earn that much in a couple of years, maybe even a couple of months if they have the right skill. Even if you just join the military, it won't take you more than ten years to save up enough to pay down the debt, and I don't need interest or anything like that. I'm confident you'll be good for it, and besides, we're friends, right?"

Though he was unsure why Sky was giving him a sour look, Mark could tell she was coming around to the idea.

"If you need time to think about it, that's fine too," he said, but she shook her head.

"No, if you're genuinely offering it to me on those terms, I'll happily take it. The chances of me getting another shot at a skill gem are one in a million. I'd be an idiot not to take this opportunity."

"All right. Well, I came up with a contract to make it a little bit more official," Mark said, sending over a short, single-page legal document to Sky's watch.

Opening it up, she scanned over it quickly, her eyebrows rising as she got to the last clause. "What does this mean?"

"Which one? Oh, six? That just means that once you get famous and powerful, you can't pretend you don't know me," Mark said with a smile, causing Sky to laugh.

"All right, Mark, you got a deal."

With a flourish, she signed the document and sent it back to Mark.

"Wonderful. That gem right there is yours now. I'd recommend absorbing it sooner rather than later. We can go to my place if you want."

"Sure." Clutching the box tightly to her chest, Sky followed Mark back to his house, and they went up to Mark's room.

"Why don't you sit on the bed," Mark said, sitting in the chair by the desk. "You'll want to cross your legs under you, hold your palms cupped together in front of your stomach, and put the gem there. Then all you have to do is concentrate on it and breathe in."

Mark would have been lying if he had said that he didn't feel a tinge of jealousy when, not even a minute later, the gem began to unravel, turning into a thick smoke that raced into Sky's nose and mouth, rapidly vanishing as her body began to shake. Not even ten seconds later, she froze in place, and her eyes snapped open, astonishment racing through them. According to what Mark had read, the average person using a skill gem to empower would need a few days before they had access to their skill, as it took that long for their body to acclimatize to mana. That clearly wasn't the case for Sky.

"Can you tell what power you got?" Mark asked, frowning. Sky shook her head.

"No," she said.

"Huh, that's interesting," Mark replied, "because I'm pretty sure I can."

Tilting her head in curiosity, Sky saw Mark point, and looking down, she let out a shriek that made Mark laugh. Currently, she was floating six inches above the bed, her body completely motionless in the air. Still startled, she hurried to put her feet down, only to find herself drifting forward as her feet bumped against the bed.

"Mark! How do I stop!? How do I stop?"

Frantic, Sky slowly started to spin as she waved her arms and legs. By this time, Mark's chuckles had grown into full-blown belly laughs as he watched her frantically pinwheeling her arms and legs.

"I don't know," Mark said, after regaining his composure. "It's your power, not mine. Just try thinking about stopping."

Immediately, Sky froze in place, as if she had been pinned in midair. Unfortunately, her head was currently pointing down, and her legs were at a forty-five-degree angle from the ceiling. Ever so slowly, her body righted itself, until she was standing in the air, four feet off the ground, her body stiff as a board, as if she was afraid to move.

"Try coming back down to the ground."

"How do I do that?"

"Again, not my power, so I can't tell you. What if you thought about it? That worked for stopping."

Even before Mark had finished speaking, Sky's feet touched down on the carpet, and in absolute astonishment, she stared down at them. "Did you see that? I was just flying."

"Yes, I saw it," Mark said. "Congratulations. Welcome to the ranks of the empowered."

Just then, there was a knock on the door, and Joe stuck his head in.

"Everything okay in here?" he asked, looking between Mark and Sky. "I heard some shrieking."

Blushing, Sky nodded.

"Yes, everything's fine," Mark said.

"Uh-huh," Joe said, watching as Sky unconsciously began to drift up off the floor. "Your feet, they're floating."

Squeaking in surprise, Sky quickly concentrated and landed back down on the ground.

"I take it this is a recent thing," Joe said, stepping inside the room and looking between Sky and Mark.

"Yes," Mark said. "She only just empowered, with a skill gem."

Raising his eyebrows, Joe looked at Mark, a knowing smile on his face, before addressing Sky. "Congratulations, you've unlocked quite an interesting power. This isn't the first time I've seen a flight power, but yours seems to want to activate on its own."

Intrigued, he stepped into the room. "Why don't you try relaxing? See where you end up."

Taking a deep breath, Sky did her best to let her tight concentration relax. Almost immediately, she began drifting into the air until she stood around six inches off the ground.

"All right, now think about moving in any direction."

Nodding, Sky drifted up, then to the side, before coming back down to her original height of six inches.

"We should go outside and test this," Joe said. "I'm curious if there are any height restrictions."

"Won't I just fly away?"

"It's unlikely," Joe said. "After all, you seem to stop at about six inches."

"If we get a rope, we could tie it around you," Mark said, his eyes lighting up. "Joe, do we have any rope?"

"Um, not that I know of, though there might be some in the storage room."

"Hold on, let me check."

After rooting around fruitlessly in the storage room, Mark settled for a long spool of thread. He brought it out and tied one end around Sky's ankle.

"If you feel yourself starting to float off, just pull on the thread."

"What if it breaks?" Sky said.

"I'm sure it won't break," Mark said, trying to reassure her. "You'll be like a kite."

Rolling her eyes, Sky followed them downstairs, walking perfectly normally, if one didn't count the six inches of air between the bottom of her feet and the floor. When she got to the door, she hesitated, but Mark gave her an encouraging nod, and taking a deep breath, she stepped outside. At first, she braced herself, drifting back down to the ground, but then, ever so slowly, she relaxed her control and floated back up to six inches.

"Interesting, so this seems to be your static point," Joe said, already taking notes. "You're going to want to go and get evaluated at the assessment center, but it's helpful to have some of this information already prepared. Let's see how high you can go."

"Float up until you're even with the second-story window," Mark instructed.

Nodding, Sky took a deep breath and drifted up into the air.

"Okay, now come back down."

Without any trouble, she floated back down.

"All right, now try the roof this time. See if you can just get up onto the roof."

A little bit more confident after her previous attempt, Sky easily flew up to the roof. With a bit of concentration, she landed on it.

"Wow, this is really pretty incredible," Joe commented. "The only person I know who can fly can only go one direction, straight, and flies via bursts of speed. You seem to just have absolute control over your direction. Here, come back down here. Let's see how fast you can move."

Having grown more confident still, Sky jumped off the roof, intending to catch herself just before she hit the ground. Instead, as soon as her legs left the roof, she just froze in place.

"Oh, weird," she muttered as she made herself fly to the ground.

"Okay, this isn't flight," Joe said, his eyes shining. "This is spatial control, something like that. It's like you're able to shift your absolute position. This is way too complicated for us to figure out here. You'll need to go and get assessed before we have a better idea. Though you should probably just call it flight. Here, let's try something."

Reaching down, he picked up a small pebble.

"Try to stop the pebble," he said, then tossed it up into the air.

Though it was clear from her focused expression that Sky was concentrating, the pebble dropped right back down to the ground without any trouble.

"Huh, what about this," he said, and picking up the pebble again, he tossed it directly at her.

With a yelp, Sky flinched out of the way, and the pebble flew past her head.

"Sorry, I shouldn't have thrown that at you," he said. "Here, we'll try it this way."

Picking up another pebble, he walked over and had Sky hold her hand out. First, he poked her palm, having no trouble doing that, and then he dropped the pebble down onto her hand. Though it was very slight, Mark noticed that as soon as the pebble came near her palm, it slowed slightly, as if passing through a field, before landing in her palm.

"Huh, this is really fascinating," Joe said. "Unfortunately, we don't have a lot of the high-tech testing devices, so your best bet is to head to the assessment center, but you should also test it on your own. Try to figure out what the limits are."

"How fast can you go?" Mark asked, and a moment later, Sky slammed into him, sending both of them tumbling to the ground.

"Ouch," she said, rubbing her head where it had nailed Mark's chin.

Mark, rather groggy, as he hadn't had time to shift out of the way before she rammed into him, slowly got to his feet and helped her up. "Okay, so you're pretty fast."

"Which is great," Sky replied. "This means that I won't have to take the train anymore."

"You're definitely not as fast as the train," Mark replied. "But who knows, maybe you'll get there. What about weight? Can you pick me up?"

Slipping her hands around Mark's waist, Sky tried to float into the air but only managed to lift him an inch or two before she couldn't go any higher. Dropping him back to the ground, she retreated quickly, her face shaded with a faint pink.

Joe, who was watching them, grinned. "So you can't carry a full person, but you can carry yourself and your clothing. That's something. Let's try other weights."

For the rest of the afternoon, they played around with Sky's power. Eventually, she grew too exhausted to fly high in the sky anymore, but what was surprising was that she remained floating at six inches off the ground, unless she focused her concentration to walk normally.

"What a fascinating power," Joe said. "Hey, it's getting to be about dinnertime. Should I cook us up something?"

"Yeah," Mark said. "That'd be great. I think I still have some meat in the fridge. We could make a stir-fry."

"Who's the 'we'?" Joe said. "The last time you made stir-fry, you nearly burned down the house."

"Oh, come on. I was twelve," Mark protested as Sky giggled.

She was currently lying in the air, her body stretched out, looking completely at ease, despite the fact that no part of her was touching the ground. Mark was astonished at how quickly she had gotten used to being able to fly, though in retrospect, it was no faster than he had gotten used to his new power.

"You know, this is really unfair," Mark said, upon reflecting. "I got a stupid arm power, and you got flight. No fair at all."

"It just means she's more talented than you," Joe called from the kitchen, causing Sky to laugh and Mark to roll his eyes.

That night, after Sky had recovered her energy and flown away, Mark headed to the warehouse to resume his training under Abrams. He was quite excited, since they were taking a break from the corpses to learn basic alchemical recipes. He hadn't found the dead man's finger fungus in the dead zone but had had enough money to buy some, and so he'd brought it to his master, who'd agreed to teach him the potion.

When Mark arrived, Abrams took him to a room he had never entered before. It was full of dust and old alchemical equipment that had not been used for years, maybe decades. Looking around, Abrams seemed sad, but all he said was "Clean it up" before turning around and walking out.

Mark did as he was commanded, and four hours later, the room was spotless. He had washed all the equipment, laid it out to dry, and cleaned every single surface that was visible and most of those that weren't. When Abrams walked back in, he had regained control of his emotions, and they got started.

"The most important thing about alchemy is precision," he said. "The potion we're going to be making is called 'Dead Man

Walking.' It's a potion that renders your vital signs inert, allowing you to pass by undetected among the Exlian swarms. Don't give me that look. I know exactly what you're thinking: 'If such a potion exists, why doesn't the military use it?' Well, simple. Exlian can still detect mana circuits, which means if you're clanking about in armor, then no matter how many of these potions you drink, they're still going to find you. This potion is very effective, but it requires that you move without any active mana circuits. That means no armor, no watch, nothing, as nature intended."

"Okay, so I can understand why nobody wants to use it."

"Exactly. Who'd be mad enough to walk out among the Exlian without their gear," Abrams said, a rather crazy grin on his face.

Mark suspected that he knew the answer to that question, but Abrams had already changed the subject.

"Precision is everything, though. Too much of the dead man's fingers, and you'll be, well, dead. It's a poison that suppresses life signals, putting you into a false coma, but your body can only survive so long in that state. The pheromone gland that the drones use happens to counteract it, and if you get the balance right, you just look dead. No heartbeat, no breathing, no body heat, nothing. Give it to an unempowered, and it'll kill them. Get me the measuring bowls and the mortar and pestle."

Retrieving the tools Abrams was pointing at, Mark watched as he broke off a piece of the fungus, mashed it up with the mortar and pestle, and then scraped it into the vial, before pulling out one of the pheromone glands sitting in a freezer container, thawing it, and mashing it up to put it in another beaker.

"Now, there's a jar of clear liquid, should be labeled 'base,' over in that fridge. Grab some of that and pull it out. We want twenty-five milliliters."

Opening the fridge, Mark saw an old jar with crust around the rim and carried it out. Carefully brushing the crust away, he poured twenty-five milliliters into a beaker and brought it to Abrams.

"Good, now we're just gonna jam all this stuff together, shake it up, filter out the sediment, and we'll see how it went."

Fifteen minutes later, Mark was staring at a gray potion that absorbed all light without turning black.

"Ha, still haven't lost my touch," Abrams said.

Picking up a book that had been sitting next to him, he waved it at Mark.

"Your next task is going to be hanging out in this laboratory until you've made an acceptable version of each of these potions. These are the most common recipes and lack a lot of the punch that modern potions carry, but what's important is that they work, and you never know when you'll need a particular potion. Get to memorizing it. Check back with me after you've completed each potion. There are materials around the room. You can figure out where they are yourself, and if there's anything you need from one of the bodies out there, you can get it yourself."

Grabbing the Dead Man Walking potion he had made, Abrams brought it over to a machine that looked similar to the one that had tested Mark's elixir. He clipped the potion into place and turned it on. A moment later, he had a readout, which he tossed to Mark.

"There's a recipe in the book for base, which you'll want to learn first, since you're going to need a lot of it. Once you've finished your potions, stick them in here, and it'll test them, and don't be nervous about failing. I'm rich enough to support even the worst alchemy student."

Waving his hand as if to tell Mark to get to it, Abrams sauntered out, and Mark, incredibly excited, opened up the book and began to peruse it. It took an hour to just familiarize himself with all the different recipes it contained. They proceeded from least complicated to most complicated, and Mark saw a couple of different potions that got him very excited. Of course, there were the basic healing potions and stamina potions, which came right after the recipe for base his master had mentioned, which was the liquid that every potion used as a catalyst. From there, the potions grew in effect and rank until, at the end of the book, Mark saw one that left him staring in shock.

It was called Second Awakening and claimed to allow someone to undergo a second empowerment, gaining a brand-new power. He had never heard of any of the materials that it required, and a quick search on the forums turned up nothing. Confused, Mark thought about going and asking his master but figured there was time enough for that later. For the moment, what he needed to do was start from the beginning.

Flipping to the front of the book, Mark began to study the recipe for producing base in earnest, and over the next few hours, he made attempt after attempt, each one a failure. Very quickly, he realized that if he was going to learn from his mistakes, he needed to keep detailed notes, and so he began to slow down, writing digital notes in his watch between each attempt. He still hadn't managed to make a successful batch by the time he went home, but he felt that he was getting close.

The sun was high in the sky the next day when he finished his morning training, and after grabbing a quick shower, he sent a message to Sky to check in on her. She had said that she was going to go to the assessment center, but he hadn't heard anything from her yet, so he figured she was probably there and undertaking the assessment. Ordering a taxi, he gave the driver the address Phoenix had given him, and half an hour later, they pulled up in front of a tasteful villa, squirreled away in a large park.

He was met at the door by an elderly gentleman dressed in a suit who wore spotless white shoes. Ignoring the look of astonishment on Mark's face, the elderly man informed him that he would find the party on the back porch and directed him through the house. Wandering through the hall, Mark was quite impressed. Everything in the home was made with exquisite craftsmanship, and he saw numerous pieces of art that he could only imagine cost a fortune. It was a different type of wealth from what he had seen in the club during their last party. That had been designed to impress, while this home had been designed to enjoy. He was just pausing to enjoy a beautiful painting that showed the setting sun glittering across a windswept sea when he noticed a man coming out of a nearby room. Catching sight of him, the man's eyes lit up, and he gestured to the painting.

"Philippe Gorgon," he said. "It's an original, one of three that still remain after his home was lost."

"It's astounding," Mark said. "There's so much emotion in it."

"There is. It's why I like it. My name's Matthew. Matthew Borner. You must be . . . Wait, let me guess. You must be Mark."

Seeing Mark's surprise, Matthew laughed. "In truth, I'm cheating a bit. Noah and Glenn are both here and already introduced themselves, and from what I understand, Danny is unmistakable."

Just then, they heard a low, rumbling voice at the entrance to the house, and Mark nodded, jerking his thumb toward the door. "He certainly is, and it seems he's arrived."

"My daughter, Phoenix, has told me a lot about you. It's a pleasure to have you here."

"The pleasure's mine, sir," Mark replied, bowing slightly.

"No need for any of that," Matthew said, waving at Danny, who was thudding his way down the hall. "You're Danny, right? My name's Matthew. I'm Phoenix's father."

While Mark hadn't reacted particularly, Danny's eyes went wide, and he quickly hurried forward, nearly knocking over a vase. He grasped Matthew's hand and shook it firmly. "A pleasure to meet you, sir. Your new Titan VI is an amazing suit."

"I can imagine you'd appreciate it," Matthew said, taking in Danny's size. "In fact, Phoenix has already mentioned to me that you'd be a good candidate to test some of our heavy suits in the future. We've got a couple that require a build a good bit bigger than even yours, but you said you have a growth power, right?"

"Yes, sir." Danny nodded furiously.

Watching Matthew and Danny interact, Mark couldn't help but grin. In truth, though he appreciated the armored suits the military used, he wasn't that big of a fan, as they brought with them a stifling feeling he couldn't quite shake. He much preferred to be without one, though the armor was nice. After Danny had finished fanboying, Matthew took the two of them to the back porch, where they found the others waiting.

"Here they are," Phoenix said, grinning. "Let's get the party started."

"If you need anything, let me know," Matthew said, patting his daughter on the shoulder. "It was a pleasure to meet all of you, and I'm sure we'll see more of each other in the future."

"Bye, Dad," Phoenix said, giving him a quick hug.

As attendants brought out food, Phoenix introduced the grounds to them. The large porch overlooked a beautiful, naturally sculpted swimming pool and a small, well-manicured garden. There were various spaces for games beyond the garden, and even a gymnasium that doubled as a training center.

"All this is great," Glenn said, "but I want to know what kind of powers you guys unlocked."

"I didn't use my gem," Phoenix said with a smile. "My slots are already full."

"Hey, I wanted to ask about that," Mark quickly interjected. "If your slots are full, what happens if you try to absorb a new gem?"

"The same thing that happens normally," Phoenix replied,

giving him a slightly odd look. "It'll turn into mist. You inhale it, but then it'll come back out and reform."

That was the answer Mark had been hoping to hear the least, as it meant the problem truly was with him and not with the mana gems.

"Okay, so you didn't absorb it," Glenn said, "but what power did it have?"

"Barrier," Phoenix replied, "which isn't a bad power. It's just I'm focusing on will, so I don't need another power that sucks up will, especially when I can already make a barrier."

"Huh, I got speed," Glenn said, his hand blurring as he produced a knife from a hidden sheath. His hand twitched and it vanished, sheathed once more.

"That's really nice," Phoenix said. "It'll give you some defense."

"Exactly. What about you guys?" Glenn asked, turning to the others.

"I didn't absorb mine yet," Harper said. "I've got no room, but it seems to be a minor intelligence power. I'll probably trade it for something else."

"I absorbed mine," Danny said, and held out his hand. His activator flashed, and a massive mace manifested in his hand.

"Whoa, you got weapon creation? That's insane."

"I am pretty happy with it," Danny said. "It even scales with my growth."

"I'm so jealous," Glenn said. "What about you, Noah? What'd you get?"

"Like Phoenix and Harper, I don't have any slots," Noah said. "And I'm not sure what the power was."

"Have you not checked it yet?"

"No," Noah said, looking slightly stricken. "I kind of forgot."

"You forgot about a skill gem? Oh my goodness, what I would

give to be able to forget about a skill gem," Harper said with a groan. "Mark, please save us from Mr. Moneybags over here."

"I didn't use it," Mark said. "I gave it to somebody else, but it contained flight."

"You gave it away?" Phoenix asked, her eyes narrowing slightly. "Who'd you give it to?"

"A coworker of mine. Well, I guess former coworker."

"You gave it to that girl, didn't you? What was her name? Sky?"

Sweating slightly, Mark nodded. "Yes, that's right."

"Well, I hope she appreciates it," Phoenix said, her eyes softening. "Flight is a pretty good power."

"I think she does," Mark said, smiling. "She's always wanted to fly."

"Well, then I'm glad she got the chance," Phoenix said, raising her glass. "To new powers and new beginnings."

"To new powers and new beginnings," they all echoed, clinking their glasses together.

"So, Mark, tell me more about this girl you handed your gem to?" Danny asked.

Under Harper's and Phoenix's intense stares, Mark ignored Glenn, who was grinning and giving him a thumbs-up.

"She's gonna be joining the training camps," he said, "and I thought it would be better for her to do it as an empowered rather than as an unempowered."

"That's a seven-and-a-half-million-credit gem," Phoenix said. "I hope she appreciates it."

"How much?" Mark asked, his eyes widening.

"At least seven and a half million. Flight is a super rare power. I mean, imagine being able to just fly away when danger comes."

"Aren't there Exlian that fly?"

"Sure, but very few of them are also able to fight, and so as long as an empowered is kitted out with the right kind of suit, they'll be able to tear through any Exlian that can catch up to them."

"Oh," Mark said, scratching his chin. "I didn't realize that."

"Well, what's done is done, but you should at least know what something is worth before you just go handing it out, even to your girlfriend."

"No, we're just friends," Mark said, missing the faint relief in Phoenix's eyes.

"All right, so we all know what skill gems we got, except of course for Noah here, who's too rich to even care that he was given a skill gem," Phoenix said, shifting the subject. "So now it's time for the even more important question: Where are you all planning to apply?"

This time, Mark was the first to answer.

"Defense Force," he said firmly. "Maybe the Rangers, but I'd really like to be in the Defense Force."

"Defense Force for me too," Danny said, leaning over and bumping fists with Mark.

"I'm actually thinking about the Engineering Corps," Glenn said. "I've mostly been using my telekinesis to control knives, but there are quite a few machines that have a lot of little parts, and I've heard you can make good money doing field assembly, especially now that I have some extra speed. What about you, Harper?"

"Rangers. I think my powers would be best suited in the Rangers."

"I'm thinking either Defense Force or Rangers myself," Phoenix said, glancing at Mark as she spoke. "Noah?"

"Rangers."

"How's your dad feel about that?" Phoenix asked.

Noah shrugged. "He doesn't like it at all. He didn't want me to join the military. He wants me to take over after him, but I'd rather become Exlian excrement first."

"I'm sure he was excited when you told him that," Phoenix said with a laugh. "Well, a toast to you. A toast to all of you. May you get your heart's desire."

The party lasted until six, and after it was finished, Mark headed back to the warehouse to continue his alchemical training. He had felt the previous night that he was getting close, and his third attempt worked, leaving him with a beaker of perfectly clear liquid. Curious to learn more about it, Mark took it over to the testing machine and then spent a few minutes searching the forums to find out more, eventually stumbling on a post by an alchemist who frequented the forums and went by the name UntidyBeaker.

UNTIDYBEAKER

Base is a simple alchemical recipe, the simplest, in fact, and is a necessary ingredient in practically any other potion. While there are a few potions and indeed more alchemical creations that don't use base, it remains to this day the very best catalyzer we have at our disposal, as well as the easiest to source. Like every alchemical ingredient, base has ranks as well. Simple, complex, and exquisite. A simple base can be used for any potion D rank or lower, complex for any B- or C-ranked potion, and exquisite for A-ranked

> potions and above. When making your base, ensure that you use the correct amount of salt and water, as that is really all you need. It has more to do with how you heat and mix the liquid than with any of the supplemental ingredients.

That got Mark curious, and he quickly searched to see if he could find a recipe for base that was just salt and water. Almost immediately, he found dozens, each one claiming to be better than the last. Though he was quite curious about them, Mark decided to try them later and instead checked the printout he had gotten from the tester. It identified the pitcher of liquid as a simple base, suitable for E- and D-ranked potions. Excited to have completed his first recipe, Mark brought it to Abrams, who looked at it, grunted, and waved him off, not at all impressed.

Now that he had some base, Mark could begin testing the next potion. There were two E-ranked potions, the basic healing potion and the basic stamina potion. Since his alchemical blood affected healing potions, Mark decided to start with that, and he began memorizing the recipe.

Later that night, close to three in the morning, Mark, who was in the middle of trying to avoid having his head bitten off by a dream mantis, felt a thrum in his chest, and his eyes snapped open. He had gotten home an hour and a half ago and had gone to bed right at two, maintaining his normal schedule. The first thing he saw was the light of the mana clock telling him that it was 3:03 a.m. The second thing he saw was Mime, crouched on his bed, her hackles raised as she stared at the door.

Joe was spending the night at a friend's house, so it probably wasn't his brother who had set Mime off. His ears straining, Mark picked up a faint sound from downstairs and carefully sat up. It wasn't the sound of someone walking into a place they were familiar with, much less owned. Instead, it was the soft creak of floorboards as someone tried to tiptoe.

Reaching over to the side of the bed, Mark grabbed his necklace and slipped it over his head, activating his titanium arm as he got out of bed as quietly as he could. Unfortunately, his house was old, and the floorboards under his feet shifted slightly. Immediately, the sound downstairs ceased, and Mark's heart began to slow down, an icy calm growing in him as he took a step toward the door. He listened for a long moment, and when he didn't hear anything, he carefully eased it open.

There was no movement in the hall beyond, and as Mark slipped into the hallway, he didn't see anybody else. There was a muffled sound from downstairs that sounded like whispering, and with his eyes narrowing, Mark took a step toward the stairs. At that moment, his senses went crazy, and he realized that someone was dropping from the ceiling above him.

Twisting his hips, he dropped, at the same time thrusting his left hand up into the air, and the tips of his fingers caught the metal rod that had been chopping down toward his head. His wrist shook, the end of the metal rod sheared off, and he felt his fingers piercing flesh. Realizing he had gotten his attacker's shoulder as the figure twisted out of the way, Mark lunged forward, but there was a curse, and a wave of force slammed Mark backward down the stairs.

As he fell, his fingers dug into the wall, ripping large furrows all the way down, and he winced at the damage. It allowed him to land on his feet, though, his eyes fixed on the top of the stairs, where a woman in a mask clutched at her shoulder, her fingers splayed out in front of her.

Hearing a noise behind him, Mark ducked and kicked the steps, sliding back across the wooden floor in a sitting position as a mana-edged blade tore through the air where his head had just been. Turning over, Mark scrambled forward, slipping under the table in time to avoid another metal rod that cracked down, splintering the floorboards.

Without hesitating, Mark flipped the table, spun on his back, and kicked it with both feet, sending it slamming into the two men who had attacked him. Using his brief reprieve to scan the room, he saw the two men, who were throwing aside the table, and a second woman, who was currently pointing a rod-shaped device at him.

An intense feeling of danger filled Mark as her activator flared, shooting three puffs of air from the end of the rod. Completely on instinct, he managed to avoid the first dart, and the second he swatted aside with his titanium hand. The third poked into his chest and, with a high-pitched whine, injected its full payload into his body.

An intense burning flooded through him as he ripped the dart out, and weakness started to invade his limbs, but with gritted teeth, he turned and dove through the window, using his arm to shield his head from the glass. He landed in a heap in the yard outside and heard muffled shouts from behind him. Wondering who the people in his house might be, he sprinted forward and vaulted the fence, taking off down the alley as fast as he could. He could feel whatever had been injected into him working, spreading pain and numbness throughout his body. He knew that by running, he was hastening its spread as his heart pumped furiously, but right now, he just needed to get as far away from his attackers as possible.

Back at the house, the woman who had fired off the darts swore.

"Get after him," she said. "He took a full dart, so he should be depowered. Make sure you capture him, alive preferably, but if he won't come, just kill him. We've got an outstanding request for his body."

The two masked men nodded, raced through the back door,

vaulted the fence easily, and vanished into the night. Pulling out a set of darts from a clip on her belt, the woman felt her watch vibrate and accepted the call. A shadowed face appeared above her watch and spoke in a garbled voice. "How is it going?"

Eyes narrowing, the woman gave the shadowy figure a hard look. "Just cleaning up, why?"

"Because we just got a ping that there are alerts going out. Did you touch the younger brother? It looks like there are a lot of people keeping an eye on him, so tread carefully. Whatever you do, don't leave any evidence."

With a click, the call terminated, leaving the woman annoyed. With a shake of her head, she began to reload her rod as she walked to the stairs.

"Did you find anything up there?" she called, but there was no response.

Her annoyance mounting, she placed her foot on the first step and then froze as she saw a figure sitting at the top of the stairs. It was a simple black cat with a white face, currently licking its lips, as if it had just eaten a tasty meal. Though she didn't know why, a shiver ran down the woman's spine, and she turned and bolted, rushing out the front door as fast as she could and not stopping until she had started her car and driven away.

A panicked glance in her mirror gave her a glimpse of Mime sitting in the doorway of the house, head tilted slightly. For a moment, Mime's eyes flared, and then, almost sadly, she looked back over her shoulder in the direction Mark had run. Giving the fleeing woman a disappointed look, Mime watched until the tail-lights had disappeared around a corner, then walked back inside, shutting the door firmly behind her with her back paw.

Mark had run as far as he could. He could feel his body fighting against the toxin that filled him, producing a terrible itching feeling that numbed his limbs. With his breath coming in large gasps, he stopped to lean on a trash can and a moment later heard the pounding of footsteps, and the two men who had attacked him in his kitchen skidded to a stop at the entry to the alleyway.

"It looks like it's working," the man with the mana blade said, his voice a hoarse growl. "Come on, kid. You can either come peacefully, or I'll chop you into little pieces, put them all in a bag, and drag the bag back. It's up to you."

"Though we'd really prefer that you choose option two," the man with the metal rod said, eliciting a laugh from his companion.

Mark wasn't listening to either of them. His vision was starting to swim, and it was all he could do to keep himself on his feet. Seeing him sway, the two men exchanged glances and then approached, spreading out slightly. The one with the mana blade reached for Mark's shoulder, grabbing it tightly and hauling him up. "Hey, kid—!"

Mark's titanium arm had been hidden from their view because of the angle, but seeing the flash, the man realized something was wrong and started to jerk back. Before he could, Mark twisted his body and chopped at the man's hand. With a scream, the man jerked back farther as his hand fell to the ground, severed neatly from his wrist. At the same time, Mark's other arm twisted like a snake, and two fingers jabbed through the man's throat, cutting a hole straight through it.

So shocked that his hand had been chopped off, the man didn't notice the blood pouring out of his neck until his horrified companion let out a yell and slammed his rod into Mark's back, causing him to collapse to the ground. Darkness feathered the edges of Mark's vision, and in his delirious state, he expected the rod to slam into him again. Instead, there was a soft snick, and he saw a head with a horrified expression tumble into view. Then the darkness came, consuming Mark's mind as he fell unconscious.

Mark awoke to a blinking notification on his right arm. Blearily, he sat up, briefly wondering why he was sprawled out in a pile of trash in an alleyway. Without thinking too much about it, he opened up his notifications and saw words scrolling across his arm.

Excessive exposure to neurotoxin 7737 has caused your body to adapt. You have unlocked Minor Poison Resistance as a genetic adaptation.

A fierce cough rattled Mark's chest, and a moment later, he vomited up a glob of black slime that stank to high heaven. As soon as it was out of his body, however, he felt his mind clear up, and his recent experiences flashed through his mind, causing him to look around wildly for the bodies that should have been surrounding him. He vaguely remembered killing the first man and seeing the head of the second roll by, but neither body was in sight. There wasn't any blood either, and once again, it appeared as if a section of the alleyway had been vacuumed up, absorbing both the blood and a bit of the dirt that had been underneath.

Checking his watch, he saw that it had only been four hours, and it was now seven in the morning. A swift glance at his status showed his biofuel meter was still mostly full, likely because he had been interrupted halfway through his fight against the Exlian, and as he got to his feet, he saw a familiar figure sitting at the end of the alleyway.

"Mime, what are you doing here?"

Looking at him, Mime pointed at him with a paw and then

yawned, tilting her head to the side as if falling asleep. Then she sat up straight and looked around vigilantly.

"You were guarding me while I was asleep?"

Pleased he had gotten it on the first try, Mime nodded and then padded over and jumped up onto his shoulder, licking the side of his face with her rough tongue.

"Thanks. Let's go see how bad things are."

The sight of the damage done to the house dismayed Mark. The lock on the back door had been broken, the kitchen window was busted out, and the table had been cut in half, likely by the blade-wielding man Mark had killed. There was also a broken floorboard and five deep gouges running the entire length of the stairwell, where Mark's fingers had carved through the plaster.

Half afraid of what he would find at the top of the stairs, Mark was surprised when he saw absolutely nothing. Whoever they were, they hadn't gotten a chance to go into any of the upstairs rooms before Mark had come out. The bottom floor was a bit more of a mess. Everything in the storeroom had been thrown around, no doubt in a hurried search. Four people had come into his home the night before, and since two of them had been killed in the alleyways, Mark could only assume that the other two were still on the loose. Just then, he heard the front doorknob turn, and he spun, his arm rapidly transforming again. The door opened, and Joe stepped inside, freezing when he saw the mess. "Mark, what happened?"

"Had some visitors last night," Mark said, canceling his transformation and scratching his head. "Things got a bit rowdy."

Walking over to the table, which was sliced neatly in half, Joe let out a low whistle. "'Rowdy' seems like an understatement. Who were they? What were they here for?"

"Great questions," Mark said. "I don't know. I assumed they were coming here to rob us. I was upstairs sleeping when I heard something and walked out onto the landing. One of them attacked me, knocking me down the stairs." Mark pointed at the large furrows. "Then when I got to the bottom of the stairs, the others attacked me. There were three down here, two men and a woman. I barely avoided getting my head chopped off and threw the table at them, which resulted in, well, that."

Taking a deep breath, Mark pointed at the window.

"The lady shot me with a dart carrying a knockout potion. I managed to get out the window and over the fence and ran into the alleyway. I woke up this morning in a pile of garbage, where I must have collapsed."

"And the attackers?"

Mark shrugged. "I wounded the one woman," he said, "at the top of the stairs, stabbed her in the shoulder."

"What about the others?"

"They weren't here when I got back," Mark replied, hoping Joe wouldn't pry too deeply.

He didn't particularly fancy telling his brother that he had become a cold-blooded murderer, even though he felt he was entirely justified in each of his acts of self-defense.

Looking around, Joe shook his head.

"We better call the Defense Force," he said. "Something like this needs to be reported, especially if any of them got away and might come back."

Before making the call, Joe went up to his room while Mark

went to get dressed. Staring at himself in the mirror, he couldn't help but blink as he ran his hand over his chin. Though he still looked the same as always, Mark couldn't help but feel that he had become a radically different person. It was almost sickening how easily he had killed the man who attacked him, and he felt like he should have been more torn up about it. He had heard that everyone experienced nausea after the first time they killed a person, but Mark felt nothing of the sort. To him, the difference between the black-clothed man and an Exlian drone was the number of legs and mandibles.

He could feel himself changing, and Mark wasn't sure he liked it. Then again, the changes that had happened to his mind and body had kept him alive on more than one occasion. At first, he had assumed his cold-bloodedness had manifested from his training with Abrams, but that didn't quite cover it. As he reviewed what had happened the night before, he couldn't help but marvel at how calmly he had made each decision. Catching sight of Mime in the mirror as she sat on his bed, Mark sighed and turned around.

"You're a weird one too," he said. "I don't know what's happening or what's your deal, but we make good partners, so stay out of sight while the Defense Force is here. We don't need any more questions than we're gonna get."

Giving him an amused look, Mime nodded and then said, "Meow."

"Yeah, absolutely none of that," Mark said with a laugh.

The Defense Force arrived within the hour, five agents pulling up in a large black vehicle. Two of them headed for the back of the house, while the other three knocked on the front door. Joe let them in and spoke with one of them in a low voice for a minute before they spread out and began examining the scene.

"Hello, Mark. I'm Investigator Cram. I just have a few questions. Would you mind sitting down with me?"

"Sure, no problem," Mark said, "though I wouldn't sit on that side of the couch. The springs are sharp enough to stab you. Here, I'll grab us two chairs."

While Mark walked to the kitchen to get two of the chairs that had been knocked over in the fight, Investigator Cram, a man in his mid-thirties with a quickly receding hairline, glanced down at the couch and smiled slightly.

"Thank you," he said, accepting the chair that Mark brought over. "Reminds me of my old couch."

"Did you get a new one?" Mark said.

"Honestly, no," the investigator replied with a laugh. "I just figured having no couch was better than having a couch no one could sit on, so I threw it away. Now, I want you to talk me through what happened, in your own words, and feel free to take your time. We're not really in any rush."

Nodding, Mark began retelling the story, starting with how he had woken up in the middle of the night and felt someone was outside his door. Knowing that Joe shouldn't be home, he had stepped out and been attacked, managing to wound his attacker before getting knocked down the stairs. After that, he described his brief fight in the kitchen and how he fled. The investigator listened to him calmly, occasionally exchanging glances with a companion standing behind Mark. After Mark had finished, Investigator Cram steepled his fingers together and gave Mark a concerned look.

"It's quite the tale," he said. "Unfortunately, I'm having a little bit of trouble understanding the sequence of events. You're saying you wounded somebody in the upstairs hallway?"

"Yes," Mark said. "My left hand. Stabbed her in the shoulder."

"Her? You got a good look at her?"

"Not really," Mark said. "She was wearing a mask, but it was definitely a woman."

"I assume, then, you could identify her by body shape?"

Shrugging, Mark shook his head. "She had on a fairly heavy jacket. They all did. Heavy boots, black cargo pants, jackets, gloves, and masks."

"Did she have long hair?"

"Not too long. Drawn back in a ponytail."

"Any jewelry?"

"No."

"So you did get a good look at her," Investigator Cram said, flashing a small smile. "Identifying marks on her face? Color of skin?"

"Look, it was dark," Mark said with a shrug. "The only light was the light coming through the windows. So I really didn't get a great look at her."

"You said she tried to strike you with a metal rod?" Investigator Cram said. "And you defended?"

"Yeah," Mark said. "With my arm."

"Which I believe turns into titanium. Is that correct?"

"Yes."

"Would you mind demonstrating for me?"

"Sure."

Mark reached up and grabbed his necklace, and a moment later, his arm had transformed.

"Interesting. Then, after stabbing her with your fingers, you were blown backward and flew down the stairs."

Seeing Mark nod, Investigator Cram glanced at the person standing behind Mark, and his forehead furrowed.

"Is something wrong?" Mark asked, twisting to look back at the woman behind him.

She gave him a wide-eyed stare, as if completely innocent.

"The issue is that we can't seem to determine whether or not you're telling the truth," Investigator Cram said.

"Is that her power?" Mark asked, jerking a thumb at the woman behind him. "Telling whether somebody's speaking the truth or not?"

"Not precisely, but close enough," Investigator Cram said. "But unfortunately, we're unable to verify with you, and there really isn't any evidence of a break-in, apart from the general destruction of your house. While it is consistent with the story you tell"—the investigator paused and took a deep breath—"I'm afraid we don't have anything to go on. For example, if you wounded somebody upstairs, one would expect to find traces of blood. There are none. You claim you were hit by darts. We can't find them anywhere. Does your skin have a hole in it?"

Reaching up to touch the spot on his chest where the dart had landed, Mark realized that his healing ability had already closed up the puncture wound.

"No," he said, shaking his head.

"We could take a blood test, if you'd like. Test for the presence of toxins," Investigator Cram said, but Mark could only shrug.

"My guess is, you're not going to find anything," he said with a sigh.

"As I suspected." Standing up, Investigator Cram lowered his voice. "Look, Mark, I don't know what's going on with you and your brother, but try to get along. I know Joe can be a stick-in-the-mud, but brothers need to stick together. All right?"

Patting Mark on the shoulder, the investigator walked over to Joe. "Sorry, I don't think we can help."

"You didn't find anything?"

"No, and unless you're going to pull the psychometry team, there isn't anything to find."

"All right. Well, thanks for your help," Joe said.

A few minutes later, Mark and his brother watched from the doorway as the car pulled away.

"You believe me, right?" Mark asked, glancing at Joe, whose forehead was furrowed.

"Oh, I believe you, all right," Joe said, shutting the door. "The problem is figuring out how to find them after they erased their traces so thoroughly."

"I'd like to know that as well," Mark said, looking around in confusion. "But I do know somebody we might be able to call to help, since the Defense Force isn't doing us any good."

"Oh? Who would that be?" Joe asked.

Mark didn't answer, instead flipping open his watch and sending a short message. Forty-five minutes later, Noah was standing in the middle of Mark's living room, his eyes slowly tracing the deep gouges in the stairwell.

"How many of them were there?"

"Four," Mark said.

"And how many of them escaped?"

Biting his lip, Mark shrugged. Thankfully, Joe was outside, taking care of some trash. "At least one, maybe two."

Noah's eyes narrowed slightly as he gave Mark an appraising glance. "And you don't have any of the darts they shot?"

"No," Mark said.

"Can you sketch one?"

"Easily. I got a good look when I pulled it out of me."

"Good. Every detail helps. You don't happen to have anything of theirs, do you?"

Just then, Mime came trotting down the stairs and padded over to Noah, looking up at him. When he didn't look down, she pawed one of his feet, causing him to frown slightly and glance down. Mark was hunting for paper when he heard Noah cough behind him. "Is this the dart?"

Glancing over his shoulder, Mark saw Noah holding the empty dart that had hit him.

"Yeah, that's it," he said. "Where did you get that?"

Ever so slowly, Noah's eyes fell to the cat, sitting proudly at his feet.

"No wonder we couldn't find them," Mark said. "Mime must have grabbed them."

"Find what?" Joe asked as he walked in the door.

"Mime found one of the darts. She must have picked it up and brought it to my room. Which is why the agents didn't find it."

"If it's okay, I'll take it with me," Noah said, sticking it in his pocket. "Once I'm done, I'll return it, and you can give it to the Defense Force."

"No need," Joe said, shaking his head. "Even if they saw it, it wouldn't demonstrate anything. We could have found a dart like that anywhere."

"All right," Noah replied. "I should have something for you soon."

With a nod to Joe and another to Mark, Noah got in the car that was waiting for him outside.

Mark expected not to hear from Noah for at least a couple of days. Instead, within five hours, he had a blinking message. Opening, he saw pictures of the four people who had attacked him the night before staring at him. Accompanying the images was a file, including a location of a hideout, and a couple of other pieces of information.

The four intruders belonged to an information-acquisition organization, which was a fancy name for a gang of thieves focusing on stealing secrets. Noah didn't know anything about why they had broken into Mark's home, but the file did mention that there were at least ten people in the group, which meant that if two of them had died, eight remained. Two minutes after the file arrived, he got a call and saw Noah sitting in a chair on a balcony overlooking a beautiful garden.

"The location they're using as a hideout is an old office building. We should be able to sneak in through the roof. They're on the fourth floor, so we'll enter two floors above them and sneak down. Security's tight, but I should have a couple things that'll get us around it. I think the two of us should be enough, but if you want, we could call some of the others from the team."

It took a moment for Mark to realize that Noah was casually suggesting that they break into the enemy base.

"Is this something you've done before?" Mark asked, and Noah, flashing a small smile, nodded.

"Like I said, my dad wants me to take over the family business. I've had quite the range of training."

"I think the two of us should be enough," Mark said. "We'll pick a time when not many people are there."

"Sounds good. I'll have somebody keep watch to see when most of their team leaves."

"Thanks, Noah," Mark said, but Noah just waved him off.

"It's the least I can do. I'll keep you updated."

As the call clicked off, Mark scratched his head, wondering what on earth he was getting himself into.

Noah's call came the next night, just as Mark was cleaning up his workstation. Sliding the batch of base he had just finished making into the fridge, he accepted the call and saw Noah, dressed in dark clothing, standing in a dark room, looking every inch the professional thief.

"I think we've got our opportunity," Noah said, his eyes glancing to the side. "There should only be two people in the building until morning. You still have the address, right?"

"I do," Mark said, brushing his hands on the apron he was wearing.

"Great. How quickly can you get here?"

Mark entered the address into his watch. "Looks like twenty-five minutes."

"Then I'll see you in thirty," Noah said, and hung up.

Putting everything else away, Mark left the warehouse, making sure to lock up behind him. Since he had started working in the alchemy lab, Abrams often went to bed before he left. At first, Mark had been slightly disconcerted to work alone in the warehouse full of frozen Exlian, but as the days progressed, he found he quite enjoyed the quiet. Something about being alone in that environment made him calm. He had already called a taxi, and as he walked toward the end of the alleyway, where the car was waiting, he saw a figure emerge from the back door of the restaurant.

"Mark!"

It was Sky, just getting off the late shift. She ran over, and for a moment, Mark thought that she was going to hug him, but at the last moment, she held herself back, sliding to an awkward stop in front of him. "Hey, what are you doing? You're just getting off, right?"

"Yeah, I just finished up," Mark said, glancing down at Sky's feet.

They were planted firmly on the ground, and with a grin, she showed him the activator on her right arm.

"It's a lot easier with the activator," she said. "Staying on the ground, I mean. It doesn't require nearly as much concentration, and I've been practicing quite a bit."

Sky had gone through her assessment, and when she sent Mark the results, he had nearly cried. They had assessed her with an A-ranked power and a B-ranked potential, meaning that as she grew in strength, she was going to leave him in the dust. The fact that he had given up an A-ranked flight power didn't irk him that much, but only because he couldn't absorb it himself. Otherwise, he'd be kicking himself right now.

"Are you busy? Do you want to hang out?" Sky asked.

Mark hesitated for a moment, not quite sure how to tell Sky that he was about to try to break into the secret base of the people who had tried to kill him a couple of nights before. She saw his hesitation, and her face fell.

"It's okay if you are busy. I mean, we don't need to hang out now. We can hang out another time."

A faint feeling of panic rose in Mark as he saw the way her

shoulders slumped, and he reached out to touch her arm lightly. "Sorry, I really do want to hang out. It's just that I'm meeting Noah to handle something."

Mark wasn't sure if it was the inflection of his voice or the words he chose, but Sky noticed something was up, and her eyes narrowed as she regarded him.

"It sounds like you are up to some trouble. Let me help."

Taking a small step back, Mark shook his head. "I can't. It could be dangerous, Sky."

"I can handle myself, Mark. I'm empowered."

"Sky, I don't think you understand. We are walking into a really dangerous situation."

With a disdainful look, Sky's body blurred, and she appeared in front of Mark, her finger poking his cheek. Startled, he tried to grab her hand, but before he could, she had retreated out of reach once more. He opened his mouth to speak, but she vanished again, this time shooting up into the air so quickly he could barely follow her movement. A moment later, she was back, standing in front of him as if she had never moved.

"I'm way more likely to survive danger than you, Mark. And besides, it's not like you can stop me from following you. I'm helping."

Rubbing his forehead, Mark sighed. "Fine, you can come with me."

As soon as the words left his mouth, he regretted them, but it was too late, and she brightened up, nodding her head aggressively. "Oh, that's great. I'd love to come with you."

"Well, we gotta go. We're gonna be late," Mark said, desperately trying to figure out how he was going to explain the situation to Noah.

As it turned out, Noah didn't care one bit, barely glancing at Sky as he immediately launched into an explanation of the mission they were about to undertake.

"There are only two people in the building, and as I said in the dossier, the main part of their base is on the fourth floor. They've trapped the fifth floor, and they have security on the entrances from the ground floor. The best option is to get up onto the roof. However, that's going to be tricky, as they have both sound and pressure sensors around the door. I have a way to nullify them, but unfortunately, we have to be on the roof to do it."

Looking at the schematics that Noah sent over, Mark felt a tug on his sleeve, and glancing over, he saw Sky looking at him with wide eyes. "Are you guys raiding that building?"

"'Raiding' is a strong word," Mark said. "Right now, we're just doing reconnaissance, looking for information, trying to figure out who the people are and, more importantly, why they broke into my house."

"They broke into your house?" Sky asked.

Now, Noah did look over, his expression confused as he glanced between Mark and Sky. Taking a deep breath, Mark nodded.

"Yes, some people broke into my house, and we ended up in a little bit of a fight, and they tried to kill me. I'd like to know why, and so that's why we're here. Their main base seems to be in that building over there, and we're going to be slipping in, or at least trying to, and getting as much information as we can. The goal is to avoid engaging anybody and to just get in and get out. However, this security looks like it's going to be a problem."

Nodding, Noah gestured to a table covered in various devices. "I put gear together for us that should help us infiltrate, including a jammer that we can use to lock down the security. It's a pretty ingenious device, but unfortunately, it has a fifteen-foot range, which means we have to literally plant it on the door if we want to bypass their security."

Walking over to the table, Mark picked up the device that Noah had pointed to. It looked to be about the size of a small book, and he could see a mana gem inside of it through the clear case. An incredibly complex mana circuit filled the rest of the space, and even though it wasn't active, Mark could feel the mana around it becoming sluggish.

"Will it impact powers?"

"No, though it does feel slightly weird to be inside the field it produces," Noah replied. "Once it's activated, all it'll do is lock down other mana circuits in the area, keeping them from activating. It will mean that you won't be able to use your activators, but it doesn't actually stop powers, so long as they don't rely on mana circuits to run."

Glancing out the window at the building they were targeting, Mark scratched his head. It was six stories high, and none of the surrounding buildings were more than three stories, making it tricky to get to the top of the building without climbing up the outside.

"All you need to do is get this device on the top of that building, right?" Sky said. "That's easy."

Frowning, Mark turned and looked at her, then smacked himself in the forehead. "Oh, of course it is. Noah, you've met Sky, right? Sky has flight."

"Ah, she's the one who consumed your gem," Noah said, remembering the conversation they had at the party. "Will she be able to get close without setting off the sensors?"

"Yes, her flight isn't wind based. It only affects her. She should be able to fly up, approach from the sky, and then activate the device and slowly put it down. You said it has a fifteen-foot sphere of influence? Then as long as she drops right down on top of the door, she should be able to set it up."

"I think that's our best bet," Noah said, nodding and taking the device from Mark.

Flipping it over, he showed the back to Sky. "This is an adhesive.

You'll want to pull the tab, and then you can stick it straight to the door. It'll operate for a couple of years unless it's turned off, so we'll have more than enough time."

Handing the jamming device to her, he walked over to the table and picked up a hook.

"As long as you're going up there, you might as well help us get up too," he said. "This is a specialized grappling hook. Place it securely, and I can get a rope attached to it. That way, we can zip up."

"Sure, no problem," Sky said, her eyes gleaming. "This is just like one of those spy thrillers."

"Yeah, something like that," Noah replied with a nod. "But we have a limited window, so we should get going. Mark, let's gear up. I brought extra clothes, and you can change in the bathroom. Sky, I don't know if I have anything that'll fit you, exactly, but you'll find some darker clothing on the counter. Pick what you'd like and get changed."

When Mark emerged from the bathroom, he was starting to feel like he was in a spy thriller as well. He still had his own boots on but now wore dark military fatigues over a tight bodysuit. Noah handed him a pile of webbing that turned out to be a harness, optimized to carry all the gear Noah had laid out. Giving Mark a brief introduction to each item, Noah showed him where to attach it to his harness, and fifteen minutes later, they were standing on the roof of their building, watching as Sky shot up into the air, quickly disappearing in the darkness.

Through a pair of binoculars, Mark watched her hover over the distant building. Twenty-five feet above the roof, she flipped over, hanging upside down in the air. The strangest thing was that her hair didn't flip at all, remaining perfectly relaxed against her neck, as if she were standing right side up. This deepened Mark's suspicion that there was a force completely isolating her from the world around her.

Ever so slowly, she began to creep down toward the door, her expression locked in a concentrated scowl. There was a faint crackle of energy around the jamming device, and Mark found himself holding his breath, waiting for the alarms to go off on the fourth floor as she set the device on the door. No alarm.

"I think we're good," Noah said, listening to a bug placed outside one of the fourth-story windows. "Sky, go ahead and set the grappling hook."

Flying to the edge of the building, Sky planted the grappling hook device on the edge of the wall, as Noah had instructed her. With a faint beep, the mana circuits flared to life, and a rod extended from the device, rising five feet into the air. At the same time, the claws welded themselves to the cement wall. Noah, glancing at his watch, nodded, and Mark picked up a launcher. It was shaped like a tube, with a small aiming device. He lifted it up, sighting on the rod that extended from the building in the distance, and activated the mana circuit. There was a soft thump and then a whooshing sound as rope extended out of the launcher. With unerring accuracy, the rope shot into the distance and attached itself firmly to the rod.

Mark had never seen anything like these devices and was quite astonished at how well they worked. Noah took the launcher and planted it on the ground, activating a mana circuit on the end as it welded itself to the floor, just as the rope had.

"Let's go," he said, and grabbing one of the devices on his harness, he clipped onto the rope that now extended half a city block between the two buildings.

There was a faint zip, and then Noah was gone, carried across the rope up to the roof of the building where Sky waited. Mark was a moment behind him, attaching the device Noah had given him to the rope and tapping the side. There was a moment when nothing happened, then a strong jerk as Mark found himself dragged off the edge of the building and into the air. It only took him ten seconds to reach the top of the zip line, and at the last moment, his device disconnected, and he dropped onto the roof next to Noah.

"Looks like we're still good," Noah said. "Sky, can you keep watch?"

"Sure," Sky replied, floating a few feet above them.

"Mark, let's go."

Following Noah, Mark watched as his friend used a circular device to bypass the lock since the keypad currently didn't work. Opening the door an inch, Noah checked for an alarm again, and when nothing sounded, he stepped inside the stairwell.

"We'll be going down two floors," Noah said quietly. "You have the layout memorized?"

"Roughly," Mark replied.

"Good. I don't know the exact location of the two people on the fourth floor or where they'd be keeping their files, but since this is a permanent base, I'd anticipate there's an office, maybe even a command center. That's where we're going to start. Let's go."

Anytime Mark watched Noah operating, he couldn't help but be amazed at how easily Noah did everything. Completely silent, Noah walked down the steps, keeping an eye on the stairwells below. He was holding a short rod in his left hand and the circular lock-opening device in his right. With his chiseled jaw, striking good looks, and high-tech outfit, Noah looked as if he could have stepped out of the latest summer blockbuster, and Mark found himself genuinely jealous.

"Something wrong?" Noah asked, pausing to look back at Mark.

"Hmm? No. Everything's fine," Mark said, embarrassed.

"All right, watch out for traps."

Moving down each step slowly, Noah used the short wand to

scan back and forth. On the third step, it vibrated in his hand, and he immediately stopped. Crouching down, he scanned the step and then pointed to a thin wire stretched across it.

"Good old-fashioned trip wire," he said. "Be careful not to touch it, or you'll set off the alarm."

Once they knew it was there, the wire was easy enough to step over, and they bypassed two more the same way before arriving at the fourth floor. The door was solid, with no window, which meant they'd have to take a risk that nobody was on the other side when they opened it. As Noah reached for it, Mark grabbed his hand, frowning.

"Let me try something," he said, and closed his eyes, focusing on the faint psychic web at the edge of his mind.

At first, nothing happened, and after a minute, he felt Noah stir, but he kept concentrating, and slowly, the web strengthened. Mark saw a dull object near the center of the web. It looked like a pebble, placed precisely where Noah stood. Elated, Mark gently probed the psychic network, looking farther out to see if he could spot any other pebbles. At first, there was nothing, and then, roughly twenty-five feet away, he saw another pebble, this one rolling slowly along.

His eyes snapped open, and he opened his watch, projecting the floor plan of the building. Currently, it showed the fourth floor, including the stairwell where they were located, with a green dot representing him and Noah. Outside the stairwell was a long hallway, with rooms off to the right and to the left. Tracking the rolling pebble for a moment, Mark tapped one of the rooms nearby.

"There's someone in here," he said, "currently walking. Looks like he just entered the room, based on the direction he's going."

Nodding, Noah eased the door open and slipped into the hall, and Mark followed behind him a moment later. With silent steps, Noah crept down the hall until he was at the door of the room Mark had mentioned. The door hung open, and listening, they could both hear the sound of someone inside. There was the scrape of a chair and then a soft sigh as someone sat down.

Pulling out a small mirror from his belt, Noah held it in his palm and activated it. A moment later, an image came to life on the mirror, showing what was right around the corner. There was a man in the room, just as Mark had said, sitting on a chair with his back toward the door. He appeared to be unlacing his boots, so Noah didn't hesitate. Like a ghost, he slipped into the room, darting to where the man sat, drawing his mana blade as he went.

His left hand wrapped around the man's mouth, and his right hand slid the blade through the chair and into the man's back, cutting straight into his lungs. Even as the man jerked, Noah's blade withdrew and stabbed again, moving to the front of the man's chest and stabbing into his heart, killing him almost instantly.

Mark, who had stepped into the room after Noah and was plastered against the door, keeping watch down the hallway with his own small hand mirror, felt a twinge in his mind, once again experiencing that strange disconnect. He had just watched someone murdered in cold blood, but while it was intellectually unsettling, he found his pulse absolutely calm, as if what had just happened were the most mundane thing in the world.

Gently easing the corpse to the ground, Noah crouched and checked over the body quickly. When he had finished, he searched the room, not finding anything of value, and then walked over to where Mark was still keeping watch at the door.

"Horace McLavin," Noah said quietly. "Wanted murderer."

Confused, Mark felt his watch vibrate and opened up the message Noah had sent him. It contained a complete profile of the man who had just been killed, including the multiple murder charges he was currently wanted for.

"I've done a bit more digging on the members of the team since I sent you the first profile," Noah said. "Most of them are on wanted lists and are currently hiding from the authorities."

There was a grimness to Noah's tone that Mark had never heard before, but as he read through the reports on the ten members of the team, he found himself no longer caring how Noah dealt with them. Turning off the virtual screen, he nodded. "Let's go."

As they slipped back out into the hall, Mark focused on the psychic web again, trying to spot the other person who was on this floor. The fourth floor was large and composed of one massive office area. A set of elevators on the northern side, opposite the stairwell they had entered, was the primary way of getting in and out of the building. There was a large lobby outside it, currently home to three beat-up couches and a large table. The floor also contained several supply rooms, some rooms that were being used for sleeping, and a small armory.

Though he was tempted to take one of the fancy-looking mana swords from the armory, Mark figured they would still be there later. It took forty minutes to search through the floor, and when they finally found the office, they found the other member of the team as well. He was working at one of the desks, a series of large virtual screens in front of him, showing a variety of scenes. One of which was the outside of Mark's house.

Mark's eyes narrowed. He didn't wait for Noah. His left glove came off, and reaching up, he touched his necklace as he darted forward. The man must have heard his footsteps, because he spun around, eyes going wide as he caught sight of Mark. He started to shout, his hand dropping to a wand he kept at his waist, and Mark recognized it as the same device the woman had used to shoot him a few days ago.

Before he could get out a sound, Mark was already on top of him, his fingers flashing as they slid across the man's throat. At the same time, Mark swept the man's legs, grabbing his shoulder and pulling him forward as the spray of blood that exploded from his sliced artery drenched the floor, barely avoiding Mark. The man died in seconds, never managing to draw his weapon.

As he held the body against the floor, Mark frowned. Noah's kill had been quiet and tidy, with barely any blood leaking, thanks to how sharp the mana blade was. Mark's kill, on the other hand, caused quite a mess and was slowly filling the room with the stench of blood. Coming in after him, Noah glanced at the body on the floor and then at Mark.

"Well, that's handy," he said, and Mark realized that he was making a joke as the corner of Noah's lips twitched.

Suppressing his smile, Mark nodded. "But not nearly as neat. I need a better way to take people down silently."

"You could always try breaking his neck next time. Though, with empowered, that's hard unless your strength is considerably higher than theirs. Blood loss or destroying their heart or brain are really the only good options for taking somebody down quick, because you never know what kind of powers they have. Come on, let's see what we can find."

Crouching, Noah stripped the watch off the corpse's wrist and placed it next to the keyboard to make sure the computer didn't lock him out, then began to work, his fingers flying. Mark, who had no idea what to do to help, opted to search the desk for any physical evidence. They both worked as quickly as they could, and it wasn't long before Mark found something.

It was in a stack of papers stuffed into a drawer. As he thumbed through them, Mark caught sight of a memo. What grabbed his attention was the official logo of New Emery stamped on the top. Pulling it out, he placed it down on the desk and read over it, twice. The memo had been issued by somebody in the Defense Force, one General Carter. That wasn't a name that Mark had ever heard before, but that didn't surprise him, as New Emery was quite big, and the military occupied most of the government positions in the city.

The memo, which appeared to be a photocopy, detailed the creation of a program intended to gather information and carry out tasks of a sensitive nature. Though the term *sensitive nature* wasn't spelled out any further, it didn't take a genius to read between the lines. A bad feeling began to bloom in Mark's heart as he continued his search. If he was reading the memo correctly, then it was likely that this team wasn't working independently but instead was working for the city itself, which boded ill for Mark.

He still hadn't figured out why they'd been in his house, however, as it wasn't as if he possessed anything of value. A moment later, he paused, remembering the stacks of elixirs still sitting in a small box buried in his closet. Was it possible that they had gotten wind of his upgraded potions and had managed to trace them back to him?

Frowning, Mark shook his head. While theoretically one could trace somebody back through the Black Star Exchange, he highly doubted they had. When his upgraded elixirs were assessed, only Exlian extracts had been listed as ingredients, which meant that there was no way for anybody to know that it was his blood that was causing the change. The machine Alchemist Henley had used hadn't been able to tell that the elixir was originally a yellow C-ranked elixir rather than the blue B-ranked elixir it had become. There had to be something else that they were looking for.

Eventually, Mark exhausted his options, having searched through the desks without finding anything related to him. There were plenty of other incriminating documents, and he took pictures of most of them with his watch, dropping them all into a file to go through later.

"Hey, Mark?"

Hearing Noah call out to him, Mark looked up.

"I think you should come and take a look at this."

There was something off about Noah's tone, and with his heart beating loudly in his chest, Mark walked over. Four screens were laid out above the desk, information arranged across them, and for a moment, Mark had trouble understanding what he was looking at. A variety of profiles were pulled up on two of the screens, most of them for people Mark had never encountered before. Two caught his eye.

The first was for a familiar-looking woman, a woman Mark had only seen once, months ago, when she died in front of him in an alleyway. Her name, Mark read, was Tara Hamlin, and she had been a researcher assigned under one of Dr. Edward Graham's many projects. A red note scrawled across the bottom of her file said *Terminated for industrial espionage* and gave a date, the same date that Mark had run into her. Below it was another note, much smaller.

> Body of the deceased identified by Captain James Balin and team. However, the corpse was missing when the cleanup team arrived an hour later.

Unsure what to make of it, Mark turned to look at the profile of the other person he recognized. It was one of the twins, his brother Joe's friends, who he saw regularly.

"I think they're after your brother," Noah said quietly, pointing to a screen that held a long report detailing the explosion that had recently rocked the city.

As Mark read on, his eyes went wide. According to the report, the explosion wasn't a gas-pipe leak, as had been reported in the news. Instead, it was a bomb, planted by seditious elements in the city who sought to undermine the rule of law. Attached to the report was a long list of names, and among them were half a dozen of Joe's friends. As Mark continued to scroll down, his expression darkened. There, at the bottom of the list, was the name he'd been hoping not to see: Joseph Fields.

Swallowing, Mark clicked on the profile attached and saw his brother's military picture looking back at him. The file detailed Joe's military service and included the results of the Cerberus Battalion's last deployment. He was marked as burned out, with a note mentioning that he would still have value if reassigned to a desk job. A red note had been added to the bottom of his file as well.

> Suspected member of the Green Line terrorists. Known to be highly dangerous. Approach with caution.

Green Line was the train station where the bomb had exploded. Wordlessly, Mark continued to read through the report, trying to understand everything that was going on.

"I was trying to find the client," Noah said after a few minutes had passed, "but I haven't had any luck. Though if I had to guess . . ." His voice trailed off.

"It's the city," Mark said, rubbing his forehead. "There's a memo in one of the drawers. I took a picture of it and sent it to our folder. This group is probably being used to gather information."

Sighing, Noah shook his head. "What a messed-up world we live in. The government using a bunch of wanted killers to dig for information on a bunch of suspected terrorists. This whole thing stinks."

"It does. I can't believe they think my brother is in on it," Mark said with a frown. "There is no way Joe would do something like that. I mean . . ."

Noah didn't say anything, but he didn't have to. Mark was starting to put together all the disparaging things his brother had said about the city with the information in front of him, and though not conclusive, the case was damning.

"There isn't actually any proof in this report, just a bunch of suspicions, which is probably why they can't go through the normal investigative methods," Noah said quietly. "They have to use a team like this that can operate outside the law. After all, you can't go and search somebody's house without a warrant, and you can't get a warrant without having actual evidence, or at least a reasonable suspicion, but all of this is paper thin."

"Would that actually stop them?" Mark asked. "I mean, if they couldn't find any evidence."

"No," Noah replied with a faintly disgusted look. "In fact, I wouldn't even be surprised if the team had been hired not to look for evidence but instead to plant it."

"Mark!"

Mark heard Sky's frantic voice in his earpiece.

"There are people coming. They just pulled up to the front of the building, and they're moving quickly."

Sharing a glance, Mark and Noah turned and bolted. Yet before they had gotten more than a few steps, a sharp alarm sounded, and lights began to flash.

"There must have been a silent alarm that I didn't catch," Noah snarled as they burst through the door into the hallway.

As the alarm wailed, loud thuds echoed around them and heavy metal shutters slammed down, locking the entire floor, leaving them trapped.

"That's not good," Mark said, looking at the metal sheets covering the windows and doors.

"Not good at all," Noah replied. "Sky, how many people are coming up?"

"It looked like five."

"That's just about the whole team," Mark said, looking around for a way out. "Sky, get out of here and make sure they don't see you."

No escape presented itself, and a moment later, they heard a ding as the elevator opened up. Noah gestured for Mark to get down, and the two of them slipped into one of the rooms. Crouching by the wall, Mark focused, trying to lock onto the enemy's locations through the psychic web. They were moving so quickly that it was hard, and hearing a muffled shout, Mark saw them beginning to spread out across the floor.

"I hate to say this, but the elevator is probably our best bet," Noah said.

"We've got two people in front of the elevator," Mark replied, "and three spread out."

As he spoke, he tapped the map, pinging their locations for Noah. There was a shout from the room next to them as someone discovered the dead body, then more shouts as the second was discovered a moment later.

"Split into teams of two and search the floor. They've got to be in here somewhere. Carl, guard the elevator."

The enemy team split up to begin combing the floor, and Noah pointed to the elevator on his map and then made a slicing motion across his neck. Taking a deep breath, Mark nodded. There was nobody immediately outside the room, so they slipped out, sprinting down the hall toward the elevator, where a large man with bulky muscles stood. As soon as he saw Mark and Noah, he let out a loud shout, lifting his metal rod. At the same time, a metal shield unfolded on his arm, covering half of his body. Mark and Noah split up, Mark heading for their opponent's right while Noah went to the left in an attempt to trap him between them.

With a savage yell, the brawny man lifted his rod and slashed at Mark. Even before the attack was launched, Mark was already dodging, and it was a good thing, too, as the superstrength-empowered strike ripped through the air and slammed into the wall, crushing a large chunk of cement as it landed. Mark, having barely slipped under the blow, struck with his left hand, carving a bloody furrow along the underside of the man's wrist. With a screech of pain, he turned, wrenching the rod free and trying to slam it into Mark again. Before he could, the gleaming end of a blade poked out of his chest, as Noah got behind him and sank his knife into the man's back. There was a soft ding, and the doors of the elevator opened, and Mark and Noah darted inside, Noah dragging the still-struggling man behind them.

Mark saw a figure dart around the corner and recognized her at a glance. It was the woman he had fought in his kitchen, and as she lifted her wand, Mark realized why Noah had dragged the dying empowered through the doorway of the elevator. There was a series of puffs, and three darts sprouted from the man's chest. A moment later, the door slid closed, and the elevator started to drop. Pulling up his watch, Noah typed frantically.

"We've got to get back to my house," Mark said. "Find Joe."

"Are you sure that's a good idea?" Noah asked. "I mean, given the information we just learned, it might be dangerous."

Suppressing the flash of anger he felt at Noah's insinuation, Mark shook his head stubbornly. "We need to go and talk to him. There's no way my brother is part of a terrorist group."

Though he looked like he wanted to respond, Noah kept his mouth shut, and a moment later, the door opened into the lobby. Unfortunately, what met them as they emerged was a blast of mana that nearly roasted Mark alive. At the last moment, he felt Noah grabbing him and jerking him aside as the rolling ball of mana stormed past them, exploding in the open elevator with such force that it warped the metal walls.

"Where'd that come from?!" Mark yelled.

"Does it matter?!" Noah yelled back as they scrambled for cover behind a large potted plant.

Feeling mana gathering in the distance, Mark and Noah looked at each other, wide eyed, and then split up, each heading a different direction as the pot they were hiding behind exploded in a shower of dirt, twigs, and shards of pottery.

Dashing to a pillar, Mark risked glancing around it and saw a female empowered gathering another mana blast, staring directly at him. Taking a deep breath, Mark darted out from behind the pillar, trying to move as quickly as possible as he headed for the exit.

With a savage grin, the woman was lifting her charged ball of mana to hurl at him when Noah's foot slammed into the side of her face. Crying out, she stumbled to the ground, losing control of the mana, which exploded, throwing both her and Noah back. Even before Noah had landed, he had already righted himself in the air, though his left arm hung limply at his side, blood seeping from a badly burned patch of skin on his biceps, where he had borne the brunt of the blast.

As soon as Noah had made contact with the woman, Mark had already changed directions, sprinting toward her sliding body with all his might. Unfortunately, he wasn't quite close enough, and as he got within a few steps, he felt mana gathering again. Gritting his teeth, he pressed forward, but a mana shield sprang up in front of him. Realizing he was going to slam right into it, Mark frantically hacked out with his left hand, his wrist twisting as he executed the second stage of the Cutting Palm.

Luckily, his technique worked this time, and the air parted in front of him, splitting the mana shield in half to reveal the shocked gaze of the empowered woman on the other side. Mark's fingers flicked as she jerked her head back, and a gash appeared on her cheek. She let out a low shout, and a flash of mana propelled them apart. By this time, Noah had reached the exit. Mark borrowed the force of the explosion to chase after him, turning around in midair and falling into a stumbling run as he landed on the ground.

As they raced outside, a large black car tore down the street before skidding to a stop in front of them. Noah's large bodyguard was driving, and Noah and Mark piled in without a moment's hesitation. As the doors shut behind them, the engine revved, and the car took off, accelerating like mad. Looking through the back window, Mark saw a group of people rushing out of the doorway and piling into the vehicle that had been waiting outside.

"Shall I proceed to one of the safe houses?" Bandman asked.

"No," Mark said, practically shouting.

Taking a deep breath, he brought his voice under control.

"No, we need to get to my brother, to Joe. We have a lot of

incriminating evidence, which means that they need to silence everybody involved."

"Isn't your brother an A-ranked empowered?" Noah asked, his forehead furrowing.

"Not anymore," Mark said. "He burned out."

Taken aback, Noah tapped his watch and projected a virtual screen in the back of the vehicle as Bandman drove at a breakneck pace down the road. "You said he burned out?"

"Yes, during the last mission."

"That must be the connection," Noah replied as he began pulling up the profiles contained in the report about the Green Line terrorist group. "One of the things I noticed is that more than half of these people on this list are marked as burned out."

Looking over, Mark's eyes widened as Noah opened profile after profile that had the large red words stamped across them.

"If there is an organization planning on trying to disrupt the city and it's composed of empowered who have burned out, then it's highly likely that they contacted your brother," Noah said.

"Sir, they're on our tail," Bandman said from the front seat.

Tearing his gaze from the report, Mark looked out the back window and saw a car accelerating rapidly as it approached them.

"How are they so fast?" he asked.

"They disabled their limiters," Noah said with a sigh. "All mana-powered vehicles have built-in limiters so they can't accelerate endlessly, but somehow I don't think they care."

One of the windows rolled down, and a figure crawled out halfway. The empowered woman from the lobby still had blood on her cheek as she began to gather mana in her hand. A moment later, their car shook as the mana splashed across the back of it, the window visibly melting.

"We can only take two more hits, sir," Bandman said.

A moment later, that number dropped to one as a second

ball of mana slammed into them. The enemy was getting closer and closer, and just when Mark thought they'd lose the back of the car completely, something zipped between them. There was only forty-five feet between the two speeding cars, and the gap was constantly shrinking, so when Mark saw a figure blur between them, he was stunned. So was the driver of the enemy's car when he saw a signpost appear in their way, hanging in the air.

With a yell, he jerked the wheel, and their car skidded off to the side of the road, running up and over the sidewalk. He tried to regain control of his careening vehicle, but they were moving too fast, and before he could, they slammed straight into a building, crashing through the wall in a fiery explosion. Wild laughter broke through the voice channel, and Mark and Noah exchanged a glance.

"Sky, was that you?" Mark asked.

"Ha! Yes! I did it! It worked! Wow! I definitely thought I was gonna die. Like, really, definitely thought I was gonna die!" Sky said, slightly hysterical.

It was a while before Sky calmed down enough to explain what she had done. It had been a simple matter, really. She had cut a metal pole with a mana blade, flown with it to the two vehicles, and released it directly between them. Facing the prospect of ramming into the metal pole while going 150 miles an hour, the driver had opted to try to steer out of the way, only to lose control and slam into a nearby building.

"And that is why flight is such a valuable power," Noah said smugly. "It just takes a bit of creativity, and you become incredibly dangerous."

"Yeah, I can see that," Mark said, glancing out the half-melted back window at the empty street behind him.

A moment later, there was a soft thud as Sky landed on the

roof of the car. "Hey, can I come in? I'm kinda tired. It's rough going this fast."

"Sure," Mark said, unbuckling and scooting over as Noah unlocked the doors.

A moment later, the door opened and Sky floated in, completely at ease, as if the car weren't moving at all. She shut the door behind her and buckled up, breathing a huge sigh of relief as she brushed her hair out of her face.

"Wow, that was exciting," she said, her eyes practically glowing as Mark and Noah stared at her.

When they arrived at Mark's house, everything was quiet, and after pulling up silently, they piled out of the car. Mark hurried to the front door, punched the key code in, and stepped inside as soon as the door opened. Immediately, his senses triggered, and he bent backward, barely avoiding a hand grabbing for his throat. Instinctively, his foot snapped out, slamming against his opponent's knee, even as he struck at the grabbing wrist with his left hand.

His foot hit his opponent's leg, and Mark's body shook, feeling as if he had just kicked a steel plate. A fraction of a second later, his titanium fingers scraped across the back of his opponent's wrist, barely drawing blood as Noah's hand grabbed the back of his jacket and pulled sharply, helping him avoid his opponent's sweeping leg. Everything had happened in a flash, and when Mark's brain caught up to his senses, he found himself staring at one of the twins. Slowly straightening up, Kevin smiled sheepishly and scratched the back of his head.

"Sorry," he said, holding up his wounded hand. "I didn't mean to startle you. I was sleeping on the couch, and you know, well, instinct."

There was a clatter as a few people ran down the steps. Seeing Joe, the other twin, and a young woman he recognized from the profiles in the report, Mark could feel his heart clenching.

"You okay, Mark?" Joe asked, walking over.

"He's fine. I didn't even touch him," Kevin said. As he spoke, he showed Joe the faint cut on his skin. "He got me, though."

"Why don't you all come in," Marvin said. "No need to let the whole neighborhood watch."

Leaving Bandman outside to watch the car, the other three trooped into the house, finding seats inside. Once everyone was settled, Mark stared at his brother.

"What's the matter?" Joe asked, after looking over Mark carefully. "You look like you're dressed for war."

"Something like that. We just had a bit of an excursion. Did a little bit of digging."

"Is this about those people who broke into our house?"

"You had people break into your house?" the young woman who had been upstairs with Joe asked, her tone sharp. "Joe, don't you think you should have shared that information?"

"Who's she?" Mark asked.

Feeling the tension rising, Joe lifted his hands. "Everybody calm down," he said. "Mark, this is a friend of mine, Emily. Emily, this is my younger brother, Mark."

"Another friend, huh," Mark asked, staring at Emily with a sharp gaze. This was the young woman he had heard arguing with Joe some months back.

"Since high school. Why? Is that important?"

"I don't know, you tell me," Mark said.

"But probably not right now," Noah interjected. "We need to get to a safe house."

"Safe house," Joe asked, glancing at Noah and then back at his brother. "Mark, what is going on?"

"The people who raided our house," Mark said, closing his eyes and rubbing his forehead, "were a team that was hired to investigate members of the Green Line terrorist group."

As soon as he said the name, the tension in the room shot up, and Mark knew that his fears were right. With a groan, he opened his eyes, staring straight at his brother, whose face was pale as a sheet.

"I have no idea what you're involved in, Joe, but they just tried to murder us. Admittedly, we killed some of theirs as well. So at this point, it's just a matter of who will get the other first."

Seeing Joe's expression tighten, Mark laughed mirthlessly and shook his head. "Don't give me that look. I'm sitting on a report that says you and your friends bombed a civilian train line and killed twelve people. I don't want to hear anything from you about what I'm choosing to do."

Marvin, frowning, looked at Joe. "I hate to say it, Joe, but if your brother is telling the truth, then we need to leave. Now. We're probably all compromised."

"Fine, but then you and I are going to have a conversation," he said, pointing at Mark.

"I think that's a good idea," Mark replied, meeting his gaze squarely.

"Where are we going?" Noah asked. "My safe house or yours?"

"We should go to ours," Emily replied after a moment of thought. "My guess is that the rest of the network is compromised as well, but they won't be able to find our safe house."

Smiling tightly, Mark nodded. "There were close to forty people whose profiles were attached to the report, though a couple of them were marked deceased or missing."

"That's almost all of us," Marvin said, rubbing his hand over his close-cropped hair. "That's not good at all."

"This really isn't good," Kev added. "We need to get everybody into hiding."

"Then let's get moving," Emily ordered, and Joe and Marvin sprinted upstairs, while Kev went to the storeroom to dig out a bag.

While the others were gathering their things, Mark, Noah, and Sky looked at each other.

"What do you think?" Mark asked quietly, shooting a glance at Emily, who was across the room, pointedly ignoring them.

"I think it's risky to go with them," Noah replied. "Currently, we haven't been tagged into whatever this terrorist organization is, but the longer we hang out with them, the more likely we are to be assumed to be part of it."

"I don't think I want to join a terrorist organization," Sky whispered, peeking a glance at Emily.

"We're not joining a terrorist organization."

As he spoke, he felt something stir in the back of his mind and glanced up, seeing Mime at the top of the stairs. His cat's eyes were fixed firmly on the front window, her body tense and hackles raised. Acting by instinct, Mark grabbed Noah and Sky, pulling them to the ground with him as he yelled. Emily was far enough away that she managed to dodge in time, but Kevin, who had stepped out of the back hallway, was right in the path of the car that came through the wall. There was a crunch as he was hurled backward, his body crashing through the steps and into the bathroom on the other side.

A moment later, the doors blew off the vehicle, and four

black-clothed empowered rushed out. Hearing the commotion from upstairs, Marvin and Joe raced down the steps, quickly throwing themselves at their opponents, who wielded the dart-shooting rods Mark was growing to hate. As the entire inside of the house transformed into a chaotic melee, Mark reached over, grabbed the bottom of the couch, and hauled it up, catching one of the empowered who was trying to vault over it in midair and slamming him into the ceiling. Thrown off balance, he landed awkwardly, and Mark's fingers nearly took his head off.

The empowered who had rushed into the house weren't very strong and hadn't anticipated finding the place filled with powerhouses. There was a loud roar as Kevin came charging out of the hole his body had created and slammed into one of the men. He was barely scratched, and with heavy fists that shattered bone, he drove the man to the ground. One of the other empowered, an energy controller who shot darts of superheated plasma, was trying in vain to pin down Joe, who was simply too quick for her to catch. While she was distracted, Marvin slammed into her, repeating Kev's performance by overwhelming her with brute strength, snapping her neck.

The last of the empowered met a swift end at the tip of Noah's mana blade after Sky darted over and pushed his tube to the side before he could fire it. Tapping his watch, Noah's face paled, and he dashed outside, leaving the door hanging open. There, Bandman was locked in a fierce fight with two more assailants, and Noah launched himself into the fray, Mark following close behind. As they lost the advantage of numbers, the two empowered thugs attacking Bandman panicked and tried to run but were quickly subdued by the bodyguard and Noah. Arriving a second after the fight ended, Mark looked around. The entire front of the house had been caved in, as the car had driven straight through the front window, and sirens had started in the distance.

"We've only got a minute or two," Joe said, striding out of the house. "We have to leave now."

"Are we all going to fit?" Kev asked, brushing blood off his knuckles as he strode through the door.

"We're going to have to," Emily snapped, "unless you've got another car just hanging about."

"As a matter of fact, I do," Kevin said. "Marvin, you want to help me?"

The car that had crashed through the wall was still idling, though its front bumper was badly crumpled where it had slammed into Kevin. Wrenching off the driver's door, Kevin sat inside of it as his brother cleared the rubble behind it. There was a whine as the car kicked to life, and Kevin reversed it, pulling it onto the yard. Leaning out the window, he grinned. "If you hit me with it, it's mine. Come on, get in."

Emily, Marvin, and Joe all ran over and piled in the car, leaving Mark and Noah standing with Sky next to Noah's half-melted vehicle.

"We have a safe place," Joe said when he saw that Mark and his friends weren't moving. "Guaranteed to lose them. You don't have to stay with us, but we do need to wait until the heat blows over."

Gritting his teeth, Mark nodded. "Fine. Noah, are you okay following them?"

"Yes."

"Sky, what about you?"

Swallowing, she nodded, and together with Bandman, they got into the car and began to follow as Kev drove off. They headed toward the southern end of the city, soon entering a dilapidated neighborhood where the houses were crumbling. In the distance, Mark could see the city wall, lit by the first rays of the morning sun. To his surprise, there was a bunch of scaffolding set up next to it, and it looked like a half-finished construction project.

"What's that?" he asked, pointing toward the wall.

"That's one of the gaps from the last war," Sky responded, her voice quiet.

"It was breached during the last wave, and they haven't repaired it? It's been fifteen years."

"No, it hasn't been repaired. The project has been abandoned for some time—for as long as I can remember," Sky said.

Noticing how nervous she was, Mark reached over to grab her hand. "Sky, are you okay?"

"Yeah, yeah, I'm fine," Sky said. "It's just, it's been a bit of a wild night, and coming back here is unsettling. This is the Willow Lake District. This is where I grew up . . ."

Remembering her story about the orphanage she had grown up in, Mark didn't know what to say, so he just squeezed her hand. The car in front of them pulled into a small parking garage attached to a broken-down motel and stopped at a metal garage door. After a short wait, it rumbled up, and the two cars slipped in, entering a long, dark passage that led down into the earth. The tunnel was pitch black, and if it weren't for the broken headlights of their vehicles, Mark was sure they wouldn't have been able to see at all. They drove for over twenty minutes before they finally stopped at a large gate. After a moment more, it rose with a grinding noise, and they drove through. Kevin parked his car, and Bandman pulled up behind him. As everyone got out, they were met by a few new people, all of whom shared a military air.

"Is your message verified?" one of the older men asked Emily, and with a pale face she nodded.

"Yes. We've likely all been compromised. Everyone has to go underground. As soon as possible."

"I see. Who are they?"

Not liking the way the older man was looking at him, Mark

crossed his arms, his eyes narrowing as he met the man's gaze. Joe quickly stepped in between them.

"My brother and friends," he said calmly, trying to defuse the situation.

"If they're not members, why'd you bring them down?"

"Because they're the ones who warned us and helped us fight off the team that attacked us. We're gonna have a conversation, and then they'll either become members, or they'll go on their own way," Joe said. "Don't worry. I'll deal with it."

"See that you do. We're already in enough trouble because you picked up a tail."

"Hey, that's not fair," Emily started to say, but Joe cut her off with a wave.

"We don't have time for any of this," he said. "Let's pick up this conversation later. For now, we need to get everybody underground."

Giving Mark another dark look, the older man nodded and left, taking Kevin, Marvin, and Emily with him. Soon after they had gone, Joe rubbed his forehead and looked at his brother with a complicated gaze.

"I don't know what you found in your report," Joe said, "but we're not the Green Line terrorists. We didn't plant a bomb. We didn't kill people. That's not what we do."

"Then what do you do?" Mark asked.

Joe hesitated for a second, then took a deep breath.

"We're a group of concerned citizens," he said, choosing his words very carefully. "We're concerned about a number of things that the government of New Emery is doing with the support of the military, and we're trying to uncover evidence."

"Evidence of what?" Noah asked.

Joe glanced over but didn't respond.

"I really can't tell you anything if you're not a member," he said to Mark, "but I can guarantee you we're not doing anything bad."

"Huh. That's interesting," Mark said, "because I assume that if you ask the military or the government, they'd probably say the same thing."

"I know. Look, I get it, but if I share too much information, it increases the chance that we could be compromised."

"You're already compromised, Joe. They have an entire file with your face plastered all over it. They attacked our house. Twice."

"I know," Joe said. "I've been wondering why our people have been going missing, and I'm guessing that that file you're talking about is the culprit. If you're right and they have that much information on us, then either we have a mole inside our organization or they've just been onto us for a long time. I know this is an unfair request since I'm not giving you any information, but would you mind sharing that file with me?"

Looking over at Noah, Mark saw him shrug. "Up to you. He's your brother."

Turning back to Joe, Mark nodded. "Fine, I'll send it to you, but I don't want to join this terrorist organization or whatever it is. I don't want to be involved in any of this."

"That's fine," Joe said. "I can show you how to get out of here. You can pretend that you were sleeping over at Noah's house, and when the investigators arrive, just tell them you have no idea where I am."

Pointing to a small door set in the wall, Joe gave Mark a sad smile. "It might be a while till I see you again, but don't worry, they won't be able to catch us."

Feeling quite torn, Mark nodded and walked over to his brother, giving him a tight hug. Surprised, Joe froze for a moment and then returned the hug, patting Mark on the back. After letting go, Mark stepped back.

"I know I said I don't want to be involved," he said, "but if things get really desperate and you need a hand . . ."

He didn't finish his sentence and instead turned toward the door, the others trailing after him. Resisting the urge to look back, Mark stepped into the small corridor, where an elevator waited to take them to the surface. He had no way of knowing how deep underground they were, but he imagined that it must have been at least half a mile from how long it took the elevator to get them to the ground floor of a dilapidated office building.

Mark had noticed that his map hadn't been working down in the hidden room below their feet, and now, as it came back online, he realized that they were in a completely different part of town. Sky looked exhausted, and Noah was a bit pale around the eyes as well. For a long moment, the three of them stood in front of the elevator, simply staring at each other as Bandman went out to call a taxi.

"I'm sorry," Mark finally said. "I shouldn't have dragged the two of you into this."

"It is a bit of a difficult problem," Noah said, "but I chose to be here, and so I'll take responsibility for that."

"Yeah, Mark," Sky said, punching him lightly in the shoulder. "Don't worry about it. That was more excitement than I've had in years."

"We'll try to lay low for a little while," Mark said. "You two shouldn't have been ID'd, but there's a nonzero chance that people might come after you."

"In that case, we should set up a crisis code," Noah replied. "You can set your watch to autosend a text on command. We'll keep it to something innocuous."

Opening up his watch, he fiddled around with it for a moment and then sent a message. Mark's wrist vibrated, and looking down, he saw a message from Noah.

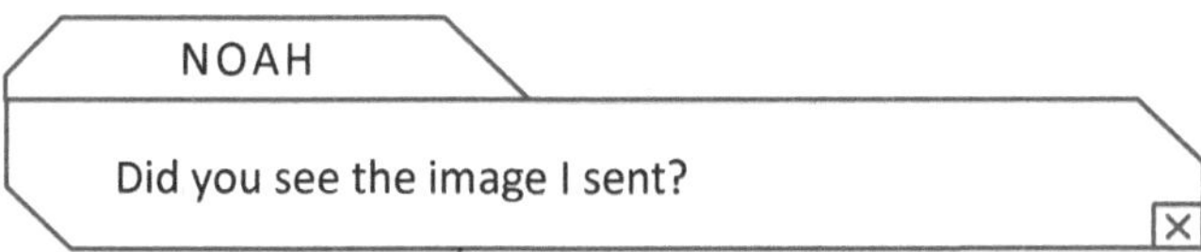

"If you get this from me, it means that I've been compromised, or someone is after me."

"Oh, that's a great idea," Sky said. "How do you set that up?"

By the time they'd finished setting their messages so that they could be sent with a quick tap along with the watch's current location in the city, the two taxis Bandman had ordered had arrived. Before splitting up, Noah pulled Mark aside and, after hesitating for a moment, spoke in a low voice.

"I know that this is a bit dumb, especially after everything we just went through, but please watch yourself. Not only do you have attention from the city, but my dad has been asking about you too, which isn't a good sign."

Frowning, Mark tried to think of a reason Noah's dad would be asking about him but couldn't come up with anything. "Do you want me to meet him?"

"No, absolutely not!"

Taken aback by the vehemence in Noah's voice, Mark leaned back as Noah continued.

"He's scheming something, and it won't be good, whatever it is. Just . . . just be careful when you go out for the next few days. Send me a message if anything comes up."

Patting Mark on the shoulder, Noah headed toward one of the cars with Bandman, while Sky and Mark got into the other. Since Mark's house was practically ruined, she had offered to let him stay with her, and forty-five minutes later, they pulled up outside a decrepit apartment building on the edge of the Willow Lake District.

"There really isn't much," Sky said, embarrassed, "but come on up."

The elevator hadn't worked for years, so they climbed seven stories up to Sky's apartment. When they arrived, Sky asked Mark to wait and then walked to the end of the hall, where she opened a window and flew out. A minute later, Mark heard the door unbolting, and Sky let him in.

"I keep the door locked," she explained, "since I can just come in and out the window now."

By *window*, she meant a hole in the side of the building. Mark hadn't seen it from the angle they had approached, but where Sky's apartment once had a large glass window and a balcony was now a gaping hole that gave them an excellent view of the Willow Lake District in the distance and the wall beyond it. The apartment was little more than a floor, walls, and a ceiling, though there was a small bathroom tucked away in the corner. A makeshift kitchenette had been shoved against one wall, and a simple mattress sat against the other. Looking around, Sky scuffed her feet.

"It's not much," she said, with forced cheer, "but if you can believe it, it's actually an upgrade from where I was before. And it's cheap. Rent's only two hundred credits a month."

"That is cheap," Mark said as he looked around. "You're pretty high up here."

"I am. There are apartments lower down, but I like being up here, away from everything. Especially now. And the view, the view's nice, especially when the sun sets. You should see the colors."

Walking over to the edge of the gaping hole, Mark stared into the distance. From this high up, he had a good view of the southern wall and saw that there were construction projects at more than one spot. Beyond the wall was the dead zone, stretching out to the much smaller outer wall. Beyond that, trees and hills, and in the far distance a smudge against the landscape that he assumed was the swamp where the murder scorpions came from. For a few minutes, they stood in silence, staring out over the city, and then Sky edged closer to Mark until her shoulder was just barely touching his.

"I'm sorry about your brother," she said. "I imagine it was pretty shocking to find out that he was involved in something like that."

Finding Sky's proximity oddly comforting, Mark sighed. "It certainly caught me off guard, but how much of it is true, I don't know."

"What are you going to do now?"

"Same thing I've always been doing," Mark replied. "I'll keep working with Master Abrams and wait for my assignment."

After another long pause, he looked over at Sky. "What about you? You got into the training camp, right?"

"Yes, I start next week," Sky replied.

"Are you excited? Nervous?"

"I am. Both, but more excited than nervous. Hey, do you want something to eat?"

With a wide smile, Mark nodded. "You know, I'd love something to eat. I'm absolutely starving."

Knowing he'd have to address his destroyed house at some point, Mark headed back home that afternoon. It had been oddly relaxing to spend the morning with Sky after their frantic adventure, and he found himself completely relaxed when he stepped out of the taxi to the ruins of his house. Already a number of Defense Force investigators were nearby, and when they saw Mark, they hurried over. Investigator Cram was with them. "Mark, where's your brother? Where's Joe?"

"I've no idea," Mark said, shrugging, his eyes lingering on the massive hole where the front window should have been. "What happened to the house?"

"We were hoping you could tell us."

Giving Investigator Cram a blank look, Mark gestured to himself. "Me? I just got here."

Investigator Cram glanced over, and Mark saw the blond young woman who had been standing behind him the last time he and the investigator chatted. Her forehead was wrinkled, and she was staring straight at Mark. With a faint look of frustration, she shrugged, which in turn caused Investigator Cram to sigh.

"Fine. I get it. You don't know what happened, and you don't know where your brother is."

"Can I go in?" Mark asked.

Taking a deep breath, the investigator nodded. "Yes. We're almost done here. We have a suspicion that your brother is involved with some nasty folks."

"Is he in trouble?" Mark asked, feigning concern.

"Not precisely, since we don't know what his involvement actually is. It's entirely possible that he's being coerced into cooperating with them, so if you see him or if he contacts you, please let us know."

"I will, sir," Mark lied.

It was another few hours before the investigators left and Mark was alone in his house. The first thing he did was slip upstairs, head into his bedroom, and open up his closet. Digging through a pile of old clothes, he saw his box of elixirs was still sealed, and he sat back on his heels, breathing out a sigh of relief. He didn't know if it was irrational or not, but as soon as he had seen the investigators combing through the house, he had had this lingering fear that they would find his elixirs and decide to confiscate them. With his brother going underground, Mark would have to bear the cost of repairing the house himself. He still had close to three million credits, but the elixirs were his secret stash in case he needed to raise more capital.

Heading downstairs, he looked around at the ruined living room and half-destroyed stairs. The couch was practically in pieces, and when he looked it over, he had to laugh when he saw Mime seated on the good cushion, watching him calmly despite the fact that the rest of the couch was broken into multiple pieces. Seeing her wrinkle her nose, Mark grinned.

"All right, we'll get a new couch," he said. "Actually, maybe we'll just move to a place closer to town."

The more he thought about it, the more Mark liked the idea. While this was the family home where he had grown up, hanging around here while he had enemies on the loose simply wasn't a good idea. Besides, Joe likely wasn't going to be back for any of his stuff anytime soon. Mark walked over to the pantry, opened it up, and grabbed a tube of nutrient paste, then slowly sucked on it as he looked at the mess.

"Yeah, let's move," he said to Mime, who nodded her agreement and came over to rub herself against his leg.

Mark had spent practically nothing since the Javesi family had transferred two million credits to him, and so, feeling quite wealthy, he called up a local contracting company and asked them to come out and take a look at the house to give him an estimate on repairs. He also contacted a cleaning company to come and help him clean up the destroyed living room. By that time, it was time to leave for work, so he called a taxi, left the cleaners to their business, and headed to Abrams's warehouse.

"I hear you've been up to all sorts of exciting things," Abrams said as he met Mark at the door.

Freezing, Mark stared at his master for a long moment, wondering how the old man had found out.

"You don't have to worry about it," Abrams said with a smile. "There's nothing wrong with getting into a few scrapes when you're young—just don't make a habit of it. And do yourself a favor and steer clear of the Green Line, or whatever they're called these days. That is an endless trap."

"Yes, sir," Mark said, snapping a salute.

"I heard your house took quite a beating too."

Realizing that Abrams must have someone keeping tabs on him, Mark relaxed. "Yes, sir. Someone drove a car through the front wall."

"Well, I've got a real estate agent who works for me, if you're looking for a place to stay," Abrams said.

"That would be very helpful, sir."

"Or you could stay here," Abrams continued, as if Mark hadn't said anything. "There's a small room on the second floor. Well, technically, it's above the restaurant, but currently it's empty."

Seeing Abrams pointing to a set of stairs, Mark was about to decline, but Mime smacked him in the back of the head with her paw and then jumped down from his shoulder, running swiftly to the stairs. Mark watched as she bounded up them and then stopped at the top, turning around to look at him and nod. Clearly, this was where she wanted to stay, and she wouldn't take no for an answer. With a sigh, he bowed slightly to Abrams.

"I think it would be great if we could stay here," he said, "as long as you're okay with pets."

"Of course," Abrams said, watching Mime with a curious gleam in his eye. "One of the benefits of staying here is that you can use the butcher table and the alchemy lab anytime you want."

Mark hadn't thought of that and perked up immediately. The training camp had finished, and he was now just waiting to hear where he would be assigned, which meant that he would have plenty of time to spend working on his alchemy.

"Thank you, sir."

"All right, enough of that. Help me dismember this great owl. We need its rib cage."

The next two days passed quietly, though Mark found himself on edge, wondering when the government would come banging on his door to tell him that his brother had been arrested. He kept an eye on the news as well, but nothing about their fight popped up. The longer the silence continued, however, the more tense Mark felt, so he buried himself in alchemy, attempting to create a healing potion over and over again. After failing his fiftieth attempt, Mark needed more materials and, with considerable hesitation, went to ask Abrams. He thought that his master would be upset by the flagrant waste, but Abrams didn't even look up from what he was doing.

"Sure, there should be a piece of paper with a contact number on it stuck to the back of the door. Just call them and tell them what you need."

Slightly let down by how casual Abrams was about everything he had just wasted, Mark went back to the alchemy lab and found the contact number. It turned out to be for one of the largest alchemy supply stores in the city, the same store that Abrams had taken Mark to previously. After he finished reading out the list of ingredients he needed, the attendant on the other end asked him if he was currently producing a large batch of healing potions.

"Well, sort of," Mark said. "Not yet. I'm still learning how to make them."

"I see. I'll make sure to include two hundred units of each material," the attendant said, his voice completely calm.

As he hung up, Mark stared at his watch, realizing that the failure rate for new alchemists was clearly much higher than he had anticipated. It wasn't until his 127th attempt that he finally managed to make a healing potion, and he nearly cried when he got the slip of paper letting him know that it qualified as a basic potion. Abrams was quite surprised when Mark came up to him and showed him the healing potion he had made, and after examining it closely, he looked at Mark with a piercing gaze.

"How many times did you attempt this?"

"One hundred twenty-seven," Mark said, slightly ashamed.

"Huh," was all Abrams said as he handed the potion back to Mark. "Well, get back to it."

Heading back to the alchemy lab, Mark checked his watch. It was nine in the evening, and since he had been working all day, Mark thought about heading upstairs. As he began to clean up the leftover material, putting each away, he saw Mime jump up onto the counter and then onto his shoulder. His cat had been spending most of her time creeping around the warehouse, not seeming to mind the cold one bit. Now, however, she seemed tense. Just then, Mark's wrist shook slightly, and he glanced down, catching sight of a blinking message. Eyes narrowing, he tapped it.

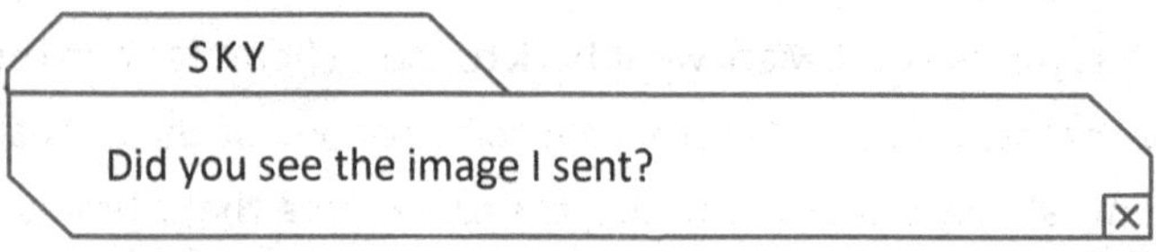

Mark felt as if his heart had been plunged into a bucket of ice, as a second message arrived with the coordinates of Sky's watch. Leaving the ingredients where they lay, Mark rushed out of the lab and sprinted toward the door, pulling up his map as he did so. A few seconds later, another message arrived, showing a new set of coordinates. Sky's watch was on the move. Hopefully, it was still attached to Sky herself.

Calling up a taxi, Mark sent a quick message to Noah, then gave the taxi driver the last location. It was in the Willow Lake District, and it was all Mark could do to sit still, biting his tongue and waiting. He noticed there were no other pings. When he jumped out of the car and raced the last few hundred feet on foot, he didn't see Sky or her watch. Mime jumped down from his shoulder, scrambling down a small embankment to a ditch filled with grimy water. With a lightning-fast paw, she slapped something out of the water that landed at Mark's feet.

Crouching, Mark saw that it was Sky's watch. It had been broken, squeezed in the center with enough force to crush it. The sight caused a chill to intensify in Mark's heart. He had no idea how he was supposed to go about finding her until Mime, looking at him curiously, said, "Meow?"

The sound Mime made sounded exactly like Sky's voice, and Mark's eyes lit up as he crouched down next to the cat.

"Yes, Sky. Can you find her?"

Mime considered for a moment, then nodded before racing off. Mark found himself having trouble keeping up as they headed deeper into the Willow Lake District toward the looming wall. They soon left the houses and arrived at a large set of scaffolding that crawled like a meandering worm up the side of the wall. Mime didn't stop, jumping up onto one of the platforms and trotting along it as Mark climbed up behind her. Noah had sent him a message saying he was on his way, and as he moved, Mark tried to keep his friend in the loop.

They continued to climb until Mark saw a large crack in the wall. As he got closer, he realized that it wasn't a crack but a place where something had burrowed out of the wall. Mark knew that there were tunnels inside the wall to facilitate the movement of troops and to store supplies and munitions for easy access during the waves. Something had burrowed out from that tunnel system, cutting a clean opening in the magically reinforced stone. He hoped that whatever it was wasn't still inside.

Mark saw Mime disappearing into the hole and entered after her. It was dark, though his eyes quickly adjusted, and after walking approximately fifteen feet, he found himself in a man-made tunnel. A faint light was coming from mana lamps stuck to the ceiling. Catching sight of Mime's tail disappearing around a corner to his left, Mark hurried after her.

When he turned the next corner, she was gone, but he heard a faint voice farther down, and so he crept closer, reaching up to activate his titanium arm.

"I'm telling you, she's worthless. We might as well scrap her for parts," one voice said.

"And I'm telling you, she's probably one of those guys' girlfriends, which means if we play this properly, we should be able to lure one or both of them out."

"I just want to know where that kid went—the one who killed Greg and Steve."

"Just relax. We'll deal with one thing at a time. After we decide what to do with the girl, we'll go find him."

Listening to the two men talking, Mark recognized their voices. They had been members of the team he and Noah had raided. Continuing to creep closer, Mark wished that he had some of the gear Noah had given him. Some of it had been lost in the fights, and the rest was currently sitting in his room above Abrams's warehouse. He had left in such a rush that all he'd brought with him were the potions he had been holding. Glancing around to see if he could spot Mime, he didn't see his cat anywhere.

Just then, the door to the room where the voices were coming from, which had been half ajar, opened the whole way, and a woman stepped out, a disgusted expression on her face. Her eyes met Mark's, and for a split second, they just stared at each other, both too surprised to move. With a yell, the woman dove back into the room as Mark darted forward as fast as he could. She managed to get clear of the door and kicked it shut, but Mark hit it at full speed, his arm slamming it back into her.

He only had a moment to take stock of the situation when he entered the room, and he saw two men, both empowered, staring back at him. One was well built, with thick muscles, making him look like one of the twins. The other was thinner and carried a weird, wavy blade at his side. Stumbling over the woman who had fallen to the ground, Mark saw the man with the wavy blade blur, and so he let gravity take hold, pulling him down to the ground, landing next to the woman as the blade slashed through the air above him.

She was scrambling at her belt, no doubt looking for her weapon, when Mark grabbed her throat and heaved, rolling onto his back as he pulled her on top of him, barely managing to block the slash aimed at his head. The wavy sword glowed as it slashed through the unfortunate woman's neck, severing her spine, and when it hit Mark's hand, it bounced off. Ignoring the sticky blood dripping down onto him, Mark kicked her body aside and rolled over, bouncing to his feet, just in time to catch a heavy punch in the solar plexus.

With a groan, he stumbled backward, somehow managing to keep his feet as he lifted his hands, his mind working furiously. The thinner man with the wavy blade had a speed power, while the bigger man had minor invulnerability. If he had had super-strength, Mark likely would have died as soon as his fist landed, but as it was, it just felt as if he was quite strong.

Unfortunately, both of his opponents were C rank, each a good bit stronger than he was. Even worse, he could see Sky crumpled in the corner, blood still oozing from a nasty gash across her temple where she had been knocked out. For a moment, the two empowered men stared at Mark, unable to believe what they were seeing. The heavier one spat to the side as he lifted his hands in front of him, clenching his fists tightly. "You're gutsy, kid, I'll give you that, but you've caused us enough trouble."

"I don't mean to," Mark said. "If you'd let me take my friend, I'd be happy to pretend we never even met."

"After you killed our whole team?" the thin man asked, his voice venomous. "You really think we'd just let you waltz off? We had a good thing going, and you ruined it."

"No," Mark said, "you ruined it when you decided that it'd be a good idea to break into my house."

"Listen, kid—!"

"Enough!" The leader of the men cut off his companion with a shout as he glared at Mark. "Say your prayers, kid."

As much as he hated to admit it, Mark thought that the brawny man might be right. Fighting against one C-ranked opponent was a sure route to death. Fighting against two was a nightmare made reality. Even worse, though he could barely keep up with the speedster's movements, he couldn't do it while also getting through the larger man's defenses.

Doing a quick inventory of everything he had at his disposal, he found himself at a loss. His only hope was that Noah would arrive quickly. To make matters worse, Sky was continuing to lose blood. Thankfully, he had stuck the healing potion he had been working on in his pocket, and as long as he could get it to her somehow, he thought she would be fine.

His thoughts were interrupted by a fierce yell as the larger of his two opponents rushed forward. At the same time, the thin man attacked, his wavy blade streaking through the air as he cut off Mark's retreat paths. Mark dodged as best he could, using his tough left hand to redirect the heavy punch coming toward his chest while kicking his legs up to avoid the incoming slash.

For a brief, frantic moment, Mark dodged this way and that, barely evading his opponent's attacks. He could feel his biofuel meter beginning to empty and found himself incredibly grateful for the intense training his brother had put him through. Currently, Mark was using every ounce of his strength to block and parry and every inch of his speed to dodge. Such exertion should have left him exhausted after only a few moves, but even as he expended his energy, the biofuel he had stored regenerated his energy levels.

Slowly, however, he was being pushed back toward the wall, where he would be trapped. Taking advantage of a backhanded slap, he grabbed the hand and threw himself in the same direction, letting it carry him through the air as he shot like a rocket toward the other side of the room. His muscles groaned as he slammed into the wall, and he could feel the bruises beginning to form almost immediately.

Trusting his recovery, Mark gripped the wall tightly with his metal hand and launched himself along it, managing to transfer some of his momentum horizontally, practically running along the wall. With a snarl, the thin man with the wavy sword flashed across the room and met him, unleashing a storm of strikes to cut Mark into pieces.

Mark's hands blurred, and for a shocking moment, he found himself able to not only keep up with his opponent but drive him back. Though the speedster held a sword, his technique was terrible, as he relied almost exclusively on moving faster than others in order to fight. Mark, on the other hand, had impeccable technique, and in his moment of crisis, it was driven to new heights.

Flipping down from the wall, he could see his other opponent thundering toward them, but Mark paid him no mind and continued to press forward, his hands moving increasingly quickly as he executed an ever-shifting flow of palm strikes. Growing flustered, the thin man tried to increase his speed once more, and Mark felt a sting in his shoulder as the blade began to slice into him. Instead of jerking back, he pressed forward, his left hand brushing across the inside of his opponent's elbow. With a scream of pain, the speedster abandoned his sword and retreated directly into the path of his companion, who slammed into him, sending him bouncing across the room.

Mark didn't hesitate and grabbed the sword in his shoulder, wrenching it out as he slashed toward his more heavily muscled opponent, who was looking dumbfounded at his companion flying away from him. Too late, the man saw Mark's sword, and with a roar, he tried to lift his arm but failed as the blade bit deeply into his skin. For a moment, Mark thought he might have a chance, and then he felt an irresistible force wrenching the sword out of his hand. Completely enraged, the empowered brute snapped the sword in half and tossed it to the side, his body beginning to grow and swell as he reached for Mark with an ever more giant hand.

Mark started to backpedal, and then, as his opponent took a step forward, he reversed his direction, using a double-handed palm strike to push the grasping hand away as he dove through the brute's legs and scrambled across the room to where Sky lay. Barely stopping, he picked her up and fled. Completely enraged, the brute turned around, his head scraping on the ten-foot ceiling, and with a roar, he threw himself at Mark, batting him across the room. Mark slammed into the ground, holding Sky tight as he rolled over and over, until he bumped into the wall.

The brute, whose skin had turned red and was covered in protruding veins, began to stomp toward him as Mark, groaning, tried to push himself to his feet. When that failed, he did the next best thing, reaching in his pouch to try to find something, anything, that might be helpful. He felt the potions he had stuffed into his bag before leaving the alchemy lab, but there was nothing else.

With another step, his enemy towered over him. "I told you—you are dead, and the girl will follow after."

Mark, fear blooming in his eyes, suddenly blinked, his gaze dropping.

"Oh, thank goodness," he said, staring past the giant.

With a roar, the giant stepped back and spun, his hand sweeping through the room, only to find himself facing nothing. Mark, unable to believe that baiting the brute had worked, took the opportunity to dart toward the door, his brief moment of reprieve having refilled all his energy. Moving as fast as he possibly could while still holding Sky, he scrambled over the dead woman's body, grabbing the tube she had at her waist, and slipped out of the door as the giant lunged for him.

He managed to make it down the hall, barely avoiding the

giant's fingers as they grabbed and scrabbled against the wall. The giant was too big to fit out the door, but his roar shook the hallway as Mark ran as fast as he could. He only realized he was going the wrong direction when it was too late. He could hear the shouts behind him, and so he kept going, winding his way through the twisting passages, until he came across a massive gaping hole in the wall. The stone was melted, blocking most of the passage ahead but leaving a large gap.

Pausing for only a second, Mark stared out over the dead zone, and then, fearing his opponents would catch up soon, he ran to the edge. Holding Sky with one arm while trying to keep her head steady, Mark looked at the long trail of melted stone that dribbled down the side of the wall. Taking a deep breath, he stepped off the ledge. For a terrible moment, he fell through the air, but then his arm caught hold of a small ledge and with a wrench he stopped in place, swinging nearly four stories off the ground.

He could feel the pain in both his arms. His right arm, which was currently holding Sky, was badly bruised, and his left shoulder ached from the pressure he had just put on it. Carefully feeling around for some footholds, he took a deep breath and began to descend. If either of his enemies spotted him on the outside of the wall, there was no way he'd be able to defend himself, so he wanted to get to the bottom as fast as possible.

Back in the room, the speedster was finally stirring as his companion shrank back down to a normal size. "Come on, he's getting away!"

Dazed, the speedster staggered to his feet, his hand instinctively going to his side, where there should have been a wavy blade. Not finding anything, he stared around dumbly as the brute took off, racing down the hall after Mark. When he located the handle to his sword, the speedster picked it up and saw it was snapped. His face paled, but fury soon replaced his shock. He blurred as he raced toward the door, only to screech to a halt, staring in surprise at a small black cat who sat in the doorway.

"Meow," said the cat, sounding nothing like a cat.

A prickling feeling raced up the speedster's back, and he slowly took a step backward. His eyes blinked rapidly as he tried to figure out if the cat had two eyes or three. What he did know was they were glowing red, and its mouth held entirely too many teeth.

Mark reached the bottom of the wall rather quickly and began to limp away. Hearing a thud of footsteps from up above, he looked over his shoulder and caught sight of the brute appearing in the gap he had just descended from. Though he had only walked thirty steps, Mark had once again recovered fully. He could feel the damage that had been done to his arm and his shoulder healing as well, and he broke into a flat-out sprint, quickly vanishing into the tangle of buildings beyond the wall.

There was an angry roar and a loud boom behind him as the brute jumped down, forming a small crater as he landed. Though the difference between them was only one rank, that rank was practically insurmountable in a one-on-one fight. That didn't mean, however, that the brute beat Mark in every category, and Mark hoped his speed would allow him to stay ahead.

As he ran, Mark reached behind him and pulled out one of his potions. Glancing at it, he shoved it in his pocket and then pulled out another. This time, he grabbed the healing potion, and as he continued to sprint down alleyways and across small courtyards, fleeing with all his might in a zigzagging pattern that he hoped would buy him a little more time, he popped the top open.

The sounds behind him had begun to fade, and so Mark paused for just a moment to slip into a small building, where he put Sky down. Reaching up, he dug his fingers into the wound on his shoulder, grimacing as it began to bleed again. Holding up the vial, he captured a few drops of blood, recapped the potion, and shook it up. Immediately, the red of the potion grew brighter until it was positively gleaming.

Mark had only been able to create an E-ranked potion, but the addition of his blood had raised it to D rank, making it more than twice as effective. Opening the vial once more, Mark turned Sky's head and poured a bit of it into the cut on her temple, and then, forcing her mouth open, he poured the rest down her throat, keeping her head up to ensure she wouldn't drown. As her body instinctively swallowed, he pulled out the Dead Man Walking potion from his pocket and forcibly fed that to her too.

Almost immediately, the change took effect, her vital signs fading and then vanishing altogether. Leaning her up against the wall, Mark could only marvel at the effect of the potion. If he'd passed her by, he genuinely wouldn't have been able to tell that she was anything but an old, dried corpse. Thinking for a moment, he pulled off his watch and strapped it around her wrist, hoping that if Noah arrived, he would find her from the constant pings that it was sending out. There was a boom from nearby, and Mark, not trusting that he'd be able to hide from the brute, took off, running low to avoid being spotted in the windows. He paused for half a second at the door and then darted through, crossing the street as quickly as he could.

He heard a yell from behind him and knew that he had been spotted. Heart pounding in his chest, Mark ran for all he was worth, until his heart beat in his ears like a war drum and every breath ripped painfully at his lungs. Even then, he didn't stop, trying to put as much distance between himself and Sky as possible. He wasn't running aimlessly, however, but instead was using the faint pings of the psychic network to figure out where the Exlian were.

The farther out into the dead zone he got, the more Exlian he located, and he did his best to use them to his advantage. When they were directly in his path, he would detour around, then cut back to try to put them between him and the brute. A few times, he even managed to lure groups of drones into chasing him before using his speed to lose them, causing them to turn around and target the brute behind him.

Eventually, however, he couldn't run anymore, and he slowed to a stop, leaning heavily against a brick building. His breath came in massive gasps that echoed loudly in the still air of the dead zone, and Mark could feel Exlian all around him. The brute arrived a moment later in another small crater and a pile of broken concrete.

"You didn't really think you could run away from me, did you?" the brute said with a laugh. "It always catches people off guard, but I've got quite the nose, and I can sniff you out no matter where you try and hide."

"Chop off your nose. Got it," Mark said with a grin.

"Ha, as if you could."

Laughing, the brute walked into the alleyway where Mark was resting, casually slamming his fist against one of the walls and causing a shower of bricks to fall beside him. He dragged his hand along the wall, tearing out chunks of stone as he headed for Mark. Lifting his fists, Mark took his stance, then abruptly held out one of his hands.

"Hold on," he said. "Just wait."

Taken aback, the brute looked at him for a second and sneered. "No amount of begging—"

"Okay, you can come," Mark said, interrupting the brute and gesturing for him to step forward.

With an angry roar, his skin so red it looked like it was being cooked, the brute lunged forward, lifting his fist to bring it down on Mark's head. Just before it landed, there was a loud screech, and a large, multilegged figure dropped just as Mark leaped out of the way. Unable to stop himself, the brute hammered his fist down on the Exlian warrior who had suddenly appeared in Mark's place. The blow was so hard that it managed to crack the warrior's carapace, and with a shriek of rage, the warrior's two mantis blades stabbed into the brute's chest, trying to skewer him.

The blades only made it a couple of inches into his skin before the brute managed to react, shoving the mantis away as he stumbled backward, staring in fury down at the bleeding wounds on his chest. Mark, who had stumbled to the side, was forced to roll out of the way as the Exlian warrior casually snapped a claw in his direction. Deciding that the brute was a bigger threat, the mantis let out a shriek and charged, its claws opening wide as it got ready to clamp down on him.

Mark gulped in air, trying as best he could to recover his energy. His biofuel was starting to bottom out after his frantic escape, and he only had enough to recover partially two more times. Though he wanted to slip away, Mark could feel more Exlian closing in and knew that doing so would just pit him against the endless swarm. The brute and the mantis were at it like hammer and tongs, bashing and slashing at each other with reckless abandon. Mark slowly backed up, trying to think of a way to help the mantis without immediately being set upon and eaten for his trouble.

Unfortunately, he didn't have a chance. As the brute suddenly let out a roar and lunged forward, the mantis responded with a double stab of its blades, only to find that one was dodged and the other grabbed. Planting a foot on the mantis's carapace, the brute yanked as hard as he could, ripping the Exlian's blade arm from his back and casting it aside. The sight of blood sent him into a frenzy, and he grabbed the mantis, lifting it up into the air and smashing it against the wall, even as its blade slashed at his back, making dozens of shallow cuts. Knocked silly by the successive blows, the mantis could hardly resist as the brute took it apart piece by piece.

Unsure what to do, Mark remembered the tube he had picked up from the dead woman and tried shooting it at the brute. Two of the darts simply bounced off his hard skin. The third managed to prick one of the wounds on his back, but he hardly even flinched as it injected its poisonous payload into him. Mark was running out of ideas, and as the brute finished tearing the mantis to pieces, he slowly turned and stared at Mark, his face the very picture of savagery.

"I'm going to enjoy this, kid. I'm going to tear your fingers off one by one and feed them to you."

Mark flashed a lopsided smile at the brute and pointed up. "You should worry about him first."

The brute wasn't about to fall for the same trick twice. Unfortunately for him, the mantis dropping onto his head from the roof of the building above was as real as real could be. It slammed down on him with bone-crunching force, driving him to one knee. Backing up a few steps, Mark decided that now was the time to escape, but as he turned around, he spotted swarms of drones heading toward them, blocking his only exit. His options now were to cut his way through a sea of drones or backtrack and squeeze past the titanic battle happening behind him.

In order to save energy, Mark had undone the titanium transformation on his arm. Now, as he reached for his necklace, he was horrified to find it was gone. Frantic, he looked around. He could transform his hand into cement, but that was heavy, and his martial arts required speed, not weight. Unfortunately, there was no metal in sight. Feeling he had no other choice, he crouched, only to feel something bump into his foot. It was the blade of the mantis that had been torn from its back. A crazy idea bloomed in Mark's head, and pressing his fingers against it, he activated his power with all his might.

Behind him, his shadow stretched long. There was a shimmer, and three crimson eyes blinked on it as it began to stretch even longer. A shadowy mouth with far too many teeth appeared as his shadow split open, swallowing the dead mantis corpse with a faint crunch that was lost in the bellows of the brute fighting in the alley behind Mark.

Mark felt a strange power flooding through his body, bringing with it searing pain, and his biofuel meter fluctuated wildly. The faintest of sounds rang out as his bones twisted and then settled, and he felt the familiar shake of his wrist as a notification appeared. He had no time to read it, however, as the drones were upon him. He lifted his hands and, half despairing, lunged forward to meet the first one, his right hand flicking out, two fingers extended as a blade.

They met the mandibles of the drone, slicing straight through its body with ease, splitting it apart as if his fingers were the sharpest knife in the world. He had no time to process what was happening, as more drones were upon him, and in a blur, he danced around them, right and left hand rising and falling in a deadly dance that left them in pieces on the ground.

In shock, he stared at his hands as the tide of drones subsided. Both hands appeared to be made from gleaming bone, the same material the mantis's razor-sharp blades were formed from. Instinctively, Mark understood that his hands were far harder than the titanium he had used before, and he could feel a faint thread of mana running through them.

Strangest of all, the mana wasn't his but rather was pulled from the atmosphere, naturally improving the bone's durability to an almost impossible level. Both of his arms, from the tips of his fingers to his elbows, were formed from the same material, leaving Mark ecstatic and, more importantly, meaning that he actually had a chance to wound the brute.

Had Mark been thinking about the situation rationally, considering the pros and cons, he would have turned and fled with all his might, but his mind was floating in a strange place, unconcerned with thoughts of ranks or power levels. Instead, all he knew was that he had been hunted and now had the strength to become the hunter.

More drones began to pour into the alleyway, but Mark ignored them, slowly turning to stare at the brute still locked in combat with the second mantis. Taking a small step forward, Mark watched the battle carefully. As strong as the mantises were, they were ultimately only D-ranked monsters, and the brute, though not impervious to their blades, was strong enough to tear through their carapaces with his bare hands.

A dozen wounds marked the brute's body, but even as Mark watched, they were starting to heal. With a roar that shook the walls, the brute pounded his fist into the mantis's head, knocking it to the ground. He lifted a massive foot and brought his heel down on the monster's carapace, cracking it in half. Two more heavy stomps put an end to the mantis, and with heaving breath, the brute looked around wildly, only to catch sight of Mark.

The tiny part of Mark's brain that was still operating normally caught the look of confusion and then growing terror on the brute's face and wondered what that was about. Blinking his three eyes, Mark slowly began to stalk forward, his focus absolute. Behind him, the drones hissed angrily, swarming into the alleyway. Yet none of them attacked, wary of the leering shadow that swayed unnoticed behind Mark. Drones who didn't manage to withdraw before the shadow fell over them would vanish with a faint crunching sound.

"You—!?"

That was as far as the brute got as Mark launched himself forward, moving faster than he ever had before. Even as his muscles screamed, power flooded through them, and as the terrified brute tried to crush him with a slap, Mark danced around the blow, his fingers flashing as they transformed into a dozen blades that tore the brute's arm to shreds.

With a roar of pain, the brute tried to crush Mark with pure force, but he was too quick, darting in and away as his hands left deep gouges in the brute's skin. Finally, terror set in, and the brute turned to run. Sensing an opportunity, Mark launched himself forward, landing on the brute's back, his hands transforming into blades that stabbed deep into his opponent's swollen neck.

The skin that had bounced his hand away so easily before now parted like water before Mark's palm strikes, and shuddering, the brute fell as Mark cut through his spine. With a thud, his body slammed into the ground, Mark jumping lightly to land beside it, his eyes blazing. A low, guttural growl escaped Mark's mouth, and he turned to look at the swarming drones. They froze for a moment, then fought each other to flee, emptying the alleyway in a few short seconds. Taking a step forward, Mark's legs failed and he dropped, landing face-first on the ground as he passed out.

When Mark came to, the first thing he saw was Sky's tearstained face. She was shaking his shoulders, saying his name repeatedly. As the haze in his head cleared, he blinked, trying to process what had happened. The last thing he remembered was facing down a swarm of drones, trying to absorb the traits of the mantis's bone blade. Whether he had succeeded, he honestly wasn't sure. His body, covered in blood, ached with a deep, burning feeling.

Hearing a crunch, he snapped his gaze up, half afraid he would see the brute bearing down on them. Instead, he saw Noah, dressed in a sleek mana suit, with four well-built companions, each armed to the teeth. Noticing that one of them was Bandman, Noah's bodyguard, Mark let out a sigh of relief. Noah was staring at the alleyway, puzzled.

"It looks like there was a fight in here," he said.

"There was," Mark replied, "between a couple of mantises and the guy who was chasing me."

There was a long, drawn-out silence as everyone turned to stare at him.

"And where are they?" Noah prompted. "Shouldn't there be bodies? Or at least blood?"

With a strained laugh, Mark accepted Sky's hand and pulled himself to his feet. "Your guess is as good as mine. The fight was still in full swing when I went unconscious. I don't remember anything else."

There was a noise from behind Mark, and as the bodyguards lifted their weapons, Mime jumped up onto his shoulder.

"There you are," Mark said, reaching up to scratch the fur under Mime's chin. "I wondered where you went."

"Mime led me to you," Sky said, noticing how the bodyguards were relaxing.

Mark glanced at Noah, who nodded. "We found Sky, thanks to the watch you gave her, but we had no idea where you were. Mime suddenly showed up out of nowhere, and Sky insisted we follow her. She led us straight to you. She's awfully smart for a cat."

"Maybe she's empowered," Mark said, cracking a grin. "But as much as I'm enjoying standing here in the middle of the dead zone wearing nothing but rags, what do you say we get back to the city?"

"I think that's a good idea, sir," Bandman said. "We haven't run into any Exlian, but they're more active at night, so the sooner we're back in the city, the better."

"How'd you guys get out here?" Mark asked. "Don't they keep the gates shut at nighttime?"

"Rules for thee and not for me," Noah replied with a small smile as he waved one of his bodyguards forward. "I brought you another suit."

"I don't need it," Mark said. "Give it to Sky."

"You need it more than I do," Sky said. "If I hadn't been hit in the head, they never would have got me."

"Speaking of which, what happened?" Mark asked as they started the journey back to the city wall.

"They ambushed me in my apartment," Sky said. "Somehow they'd gotten inside, and when I landed, that woman hit me with a dart of some sort. That took away my power. And then the speedster slapped me in the side of the head with his sword. The next thing I knew, I was waking up in the dead zone, smelling all funky."

"The healing potion you fed her kept her stable," Noah said, "and we brought some additional healing potions and something to fight neurotoxin. Neurotoxin 7737 is nasty but fairly common.

It shuts down the body's ability to use mana temporarily, which is why Sky couldn't fly away."

"Which is also why you should be wearing a suit," Mark said. "Can you imagine what would happen if you were flying and you got hit by one of those darts?"

"Certainly wouldn't be very pretty," Sky said with a grimace. "I'll think about it."

"Please do. I don't think I could be friends with a human pancake."

"Ew, gross," Sky said, wrinkling her nose.

Shrugging, Mark glanced at Noah. "Thanks for coming. You keep pulling me out of the fire, and I'm not sure how I'm going to repay you."

"I don't do it because I want repayment," Noah said, his tone growing cold.

"I know," Mark said hurriedly. "That's not what I'm saying. It's just, I feel like you're really going out of your way for me, and I keep putting you in these really dangerous situations."

"No more than you'd do for me," Noah said, his tone relaxing slightly. "Sorry, I don't mean to be tense. It's just, I haven't had the greatest luck with friends."

Though none of his bodyguards said anything, Mark caught more than a few sharp glances. Thankfully, Sky was there to rescue him.

"Well, I think it's great," she said. "The fact that you are willing to come rescue us in the dead zone in the middle of the night, that's exactly how friends should be."

"I agree," Mark said, "and I'm glad we're friends. Not just because you saved my skin."

It took two hours to get back to the wall, and Mark could only marvel at how deep he'd gone. Admittedly, they took their time, not wanting to accidentally upset any swarms of Exlian drones that might be lurking around. They were met by another team, which had set up a small defensive position closer to the wall to act as a forward base. Its members were dressed in the same armor that Noah wore, and after greeting Noah, they quickly tore down the camp before heading back to the gate. There, one of them scanned in, and after a moment, the gate opened and the team slipped through. There should have been guards on the other side, but there was nobody in sight, giving Mark just another taste of how the real world actually operated. Splitting up, they piled into three cars and took off, heading back into town. Sitting in the front seat of one of the cars, Noah turned and looked at Sky and Mark.

"Where do you want to go?" he asked. "You're both welcome to come stay with me if you need a place."

"Well, I'm certainly not going back to my apartment," Sky grumbled.

"You could come stay with me," Mark said. "Well, not really with me, but with my master. He's got a couple of extra rooms, and I'm sure he'd be willing to give you one."

Eyes brightening, Sky nodded. "Sure, that sounds good. Sorry, Noah, I'm going to stay with Mark."

A ghost of a smile slipped across Noah's lips, but he quickly turned his head away.

"That's fine," he said. "The offer's always open."

"Thanks," Mark said, reaching up to pat Noah on the shoulder.

When they arrived, Master Abrams was waiting outside, his eyes cold as the Arctic. Seeing the way that he was looking at Noah and Noah's bodyguards, Mark realized there must have been a misunderstanding, and he quickly stepped forward and bowed.

"I'm sorry for running off, sir. I should have said something, but I got a distress signal from Sky and found out that she had been captured. I went to rescue her, and Noah and his men came to back us up. They were instrumental in helping us get back to the city in one piece."

"You went outside the city wall?" Abrams asked, his forehead furrowing as the cold look in his eyes began to thaw.

"Yes, sir, there's a gap in the southern wall where all that construction is taking place. The people who kidnapped Sky had gone through that gap, and I followed after them, ending up outside the city," Mark explained.

Abrams looked at Sky.

"You gave her a Dead Man Walking potion," he said to Mark with an amused smile. "I told you it would come in handy."

"It did, sir. Saved her life, probably, as it allowed me to lead the enemy away."

Feeling no need to explain what had happened after that, Mark fell silent as Abrams looked everyone over once more and then nodded.

"Fine, but no more of this messing about, okay? I can't have you throwing yourself into dangerous situations over and over again."

"Yes, sir. I understand, sir," Mark said, bowing again.

"He says he understands," Abrams muttered under his breath, looking at Sky and rolling his eyes. "You just watch. Next week it'll be something else. Kids this age, they're all alike."

Unsure quite how to respond, Sky just nodded.

"All right, well, say bye to your friends and come inside. You've got work to make up."

It was only then that Mark realized that the reason his master was angry was that he had skipped out on finishing his training, not that he had nearly died a dozen times that night. Feeling Sky poke him, Mark remembered that he wanted to ask if she could stay with them and hurried to take a step forward before Abrams disappeared into the warehouse.

"Sir, would it be okay if Sky stayed with us?"

"I don't care," he said with a grunt. "She's your girlfriend. Do whatever you want."

Too dumbfounded by his master's retort to notice Sky's blushing face, Mark opened his mouth, but nothing came out. By the time he turned around, she had already regained her composure.

"Well, I'll leave the two of you lovebirds to it," Noah said with a small smile. "Call me if you need anything."

Jumping back in his car before Sky could hit him, Noah took off, leaving Mark and Sky standing in the alley, watching the taillights vanish into the night. Letting out a deep sigh and glancing up at the night sky, Mark shook his head. "What an eventful night. Come on, I'll show you where the rooms are."

Mark brought Sky upstairs, and she picked a room next to his. Mime had gone off to explore somewhere, but Mark was well past worrying about his cat. She either was really good at surviving or had a lot more than nine lives, because she always showed back up. He was exhausted after going through such an intense experience, and as he lay in bed at close to three in the morning, he couldn't help but wonder at how strange his life had become.

That reminded him that he had a notification on his status that he had missed. Opening it up, he blinked, then blinked again, unable to recognize the strange symbols running across his arm. Suddenly, they began to shift, twisting and merging and then expanding outward again, until they had formed words he recognized.

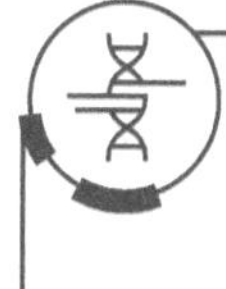

Sufficiently advanced genetic material acquired. You have unlocked the ability Genetic Memory.

Taking a deep breath, Mark saw that he had a new skill. Focusing on *Genetic Memory*, he read the words that popped up carefully.

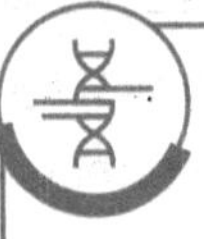

Genetic Memory (1/2): Your body can store trace amounts of specific genetic sequences, allowing you to acquire their traits at will.
Slot 1: Bone Blade
Slot 2: Empty

If what Mark was seeing was correct, then he had somehow absorbed the essence of the mantis blade, allowing him to recall the makeup of the substance at will. His eyes flashing, Mark held out his arms and watched as his skin transformed into the shiny bone material Exlian mantis blades were made of.

"Okay, that's cool," Mark whispered.

Closing the window, he saw there was another notification and opened it up.

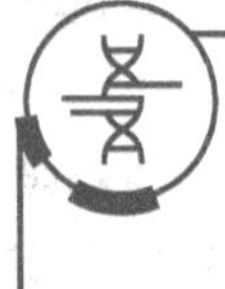

Sufficient specialized genetic material acquired. Would you like to remember Bronze Skin?

Mark stared at the message for a long time, his mind all jumbled up as he tried to make sense of it. He had no idea what bronze skin was, though he suspected it was the red skin that had covered the brute he had faced. How he had managed to get enough genetic material to be able to acquire it was something Mark desperately didn't want to think about.

Though it seemed like a useful skill, as the brute's skin had been almost as tough as armor, Mark decided against it. At this point, he could only transform his two arms, and the mantis blade material was already tougher. Selecting *no*, he felt a shimmer inside of him, and a bit of power that had been condensed in his chest spread out through his body, subtly reinforcing his skin.

It was a shame to leave the slot empty, but Mark was sure that the opportunity to add something else to it would come up in the future. For the moment, he was simply ecstatic with the changes to his abilities. Feeling full of energy, he jumped to his feet and began executing the second stage of the Cutting Palm technique, Fingers as Knives. This wasn't the first time he had used it, but it was the first time with both hands. As the technique he had been practicing in his dreams for months made its appearance in the real world, Mark could feel the patterns and movements solidifying, burning into his muscle memory. In that moment, everything clicked, and Mark lost himself in the motion.

Later that night, when he stepped into his dream and saw the mantis charging toward him, he smiled. His arms thrust out in front of him to meet the mantis's blades. The creature was still much larger than him, and he was still thrown back by the collision, but this time, his hands bore no cuts. With a grin, he surged forward, unleashing an unending storm of strikes to overwhelm the Exlian warrior.

The next morning, he was up early doing his exercises when Abrams wandered down and began poking around among the frozen corpses, always keeping half an eye on Mark's training. After watching for about an hour, he walked over.

"How is your technique coming?" he asked.

"I wouldn't say I've mastered it, sir, but I am able to use the second form," Mark replied.

"Really?" Abrams said, with a skeptical look. "Go ahead and show me."

"Yes, sir."

Pressing his hands forward, Mark transformed his arms and sank into his stance. Before he could begin, however, he felt Abrams's tough fingers clamp down on his wrist.

"Where'd you get this material?" he said, his eyes narrowed. "This is Exlian bone blade."

"Yes, sir. The mantises have it," Mark said, pointing toward the corner of the warehouse where a few mantis corpses were stacked.

"Huh. I thought you could only transform into metal."

"No, sir. And it's not technically a transformation. It's simply absorbing helpful characteristics. So while my arms become the same as that material, they still have full flexibility and range of motion."

"Fascinating. And I see you can now transform with both arms."

"Yes, sir."

"Then let's see your technique."

Mark went through the kata slowly, demonstrating each form with as much precision as possible. Then he went through the forms again, this time putting full power behind each strike and moving as quickly as possible. The entire time, Master Abrams watched him, his face expressionless, his eyes taking in everything. When Mark had finished the second pass through the kata, he stopped, clasped his hands in front of his chest, and bowed.

"You're correct in saying you haven't mastered it, but you are getting close. From now on, we'll start your training with practice, and I'll teach you personally," Abrams said, clasping his hands behind his back. Mark could see the excitement his master was trying to conceal, and it felt really good.

"Thank you, Master," Mark said. "Though I am expecting to get my military assignment any day now."

"That's fine," Abrams said, waving his hand. "Once you get it, you'll be doing some basic training, but that'll only last a couple of weeks. Even if you're deployed, you should still be able to come and train, and if you can't, that's fine; I'll come to you. You're going for the Defense Force, right?"

"Yes, sir."

"Good. That means you won't be crawling all around the wilderness. Though, if I do say so myself, the Engineering Corps is a much better branch."

"Were you in the Engineering Corps, sir?"

"Of course I was. I process Exlian corpses for a living. If that's not a job for the Engineering Corps, I don't know what is. Which reminds me, I could probably get you a pretty lucrative job. My word still holds some weight with the Engineering Corps generals."

"Thank you, sir, but I really would like to be in the Defense Force."

"Why is that?" Abrams asked. "Given your skill set, I would have pegged you as a Ranger."

"In truth, sir, it's because of my dad. He was a member of the Defense Force and protected our city. And I don't know, I've just always wanted to do that as well."

"Fair enough," Abrams said with a shrug. "Let's get to work."

The days passed by quickly, as Mark was constantly busy. In the morning, he would do his own physical training, and then work with Abrams, polishing his Cutting Palm technique. There were three levels to the Cutting Palm: Hand as a Blade, which Mark had mastered; Fingers as Knives, which he was close to mastering; and a level that didn't have an official name but that Abrams called Body as the Sword, which Mark couldn't wrap his mind around, no matter how many times his master explained it to him. Instead of getting frustrated, however, Abrams just smiled and told him it was normal and that maybe when he had a little bit more life experience, he'd be able to understand it.

After training in the Cutting Palm, Mark would get to put it into practice. He spent the rest of the morning and most of the early afternoon cutting apart corpses and retrieving alchemical ingredients. Thanks to his new genetic memory skill, his bone blade hands had become perfect tools for extracting alchemical ingredients, since there was no chance of cross contamination. Once he had filled all the day's orders, Mark would spend the rest of the day squirreled away in the alchemy lab, only coming out to eat dinner, usually with Sky, and occasionally hang out with Noah, Phoenix, and the others.

Soon the days had turned into weeks, and Mark hadn't heard anything about his assignment, or from Joe. One by one, the others had gotten their assignments, heading to the various branches of the military they had requested, until only Mark remained. It finally got to the point where he decided to go track down Lieutenant Cox to see if something was wrong. He eventually managed to learn Cox was at Training Camp 7, and after requesting him at the gate, Mark saw him jogging over a few minutes later.

"Sir," Mark said, saluting.

"How are you doing, Mark? What brings you here?"

"I had a question, sir, about my assignment. I haven't received anything yet, and I was wondering if there was any issue."

Smiling ruefully, Lieutenant Cox rubbed the back of his head. "Actually, I'm afraid there is. I was going to say something to you, but I wanted to see how it would shake out first."

"It's about my brother, right?"

With a sigh, Lieutenant Cox nodded. "Yes, because your brother's disappeared and is now wanted, they put a flag on your profile. It's not necessarily going to stop you from joining the military, but until the investigation is over or an unreasonable amount of time has passed, they can keep you in stasis."

"Who's 'they,' sir?"

Looking slightly uncomfortable, Cox shook his head. "I don't have any names, and even if I did, I wouldn't share them. Military secrets and all. Just know that there are some people paying special attention to your brother and his friends. I think they're waiting to see if he contacts you or you show signs of joining the Green Line group. The best thing you can do for now is lay low."

Troubled, Mark nodded. "Thank you, sir. I appreciate you telling me."

"I really shouldn't," Lieutenant Cox said. "But I like your brother, and I like you. This is all hush-hush, though, so don't go blabbing that I told you."

"Of course, sir. I'll keep my mouth shut."

On his way home, Mark stopped by his house. The giant hole in the front wall had been repaired, and everything had been cleaned up and set back in order. Punching the key code into the lock, Mark heard it whine and fail to unlock, causing him to laugh. He remembered how the failure of the lock had once been his biggest trouble in life. It certainly wasn't anymore. On the fourth try, it let him in, and walking into his house, he looked around, catching sight of the picture on the wall. It had fallen during the fight, the frame shattering, but he had had the cleaners fix it and hang it back up.

Heading up to his room, he looked around, checking to see if anything had been disturbed. Then, for the first time in a very long time, he walked across the hall and entered Joe's room. It was nearly empty, containing nothing but a simple bed with a light sheet and no cover, a desk, and a closet with a few pieces of clothing hanging inside. There were two pictures on the desk, one of Joe and their parents and another of Joe and Mark. Nine years separated the two pictures, and on a whim, Mark snapped open the frame holding Joe and Mark's photo and pulled it out, only to realize there was a second picture behind it. That one showed Joe and Emily and looked as if it had been taken in high school.

"No wonder he got involved with her," Mark said, feeling like he had discovered his older brother's dirty secret.

Glancing down at the picture in his hand, he caught sight of something on the back and, turning it over, saw a contact number that he didn't recognize scrawled out on it. After memorizing the number, Mark shoved the picture into his pocket. He had no idea what it was for, but he had a feeling it was probably important.

He spent a bit of time going through his parents' room, looking through their things and trying to recall memories about them. In truth, he didn't remember much, more feelings and vague impressions than anything else. And as much as he loved his brother, it wasn't as if he had spent a lot of time with Joe. Between Joe's military training and deployments, Mark had spent more time alone than with family. Still, it stung that Joe had left, and it stung even more that Joe's decisions had put Mark's dreams at risk. As he took a taxi back to the warehouse, he stared out the window, watching the warm golden rays of the setting sun as they danced across the buildings.

"It's a pretty sight, isn't it?" the taxi driver said, glancing at Mark in the rearview mirror.

"It is. Do you ever get tired of it? I mean, you must see it a lot."

"Sure, I see it a lot, but life is what you make of it. Even the most magical thing can be mundane, and the most mundane thing, well, it can be magical."

The next day, when Mark got up, he didn't worry about when his assignment would come or even if it would come. He currently had an amazing opportunity before him, and he threw himself into it with renewed vigor, pouring his heart and soul into his training. Little by little, he was beginning to master the basics of alchemy and understand instinctively where best to cut through the frozen corpses of the Exlian to deal the least amount of damage to the surrounding tissue, improving the quality of the materials he harvested.

Each day's practice with Master Abrams brought him closer and closer to mastering the second stage of the Cutting Palm technique, and the time he spent with Sky after she got done with her training was extra sweet. Days turned into weeks, and weeks into months, until the mad scramble outside the city walls seemed like nothing but a memory of a life long ago.

One day, Mark was in the middle of crafting a D-ranked potion when he felt his watch vibrate. Expecting to see an invitation from Phoenix now that she was back from her basic training with the Rangers, Mark instead saw an official-looking notice. Puzzled, he opened it up, and his eyes went wide. It had been six months since he had talked to Lieutenant Cox, and he had all but given up on ever getting an assignment. Yet now the letter was in his inbox, but the more he read, the uglier his expression became.

"Engineering Corps? Why did they put me in the Engineering Corps?"

Dismissing the message, Mark frowned and then continued brewing his potion, smoothly completing all the steps. After running it through the testing machine, he took the paper with him and went to find Abrams. His master was currently sitting on the head of a massive bull-like Exlian with six sets of wide horns, carefully digging a horn out. Mime was next to him, eating the small tidbits of meat that Abrams was feeding her.

"Master?"

"What is it that's so important you interrupt my time with Mime?"

Suppressing the urge to roll his eyes as his master reached over to scratch Mime behind the ears, Mark took a deep breath. "I've gotten an assignment."

"Have you? It's about time." Master Abrams jumped down from his frozen perch. "When do you go to training camp?"

Frowning, Mark opened up the message and pressed a button on his watch to flip it around. "They're not sending me to a training camp. They're attaching me to an existing unit that's set to deploy in a week to a mine five hundred miles northwest of the city."

"What? Weren't you joining the Defense Force?" Abrams stepped forward and began reading through the message, the furrows on his forehead deepening the further he read. "Have they given an explanation?"

Biting his lip, Mark shook his head, trying to sort out his conflicting emotions. "No, sir. They haven't."

"Huh." Abrams scratched his chin. "I can help you fight it if you want, but it'll mean never setting foot in the military again. Unfortunately, if you want to join, this is your chance, but as long as you complete one deployment, you can always request transfer to another branch. I know the Engineering Corps isn't your first choice, but because you're my apprentice, they may have thought that it would fit you better than having you crawl around the walls with the Defense Force."

While it wasn't wrong to say Mark was disappointed, he found that he wasn't nearly as torn up about it as he would have expected. The Defense Force had been his first choice, the choice he had focused on for the last ten years, but the thought of having the chance to go into the wilds outside the city lit a fire in him he hadn't known was there. There had been something natural about the dead zone, and he had enjoyed his time in it quite a bit. Now the opportunity to head out of the city for a more distant location made him giddy.

The door opened, and Sky walked in, looking completely exhausted. "Hey, Mark. Hey, Mr. Abrams. Hi, Mime." After greeting everybody, she stopped and looked at Mark. "Did something happen?"

"I got my deployment letter," Mark said.

"Oh, where are you going to be assigned? The Defense Force?"

"Deployment, not assignment," Mark corrected. "They're sending me into the wilds with the Engineering Corps."

Recoiling, Sky stared at him. "That doesn't seem right. You haven't even been to basic training."

"Yeah, that's what I thought too," Mark said, scratching his head. "But this specifically says that I'll be skipping it. The training camp, I mean. Instead, they're expecting me to learn on the job. I'll get mission details tomorrow morning."

Wrinkling her nose, Sky shook her head. "Something about this stinks. Though that could just be me. I really need to take a shower. They had us crawling through ditches all day."

"Oh, I remember that training," Mark said, grinning. "Good luck getting the smell out. It took me a week."

The next morning Mark was up bright and early, standing in front of a dark-brown building that squatted among the rising skyscrapers in the central district. This was the Engineering Corps headquarters, and nothing about its appearance inspired confidence. Walking inside, Mark found it nearly empty, with only one of the six front desks occupied. Going up to the soldier sitting behind it, Mark scanned his watch on the terminal and introduced himself. "Mark Fields, reporting for a briefing about the Felwer Mine."

"6C."

"Thank you."

Stepping into one of the elevators, Mark saw close to a hundred floors arranged from lowest at the top to highest at the bottom. Curious, as the building only had three floors from what he could see, he punched the button for floor six and scanned his watch to confirm his identity. Entirely silent, the elevator dropped through the earth, and a moment later, the doors opened, and Mark found himself in a tastefully decorated yet subdued lobby. Looking around, he spotted an attendant at another desk and walked over.

"I need to get to 6C," he said.

"Ah, you'll want to take Tram 2."

Following the man's pointing finger, Mark walked down a short hallway until he arrived at a tram station packed with people. Looking at the map on the wall, Mark realized that what he'd thought was a simple building was a massive complex sprawling under the city and going down into the earth for miles. There was a complete tram system that he'd had no idea existed up until this moment, and new trams arrived and departed every three minutes.

It didn't take him long to figure out which platform to wait on, and when Tram 2 arrived after a three-minute wait, he stepped on and rode through a dark tunnel to another platform in the C building. Getting off the tram with everyone else, he made his way up to the attendant and scanned his watch. She directed him down a flight of stairs to a long hall filled with briefing rooms. He was early, so he took a seat on one of the benches near the meeting room and pulled up his status to pass the time.

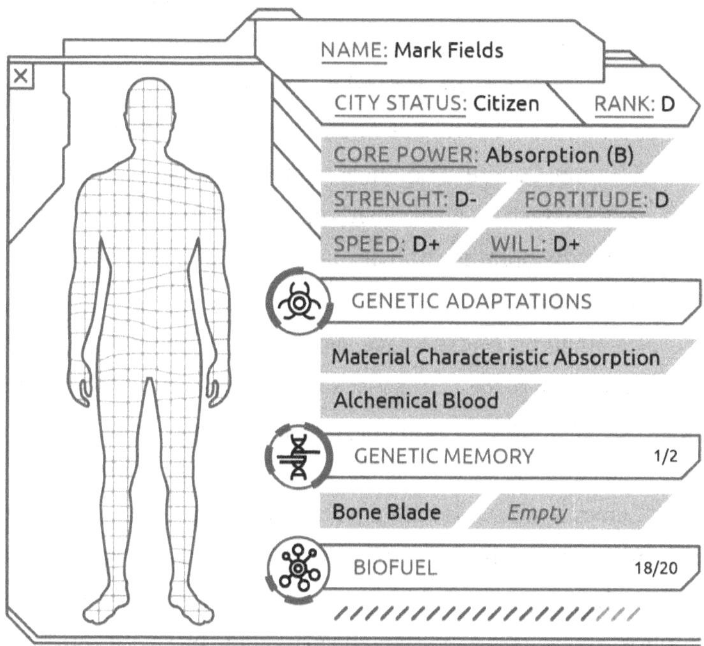

Nothing much had changed over the last six months, but Mark could feel that his stats were getting close to increasing, and once he finally mastered Fingers as Knives, he thought he might see his speed increasing again. After a few minutes, the door opened and someone stuck his head out, looking around, so Mark jumped to his feet.

"Are you Mark Fields?"

"Yes, sir," Mark said, saluting.

"Great, come on in. My name is Lieutenant Moran, and I'll be running the briefing. Welcome to the Black Mountain Battalion."

Far underground, a man who had been watching Mark on a floating screen frowned. As the door clicked shut behind Mark, the man reached up and scratched his graying mustache.

"I don't like this," he said without turning around.

"What is there to dislike?" Andre Javesi asked from behind him.

Turning around, the general fixed a hard glare on the councilman's handsome face, but Andre just grinned and held up his hands. "Come, General. Enough of the morality play. You get what you want; I get what I want. That's all there is to it. A simple exercise, all for the greater good of our city."

"But why him?"

The smile on Andre's face slipped for a moment and then returned in full force. "Let's just say that I've discovered my son does better when he doesn't have close friends."

"You're gonna kill that kid just because he's your son's friend?"

"General, my son is being groomed for something very specific. Something we cannot allow to fail if we want humanity to thrive. He does not need friends. He needs subordinates, loyal hounds who will do everything he says when he says it. Anybody who doesn't fit into that category will be removed. And besides, I'm not going to do anything."

Standing up from his seat, Andre straightened his jacket and tugged on the cuffs of his shirt. "I don't have to do anything. After all, that's why I have you, isn't that right?"

Walking to the doorway, the councilman paused for a moment before he opened the door and turned back, his eyes bright and hard. "But you don't have to feel too bad. Nature will do our dirty work for us. We'll do as we always have. Deploy the unit to the mine and let the Exlian do the rest. By the time we come in to save the day, the world will be right again, and you will be one step closer to being free. Just don't forget to recover his body."

Flashing a wide smile, Andre spun on his heel and walked out the door before closing it with a firm click.

To be continued . . .